P9-DTR-605

The experts applaud
Between the Hunters and the Hunted

"*Between the Hunters and the Hunted* is a tremendously exciting read. The characters were well drawn; the action riveting. I couldn't put the book down."
—Allan Topol, author of *Conspiracy*

"A gripping, superbly told story of war at sea. A masterful blending of fact and fiction that thrusts the reader into the center of white-hot action and the heart of momentous events, which, had they been real, would have changed the course of history."
—Peter Sasgen, author of *War Plan Red*

"Wow! What great page-turning action and captivating characters. Wilson will keep you enthralled and on the edge of your seat."
—David E. Meadows, author of the *Sixth Fleet* series

"A fine adventure novel in the tradition of Alistair McLean; once you pick it up you won't put it down."
—Tom Wilson, author of *Black Serpent*

"Steven Wilson takes us on a taut, suspenseful, engaging and frightening saltwater thriller to the secret, dangerous undersea horrors of WW II submarining, where his war machines are as deeply soulful—and as realistically lethal—as his combat-weary yet inspired characters. No submarine fiction fan's bookcase is complete without Wilson's *Voyage of the Gray Wolves*. Bravo zulu and good hunting, Steven."
—Michael DiMercurio, author of *Emergency Deep*

Also by Steven Wilson

Voyage of the Gray Wolves

BETWEEN THE HUNTERS AND THE HUNTED

STEVEN WILSON

PINNACLE BOOKS
Kensington Publishing Corp.
http://www.kensingtonbooks.com

PINNACLE BOOKS are published by

Kensington Publishing Corp.
850 Third Avenue
New York, NY 10022

All Kensington Titles, Imprints, and Distributed Lines are available at special quantity discounts for bulk purchases for sales promotions, premiums, fund-raising, and educational or institutional use. Special book excerpts or customized printings can also be created to fit specific needs. For details, write or phone the office of the Kensington special sales manager: Kensington Publishing Corp., 850 Third Avenue, New York, NY 10022, attn: Special Sales Department, Phone: 1-800-221-2647.

Pinnacle and the P logo Reg. U.S. Pat. & TM Off.

First Pinnacle Books Printing: November 2005

10 9 8 7 6 5 4 3 2 1

Printed in the United States of America

DKM SEA LION

HMS PRINCE OF WALES

HMS FIREDANCER

HMS PROMETHEUS

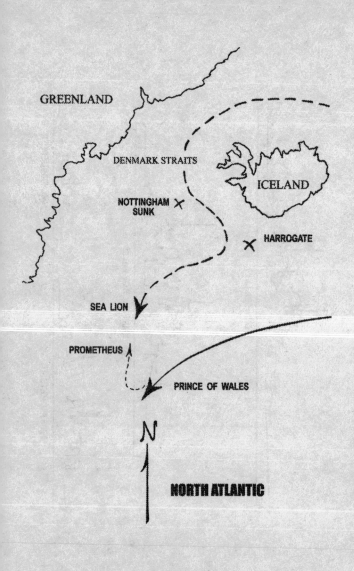

GREENLAND

DENMARK STRAITS

ICELAND

NOTTINGHAM
SUNK ✗

✗ HARROGATE

SEA LION

PROMETHEUS

PRINCE OF WALES

N

NORTH ATLANTIC

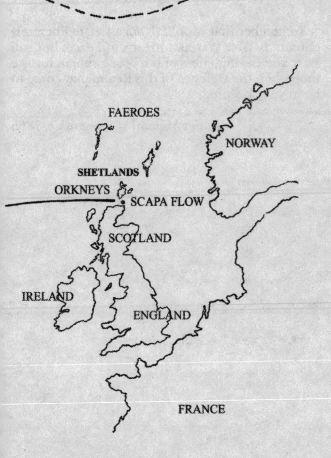

FAEROES

NORWAY

SHETLANDS

ORKNEYS

SCAPA FLOW

SCOTLAND

IRELAND

ENGLAND

FRANCE

Remember that your life's vocation, deliberately chosen, is War: War as a means of Peace, but still War; and in singleness of purpose prepare for the time when the Defence of this Realm may come to be in your keeping.

Alston's Manual of Seamanship, 1865

Chapter 1

Warm Springs, Georgia, 3 July 1941

Louis Hoffman walked up the slight grassy knoll leading to the large swimming pool, removing his sweat-drenched jacket and undoing his tie. He'd already unbuttoned his vest and taken off his battered hat, but it was still too damned hot for a civilized man to be out in this uncivilized country. His suit, which always looked as if he slept in it, was as limp as the damp hair that plastered the back of his neck.

Hoffman was irritated, which was a natural state of affairs for the diminutive aid to President Franklin Delano Roosevelt. He was hot and he was disgusted that he'd had to travel from Washington down to this godforsaken country because Franklin told him to come to Warm Springs as quickly as he could because it was "important." Everything with Franklin was important because Franklin made everything important, and when anyone around the president exhibited the least bit of consternation over the endless barrage of edicts, Franklin would flash that patented smile of his and airily wave off any concerns.

That is, to anyone but Hoffman. Louis Hoffman was the only one who ever told the president, "Franklin, you're full of shit," and could get away with it. Hoffman was granted that privilege because he and Roosevelt were ambitious, brilliant, and implacable. They shared one other similarity: physically they were broken men, but neither accepted that as a detriment to achievement.

Hoffman didn't like to travel and he didn't like to leave Washington and he had a rotten cold anyway. Most people made the mistake of considering him inconsequential, a disgusting gnome who had somehow insinuated his way into the patrician Roosevelt's good graces. They were mistaken. "I don't like you very much, Mr. Hoffman," Eleanor Roosevelt had said to him in her very cool and cultured voice, making it seem as if it were his fault, "but Franklin thinks well of you and I suppose that I shall have to be satisfied with that."

Franklin thinks well of me, Hoffman snorted as he reached a cluster of wooden deck chairs scattered around the pool. *Nobody, including me, knows what Franklin is thinking. I take what he tells me on faith because I have to and Franklin takes what I tell him on faith because there are too many two-faced sons of bitches fluttering around him who wouldn't tell him the truth if it meant their lives.* A coughing spasm overtook Hoffman and he quickly pulled a stained handkerchief from his back pocket and pressed it over his mouth. He could taste the phlegm as it shot out of his lungs and filled the handkerchief, and he felt his chest burning with the eruption. He would be weak after the attack, he knew that, and short-tempered, others knew that all too well, but he would be able to breathe better. For a while.

"Louis!"

Hoffman looked up to see a strange shape floating on the pool, distorted by the rays of the sun flashing across the water. He held his hand up to cut down the glare. It was the torso of a man. The man was waving at him.

"Louis," Franklin Delano Roosevelt called again in that famous vibrant voice that never seemed to lack confidence or calm authority. "Good of you to come."

Hoffman jammed the handkerchief in his back pocket and dropped heavily into a deck chair. "You ordered me to," he said, curtly. He watched as Roosevelt maneuvered the floating chair through the water, his powerful shoulders, arms, and chest, white against the blue water, driving him closer. Hoffman knew that the president's legs, crippled by polio, dangled uselessly below the surface.

Roosevelt's chair, a unique cork and canvas and web device, bumped up against the edge of the pool. The president stuck out his big hand and beamed. "Good to see you, Louis."

Hoffman pulled a cigarette from a pack and lit it. "I hate this fucking place." He stuck the cigarette in Roosevelt's ebony holder and handed it to the president.

Roosevelt threw his head back and laughed heartily. "We do need to get you out of Washington more often, my old friend."

"How about Times Square and Second Avenue?" Hoffman said, lighting a cigarette for himself. "Where's a guy get a drink around here?"

"Ring the bell, Louis," Roosevelt said, pointing to a small bell on a table next to the chair. "When Charles comes, order whatever you like. I'll have iced tea, lots of lemon, unsweetened." He pushed himself away from the edge of the pool and clamped the holder in his teeth at a jaunty angle. "I've got two more laps and then we'll talk. Go to the lodge and get refreshed. I'll meet you in an hour. In your room is a folder with the latest dispatches from England." He was almost shouting as he neared the center of the pool. "No improvements, I'm afraid, but we'll talk about that later. Oh, and, Louis?"

Hoffman looked up.

"Try not to be unpleasant to the staff, will you? They don't understand you the way I do."

It was two hours before the president was wheeled into his tiny office. By that time Hoffman had showered, changed, drunk three scotch-and-waters, smoked a dozen cigarettes, and read the cables in the folder. His disposition hadn't improved.

A servant took Hoffman to Roosevelt's office. The president, dressed in lightweight slacks, a knit shirt, and canvas deck shoes, motioned Hoffman to a chair next to him.

"Louis," the president began thoughtfully, sliding a cigarette into a holder, "we've a problem."

"Is this a one-drink problem or a two-drink problem?" Hoffman asked.

"Hear me out and you can decide for yourself." Roosevelt moved the wheelchair closer to Hoffman. "I don't think England can last much longer on her own. Adolph is too strong. The British rescued the bulk of their army at Dunkerque but left their supplies on the beach. No tanks, artillery, or trucks. They might as well be a nineteenth-century army. Mr. Hitler's U-boats are starving her. Her convoys see fifty or sixty percent losses. Whatever is getting through is not enough. We have given her fifty old destroyers and whatever else we can spare short of going to war ourselves." He examined the end of the glowing cigarette. "I'm afraid, and I mention this only to you of course, that Great Britain is dying."

"Franklin," Hoffman said irritably, "you're giving me a laundry list of headlines over the past six months. I know this, and you know that I know this, and we've talked about all of it until the cows come home. Now if you're preparing me for something, just say it."

"Britain needs more help than we've given her to date."

"Yeah," Hoffman said, tossing the folder onto Roosevelt's desk. "I think they need a miracle, Franklin. You've done all you could do without declaring war on Germany. And that is a bird that isn't going to fly right now. You just don't have the support. Every time I turn on the radio some idiot from the American First Party is giving you hell about something or other. If I had my way, I'd deport every single one of them to Germany. But there's no other way to say it—they want your blood. You put one foot over the line, and I mean the line that says what you should do versus what we can legally do, and you'll have a hell of a lot more time to listen to the birds singing on that godforsaken island."

"I thought you liked Campobello, Louis."

"Franklin, the last time I was up there I saw a fucking

rabbit. Look. Your hands are tied. You'd better be careful about more aid to Britain."

Hoffman watched Roosevelt ponder the comment: it was a signal for Hoffman to continue speaking. The president was absorbing what he heard, calculating, analyzing, and occasionally, his dreamy eyes never leaving the ceiling, he would ask a question. But now he wanted to hear how Hoffman saw things.

"Franklin, I'm on your side and you know it. A lot of people see Britain as a lost cause," Hoffman said. "They say that we don't have any reason to be in a war that's three thousand miles away. Hell, some of your strongest supporters have gone on record saying that if push comes to shove, they can still do business with Hitler. The almighty dollar is dictating how a lot of people think. Forget the immorality of Nazi Germany and the pure evil of that son of a bitch Hitler; a majority of Americans are convinced that this isn't our fight. You could have a hundred Fireside Chats about garden hoses and Lend/Lease and not make a goddamned difference. The way I see it, the only things keeping Britain from toppling over are Winston Churchill and the Royal Navy. Their army's shot, their air force is too small, and they have the most tasteless food I've ever eaten."

Hoffman seldom smiled and most people said that he had the perpetual look of a man who sniffed something pungent. But now, if someone took the time to look beyond the scowl and deep into the sensitive eyes that yielded every emotion the man felt, they would see real concern. "This may be the greatest struggle of good against evil in the history of mankind. I'm not certain that evil won't triumph," he added, allowing an uncharacteristic note of alarm into his statement.

"You know, Louis," Roosevelt said, watching a cloud of smoke curl overhead, "if you aren't careful, people might believe that you really are a cynic."

"It's worse than that, Franklin. I'm a Republican." Hoffman downed his drink and made himself another. "You know, the time will come when you'll want those fifty destroyers back. Obsolete or not."

Roosevelt pulled the spent cigarette from its holder and crushed it in the ashtray. "We can build more, Louis. Britain can't. She's expending her blood. The very least we can do is provide her with arms."

"Yeah, but you didn't order me down here to talk about the least we can do, did you, Franklin? You've got something going on in that upper-crust head of yours."

"How's your drink, Louis? Does it need to be freshened up?"

"My drink's fine, Franklin. Now cut the bullshit and tell me what you have on your mind."

"I've been speaking with Winston for some time. Cable and telephone. I've gotten to know him well enough. I feel that I have a sense of what Winston is like, in essence, who he is. A fellow likes to know about the members of his team, don't you know? Especially before the big game."

"Yeah. Me and my pals said the same thing about stickball," Hoffman said wryly. "Just after the cops ran us off."

Roosevelt turned grave, one of the few times that Hoffman had seen him like this. "When we go to war, Louis—when and not if, because I fully believe it will come and much sooner than anyone anticipates—I have to be absolutely sure of the other fellow on the team. Absolutely."

"You need an eyeball-to-eyeball meeting. Some place that you can sit down and get to business. Very private. Very isolated."

"Yes. There is far too much at stake here. If we align ourselves with Britain in a shooting war and she is not able to survive, that would leave the United States in a most unfortunate position."

"Speaking politically, it would be the end of your career."

"Is it fair to bring politics up in the context of this very crucial question?"

"You're an elected official, Franklin. In office you can affect changes. Out of office you're just a has-been. You've been able to accomplish a great deal as president of the United States. I'd hate to see you lose that if Britain goes down the toilet."

"As would I, old friend."

Hoffman suddenly realized why he had been called to Georgia. "You've already set this thing up," he said.

"Yes, I have, Louis," Roosevelt replied evenly.

Hoffman exploded, "Without telling me about it? Where the hell do I fit in this escapade, Franklin? You couldn't trust me, is that it?"

"Of course I trust you, Louis. I've always trusted you."

"You sure have a funny way of showing it, Franklin. Special adviser to the president, my ass. When do I advise you about this one? When the whole thing's over? What have you got up your sleeve this time, Franklin? Another New Deal but this time it's for the British?"

Roosevelt reached across the small desk, picked up the telephone, and dialed a number. "Hello, Marie? Fine, thank you. Is there any chance that we might have lamb for supper tonight? Splendid. Yes. Fix it any way you like, I trust your judgment implicitly. Thank you," he said and hung up the telephone.

"You son of a bitch," Hoffman muttered.

"Mama would be very disappointed to hear you describe her son in such terms, Louis."

"Why'd you leave me out of this, Franklin? If you already had everything figured out and a meeting planned, why did you even call me down here in the first place?"

"I called you down here," Roosevelt said, carefully inserting a cigarette into a holder, "because I need your help. Yes. The meeting is scheduled, planned, and will take place. From it, I hope that England and the United States can develop a treaty, a charter of some sort to address this crisis. I have every confidence that we can."

"I'm waiting for the other shoe to drop," Hoffman said.

"I didn't tell you anything about the meeting or the circumstances surrounding it because I need an absolutely fresh set of eyes on this. I need someone unburdened by preconceived ideas or notions to be my devil's advocate."

"Terrific," Hoffman said. "I'm a Jew and you just made me the Antichrist."

Roosevelt smiled. "Louis, you're not much of a Jew."

"Yeah," Hoffman said wryly. "This is definitely a two-drink problem." He rubbed his forehead with a bony hand. He looked up quickly, the thought jumping out at him. "Why, you tricky bastard. You're sending me to England."

"Yes, I am, Louis," Roosevelt said. "Talk to Winston. Get a sense of what he wants. What kind of man he is. I can't go, for obvious reasons. Any visit by the president of the United States or his official envoy would have diplomatic and political consequences that, at present, I do not wish to encounter. So you must go as my unofficial envoy. You're going on holiday."

Hoffman grimaced. "I haven't had a 'holiday' since I was eight years old, and if you think that the newspapers aren't going to pick up on this, you're nuts."

"Let them. They'll see through your holiday as nothing more than a ruse, but they won't have any idea for the real reason for your visit."

"You remember I don't like boats, Franklin?" Hoffman said sourly. "I get seasick."

Roosevelt smiled broadly. "Of course I know that, Louis. That's why you're taking the *Clipper*. She leaves Miami tomorrow afternoon. Simply relax and watch the Atlantic glide by thousands of feet below you." Hoffman was about to protest when Roosevelt added, "Would you like those two drinks simultaneously or sequentially?"

"Just put them in a goddamned glass," Hoffman said. "I'll do the rest."

Chapter 2

Over the Kattegat, between Denmark and Sweden,
11 July 1941

N-for-Nancy, a Lockheed Hudson MK IV reconnaissance plane, plummeted three hundred feet in the turbulent, iron-gray skies.

"Jesus Christ, Bunny!" bomb-aimer/navigator Peter Madsen shouted. "Hang on to it!"

Pilot Sergeant Douglas "Bunny" Walker pulled back on the yoke and clawed for the handle next to him that would drop his seat. He knew that in the storm he was certain to be bounced about, regardless of the seat belt, and smash his head on the roof. His hand clamped on the lever and pumped it down. Satisfied that his head was safe, he gripped the yoke attached to the steering column, trying to control the wild yawing and pitching of the aircraft. He drove his feet into the rudder pedals and yanked back on the yoke, fighting the full force of the gale. He felt the tension of the hydraulically assisted control cables through the pedals as they pulled the rudders to the right or left. That was really what flying was about—*feeling* your airplane: how she responded to the controls, whether she was sloppy or crisp or sluggish. But against this tempest was a pure muscle job—just keep the damned thing from flipping over or going into a stall.

The two 1,050-horsepower Pratt and Whitney Wasp engines barely gave *N-for-Nancy* enough power to maintain headway in the storm. It was always dirty weather over this miserable stretch of water—ice, sleet, snow, and rain, or a combination of anything always seemed to drive up from somewhere to batter *N-for-Nancy* so that the crew climbed out of the twin-tailed aircraft with bruised bodies and numbed senses. It was a contest of mind and skill between Bunny and the storm, and the prize was the ugly little Hudson and the four frightened men within her. All of this for a few pictures.

Bunny clamped his oxygen mask close to his mouth so that he could be heard on the intercom above the roar of the wind. "Johnny? See anything?"

Gunner Johnny Thompson, in the Boulton-Paul dorsal turret at the rear of the aircraft, said, "Lightning, Bunny. Very impressive."

Suddenly a great burst of air slapped the plane and threw it toward the earth. *N-for-Nancy* fell through the hole in the sky and Bunny struggled to bring it back to altitude. Continuous sheets of ice and rain beat against the windshield so that he was flying virtually blind. His arms ached from fighting the Hudson and he began to curse both the aircraft and the storm softly. "How much farther, Peter? My bloody arms are falling off."

"Weather Ops said we should have had this for only thirty minutes or so and then clear sailing."

"Weather Ops is wrong again," Bunny said. "I've been at it for close to an hour." He could hear things tumbling around inside the aircraft and he was glad that they weren't carrying anything more than a bomb bay load of cameras. That's all that they ever carried and frankly, he was getting sick and tired of it. Some genius had pulled them out of Royal Air Force rotation and handed them over to Royal Navy Coastal Command, so all that they did now was run about this disgusting straight and take thousands of pictures. He watched the sky through the maddeningly slow windshield wipers, searching for the slightest hint of clearing. The thick film of rainwater covering the windshield obscured the sky. The wipers should have taken care of it, but they were never designed for gales like this. Bunny was flying deaf, dumb, and blind, he decided, like those little monkeys he had seen at a carnival in Bournemouth. Hear no evil, speak no evil . . . The yoke tried to jerk itself out of his hands and it became a personal contest again—no longer the plane or the storm, just Bunny Douglas and that bloody yoke that threatened to break his wrists and twist his fingers off—taking a perverse pleasure in revealing that it was no longer an inanimate object; it was alive. *See no evil*, Bunny thought, completing the triad. *N-for-Nancy* yawed sharply and Bunny kicked the rudder to bring it back on course.

For God's sake, Bunny thought, *get a grip on yourself*. It was fatigue, he knew. When your body gets tired and your mind loses its ability to function, your thoughts wander, float really, and reality and common sense simply disappear.

He felt the yoke begin to relax. They were coming

out of the storm. He quickly pumped the seat up so that he could see clearly over the nose of the Hudson. The fourth member of their crew, Radio Operator Prentice Newman, was at his side.

"Wasn't that a ride, Skipper?" Newman said in a voice that Bunny knew all too well. A man sometimes forced nonchalance into his voice to hide the fear that ate at him.

"Would you like to go back, Prentice?"

"Skipper, no!" Prentice Newman never called Douglas Bunny like the other members of the crew. "It just doesn't seem right," he had said.

"Bunny," Peter called. "I see sunshine ahead. Time to go upstairs?"

"Right you are, Peter. Angels twenty in ten." Bunny turned to Prentice and jerked his thumb toward the rear of the aircraft. "Go roost now. Things are going to get busy."

The camouflaged Hudson slipped out of the remaining clouds and began climbing to twenty-thousand feet, as Bunny adjusted the flaps. *N-for-Nancy* had been lucky. The storm had been poised on the edge of Leka Island and had hidden the plane's approach from the Germans. Now all that remained was to make three flights over the island, cameras rolling, and run for home. That was all there was to it. Simple as that.

"Keep your eyes open, chaps," Bunny said. He knew Peter was prone in his bomb-aimer's position, tracking the approach, ready to open the bomb bay doors and squeeze the tit to start the cameras rolling. He felt the vibration of the Boulton Paul turret revolving to search the skies. It mounted twin 7.7-mm machine guns and Johnny was a fine shot, but the guns were too light and their range was too limited. And the German fighters that flew up to kill them were too fast. *N-for-Nancy* had to get in and out before the fighters appeared as tiny, lethal specks in the sky.

"Flack's up," Bunny said, watching the powdery brown flowers appear in the distance. They were searching for the Hudson, a few odd shots seemingly cast into the sky as if the German antiaircraft crews were going through the motions. But these shots were more than perfunctory—they were exploratory. When the crews found the altitude and range, more little brown flowers would follow, and creep closer to the aircraft. "How are you, Peter? Ready to go?"

"Straight on, Bunny. Just a few seconds more."

Bunny Walker looked at his watch. They had eighteen minutes from the time that they sighted the target to the arrival of the fighters. Three passes and then they were out.

"Doors open!" Peter said. Bunny heard the soft hum of the door motors. "One, two . . . three. Shoot," the bomb-aimer said, and Bunny knew that a dozen cameras were rapidly snapping images of Leka Island.

Suddenly flak exploded a hundred yards to the left of the aircraft. More bursts followed just behind and to the right. Bunny heard shrapnel strike *N-for-Nancy*. It was the sound of hail falling on a tin roof and on a summer's day at home would have been nothing more than comforting. But it was not hail and there was nothing comforting about the shrapnel punching holes in *N-for-Nancy*'s thin aluminum skin. There was vengeance in the dark flowers as they tracked *N-for-Nancy* across the sky. Bunny felt his beloved plane shudder and the tempo of the flak increased.

"Anyone hit?" he asked.

"Been practicing, haven't they?" Johnny said.

"I think those chaps mean to kill us, Skipper," Prentice said. It was a joke but his voice was a little too high pitched and strained, and it quivered noticeably.

"Bring us around, will you, Bunny?" Peter said. "Ready for another run. Stay away from those bloody brown flowers. They make me nervous."

"Right," Bunny said. "Here we go." He had eased the Hudson into a sharp bank when the port engine began to shudder. Bunny felt himself go cold as his eyes shot to the engine. He saw a thin black stream trailing along the upper edge of the wing through his window. He searched the instrument panel for the port engine oil-pressure gauge. The pressure was dropping rapidly—they were leaking oil from the oil tank bay. He quickly switched off the engine and feathered the Hamilton Standard propeller. "We've lost the port engine," he said.

"What?" Peter said. Bunny heard the fear in his voice. He had every reason to be afraid. At best *N-for-Nancy* could get 177 miles an hour. On two engines. Now she had one. When the fighters showed up it would be a slaughter.

"We're going home, chaps," Bunny said. "Close it up. Peter, get ready to throw out everything not nailed down. Prentice, tell base what's happened and then help Peter. Stay away from the rear door once you've popped it off. I don't want either one of you going out. Lie on the deck, one passes to another who chucks it out the door. Johnny, you're our eyes."

"Yes, Bunny."

"Don't fail us."

"No, Bunny."

Pilot Sergeant Douglas Walker reached inside his flight suit and squeezed the tiny stuffed rabbit that he kept there, three times. It was a ritual before each flight: three squeezes and everything would come out splendidly. Now he felt his hand trembling inside his suit and he realized just how frightened he was. They were hundreds of miles behind enemy lines in a damaged aircraft barely capable of keeping itself in the air. Still, it would do no good to let the other fellows know how afraid he was. He pushed the rabbit deeper into his suit and zipped it closed.

"Peter? You mustn't forget to throw those devilish cameras out, will you? Bit of irony there."

"The cameras, Bunny?"

"Every last one of the bastards."

"What a splendid idea."

"Bunny!" Johnny said. "Five o'clock. Three aircraft."

"How far out, Johnny?"

"Ten miles."

They would be on the Hudson IV in minutes and then the damaged aircraft would be doomed. Johnny could keep them at bay for a moment or two; he was a game shot with a good eye. But the end would be the same: the ME 109s would line up and come in fast and it would be three hawks on a very plump pigeon with an injured wing. *N-for-Nancy* had no place to go—nowhere to hide.

The storm!

It hung in front of him, a great gray wall of boiling

clouds, and wind and rain that provided the only shelter they could hope for. If they could reach it they could escape the German fighters. But if they reached it, they had to survive its fury. They had half the power that they needed in a storm that could tear them apart. But what choice did they have?

Bunny began to ease the yoke down, diving to build up speed.

"Johnny? Can you keep them away from us until I reach those clouds?"

"I'll try, Bunny, but don't take too long, will you? They look angry to me."

Bunny kept the Hudson's nose pointed toward the ominous mountain of clouds before them. Bolts of lightning flashed across the face of the dark mass illuminating fissures, valleys, and peaks so dense that they might have been solid. More lightning glowed deeply within the body of the storm as it hungrily anticipated the arrival of the damaged aircraft. The clouds seethed across the sky with violence, promising an endless wave of assaults should *N-for-Nancy* survive the first encounter.

N-for-Nancy was behaving sluggishly with just one engine turning. There was more than that. She was a fine ship, one of the first to come over from Lockheed in the States, but she was past her prime and she wanted nothing more than quiet duty along the English coast, looking for downed bomber crews or scouting for E-boats. Even with everything thrown out that could be and Bunny's right hand nursing the throttles to the starboard engine up for more power, she had reached her limit.

The twin 7.7-mm spat a burst and two dark streaks

flashed by Bunny, one on either side of the Hudson. Their roar startled him. This would be no contest.

"Peter, Prentice! Get to the beam guns. Keep those bloody bastards off us," Bunny said. He glanced at the clouds. God, were they moving away? Trying to elude him? Playing a devilish game of keep-away now, when he needed them to stay alive?

"Here they come," Johnny called. "Nine o'clock. Six o'clock high."

Bunny heard the hammering of the Hudson's guns and felt the vibration run through the fuselage. Suddenly he felt the unmistakable tremor of bullets striking *N-for-Nancy*, sharp blows from the 20mm cannons aboard the German fighters. The starboard window exploded and cold air rushed in with the force of a hurricane. They'd be chewed up. Fuselage, engines, controls, flaps, elevators, wings . . . men.

Bunny's hands were numb and his eyes were watering from the frigid air blasting into the cabin. He looked over the nose of *N-for-Nancy*, searching for the best place to enter the storm. They were running out of time. Too far to go. The clouds were too far away. He needed the port engine; without it they had no chance.

Bunny reached down and flipped the magneto on the port engine, adjusted the fuel mixture, and pressed the starter. She'd been leaking oil all along. There might not be any left in the oil tank bay. But there might be enough left in the engine—just enough to turn her over. Just enough to keep her going. Just enough to get them to the clouds.

He felt cannon shells slam into the plane and heard the sound of metal being wrenched apart. The Hudson shuddered under the impact of the shells as they punched holes in *N-for-Nancy*'s body. But his eyes were on the port engine. He adjusted the throttle and switched the starter again.

He saw the propeller turn slightly, stop, and turn. The engine was kicking over. It turned again and suddenly blasted to life with a growl and a cloud of black smoke. He eased the throttles up and felt *N-for-Nancy* respond.

"Port's on," he said and he heard the crew cheer.

"That's lovely news," Peter said calmly. "Now would you kindly get us the hell out of here?"

Bunny pushed the yoke well forward and the Hudson dropped like a brick, gathering speed as she approached the clouds. The German fighters realized what the Hudson had planned and dove on her viciously, tearing into her with cannon and machine-gun fire. Bits of metal and fabric skin flew off the plane—flesh from a wounded animal fleeing for its life. *N-for-Nancy*'s crew fired back, but they could only annoy the fighters who rushed in, fired, twisted out of range, and spun around for another attack.

Bunny smelled smoke, the ozone-spiked stench of an electrical fire. He glanced at the port engine and was relieved to see its propeller biting happily into the air. He felt a sudden jolt and a cry from one of the men.

"The bastards got an oxygen canister," Prentice said, and Bunny heard the loud hiss of a fire extinguisher. "That's got it."

There it was: the storm.

"Here we go, chaps!" Bunny shouted. The Hudson smashed into a huge wall of black clouds. They were thrown up and down and twisted back and forth as lightning flashed through the darkness.

The storm greedily accepted the Hudson as a sacrifice: sheets of rain pummeling the aircraft, ice crystals clattering against the skin like bullets. But not enemy bullets.

"Everyone to their positions," Bunny ordered. "For God's sake strap yourselves in." He looked down and saw the temperature gauge needle on the port engine climbing steadily. She was out of oil and in a few minutes the engine would seize. He cut back the throttle, turned off the fuel, and feathered the propeller.

"Bunny," Johnny said. "With your permission I'm going to get screechers tonight."

Bunny suddenly realized that his entire body ached. He relaxed and lowered the seat. "I took you for a shandy man," he said, trying to keep his voice steady.

"Whiskey, Bunny, and lots of it. None of that watery filth for me."

"You know, fellows . . ." Peter said, trying to find what was left of his navigator's instrument panel in the mess that had once been his station. "Oh, look, here's the bloody compass all shot to pieces." He threw it on the floor and continued to straighten things up. "We haven't any reason to celebrate."

Bunny looked down at the starboard nose compartment entry tunnel that led to the bomb-aimer/navigator's position. "Any day that I am not killed is a day for celebration, Bomb-aimer/Navigator."

"That's telling him, Bunny," Johnny said.

"Oh, I agree wholeheartedly, Pilot/Sergeant," Peter said. "But you're forgetting the obvious."

"Yes, I know. We're not home yet."

"I have all the confidence in the world that you will get us home. It's the other thing that bothers me."

"Now you have my interest, Bomb-aimer/Navigator," Bunny said.

This time Peter's voice was subdued. "We didn't complete the mission, Bunny. Those heartless bastards will send us back out here."

No one said anything and there was no reason to. Bunny knew that Peter was right. They would have to come back. He unzipped his flight suit and searched for the small plush rabbit safely nestled next to his heart. He squeezed it three times and closed the flight suit. He wondered how many times his talisman would return him to base. How much time that he had left.

Chapter 3

Lieutenant (j.g.) Jordan Cole, United States Naval Reserve, Office of Naval Intelligence, straightened awkwardly and rubbed the stiffness out of the small of his back. He shook his head in disgust at the notion of his only injury in this war coming as a result of hanging over light tables, his eye pressed to a stereoscopic eyepiece, looking for enemy ships hidden in black-and-white photographs. Not even for his own navy either, but for the Royal Navy. He was dispatched as an observer to the Royal Navy, his orders had read, as a part of an exchange program between the two services. That was a lie.

He was dispatched to the Royal Navy, his commander at Norfolk had told him, because: "You wear the uniform of a naval officer but you aren't a naval officer. You're a dilettante, Cole. You may be a college professor outside of the navy, but you're a waste of time in. You're going to England, my fine young friend, as a special observer, and you're going to do whatever the Limeys want you to do. Maybe you'll grow up over there."

His commanding officer had said other things: comments about the navy not having to settle for officers just because there was a war on, even if it wasn't their war. Things like that.

Strangely, Cole liked the navy. He liked the regulation and stability, and for some reason he felt protected within the structure of the navy. He didn't always fit and he sometimes said too much or even just enough at the wrong time. "If you would just learn to keep your goddamned mouth shut!" someone had told him. It couldn't have been Ruth. He hadn't heard from her in months.

He pressed the heels of his hands into his eyes and rubbed them gently. He figured out the routine. Take a break, get a cup of tea, swing your arms about, and then get back to the photographs. Bend over the table, adjust the glass, and begin searching. If he found something that looked interesting he circled it with a red grease pencil so that Sublieutenant Richard Moore could look over it. Dickie Moore—all arms and legs with a mass of blond hair that defied control. A good man.

"Active Service," Moore had informed Cole. "What you Americans call Regular Navy, although I must confess that there is nothing very regular about me. Most irregular, in fact. Thank God my family is filthy rich and my father is rather keen on the navy."

"Here we are, sir," Petty Officer Markley said, bringing a bound folder into the photograph analysis room. "Bit of a mess down there, sir. Those blokes aren't as organized as they should be. Time at sea would cure that right off." He set the thick folder on the table with a thump. "Raised a lovely protest, sir. I was forced to employ my rating and flex my muscles a bit. If you know what I mean, sir."

"That should have done it," Cole said, smiling at the hulking man with the ludicrously large, red moustache that sat perfectly straight on a square face. Markley moved carefully through the strata of the Royal Navy, as any good petty officer should after years in the service. He was here only because a shipboard accident ended his career at sea and forced him to take an assignment in the quiet confines of Photo Analysis Operations. It took him a while to become used to Cole's relaxed manner of doing things. "I don't get excited," Cole had once told the wary Markley, who eyed the young American with suspicion, "until there is blood on the deck." Now they were—within reason and the restrictions of officer and noncommissioned officer, and cautiously on Markley's side—friends.

"Indeed it did, sir. Indeed it did. So here they are, After Action Reports."

"Just the Kattegat. Leka Island."

Markley straightened as if called to attention. "Not entirely, sir. The place was in a right mess, as I reported, sir. I took it upon myself to hurry the blokes along and in the confusion they gave me everything they had. Sir."

"I didn't need everything, Markley. Just those flights pertaining to Leka Island."

"Exactly my words to those—"

"That means that I'm going to have to have someone help me go through this mess."

"Sublieutenant Moore is just the man to assist you—"

"Markley," Cole said. "He isn't here. He won't be back for a couple of weeks, if we're lucky. Take a look around, Markley. You'll find you, ten thousand photographs, that folder, and me. I want the After Action Reports for reconnaissance flights over Leka Island, and as I always say, call it done when Markley is on it."

"Yes, sir," Petty Officer Markley said, rubbing his mustache in disgust. "Begging your pardon, sir, but I haven't a bit of experience manning these photographs, sir."

"You're in luck, Markley. In the U.S. Navy we call this OJT."

"Sir?"

"On-the-job training. Let's get cracking."

"Sir," Markley said, recognizing his defeat. He pulled bundles of papers out of the folder. "If you don't mind me saying so, sir, you American chaps are a colorful lot."

"Practically red, white, and blue, through and through." Cole opened a drawer from under the light table and produced a fifth of whiskey. "Petty Officer," he said, and tossed it to Markley. "This might help."

Markley acknowledged the gesture with a tip of the bottle and: "To your health, sir."

Cole had the photographs of Leka Island and a one-hundred-square-mile area around it carefully arranged on the table. Some of the photographs were clear, some obscured by haze, and some angled so that the images were distorted. It was detective work, interpreting photographs. Cole laughed to himself and shook his head. No, it was scholarship— some sort of ironic punishment for a failed associate professor of history. Instead of facts and figures, instead of primary and secondary documents, he studied photographs taken thousands of feet above islands, ships, roads, canals, mountains, and railroads. From all of that, with the loyal Dickie Moore at his side and the square-rigged Petty Officer Markley manning the slide projector, he briefed his superiors. He was off to war armed with a pointer, clad in chain-mail armor of reports and memorandums, and mounted on a podium in the darkness of a smoke-filled room cut neatly in half by a shaft of light thrown by the projector. And his audience: relaxed potentates of high command and senior officers who might have once been charged with ambition when they were younger but had since exchanged that attribute for comfort.

The rewards for Cole's service, however, had been considerable. The other day he had gotten a clap on the back from Commander Harry Hamilton, Royal Navy Intelligence Operations, Coastal Command, and his immediate superior.

"Excellent job," Hamilton had said. "Damn fine analysis." That was when the slap on the back came. "Learning a bit, are we?" Hamilton had continued, hardly waiting for an answer. "Brilliant idea, this exchange. Americans observing how we do things. The only way to gain experience. Good thing, too. We'll all be in it soon enough. Together again against the Hun, as it were." Then Hamilton had decided to address the delicate issue of Cole's temperament. "See here, Cole, you came with a bit of baggage, if you know what I mean. Must have been some bad blood back home, but let bygones be bygones, I always say. Carry on with the same spirit you've shown us and things will look up for you."

Cole straightened several of the photographs and

planted his hands on the table, peering at the images. His eyes traveled over the black-and-white landscape, almost willing them to assume three-dimensional form, for valleys to sink, mountains to rise, seas to run in some sort of lazy motion under the watchful gaze of drifting clouds. He watched as details emerged from backgrounds to become things. Other times they buried themselves in shadows offering only questions. Is that a bridge? Are there two destroyers in that fiord?

"What is so important about Leka Island?" Cole asked the photographs.

"How's that, sir?" Markley said, papers in hand.

Cole straightened. "Find anything yet? About Leka?"

"Yes, sir," Markley said, handing a report to Cole. "*N-for-Nancy*. Coastal Command Hudson that went out several days ago, sir."

Cole took the report and quickly scanned it. He found the section marked *Enemy Defenses*. He read it carefully. He sensed Markley standing by expectantly. "Come here," he said to the petty officer. Markley followed him around the table to a light board covered with photographs, mounted on the wall.

"Hit the switch," Cole ordered, motioning to a wall mount. Markley did and the board flickered to life, the photographs glowing from the soft aura of the light behind them. "All of these are photographs of Leka Island," he said, "which is really a collection of islands. This large island"—he pointed to a photograph—"and this grouping of islands."

"Yes, sir."

"Take that glass"—he pointed to a stereoscope on the table—"and look over these photographs."

"Yes, sir," Markley said hesitantly. Cole knew that Markley was old-sailor enough to be wary of an officer trying to entrap him. Even if he were only a Yank. Cole smiled to himself—they had the same kind of petty officers in the United States Navy.

After several minutes Markley turned to Cole.

"Well?" Cole said.

"Begging your pardon, sir, but I'm not entirely certain—"

"Just tell me what you see."

Markley took a deep breath. "Well, sir. Nothing. Some little squares and a thread or two, but if there is anything there, it's well hidden."

"Those are buildings. The squares. The threads are roads. But you're right. There is nothing else on Leka Island or around Leka Island worth a damn."

"Yes, sir," Markley said, relaxing.

"If that's the case, Petty Officer Percival Markley, former gunner's mate of the watch aboard His Majesty's Ship *Nelson*, why do the Germans care so much about it?"

"Sir?" Markley said.

"*N-for-Nancy* made two flights over Leka Island. These photographs are the result of the first mission. I got a call from one of the base officers wanting to know if anything turned up because, as he put it, 'Our chaps had a most unfortunate go of it.' I told him that we didn't find a thing but to be sure, could he schedule another mission? He did and this After Action Report is from the second mission. No photographs will be forthcoming because the plane had to jettison the cameras. Along with just about everything else."

"Yes, sir."

"Yeah," Cole said. He reached around Markley and turned off the light. "Percival," he said to the petty officer, "there's not a goddamned thing on those islands except some old fishermen's shacks and a couple of dirt roads, but when a reconnaissance plane shows up all hell breaks loose. They don't want us to see something. Whatever is there and however it is skillfully camouflaged, the Krauts are afraid that we'll figure it out. They don't want us anywhere near Leka Island. Why do they care so much for a bunch of rocks in the middle of nowhere?"

"That's a question for a better brain than mine, I'm afraid, sir."

"Yeah," Cole said, thinking. "Mine, too, except . . ."

"Yes, sir?"

"I sure hate to give up on something when I smell a rat. And I smell a very large German rat. Get me?"

"No, sir, I'm afraid that I don't."

"We've found the hornets but not the nest."

"I see what you're getting at, sir. Things don't add up. Still, begging your pardon, maybe we ought to shift from port to starboard."

"Go on."

Markley tapped his index finger against his chin as he studied the photograph. "What isn't there, sir? Barracks, antiaircraft batteries, gun emplacements. Everything that the Coastal Command chaps claim is making their life miserable."

"No," Cole said. "I saw three emplacements along a ridge."

"Yes, sir. Three emplacements. But those chaps are talking about a dozen or more guns. I know guns, sir. As good as any seaman afloat. I didn't see them, sir. Big or small, I—"

"I'll be a ringtailed bobcat," Cole said. "I couldn't see the forest for the trees. Where the hell are the other guns?"

"Not your fault, sir," Markley said, without emotion. "We all make mistakes, now and again."

"I'll keep that in mind, Markley," Cole said. "But why bother? Why defend this island in the middle of nowhere at all? There's more here than meets the eye. They've got to go back over Leka, Markley."

"I'm afraid that you're going to make some Coastal Command blokes very unhappy, sir."

"It can't be helped. The answer is down there somewhere. I'm going to find it."

"If you don't mind, sir. It's customary at times such as this to toast brave men. The Coastal Command chaps, I mean, sir."

"It is, is it?" Cole said, certain that the tradition was newly minted by the thirsty petty officer. "Okay, go ahead."

Markley held up the fifth that Cole had thrown him earlier. "To the good health of the poor bloody bastards that will have to go take its picture again. May God grant them a safe flight and speedy return with everything in its proper place and functioning as the Almighty intended."

"You just want an excuse to take another snort."

"Nothing of the sort, sir," Markley said, without cracking a smile as the whiskey burbled into his glass.

Chapter 4

London, England

Cole threaded the little MG through piles of rubble in the street, stopping occasionally as work crews loaded the remnants of people's belongings in lorries and horse-drawn wagons. He tried not to stare. It was impolite somehow to watch families scour what they could from shattered buildings that had once been their homes. A lifetime of things, photographs, books, records, and furniture . . . *What if I lost all of my books?* he had once asked himself. He preferred not to think of it. Besides the books, his collection of records was the only thing he had that he cared for, his music, and then he realized that they were inanimate objects. No *one* to care about, he thought. Perhaps that was just as well.

He pulled up across from the dingy facade of St. Elias Hospital, a hulking building of stone and brick. A century of London's coal fires had turned its facade a mix of dismal gray or a brooding black.

Add now the smoke of the fires that burned from the air raids and you had another layer of filth.

An elderly matron at the ornate front desk directed Cole to ward 18 on the second floor. *You must take the stairs at the end of the hall,* she insisted. *The lifts seldom work, so you must take the stairs at the end of the hall. Okay,* Cole assured her, *I'll take the stairs.* He found Dickie Moore stretched out in his bed, his left leg in a cast, suspended on some sort of elaborate contraption attached to the framework of his bed. There were seven other beds in the ward—six were occupied.

"Anything to get out of work," Cole said.

"Why, if it isn't my Yankee friend," Dickie said cheerfully.

"Don't you 'friend' me," Cole said. "I'm up to my eyeballs in work and Uncle Harry won't give me any help."

"It wasn't my fault the filthy Hun broke my leg," Dickie said innocently.

"Why weren't you in a bomb shelter?"

"I was entertaining a young lady."

"That's no excuse."

"Cole," Dickie said, glancing about, "I was actively entertaining her, if you catch my meaning."

"Gentlemen?"

Cole turned around to see a nurse enter the ward. Her light brown hair was tucked carefully under her nurse's cap and her eyes were a very pale green, almost clear, Cole thought.

"Rebecca, dear," Dickie said. "Here is my good friend, Jordan Cole. Jordan, here is the most charming sister of mercy that I have ever had the pleasure to meet."

Cole watched as Rebecca smiled broadly. "How do you do . . ." She quickly studied his uniform. "Oh dear. Now that's one that I haven't seen."

"Lieutenant, J.G.," Cole said. "United States Naval Reserve." He held out his hand and she took it, her touch light, and her fingers slender and graceful.

"J. G.?"

"Junior Grade," Cole said. "That means that they don't quite trust me with anything important."

"That hardly seems right," she said with a smile.

"Maybe, but there's three ways of doing things. The right way, the wrong way, and the navy way."

"I'm Rebecca Blair," she said. She nodded at Dickie. "The sublieutenant's keeper."

"Oh, I say, Rebecca. Be kind to me today."

"I am kind to you every day," she said in a soft voice. There was a breathless quality to her voice, making her words sound quaint and charming. Cole found himself wanting her to say more. "I shall return after they have taken you downstairs for X-rays. Nurse Noonan informs me that you are healing nicely."

Dickie made a face at Cole as Rebecca moved to another bed. "Noonan. Lovely mustache. Size of an elephant. An angry one. I think she fancies me. Cole? Are you listening?"

Cole turned back to Dickie. "What?"

"Yes, Rebecca is sweet, dear boy, and rather a looker. I could listen to her talk for hours, but she has a husband and those usually mean trouble. Some place in North Africa, I'm told."

"She's very pretty," Cole said, watching Rebecca gently brush the hair of a sleeping patient off his forehead. He watched her speak to another man and when he was reluctant to speak back, she pulled a chair up next to his bed and began to talk to him. Cole could almost feel her compassion and then he thought of Ruth's comment: *You have no empathy. You don't care about anyone but yourself.*

"She's beautiful," Dickie said. "And she is a very charming creature. You mustn't make her one of your conquests, Jordan."

"Okay."

"No. I insist, old boy."

Cole turned to Dickie. "Have I ever lied to you, Dickie?"

"Oh, that's a very stupid question. Of course you have. And I've lied to you."

Two orderlies and a large, round nurse that Cole took to be the infamous Noonan appeared to take Dickie off to X-ray.

"Wait for me, will you, Jordan? It gets terribly lonely here."

"Sure. How long?"

Dickie looked at Noonan for an answer.

Noonan nailed Cole with a defiant glare. "Well, it won't be five minutes, I can tell you that. We don't run St. Elias just to make you sailor boys happy. Forty-five minutes and not a second less, and if we're stacked up like we were yesterday, it'll take as long as it takes."

Dickie rolled his eyes and said, "There's a lovely little square just to the rear of the hospital. Go and have a quiet smoke and then come and see me." Dickie quickly cupped his hand and brought it to his mouth several times, flashing a ridiculous grin.

Cole smiled and nodded. He left the hospital and

found a small store run by an ancient man that sold spirits. He bought an overpriced bottle of gin that the storekeeper grudgingly slipped into a paper bag, after examining his ration coupon. "Most don't have need of a bag. They just slip it under their arm and go about their business," he said, fixing Cole with a cold eye.

Cole found the square that Dickie mentioned, a carefully tended patch of grass and shrubs around a ring of wrought-iron benches, and sat down, glancing at his watch. At least a half hour to kill before Dickie was safely returned to his room. He was just lighting a cigarette when he saw her enter the square. "Rebecca?" he called out. "Mrs. Blair?"

She stopped, puzzled. Then she realized who had called to her and walked toward him.

"Lieutenant Cole, is it?" There was that voice again.

"Yes," Cole said, standing as she approached. "Dickie's friend. Are you playing hooky?"

"I beg your pardon?"

"Sorry," Cole said. "It's an American expression. When you skip school. Please, join me."

"Oh," she said, smiling. "I see. No, I'm not playing hooky, but I should like to very much. I've worked my first eight and I have an entire thirty minutes before I start my second."

"Sixteen hours?" Cole whistled.

"Don't tell me that you've never worked those sorts of hours."

"Yeah," Cole said, "I have but—"

"You think it's different somehow because I'm a woman?" she said without malice. "Is that it?"

"How do I get out of this?" Cole said playfully.

"Raise your right hand," Rebecca said. She waited until Cole did and then she said, "I faithfully promise never to underrate women as a class and any woman that I meet, so help me God. Say it."

"I faithfully promise," Cole returned with a smile. "Coming from you, that doesn't seem like such a difficult promise to uphold."

Rebecca's cheeks tinged red with embarrassment. She fumbled for a cigarette.

"You really care about those guys in there," he said, trying to ease the awkwardness that he had created. "It's not just a job with you."

"Sometimes I wish that it were," she said, taking a light from Cole. "Before the war it could be rough at times, but this . . ." She stopped and shook her head.

Cole knew immediately that she was overwhelmed. He saw her immersed in a world of death and suffering, and then he thought how trite the two words sounded, linked to describe the horror that she must see every day.

"Rough?" Cole said because he could think of nothing else and because he wanted her to continue talking.

She chuckled dryly and he sensed the worn condition of her soul. "Rough. Yes, that's it. I often go home and have a good cry." She dropped the cigarette at her feet and looked at him, making a valiant attempt to mask her pain. "Anymore, that doesn't seem to be enough. Sometimes there are simply no tears left." She wasn't embarrassed about her emotions, that she felt so much of what she saw. "What about you, Lieutenant Cole? Have you seen the effects of war, firsthand?"

"No," he said. "Not really. I've seen what everyone else has seen, I guess. The destruction. I've seen dead people laid out on the sidewalk. I just control my emotions."

She smiled in wonderment. "Control your emotions? How does one do that?"

"I don't know," he said honestly. "Just something that I learned as a kid. Keep an even keel." It was his turn to smile, watching her eyes respond to his words. "Why? Don't tell me you let everything get to you. If you do that, Rebecca, you're going to end up a basket case." He thought calling her by her first name sounded natural.

"Basket . . . ?"

"Nuts."

"I should think it would be the other way around, Jordan."

When she said his name it was as if he were hearing someone else say it for the first time. He berated himself for acting like a child, for letting his feelings run away with him. But it felt wonderful, somehow, her soft voice speaking his name. He tried to calm his emotions.

"I suppose that I should be going," she said.

"Don't you have a few more minutes?" he pleaded carelessly.

She stood and looked down at him, smiling. "I cannot run in these silly shoes and I must not be late. Noonan, you know."

"Can I walk with you?" He held up the bottle. "I've got to see Dickie anyway."

"I shouldn't let Noonan see that," Rebecca said. "Regulations state that I must inform the head nurse of all irregularities."

"Can you be bribed?"

"Do you have an extra pair of silk stockings?"

Cole laughed and began to walk with Rebecca, feeling her presence at his side. Silk stockings were nearly impossible to obtain, except through the black market, and even then they cost most people nearly a week's wages.

"Is your wife here with you?" she asked as he basked in the warmth of the weather and the comfort of having her nearby.

"No," he said. "I mean I'm not married. Engaged once but it didn't work out."

"I'm sorry," she said. As they walked Cole felt suddenly very protective of her. He wanted to put his arm around her small shoulders and draw her close to him so that nothing could harm her. He folded his arms clumsily behind his back, fighting back the impulse.

"Nothing to be sorry about," he said. "Better to find out before the marriage than after it."

They walked slowly, neither in a hurry to part—their pace evenly matched despite their difference in height.

"That's an oddly detached way of putting it. Almost clinical, in fact," she said.

"Nothing else to it."

"Who . . . ?" she began and then quickly added, "Oh, now I'm being much too nosey."

"She did," Cole said. Ruth was taller than Rebecca, her hair much darker and her eyes equally as dark. Overbearing, Cole had reported to his friends, but that was his excuse. *You never talk*, she had said to him, *you never tell me what you're thinking. What you're really thinking. Nothing*, Cole responded most of the time, brooding over her attempts to intrude on his thoughts, on the feelings that he so carefully tended and cultivated until they were stunted and withered. "Funny," he said. "That's the first time I ever told anyone the truth about my engagement."

"That's understandable," she said. "I'm sure the parting was very painful."

"No," Cole lied as he felt Rebecca's caring eyes examining him. "It wasn't."

Chapter 5

Aboard H.M.S. Firedancer, *escorting Convoy*
EBX-740, the North Sea

Captain George Hardy was blinded as the detonation destroyed his night vision and devoured the darkness. An instant later the shock wave from the exploding freighter shook *Firedancer* viciously. Flaming debris shot crazily into the air, fantastically graceful arcs of fire that ended abruptly in the coal-black North Atlantic.

Hardy clapped the 7x50 Barr and Stroud binoculars to his eyes, straining to make out the dying vessel across the columns of the convoy.

"Bridge, W.T. Bridge, W.T.," the wireless/telegrapher operator called through one of the brass voice tubes banded together on *Firedancer*'s tiny bridge.

Lieutenant George Land, number one of *Firedancer*, pulled one flap up of the Russian sealskin helmet. He had been feeling sorry for himself because he was tired and cold, and the oil-skinned duffel, overcoat, oilskins, scarves, balaclavas, and that damned helmet didn't help keep the frigid air of the North

Atlantic from stealing into his body. All that was
gone now. Men were dying out there.

"Bridge, W.T. What is it?"

"Merchant ship *Mecoy* struck by torpedo. Requests immediate assistance."

Hardy, his grim features frozen in the phospho-
rescent glow of the emergency action station switch,
shot Land a glance before the officer could speak.
"We do not leave this station, Number One, until
ordered to do so. Has he heard from Captain D?"

Land leaned into the voice tube. "W.T. Bridge.
Have you any orders from Captain D?" The captain
in command of the destroyer flotilla would have to
give them permission to abandon their station and
precede either to the assistance of the *Mecoy*, or to
hunt for the U-boat.

"Nothing, sir," W.T. replied.

Land looked at Hardy, who merely turned away.
"Right," Land said softly into the tube. How heartless could the man be? Couldn't he signal Captain
D and request permission to leave his station and
go help those poor bastards on the *Mecoy*? They
couldn't last more than a minute or two in the
freezing water.

Another blast tore the darkness far on the port
beam of H.M.S. *Firedancer*. Land found that he
could not help himself; his eyes were drawn to the
bright death that glowed seductively in the night.
He noticed Hardy watching as well and wondered
what the man must be thinking.

"St. Luke, Number One, chapter fifteen, verse
four," Hardy said into the darkness, but it was obviously meant for Number One. "'What man of you
having an hundred sheep, if he lose one of them,

doth not leave the other ninety and nine in the wilderness, and go after that which is lost until he find it?'" Hardy adjusted his duffel and pulled his scarf tight around his neck. "Well? Are you that type of officer?"

"Bridge, W.T. *St. John* struck by a torpedo. Captain D advises he expects an attack in *Firedancer*'s quadrant."

Hardy leaned over the voice tube, his eyes still on Land. "Reply, 'Signal acknowledged. Standing by.' Well, Number One. I see by your silence that you have not made a decision. 'Indecision' is not good enough out here. 'Indecision,'" Hardy added, "kills sailors and sinks ships."

Land felt warmth spread over him despite the cold as he fought back his anger. There were times when he found Hardy tolerable and once or twice he actually enjoyed the man's company. There were other times, most of the time in fact, when he couldn't stand to be around the sharp-tongued, ill-mannered officer.

Hardy slid the binoculars to his eyes again and said, "We'll speak about it again when you do know how to make decisions."

Chief Torpedo Gunner's Mate Sandy Baird, standing next to the MK 1 Depth Charge Rail sandwiched between the two TSDS Davits at *Firedancer*'s stern, removed his gloves, blew on his fingertips, and examined the fuses in the six depth charges. His shivering crew, bundled in every bit of clothing that they owned so that they looked more like a band of unemployed dock workers than sailors of the Royal

Navy, stood near him, awaiting orders. "'The Lords Commissioners of the Admiralty hereby appoint you captain of His Majesty's Ship *Firedancer* and direct you to repair on board that ship.'" He slipped on his gloves. "Now of course," he continued, as the men around him tried to rub some warmth into their torsos, "everyone bloody well knows that you've got a case of the shakes. And everyone bloody well knows that your Jimmy the One—"

Another explosion racked the *St. John*, and Baird's eyes narrowed in hatred as he watched the flames roll into the darkness. "That your Jimmy the One," he continued, using lower-deck slang for Number One, "is sailing 'two balls at the yardarm.'"

"What's—" Seaman Tommy Blessing began.

"'Not under control,'" Torpedo Gunner's Mate Engleman said. "Sandy there knows all there is to know about our officers, Sandy does. Ain't that right, Sandy?"

"Young Seaman Tommy has a right to know," Baird said. "It wasn't long ago that the lad was just a boy seaman straight off of H.M.S. *Ganges*, and God bless all that sailed on her."

"You men," Sublieutenant Morrison said, "quit your loafing and make ready in case we're called in."

"Right you are, sir," Baird said sharply, and then watched as Morrison made his way along the starboard gangway to the Y-throwers. "Lord Nelson himself come back to life."

"Sandy's never had a kind word for anyone," Engleman said to Blessing. "How he's managed to stay chief torps this long is a mystery. Every P. R. O. in Andrews wants a short talk in a dark room with

Torps Baird. Enemies he's got all right. Thirty years of them."

The deck telephone rang three times in quick succession. Sublieutenant Morrison slid back along the icy deck and barely stopped himself long enough to pick up the receiver.

"Depth Charge, Morrison."

Baird felt a change in the timbre of the ship's engines and a slight list to starboard as *Firedancer* changed course. He smiled at the others and gave them a thumbs-up. They were going after U-boats now.

Morrison laid the receiver down on the cradle, his face strangely white and pinched with fatigue. He was afraid, Baird knew, maybe not afraid of the enemy or even death, but chances there was some of that for sure. He was afraid of not doing his job and doing it properly—he was afraid of letting his chaps down. *Ah, he's a boy,* Baird told himself in a brief moment of understanding, but then the chief torps realized the truth of the matter: there was no place for boys in this business. They came to Andrews all proper and polished, stiff with loyal indignation and clear faces and pressed uniforms. Boys, just boys.

"Depth Charge Party, close up!" Morrison shouted, trying to sound brave. "Captain's orders. Spread of six at his command. Depth, 150 feet. Baird, see to it. I'll notify the Y-mounts."

"Yes, sir," Baird said, digging into his duffel and pulling out the depth-charge-setting key that hung from a chain around his neck. "All right, chaps. Remove the blocks." Wooden blocks were used to wedge the fuses in place prior to dropping the charges. It prevented premature explosion of the squat drums packed with three hundred pounds of TNT. When that happened it would be a brush and shovel job. If the explosion didn't sink the ship, that would be the only way to retrieve the bloody pieces of the men's bodies from the scorched and twisted stern of a smoldering hulk.

Baird knelt down, inserted the key into the tumbler, and dialed 150 feet. When he stood he noticed the others watching him nervously. They'd never been in battle before. Most where Hostilities Only and they depended on the leadership, wisdom, and just the physical presence of Active Service men like Baird, Engleman, and the others. Even Jimmy the One and Morrison were H.O. And Hardy? Hardy was Active Service and had come out of the Royal Naval College at Dartmouth, but there were too many questions about him. It was said that he'd taken a corvette into some French port and had it out with German tanks but then his nerves began to fail him. No one could say for sure that's what happened, but the fact that it was even reason for talk belowdecks over a steaming hot cup of kye was cause for concern. Baird and his chaps could forgive anything except a man on the bridge that they did not respect.

Baird forced himself to laugh. "Is it a wake you're going to? Why, we'll have this over in no time and then it's Splice the Main Brace. Rum is bound to make anyone feel better. Even our own Lord Nelson."

Firedancer rolled to starboard again and the deck danced beneath their feet as the engines increased. Then there was a quick turn to port and another shift to starboard.

"Well," Baird said loudly with a confidence that he

did not feel, "the old man has found something, all right. Maybe old George is a proper seaman, after all."

There was an explosion a thousand yards on the starboard bow and Baird watched with amazement as a tanker disintegrated in a mass of flames. He could think of nothing else except the word *volcano*, although he'd never seen one or even a moving picture of one, but he'd heard talk of them and they must surely look like this. The fire was alive and feeding on the ship as if it had been imprisoned at one time within the ship's hull and now suddenly let loose and wanted to destroy with a vengeance the thing that held it captive. It rolled and licked and boiled high into the air, over the deck and superstructure, and dripped from the ship's scuppers into the inky water. This must be hell.

The telephone rang again and Morrison was at it in an instant.

"Depth Charge Station, Morrison."

The others waited, watching for any hint of action from Morrison's face.

The tanker continued to explode, showering the surrounding sea with flame.

"God help those poor sailors," Baird heard Engleman whisper. He turned his attention back to Morrison. He could see the telephone receiver tremble in the young officer's hand.

"Yes, sir. Right, sir. We're ready, sir." Morrison's eyes found Baird's in an unspoken plea.

Baird turned quickly. "All right, you Jack-my-Hearties, stand by. Smartly now or it's over the side with the depth charges you go. When these splash I want six more on the rack faster than you can light a Woodbine." He made sure that his crew was in place before turning back to Morrison. The officer replied with a tiny nod, or perhaps it was nothing more than a tremble. Suddenly his hand tightened on the receiver.

"Yes, sir," he said and then raised his arm and shouted to the crew. "On my mark!" Baird gripped the gate release handle and rested his foot on the gate lock pedal.

"Now!" Morrison shouted.

Baird stomped on the pedal and jerked the lever back. The gate flew open and depth charges began to roll out of the rack. He heard the sharp crash of the port and starboard Y-throwers as the charges propelled the depth charges far away from *Firedancer* and into the darkness. The depth charges at his feet clattered down the track, a tiny train in motion, and suddenly they were gone. He knew that somewhere in the darkness below him they sank innocently, indifferent to the cold.

Astern, the sea boiled and vomited white, throwing frothy water far into the air. Immediately after there was a low boom in the darkness as the sound of the explosion reached the surface. The depth charges from the Y-throwers exploded seconds after and Baird felt the exhilaration of battle—that sharp, hot burst of power that tightens your muscles as taut as bowstrings.

Training does it—routine, step after step until it becomes as natural as breathing. Rote, don't think, don't consider, fall into the rhythm of action until nothing exists but the immediacy of duty. Training does it—make sure that everyone knows where to be and what to do and when to do it so that no moment, no movement is lost. Flesh-and-blood machines,

Baird called them, unfeeling beasts whose shouts and commands fill the air to accompany the sounds of actual machines swinging into action.

He looked at Morrison for further orders and saw the officer hang the receiver in the cradle with a dejected look.

"We're to stand down," Morrison said morosely.

"Stand down?" Baird said.

Morrison exploded. "Yes, damn you!" He was turning to make his way to the Y-mounts when he stopped and looked back. "And you'll address me as sir, Chief Torpedo Gunner's Mate Baird! Is that clear?"

"Yes, sir," Baird said, "it is." Torps Baird cocked an eyebrow at his depth charge party and pulled a packet of Churchman's Number 1's from his duffel.

Blessing's eyes grew large as Torps lit the cigarette.

"That's a captain's table for sure. Smoking without permission."

"Oh, and you think Johnny's going to pick out my Churchman in the light of a burning tanker?" Baird shook his head in disgust, snuffed out the cigarette, and threw the carcass over the side. "Here? Engleman. Go track down Lord Nelson and see if he wants us to reload these racks." After Engleman left, Baird took Blessing by the shoulders. "Boy Seaman, I'm twenty-eight years in Andrews and this is the closest that I've ever been to a goat fuck. Heed my words, Boy Seaman, for every word is true and certain. If we come out of anything that we go into, it won't be because of the sawdust heads on the bridge." He blew a breath and watched the vapor snatched up and carried over the stern. "Next time that we tie up I'll sign aboard as a counter hand at a wet fish shop in Clacton."

Hardy looked at Land in shock. "Cease fire?"

"Yes, sir," Land said. "Captain D's signal."

Hardy pushed Land to one side and called down the voice tube, "W.T.? Read that signal."

"W.T. Bridge. From Captain D, 'Break off action immediately. Proceed Scapa Flow.' End message."

"Surely he can't mean that. What is all this nonsense? We've got the bloody bastard dead-to-rights." Hardy slapped back the cover on the voice tube. "W.T.? Bridge."

"W.T. here, sir."

"Make to Captain D, 'Your last transmission garbled. Resend. *Firedancer*. End message.' Understood, W.T.?"

The wireless/telegraph operator read back the message to Hardy's satisfaction.

"Those bloody U-boats will swarm in and out of this pack of sheep all night long," Hardy said to no one in particular. "They'll bite a hunk out of the convoy's body to port and one to starboard and come astern when it suits them. The whole thing will bleed to death until there's nothing left. And now some idiot dispatches *Firedancer*, fully ten percent of this convoy's protection, to Scapa Flow—"

"Bridge. W.T."

"Yes!" Hardy shouted.

"Message from Captain D."

"Yes, you bloody imbecile!"

Land could tell that the sailor on the other end of the voice tube was hesitant. "'Come on, *Firedancer*.

No one uses that old dodge anymore. Orders are orders. No matter how asinine. Now go and do your duty.' End of message."

Hardy walked to the windscreen in frustration. He stared across the darkness, past the flaming tanker, and was somehow lost. He turned to Land. "Acknowledge, 'Received, Captain D. Proceeding as ordered.'"

He moved back to the windscreen and watched the little red dots bob up and down in the water. There were hundreds of them, floating about in a random pattern of death. He felt sick, standing high above them, as if in life he were given some sort of superiority over the little red dots. And secretly, he was glad that he was far removed from the lights. That only added to the guilt of course, not only that he was alive and they weren't, and he shouldn't have felt superior? He felt that he had somehow allowed them to die and the voice of reason that could have reassured him that of course that was nonsense went unheeded. His shame sprang from guilt, like some horrible flower from the putrid earth. If he had done his job then—if he had done his job before—men would not have died.

The ideas, the horrible pronouncements swirled around his mind like waterspouts chasing across the sea. No end to one, no beginning to another—just existence and with it the knowledge that he was responsible, somehow.

Each of those hundreds of silent, little red lights was attached to a cork life vest, and each vest held a dead man. They were men who had abandoned their burning ships and sought the false sanctuary of the frigid sea. But they had only forestalled death and not escaped it. The cold killed them in minutes so at best they had not suffered the horror of being burned alive, or the slow agony of drowning, trapped deep belowdecks of the dying ship.

These lights, to Hardy, were marks upon a tally sheet of his failures. He was responsible for saving those men—he did not, a mark against him. He should have sunk the U-boat—he had failed, another mark.

Hardy turned away from the floating lights. It was the Second Night all over again.

Cole waited impatiently, a debate raging in his mind. *Ask her, hang up, you idiot!* He heard the muffled sounds of the nurses' station coming through the telephone after a nurse with a squeaky voice said, "Rebecca? Yes, she's here. Who shall I say is calling?"

Cole suddenly panicked, not out of a sense of guilt but propriety. A married nurse receiving a telephone call from a man when her husband was missing in action might lead to gossip. The kind that would hurt Rebecca—something that Cole did not want to do. He threw together a plan that sounded weak and transparent.

"I'm a friend of Sublieutenant Moore's," he said. "I'm just calling to see how he is."

"If you'll give me just a minute I'll be happy to check his chart—"

"Just let me talk to Nurse Blair," Cole said, exasperated. To hell with it; let people talk. He was never good at being subtle anyway. He heard her voice in the background, speaking first to someone about a patient's condition, and then to another nurse about doctors' incompetence, and finally he heard the telephone being picked up.

"Rebecca Blair," she said, the voice hesitant and a little puzzled. "You've a question about Sublieutenant Moore's condition?"

Cole was relieved and excited at the same time. He realized how important it was to him to hear her voice again. "Kind of," he said.

There was a moment of silence before Rebecca said, "I beg your pardon?"

"Rebecca?" Cole said. "This is Jordan. How are you?"

There was even a longer silence before she replied and Cole could tell that she was startled. Now he really did feel like an idiot. He'd get out of this somehow; make up some excuse, or blame it on work. . . .

"I'm very well, Lieutenant Cole. How are you? It's so kind of you to inquire about Sublieutenant Moore. He's doing much better. He should be up on crutches shortly."

He was thrilled. She was covering but she kept the conversation going, and every word was a chance to Cole—a chance that she might accept.

"Look, I'm sorry to call you at work but I didn't know your home number." He spoke quickly, hoping that she would not hang up. "I'd like to see you again."

Silence.

"Maybe this isn't right. Maybe you have every right to tell me to go jump in the lake, but I just wanted to see you again."

Silence. Then it was interrupted by muffled laughter and he heard Rebecca's name called several times and the sound of papers ruffling and the telephone being knocked about before he heard her voice again.

"Yes," she said, her voice even softer than before. His heart soared and he tried to calm himself.

"The weather's nice. At least nice for England. I can get my landlady to fix a picnic basket for us. Is that okay?"

"Yes," she said, and then her voice dropped nearly to a whisper. "I would like that very much. Have you a pencil?"

Cole snatched a pen from its holder. "Yes."

"Is two o'clock today all right? I have a few off hours that I can take."

"That's great."

"Warren Square. Number twenty-two. Can you find it?"

"I'll find it," he said. Cole heard her name called with playful urgency and heard someone try to take the telephone away from her.

All Rebecca managed was: "Good-bye, then."

Cole had a hell of a time finding the row house in Warren Square. He rang the doorbell and waited. The door opened and she appeared, and her quick smile made Cole smile in return. She was as glad to see him as he was she.

"I hope that I haven't kept you waiting," she said, unnecessarily.

"You haven't," Cole said and there was much more emotion in his voice than he had intended. "My car's just over there. I bribed my landlady to fix a picnic lunch. No potato salad but we've got some kind of noodle salad."

They drove to Hyde Park, Cole excited that Rebecca sat next to him in the tiny car, Rebecca silent, watching all that swept past them. So much destruction, notices posted on telephone boxes and lampposts—*Have you seen so-and-so? So-and-so, come to your cousin's.* People displaced, families missing; a list of dead next to a list of those who were luckier—in the hospital.

When they arrived and found a quiet spot near a stand of trees Cole spread the blanket, and Rebecca began setting the places and unpacking the food. It was natural for them to do that, Cole thought, and for an instant he saw them married but quickly dismissed the idea. He was being foolish. They sat for some time without saying a word, watching a group of children play across the way.

"My husband and I used to come here quite often," Rebecca said.

Cole was disappointed to hear her mention her husband. No, it was more than that—he didn't know anything about the guy and Cole hated him already.

"Gregory," Rebecca continued. "He prefers Greg. He's a banker. Well, not now of course. He's with the army . . . in North Africa. Missing in action."

"I guess this was a bad idea . . ." he started to say but he didn't mean it. He was selfish enough to want Greg in an Italian prisoner of war camp for the duration.

"No," she said. "No, I'm very glad that you asked me. I've been thinking about you since we met at hospital. I suppose that's a bit bold, isn't it?"

"No," he said. He'd been doing a lot of thinking as well.

She looked at the sky. It was a soft blue and the barrage of balloons drifted about easily on their long tethers, as if they had always been there and had not come because of the war. "It is a lovely day, isn't it?" Rebecca said.

"Yeah," Cole said, following her gaze. "Maybe I ought to take a picture since these days are few and far between."

"The vagaries of English weather," she teased.

Cole returned her smile. "Why'd you go into nursing?"

Rebecca handed Cole a bottle of beer and took a drink before speaking. "My father, really. Daddy is very rich and very powerful. Because of the war he will become more so. Manufacturing. My mother, who is beautiful and refined, dotes on Daddy. He in turn keeps mistresses. I suppose that I just needed to find a place in life."

"Look," Cole said, the words tumbling out, "I've been around. I just wanted you to know that up front." He felt awkward and stupid. He was a young man again, trying to be sincere but all he managed was clumsiness.

"You say up front," Rebecca said softly, "as if you expect that there will be more to follow."

Cole took a drink of beer and then examined the label on the bottle.

"You have difficulty talking, don't you?" she said.

Cole shook his head. "Not really. Some people even call me glib."

"I don't mean that," Rebecca said. "I mean sharing what's inside you. Telling people how you feel."

"Yeah," Cole said. "I've heard that before. Maybe. I don't know. I guess I have trouble getting things out. But if people don't know how you feel," he added, "they can't use it against you."

Rebecca took Cole's hand. Her touch was almost electric. "Jordan," she said, those caring eyes searching his, "that's half a life."

Cole heard the children's laughter but he never took his eyes from Rebecca's. The children were shouting and running and screaming with joy because no bombs were falling and they did not have to spend time in the dank, putrid bomb shelters. They could be children again and play as children should and worry about nothing.

Cole leaned closer to Rebecca and kissed her gently. He drew back and saw tears in her eyes, which made him want to tell her that everything was going to be all right, but when he began to speak, she pressed her slender fingers against his lips. He nodded, knowing that words were unnecessary. Rebecca removed her hand and leaned into Cole, kissing him deeply.

When they parted Cole said, "Why are you crying?"

"I've been on a raw edge lately. I'm so sick and tired of seeing dead and dying. The men are bad enough but there are women and children. Babies. I cannot let them see me cry. They bring people in missing arms and legs, horribly burned . . . they must not see me cry."

Cole watched her take another drink of beer and fish through her purse to find a handkerchief. She patted her eyes, careful not to smudge her mascara. "I must look a dreadful sight," she said.

"No," Cole said, "you look fine."

"Makeup costs a bloody fortune and if I've cried any off I shall be very cross."

"Everything's right where it should be."

"I love my husband, you see." She wiped away a stray tear.

"It was only a kiss," Cole said, trying to help, but he saw immediately that he'd said the wrong thing.

"Is it very common for you?" she said, her voice strangely sad. "To be with women?" She saw the hurt look on his face. "Oh, I'm so very sorry. What a perfectly horrible thing to say. Please forgive me."

"Maybe you're right," he said, suddenly ashamed of himself. He hated himself for the answer but he didn't want to lie to her. "I just never thought of it that way."

"I've never . . ." Rebecca searched for the right words. "I've never been unfaithful. In a way . . . please understand what I mean and not how I say it. In a way it seems that you're still a child."

"Why?" Cole said sharply. "Because I want to be with you? What's wrong with that?"

"We've just met," she said gently. "How could you . . . ?"

"I don't know," he said. His own anger surprised him, but he felt that she was finding fault with him—dissecting his emotions so that they could be revealed, one by one, as false.

"Don't be cross with me, Jordan. I was only trying to explain. It's like you're looking for something, that's all I meant," Rebecca said. "It just seems so apparent to me."

"Okay," he said, feeling the anger subside. "Maybe I am looking for something." He regretted that he

had called her, and he realized that no, that wasn't
it. She was prying, he thought, like Ruth used to do.
"You make it seem like I'm trying to get you into
bed or something." It was a harsh thing to say but
he felt the need to shock her as payment for how
she made him feel. "It's a picnic and it was a kiss.
What's the harm in that?"

"You don't know anything about people's emotions, do you? Do you think that you live in a vacuum
and that whatever you do has no impact?" She
would not let go. "Perhaps it never did before."

She looked at him with tenderness but pity as well,
and he wanted to say something to hurt her for it,
but the words did not come.

"The harm, Jordan, is how I feel about you," she
said. "It's so very odd, isn't it? A chance meeting and
then suddenly I find myself thinking constantly
about you. Not of my husband, Jordan, but of you.
The war does that. It causes everything to race
ahead. Everything becomes unnatural, out of balance, forever tumbling. The covenants of life evap-
orate and leave only the urgency of living. It
distresses me, Jordan, but I cannot turn away." Then
she stood and said, "Please take me home."

Chapter 6

Admiral Karl Doenitz stood uncertainly in the stern of Grand Admiral Erich Raeder's barge as it slipped under the huge complex of camouflage netting suspended far about the surface of the Kattegatt, and neared the reason for his visit: the H-class D.K.M. *Sea Lion*, the most powerful battleship afloat. According to some.

"Think of it, Karl," Raeder had boasted to him on their miserable journey to this barren island. "We have built and hidden it from the English. Larger even than my *Bismarck*. Everything is bigger and better. And more deadly, Karl. She will charge into the English fleet and deal death with impunity. The Fuehrer cannot wait to see it in action."

"Yes," Doenitz had said, wanting to get back to Berlin and his U-boats. When he heard about the project and saw the plans four years before, he had remarked to his chief of staff Ernst Godt: "Such an expensive coffin." To Doenitz, nothing was as important or as effective as his U-boats. Large surface ships such as *Schranhorst, Tirpitz, Gneisenau,* and *Bismarck* were wastes of Germany's limited resources. They were obsolete giants, ponderous, clumsy vessels that floundered about the North Atlantic until they blundered into battle. And now, once more, the same mistake, except on a much grander scale—the H-class *Sea Lion.*

But as the barge sailed deeper into the vast cavern created by the camouflage, Doenitz began to have doubts about his own first impressions. God, she was huge! Her hull was a vast, gray, solid fortress that dwarfed the barge as it maneuvered to the ship's side. Dazzle camouflage, wild patterns of gray, black, and white, slashed across her hull in jagged bands—a simple device to confuse enemy gunners and spotters. Perhaps she might one day lose her exotic look and be painted all-over outboard gray, a practical but uninspired acknowledgment of her primary role as a warship.

Sea Lion's complex superstructure towered over him and could only be compared to a mountain range. He had seen the four main turrets and their twelve guns from a distance and he thought how menacing they looked in repose, sleeping along the centerline of the vessel.

When the barge nestled against the duty platform, Doenitz stepped aside to allow the handful of reporters and a dozen or more party officials, resplendent in their pseudo-military uniforms, to clamber aboard. When that pack of rats had cleared the ladder he mounted the steps with dignity, his fragile hands clad in soft leather gloves falling lightly on the rail with each step. His staff followed him at a discreet distance.

When Doenitz reached the deck he saw what must have been the entire ship's compliment drawn up at attention, vast ranks of deep blue, double-breasted peacoats and caps, impervious to the stiff winds of the Kattegatt. It thrilled him to see Kriegsmarine sailors, rigid as steel, their ranks formed directly along the joints of the deck beams, and their silent lines shadowing those of the *Sea Lion*. Here was the pomp and ceremony of the Kriegsmarine that he so often eschewed publicly, preferring quiet meetings with his U-boatmen. But, deep within, as the band played "*Deutchland Uber Alles*," and he saluted the ensign astern, the officer of the deck, and then Grand Admiral Raeder—he felt like a cadet fresh from Flensburg. He stepped aside to allow his staff to pay their respects. As they did he admired the long graceful lines of the freshly scrubbed oak main deck. Well, she was beautiful in design and execution, but was she a warship?

He remembered the sixteen-inch guns of the main armament and decided wryly that they were certainly in her favor. From where he stood he took an inventory of the weapons dotting the superstructure. He counted five heavy antiaircraft batteries, each with a pair of 10.5cm/L65 C33 guns. He knew that there were five on the port side as well. He calculated the medium antiaircraft batteries as well and came up with thirty-two 3.7cm guns. Doenitz gave up trying to count the light antiaircraft guns; there were far too many, and they were too widely dispersed.

Despite his own reluctance to admit it, Raeder's *Sea Lion* was a formidable vessel and he had taken *Bismarck*'s inadequacies into consideration in arming

Sea Lion with a forest of antiaircraft guns. *Bismarck* had been destroyed, regardless of who claimed credit, by British Swordfish torpedo bombers—obsolete wood-framed, and fabric-covered biplanes that flew no more than a hundred miles an hour. An elephant brought to its knees by a gnat.

"Ladies and Gentlemen," Kapitan zur See Wilhelm Mahlberg, *Kommandant* K. of *Sea Lion*, said. "If you will please follow these officers, they will lead you to the wardroom. There you will be briefed and plied with mugs of hot chocolate. Nothing stronger, I'm afraid." The half dozen civilians laughed and trailed after the officers, talking excitedly.

Raeder made his way to Doenitz.

"Well?" he said excitedly.

"When I saw her in the ways," Doenitz said, choosing his words carefully, "I had no idea that she would grow this large."

"She was fed on good German steel, Admiral." Raeder laughed. "Isn't she something? And her *Kommandant* and officers are handpicked. You know Frey?"

"Otto?"

"Yes. He is *Erster Artillerie Offizier*, I.A.O."

Doenitz looked over the vessel again. She seemed to grow even larger.

"Yes," Raeder said. "She does take your breath away, doesn't she? Twenty-eight watertight compartments, a top speed of thirty-seven knots—"

"Good Lord! *Bismarck* could do only—"

"Yes. Thirty-one knots," Raeder said, but then he hesitated, as if there were much more to what he had to say. He guided Doenitz in a friendly manner and walked the admiral along the deck, toward the bow. Raeder looked overhead at the vast field of camouflage netting that stretched from pylons driven deeply into the shallow ocean floor, suspended at a dozen points on the superstructure of the *Sea Lion*.

"We shall go to the briefing in a moment," Raeder said. "I want to spend as little time with those hyenas as I have to. Tell me, Admiral Doenitz, haven't you wondered what *Sea Lion*'s first mission is to be?"

Doenitz had not. All of his time was taken up with U-boat operations or the War Production Board trying to get U-boats built, or investigating the newest British antisubmarine measures, or trying to avoid the endless round of meetings that somehow required his presence. But he knew how to answer the question.

"I did not feel it appropriate to ask, Grand Admiral. I must confess it was constantly on my mind."

Doenitz was relieved to see that Raeder was pleased with the response. The old man could be brittle and mercurial. The grand admiral patted Doenitz on the hand, as if Doenitz were the naughty student and Raeder the wise old schoolmaster. Raeder's attitude irritated Doenitz, but it was one that he had to suffer. The most difficult of all of Raeder's condescending manners to accept was that U-boats would always be greatly inferior to surface vessels. Raeder was of the old school—the unfinished business of Jutland when British and German coal-burning behemoths had tried to destroy one another and the old kaiser had dreamed of *Mare Germanica*. If Raeder had the same dreams, twenty years removed, he was a fool, Doenitz decided. But Doenitz knew that Raeder was a superb tactician and brilliant seaman and could not be easily cast as a fool. *Perhaps a man who does foolish things,* Doenitz said to himself, *but we are all guilty of that.*

"We are going to kill Winston Churchill," Raeder said, and then he smiled at Doenitz's shocked expression.

Mahlberg smiled with indulgence as the civilians and party officials found seats around the unadorned wardroom table. He had ordered that the decorations and other amenities be kept to a minimum so that the visitors would not forget that they were aboard a vessel of war. The only concession that he made was to have the heavy, dark blue blackout curtains over the portholes pulled back and held in place with white cotton rope. Raeder had insisted on an additional flourish—the Kriegsmarine and Nazi flags hung side by side on the bulkhead behind him. Mahlberg wondered if they stood in silent competition to one another.

As the group settled in, Mahlberg's eyes fell on Ingrid May and he allowed himself a sliver of a smile. He saw that she, in turn, let her eyes casually signal that she knew he noticed her. It was difficult not to notice the only woman in the group—a woman whose blond hair, almost white against her black sweater and slacks, was pulled back in a ponytail. The look was casually provocative and not lost on the older men sitting around her who struggled to hold in their stomachs and look important. She ignored them as she laid two twin-reflex cameras on the table and took a reading of the room with a light meter.

She was known as the finest photographer in Germany, able to capture images of the Fatherland's leaders that no one else could. It was because she slept with most of them, her competitors said, or the jealous wives of the leaders. And Mahlberg's wife. Mahlberg was not sure of how many men she slept with—he knew of only one, and he found the experience delicious and decadent.

"I can help you, Wilhelm," she had said as they lay in bed one evening, spent from lovemaking.

"Can you?" Mahlberg had replied, his hand playing over her flat stomach to her breasts.

She turned on her side and looked at him, allowing his wandering hand free rein. "I have the ear of many well-placed party officials."

He remembered thinking to himself: *you've had more than their ears.* But instead he had replied, "How can you help me?"

She gasped slightly as his hand found the moist region between her legs. "Raeder has disappointed the Fuehrer many times. It is said that he will be replaced soon."

"That's common knowledge," Mahlberg had said as he began to tease her, his fingers seeking her most intimate area.

She moved closer to him, her breath hot with passion, and said, "Is it common knowledge that Wilhelm Mahlberg might be the next grand admiral?" She had closed her eyes, savoring his touch. "You must know," she had continued, the words escaping her in a rush, "that I was instrumental in that decision."

Mahlberg returned to the present, scanning the wardroom.

"May I take photographs, Kapitan?" Ingrid asked, her manner entirely professional.

"Of course," Mahlberg said. He looked over the assembled group. "Welcome to the finest ship, the largest ship in the Kriegsmarine." Mahlberg began his presentation as he heard the shutter snap and the film advance. He found himself suddenly ill at ease as she moved about—it felt too much as if she were stalking him. "You reporters, and of course our lovely photographer, have been honored to accompany *Sea Lion* on her first voyage. A voyage, I assure you, that will live in the annals of the Kriegsmarine as the greatest of its kind. When we return, you will report our triumphs to the German people. From those reports will they draw inspiration to conquer the world."

"But first, England," a fat Nazi Party official reminded Mahlberg.

"Yes," Mahlberg said, wondering how many such idiots filled the party ranks. "England first." He felt Ingrid on his left, the camera lens centered on his face, and he grew warm. There was something oddly voyeuristic about her proximity. He nodded to a *Leutnant zur See*, who handed each man around the table a neatly bound leather folder embossed with the name of the ship, the date, and the recipient, in gold letters.

"Before you is statistical information about *Sea Lion*. In it you will find her displacement, dimensions, armor protection, armament, propulsion plant, complement . . . Well, I could go on but I have no desire to delay our departure, so I will summarize much of what is contained in the folder. She is faster than the *King George V*, *Prince of Wales*, and *Rodney.* Her guns have a greater range and power than those vessels. She can steam 11,320 nautical miles at a speed of sixteen knots, or 5,750 nautical miles at a speed in excess of thirty-five knots. If *Sea Lion* were called upon to defend the Fatherland against the American Navy, she could just as easily destroy the U.S.S. *North Carolina,* one of their newest capital ships. So would she treat the French battleship *Richelieu,* and with apologies to our Italian allies, the *Vittorio Veneto.*"

There was a polite round of superior laughter around the table for the inadequacies of anything Italian, except perhaps food and women.

Ingrid returned to her seat and snapped the lens cap on her camera.

"Kapitan?" one of the reporters asked. "Can you tell us when we sail?"

"All I can say is that it will be shortly. I cannot give you the exact date and time, for security reasons."

"Well then," another said, "can you tell us what the mission is? Surely we who sail with you cannot possibly disclose that information."

"Regrettably," Mahlberg said, "I cannot reveal that as yet. The mission and your other questions will be answered when we are at sea."

"Kapitan Mahlberg," Ingrid said, "should I have packed a wardrobe for winter or summer?"

Laughter again and Mahlberg felt it was directed at him. She was an expert at subtle humiliation, with either her words or her tone. He looked away from her to the opposite side of the table. He needed her because she could move subtly through the intrigues of Kriegsmarine High Command and the complexities of Nazi Party politics. But at times, he despised her.

"I can tell you this," he said. "When we leave Leka we will proceed up the Kattegat, and enter the Norway fjord system through the Korsfjord. We will refuel in Grimsfjord, sail on to the Hjeltefjord near Kalvenes, and pick up our escort." He was satisfied to see the reporters scribbling furiously, but he had revealed more than he had intended. That was Ingrid's fault; her attitude had angered him. "Upon reaching the North Sea we have one of four options to enter the North Atlantic. We can run between the Orkney Islands and the Shetland Islands. That is the shortest but most dangerous route. We can attempt to slip through between the Shetland Islands and the Faeroe Islands. Although farther north, we are still within range of British patrol aircraft. We can drive between the Faeroe Islands and Iceland. Here we face minefields and surface vessels, but the weather is generally overcast or the sea is shrouded in fog."

"'Shrouded in fog,'" Ingrid said. "Such a lovely term for a warrior to use. Are you a poet as well as a seaman, Herr Kapitan?"

"Finally," Mahlberg said, ignoring her, "there is the Denmark Strait, the channel between Iceland and Greenland."

"What's wrong with that one?" one of the party members asked, obviously bored.

"Pack ice," Mahlberg said, "thick enough to cut a ship's hull in two, even *Sea Lion.* Minefields as well and British patrol vessels. They often keep two cruisers in those waters. But . . ." Mahlberg paused, hoping that these idiots truly understood the danger. "It is the pack ice that is the greatest threat. In the winter it closes the Denmark Strait. In the summer it reduces the strait's navigable waters by fifty percent. That means that our room to maneuver is severely restricted."

"Why, you said yourself that no vessel on earth can stop *Sea Lion*," the fat Nazi said.

"That is true," Mahlberg said. "But why give away the element of surprise before we even begin our mission? How much better to be at our prey's throat before they realize we exist?"

"The poet is gone. Spoken like a true warrior," Ingrid said. "Is our prey worth all of this secrecy?"

"You can decide that," Mahlberg said, tired of the meeting, "when we are under way and the prey is made known."

Doenitz, although inwardly amazed and intrigued, kept his reply neutral. "This is a remarkable ship, Grand Admiral, but I think it unlikely that she can reach London unscathed." What was the Old Man thinking? Surely it was not some sort of ill-conceived response to the *Bismarck* disaster? Hitler had been livid when the great ship went down and vowed that he would mothball all of the Kriegsmarine's surface vessels rather than see them supply another victory to the British. Doenitz himself had to plead against the notion, gaining Raeder's gratitude and support, but leaving himself dangerously exposed to Hitler's revenge should there be another loss of a capital ship.

Raeder began his lecture. "Admiral, consider this: the British have seen each of their allies fall in turn. Poland, Belgium, Denmark, Norway—France in a matter of days. They saved their army at Dunkirk, but even Churchill admitted that you do not win wars by retreating. Your U-boats are slowly strangling England, the cordon growing tighter every day so that soon she will lie exposed to invasion. London is in flames because the Luftwaffe controls the skies over England's capital and rains bombs down on her with impunity. So. We remove the last vestige of England's invincibility. The symbol of the island nation's stubborn resistance, at least to her people, is Churchill. Destroy him aboard one of the Royal Navy's greatest vessels and the spirit that is the bulwark of England's desire to fight evaporates. If England's leaders are not safe aboard her navy's vessels, aboard a battleship of the mighty Royal Navy, they are not safe anywhere."

"That is a formidable argument, Grand Admiral," Doenitz said, and he meant it. Churchill was the British lion, truly the symbol of Britannica. Kill this one man—kill him in such a way that it shattered the mythology of British naval invincibility—and who could tell what the results would be?

"Everything is in order, Doenitz," Raeder continued. "The where of it at least. And the how, I should say, is this remarkable ship as you call it. The when is determined by the enemy's timetable, but we can respond to that at a moment's notice. We have the Abwehr and Admiral Canaris to thank for the information that sends this vessel on the first of her many adventures."

Canaris with his military intelligence network, Doenitz thought, was as unreliable as the North Atlantic in winter. He was another self-serving amateur in the army of self-serving amateurs that surrounded Hitler.

"I'm afraid that I can't say more than that at this point. Orders, you understand. But as it evolves, you shall be duly notified." Raeder pulled a pipe and tobacco pouch from his navy blue greatcoat, carefully filled his pipe, and turned away from the wind to light it. "And?" he said to Doenitz.

"Grand Admiral?"

"'And' how are my U-boats to be involved? Isn't that what you are thinking?"

In fact he was thinking that a catastrophe lay just beyond the horizon. He had faith in the ship and her crew, and he would lead them, if his heart did not lie with U-boats, anywhere. But half of the weapons available in any country's arsenal were the decisions made about when and how to fight battles. The most exquisite planning, the most detailed timetable, the most exacting and complex web of logistical support: are all worthless if the admiral's decisions are faulty.

Doenitz nodded with a smile.

"At this point," Raeder said, drawing deeply on the pipe, "I can tell you that your U-boats will be involved in two phases of the operation. When we return to Berlin we will meet and I shall give you the full particulars. Doenitz. Listen. This is an opportunity to strike a monumental blow at the enemy. Not only to the head but the body as well. The plan must be fully coordinated and nothing can be left to chance."

"Yes, sir."

"Good. Now let us go and listen to Mahlberg entertain those asses."

* * *

It was not the entire ship's company drawn up to greet the various officers, civilians, and other dignitaries as they came on board *Sea Lion*. The crew inside the dark, damp recesses of Turm Bruno, the second turret from the bow of *Sea Lion*, fought the idiosyncracies of their temperamental child. Here is where the sixteen-inch guns were located, three across, each in its own cramped compartment so that a hit on one did not destroy the capabilities of the other two guns to do battle. Behind the gun rooms, running the length of the turret like the optical nerves of a ludicrous insect, was the three-position 10.5-meter range finder; one station for each gun. From openings on both the port and starboard sides of the turret, Bruno's gun layers could call range and inclination. But that role was played only if the main fire control, the haven of the I.A.O., or first artillery officer, was damaged or destroyed. From there the I.A.O. used FuMO 23 radar, a rotating dome with an optic range finder, and his own eyesight from a vantage point almost one hundred feet above sea level to direct fire. The information from any one of the three fire-control stations was fed down through armored communication shafts to the calculation room. The calculation room then fed the information to the appropriate batteries, adjustments were made, and guns were fired. Everything in Bruno, from her huge flat turret to the deep cylindrical well that descended four decks into the vessel and from, which came the cordite and shells to feed the three guns, had been carefully designed by marine engineers. They had created Bruno, but men such as Turm Oberbootsmannmaat Herbert Statz and his crew gave it life.

Bootsmann Max Kuhn, covered in grease and sweat, looked up at Statz from his cramped quarters in the elevating cylinder hold. The yellow trouble light cast a weird glow and cut sharp shadows from the thousand hoses, extrusions, rivets, and pipes that pinned Kuhn in the tiny space.

"I can't find the goddamned leak," Kuhn said in disgust. He dug into his dungaree pocket with a grimy hand and pulled out a cigarette. He barely had enough room to do that, and if he had been claustrophobic he wouldn't have lasted five minutes in that tiny space.

Statz provided a light for Kuhn. "You bled the lines?"

Kuhn nodded in thought, going over a list of the actions he had taken. "Twice. Nothing. No air."

"Cleaned and replaced the lines?"

"Yes," he said, blinking heavily. "Give me that rag, will you?"

Statz found a clean work rag behind him and gave it to Kuhn, who wiped his face. The rank smell of oil and grease hung everywhere. It was the heady stench of machinery: steel and lubricants.

"Checked the fittings and gaskets. I checked the pumps last week so I know they are fine," Kuhn said. As he drew heavily on the cigarette, Statz nodded, considering the alternative. He could feel Kuhn watching him. "Don't you dare bring that shit Weintz down here," Kuhn said. "This is my gun." He was not a gunner from Division 2 like Statz; he was a mechanic from Division 8, but his job was to make sure that the guns operated properly; his guns, he often said, because he was just as possessive of them as the gunners.

"He might have some ideas."

"He can keep his ideas to himself," Kuhn snapped. He calmed and sat back against the bulkhead in thought. "There's no wear on the lines. No drag on the trunnion." He looked up at Statz from the dark recesses of the elevating cylinder well, white eyes smiling out of a grimy face. "Statzy," Kuhn said, "why don't you be a kind boy and ask the O.O.D. if you can take the gun up about twenty degrees?" They had known each other for over a decade and although Statz was his superior, Kuhn never seemed to let that get in the way of their friendship.

Statz knew what Kuhn had in mind. "You crazy bastard. Do you want to die down here?"

"It's a hydraulic leak, Statzy. Suppose I get squirted in the eye? You'll rescue me, won't you? Look, it's the only way that I can find the leak. I've got my light and tools. Take the gun up slowly and I'll check out the cylinder and lines. When she's at twenty, come down and check on me. If I'm dead, you can have everything I own."

"The only thing you've ever owned was the clap," Statz said. He thought it over. Kuhn was well clear of any moving parts, but Statz still did not like leaving his friend in the dark, cold confines of the cylinder well. It was too much like a grave.

"All right," he said, mostly to stop the morbid thoughts. Statz climbed out of the well, passed the huge breech of the sixteen-inch gun, up the access ladder, and climbed onto the cramped gun controller's platform. He turned aft and squeezed through the hatch leading to the range finder's room in the after section of the turret—still bending low to keep from splitting open his skull on a dozen protruding wheels, dials, handles, and jutting, unidentifiable hunks of steel. He slid under the large range-finder tube between the port and amidships positions, around the squat analog gear computer, and found the telephone on the after bulkhead. He switched the black Bakelite knob to *Bridge*, and picked up the receiver. He heard a tinny voice say: "Bridge."

"Bruno. Statz here. We're trying to find a hydraulic leak on the starboard cylinder of Number One Gun. Request permission to elevate to twenty degrees."

The *Matrosentabobergefreiter* at the other end replied: "One moment." He would have to activate the electric motors to provide power to the pumps. After a moment he said: "Permission granted," and then Statz heard the click of the receiver.

Cussing the superior attitude of the bridge watch, Statz made his way back to the gun controller's station for number-one gun. He slid onto the small saddle chair and began opening the electrical circuits for the hydraulic fluid pumps.

"Kuhn!" Statz shouted over the edge of the platform. "Ready?"

"Hell yes," Kuhn called back. "Let's get this done. My ass is freezing."

"Pumps on," Statz said. He watched the needles climbing as the ready fluid exited the reservoirs. He switched on the reservoir release and saw the elevation indicator dial begin to rise. When the reservoirs were empty, the hydraulic fluid in the cylinders, when released, could be transferred to the reservoirs. The cylinder plunger fell, sliding into the cylinder with the weight of the breech, and the muzzle of the gun would rise. It topped out at forty-five degrees, but twenty degrees would give them an idea where the problem was.

"Five degrees," he called out over the loud hum of the gun's breech nestling deeper into its hold.

"Nothing," Kuhn replied.

"Ten degrees," Statz said and adjusted the fluid flow so that the gun would fall smoothly.

"Right."

"Fifteen."

"Statzy—"

There was a soft boom, like the noise of a distant firework. Nothing dangerous, nothing frightening about it. Just a sound that came to Statz from the starboard cylinder well.

"Kuhn!" Statz shouted. "Kuhn?" He quickly shut off the circuits and swung over the platform railing. He locked the insteps of his shoes to the outside ladder railings, gripped the railings with his hands, and dropped like a rock. He landed hard on the narrow deck that surrounded the cylinder.

"Kuhn?" He found the trouble light but it was out. He pulled a flashlight from the back pocket of his overalls and played it rapidly over the dark interior of the well. He saw the ruptured cylinder first. There was a two-foot slash near the bottom of the cylinder—hydraulic fluid dripped from it like blood from a wound. "Kuhn!"

Statz found Kuhn, jammed between two support flanges, cut nearly in half. Statz slumped to the deck of the cylinder well and sat in three inches of hydraulic fluid mixed with the blood of his friend, who stared back at him with sightless eyes. He must have been right next to the cylinder when it erupted—close enough for the pressurized hydraulic fluid to rip him apart.

When Kuhn was finally pulled from the turret and his body lay on a stretcher, there was more to be concerned about for the crew of D.K.M. *Sea Lion* than the fact that they had lost a friend.

Sailors are superstitious and they know that vessels are sometimes marked as lucky or unlucky. To those who never put to sea, it may seem childish and nonsensical, but life aboard frail vessels that dare the North Atlantic are governed by laws unnatural in any case, and unrelated in all cases to the land. There are complex regulations and statutes, known and unknown, put forward by the sea and enforced with absolute dispassion. Earth gives firmness and stability and seldom rises up to attack those who travel upon it. The sea is not so considerate and demands that all sailors be wary and all ships be prepared to submit to its edicts.

Now, in all of the sections and divisions aboard this remarkable vessel, old sailors shared similar stories while serious young sailors listened, about unlucky ships and unlucky crews, and they always came back to sailors dying.

Chapter 7

The garden of Number 10, Downing Street, London, 21 July 1941

Louis Hoffman followed a butler into the bright sunshine and saw the short, stocky figure of Winston Churchill, cigar in one hand, brandy snifter in the other, comfortably enthroned on a cast-iron settee.

"Mr. Hoffman. How are you?" Churchill said, making no move to rise.

"I'm fine, Prime Minister," Hoffman said, but he wasn't. He'd been too long in England and he wanted to go home. He couldn't get a decent meal unless he went to the embassy. Thank God Joe Kennedy wasn't there to bore him to death. Franklin had recalled the former ambassador some time before because Kennedy had a way of making it sound as if he admired Hitler and the Nazis. That admiration didn't mix well at dinner parties thrown by the English.

"Care for something to drink, Mr. Hoffman?" Churchill said, as if reading his mind.

"Scotch and water," Hoffman said.

"Immediately," Churchill ordered the butler with a chuckle. "Mr. Hoffman looks as if he is in need of refreshment." He took a sip of brandy and said: "All in all, how do you think we English are faring, Mr. Hoffman?"

"All in all, Prime Minister," Hoffman said, lighting a cigarette, "I'd say that the Germans gave you the old one-two combination and you're on the ropes."

"That's a lovely boxing analogy."

"Thank you. Feel free to pass that on."

"Indeed, I shall. Louis, we English can be obstinate. We are like a bulldog; you can beat us time and again and we will come back after you. Feel free to pass that on as well, Louis."

"Thanks, Winston, I will."

The butler arrived with the drink and Hoffman took a healthy taste. "Ahhh, the breakfast of champions." He eyed Churchill. "We've got the go-ahead?"

"By all means, Louis, Parliament has approved it, my lords of the Admiralty assure me that it will be a calm and relaxing voyage." He paused and swirled the remaining brandy inside the snifter. "This may be the most important meeting undertaken in the history of these two great countries. We are the same blood, you Americans and we British. We have a common ancestry and common values, not to mention a common language. We are the last bastions of democracy and we must band together to fight this terrible evil."

Hoffman nodded, ground the cigarette out on the heel of his shoe, and stuck it in a potted plant. "You're taking a chance, you know. I don't care what anybody says, it's a big ocean and those Kraut bastards would like to send you to the bottom. But the fact is that cables and telephone conversations don't do the trick. Franklin told me that he wanted an eyeball-to-eyeball meeting with you because that's how he does things."

"To take the measure of the man, is that how it is?"

"Yeah, except we call it sizing a man up."

"The same concept, Louis," Churchill said. "I agree. The issues are far too complex and far-reaching to be relegated to cables and telephone conversations. It would hardly do them justice and may lead to confusion at a time when confusion may lead to catastrophe. We must sit and talk like civilized men."

"Franklin knows that. You know it. So we're halfway home. He wants to make this meeting count, Winston. There are a lot of people in the United States who'd just as soon stay out of this mess. They don't see this thing in Europe as our fight."

"This 'thing in Europe' is every man's fight, Louis. It is ultimately a struggle of good versus evil."

"Yeah. That's what I've heard." Hoffman took a sip of his drink. "Winston, some people in America think that Hitler is the good and you're the evil. I just hope that we can convince them otherwise before it's too late."

"So do I, Louis."

Hoffman leaned forward, resting his elbows on his tiny legs. "You've got to be straight about everything. Brutally honest. Don't hold back and don't try to gold-plate anything. Franklin's a cagey son of a bitch and he can smell a load of horseshit a mile away. Be candid. Don't hold anything back."

"I wasn't aware that I was doing any such thing,"

Churchill said calmly, unaffected by Hoffman's language.

"Maybe not in so many words, but you've been careful to add a spoonful of sugar to the answer of every direct question that I've asked you."

Churchill cocked an eyebrow and rolled the cigar around in his mouth. He pushed his considerable bulk out of the settee and walked to a brick wall covered in ivy. He turned and came back to Hoffman.

"One gentleman to another, Mr. Hoffman," he said in a soft voice, "may I ask what transpired in your communications to President Roosevelt since you arrived?"

"One gentleman to another, Prime Minister, I thought you'd have the damned phone tapped." Churchill tried to protest but Hoffman continued. "I know Franklin and he may be the president of the United States but he's also a politician. The same goes for you, so it means that both of you are going to play your cards close to your vest. I told him what I thought, which is what he wanted."

"What are your thoughts, Mr. Hoffman?"

"You folks are in a hell of a fix over here. If things don't improve and I mean quick, you'll be throwing shit balls at the Germans when they land on the beaches. You need arms and munitions and just about everything else. Sometime soon you'll need American boys to lend a hand."

"That's an accurate description of the situation, if a bit caustic."

"My advice to you, Winston, when you get behind closed doors with Franklin, is to forget all of that blood, sweat, and tears hogwash and tell him the same thing I've been saying in my cables: 'Franklin, it's the top of the seventh and they're behind by six runs.' Get me?"

"Baseball, Louis?" the prime minister inquired.

"Yeah, Winston. If something doesn't happen and happen soon, England will fall to Germany."

Churchill nodded somberly. "I see why Franklin enjoys your company."

"Nobody enjoys my company, Winston. Not even me. I'm a son of a bitch."

The prime minister expelled a cloud of cigar smoke and then brushed it away with the back of his hand. "Two weeks. We'll leave Scapa Flow aboard H.M.S. *Prince of Wales*. The meeting with President Roosevelt will be candid, forthright, and untarnished by rhetoric."

"That's good."

"You'll come with me of course, Louis?"

"Oh, hell yes," Hoffman said bitterly. "The only thing that I like more than airplanes is boats."

Churchill cocked his ear to one side when the butler appeared.

"I beg your pardon, sir, but the gentlemen from Germany have arrived."

"Yes, I thought I heard antiaircraft fire. Louis, would you care to join me in the bombproof?"

Hoffman heard the faint wail of warning sirens and saw tiny flak bursts in the distant sky. "Got anything to drink down there?"

"I wouldn't have it any other way, Louis."

Cole maneuvered the MG through crowded streets, darting around stopped vehicles. He stomped on his brakes and the tiny car slid to a stop as civilians rushed across the street to air raid shelters. He heard the coarse boom of antiaircraft artillery, as the shells exploded directly overhead. Barrage balloons swung complacently back and forth.

When the frightened crowd had passed he jammed the gearshift into first and stomped on the gas pedal.

An air raid warden shouted at him to pull over and find a shelter, but he had to get to the row house at Warren Square, Rebecca's home.

He looked overhead to see a Heinkle, the German bomber, trailing smoke in a long graceful arc, glide languidly across the sky, followed by an angry Hurricane. The British fighter was pumping bullets into the carcass of the enemy plane.

Bombs were hitting around him now; he heard the sharp explosions, and the screams of the people who had not reached the shelters in time. Dirty brown towers of smoke and debris cluttered the horizon as the bombers swept through London. Cole had seen it before and was always fascinated by the macabre slow-motion eruption of the blast and the unidentifiable remnants of houses and people as they fell to earth. He never spoke to anyone about it because he was ashamed to, but he saw magnificence in all of it, a monumental spectacle unfolding in a vast arena. Too much the historian, he had cautioned himself—removed from the reality of war by the crisp white pages and stark black letters of textbooks.

It was murder of course—civilians dying by the thousands, contrary to all rules of warfare. But Cole saw it with the clinical eye of a professional and did not invest the view with emotion. His ex-fiancée would have had a comment about that. *You're cold and calculating,* Ruth had told him more than once. *Analytical and careful,* he had said, but he thought, ironically, that that was a reply delivered with no real emotion; it was simply constructed as a response. Maybe he was a coldhearted bastard after all.

Cole whipped the MG back and forth, trying to avoid debris scattered in the street, racing frantically to get to Rebecca's. He'd followed the course of the bombers as he drove to his flat and suddenly realized that they were headed for Rebecca's portion of the city. She was at home—he knew that she was there because he had called her, wanting to talk about the other day, but she had said that there was nothing to talk about and that she would have to be going soon anyway. She was at home—directly in the path of the attack.

A bomb suddenly landed in a house ahead and Cole saw a section of a wall begin to totter. He knew it was going to fall in the street. It was going to fall on him. He downshifted and steered the car up on the sidewalk on the opposite side of the street. He heard a tire blow and he was pretty sure because of the terrific jolt he felt when he hit the curb that he'd broken a spring as well.

He saw the section of wall slowly detach itself from the burning house and begin to fall. Cole tried quickly calculating how much room he had to clear the wall—when the wall would land, where it would land.

He watched in disbelief, as the falling section seemed to grow larger, the disintegrating brick monolith trailing a swirling veil of red dust, reaching out to crush him. The MG shuddered valiantly through the debris, bumping over bricks, timbers, and bits of people's lives scattered on the sidewalk.

Cole was under the wall, caught in its shadow. He could sense it falling on him, feel its presence grow as it pushed the air out of its way in an attempt to reach him.

He was through.

The world exploded behind him. He felt the MG shake from the concussion and he was enveloped in a cloud of dust so thick he could not see where he was driving. But worse, he could not breathe as the thickness filled his mouth and nostrils. He saw a lorry in front of him and he tried to swerve to miss it, but the MG did not respond. He slammed on the brakes and skidded into the heavy rear wheels of the vehicle. He was dazed but he managed to climb from the vehicle.

He looked around to get his bearings and heard the drone of aircraft engines. He had to get to Rebecca's house. If he was caught out in the streets he wouldn't last five minutes.

Cole was three blocks from Warren Square and sanctuary when he began to run. He could hear the demonic whistle of the bombs falling from the sky and then the blast as they crashed into the ground, spewing debris into the air. The horizon was a false sunset with a red and orange tint, flickering as fires raged throughout the city. Above it was the true sky, a natural blue perverted by columns of dirty smoke that rose as monuments to destruction.

Cole tasted the dust and the smoke stung his eyes and nostrils and he heard the frantic clanging of the fire bells. He knew that firemen dressed in long coats and archaic helmets, like those worn by ancient warriors, were out, fighting the fires. But it was no use—the fires were too numerous and widespread and the gallant men in their quaint little helmets must have known that they could not win.

He saw Rebecca's house and ran across the square, barely avoiding a speeding fire truck. He bounded up the few stairs and tried the handle. The door was locked.

Cole looked up and saw another wave of enemy bombers headed toward him, their throbbing engines echoing off the buildings.

"Rebecca?" he shouted, pounding on the door. "Rebecca? Open the door." He slammed against it in desperation but it wouldn't budge. "Rebecca!" He jammed his elbow into the narrow windowpane, breaking the glass. He reached through and found the lock. He flipped it and threw the door open. "Rebecca? Where are you?" He heard the rumble of the approaching planes and knew that they had only moments to reach a shelter. The flak guns began firing, sharp cracks that increased in tempo as they found the range.

"Rebecca?" he called, moving into the drawing room from the hall. He saw her, a filthy, dust-covered ball curled up in the corner, her head pressed tightly between her knees.

He ran over to her and grabbed her wrist. "Come on. We've got to get out of here."

She jerked free and pushed herself back into the corner like a trapped animal, trembling. Rebecca was wild with fright and began to bat and scratch at Cole. He tried to trap her in his arms and lift her to her feet as he heard the bombers getting closer. They were out of time.

"You're going to get killed unless you get your ass moving. Now get up!" He tried to lock his arms around her waist, but she fought back, slapping at him.

"Leave me be," she screamed at him. "Go away!"

He stopped and looked up, as if he could see through the roof of the old building, as if the bombers were visible. It was the high-pitched whine of the falling bombs that stopped him. The bombers were here.

Cole's eyes searched the drawing room and through the open French doors, the dining room, looking for some protection. He made his decision.

He ran into the dining room and pulled the heavy oak table into the opening between the two rooms. With the heavy table and the load-bearing overhead they might just have a chance.

He heard the bombs exploding and the house shook heavily in response.

He took Rebecca by the wrists, jerked her to her feet, and dragged her to the makeshift bomb shelter.

The front windows disintegrated with a blast as Cole pulled Rebecca to the floor and rolled under the table.

The house trembled and clouds of dust filled the room as the world outside exploded. Cole pulled Rebecca close to him as she screamed in fright, her body shaking. The bombs were a constant crescendo, one melting into another until it seemed that there was nothing but one deafening rumble, punctuated only by the high-pitched whistle of the falling bombs or the screams of the terrified little form in his arms. He heard things falling, crashing—he heard the destruction of the world and it went on.

He realized that he was trembling as well and he pulled Rebecca closer. He did not feel frightened, he did not *think* that he was frightened, but his body shook uncontrollably. He saw Rebecca's face, saw the tears slowly sliding over her checks, and began frantically kissing her hair and face, hoping to drive the fear away, trying to tell her that he was here, that everything was going to be all right. He tasted dust, tears, and sweat and his kisses became more passionate. She responded and suddenly her mouth was on his and her arms clenched so tightly around him that he found it difficult to breathe.

The explosions continued and the air became heavy with a thick fog of plaster dust. The heavy table bounced into the air several times from the impact on the foundation of the house, and Cole felt the floor shift with each explosion.

Then it was silent in their little shelter.

They lay still and outside all that remained was the mad clanging of the fire engines, the shouts of people, and the roar of a hundred fires. Cole inhaled a mouthful of dust and began coughing uncontrollably. "Are you all right?" he finally managed.

"Yes," came the muffled reply, her face pressed against him. "I think so." Rebecca pulled away from him. "I've never been so frightened in my life."

"Join the club," Cole said. He spat out what he could of the plaster dust. "Sorry. I think I inhaled the living room."

"There's soda in the liquor cabinet. Unless you fancy a drink."

"After that, I fancy two drinks." He smoothed her hair back out of her eyes. "When I saw those bombers headed for your house . . ." He couldn't finish.

"You shouldn't have come," Rebecca said, getting up. She looked around. "My poor house." The clanging of fire bells caught her attention. "I've got to be going. They'll need me at hospital."

Cole stood. He pulled a sliver of wood from her hair. "You'd better give yourself a minute. You've just been through hell yourself." He didn't want her to go.

"Why did you come?" she asked.

He looked at her, dumbfounded. "That's a hell of a question to ask at a time like this."

Rebecca said, "I wasn't very kind when we last spoke."

"I'm just being chivalrous. Don't read too much into it. You were a damsel in distress, that's all." That wasn't enough—it was much more than that. "It's just . . ." He couldn't find the words and knew that anything that he tried to say would sound false. He laughed. "Yeah, I'm glib all right. I can't string two words together."

"You puzzle me at times. I was dreadful to you and yet you came to rescue me. Is that it?"

"Why do you care why I came?" he said.

"That's the problem, isn't it, Jordan? I do care." She brushed herself off and moved into the parlor, pulling debris away from the liquor cabinet before opening the shattered glass doors. "This was a present from Daddy for my marriage. Not just the cabinet—the house and everything in it. I never fully explained why I became a nurse. I became a nurse because I wanted my own life. I didn't want to live in my father's shadow. I wanted to feel needed, that what I did mattered." She handed Cole a glass. "You can understand that, can't you?"

"Yeah," he said, remembering. *I feel like an ornament on your arm,* he had told Ruth after a few drinks one night. *Don't be a fool,* she had replied, rolling over and going to sleep. He never spoke to her again about his feelings.

"Greg was the most charming man that I ever met. Handsome, educated, a vast circle of friends. We had a storybook romance, married, honeymooned in Italy, and when we returned home to this house, which Greg would only live in as a concession to my daddy's wealth, I prepared to go to work one day. 'We'll have none of that,' Greg said. 'Not for a wife of mine.' I love him but I realized that I was just another part of his perfectly balanced, carefully chosen life. I was well on the way to becoming my mother. I was certain, there was no doubt in my mind, that Greg would soon follow the same path that my father had chosen, that eventually I would not be enough for him."

"You're working. That should mean something. . . ."

"Greg's in Africa. Perhaps he's dead. No one is certain. Now you've come into the picture. Am I a part of your perfectly balanced life thousands of miles from home?"

"Is that what you think?" Cole said, his temper rising.

"I don't know," she said. "You reveal so little of yourself."

"Lady," Cole said, "it's not like that. Don't lump me in with anybody else—not your daddy or your husband, because I'm neither. I'm just a sailor. Okay, I've played the field. I told you that. I never hid the fact that I did. I'm here because I was scared to death that you were in danger. When I'm not with you I think about you."

"That's all very—"

He moved closer. "I'm not done yet. You talk about need. No one ever needed me. Not ever. I could have been another sofa in the living room for all that mattered. And I've made it my business to make sure that I never needed anyone. You said something about half a life. Maybe you've got half a marriage, Rebecca, and I didn't figure that out until just now." He set the glass on the liquor cabinet and pulled Rebecca into his arms and kissed her deeply. She resisted at first but finally gave in, her soft lips yielding to his.

"Jordan—"

"Listen to me," he said. "I was alone before I met you. I'm not now. Maybe I'm being selfish about the whole thing but I don't care. I've never felt this way about a woman before. I couldn't stand to hurt you. I don't want to lose you. I don't want to be alone again."

"You say 'I' so very much. Does your world revolve around only what you want? What you need?"

"Okay. So that makes me selfish."

She laid her head against his chest. "You must understand, darling, not everyone can live their lives for themselves alone. I cannot be that way. Regardless of my feelings for you. Please understand. Please know that I want nothing more than to be with you. It is not as simple as you think."

Cole held her at arm's length so that he could look

into her eyes. "It is," he said defiantly, ready to fight to keep her. "We care about one another. That's all there is." He wrapped his arms around her protectively, the thing that he had most wanted to do in the square when they first walked together. "That's all there is," he said again, but he knew that it wasn't. There was Rebecca's devotion to a man who might be dead.

Chapter 8

Coastal Command Headquarters, 21 July 1941

Cole stayed with Rebecca as long as he could before she went off to work. He wanted to make love to her, but he knew it would have been wrong—she would have to be the one to say when. He'd salvaged his MG, changed the tire, and after skirting the worst areas of destruction, pulled up to the sentry post and presented his credentials.

"The Old Lady got it tonight, didn't she, sir?" the sentry asked.

Cole followed the sentry's gaze and looked over his shoulder at the glowing horizon. London was burning again. "Yes, she did," Cole said, thinking of Rebecca.

"Still," the sentry said, "she's a tough old bird, she is. She'll come out of it."

Cole agreed but the sentry had not seen the carnage that he had seen, and it was that and nothing more: carnage. A woman's torn body, one arm gone, her head lolling back and forth as if to protest her death as she was passed down from the rubble of what once was her home. A fireman tried to provide the last bit of dignity to the corpse by keeping her legs closed and her tattered skirt wrapped close to her body; there were no words fit to describe that single incident. One of a dozen that Cole saw as he drove back to the base and that stayed with him as he entered the photo analysis room.

He found the bottle that he and Markley had shared earlier. He held it up to the light. A thin film of liquid covered the bottom. Markley had been more than generous to himself.

He took a swig, pulled the bundle of Leka Island photographs from a file drawer, and began methodically laying them, one after another, a studied cadence, on the light table. When he reached the end of the light table he began again, and again, and again until Leka Island covered the surface table. He flicked on the light, lit a cigarette, and began to study the photographs.

Something was going on there, he knew. Or something was going to go on there. He laid the lens on the prints and began his journey up and down the rows of photographs. Antiaircraft sites. He reached without taking his eyes off the images and found a red grease pencil in the track at the end of the table. He marked the site—three of them, all on the east side of the island, covering the cluster of smaller islands. He continued on and found new buildings barracks or structures of some kind. These were better quality photographs than anything he'd seen before. He turned one over and read the stamped date, time, and sortie number. This had to have been *N-for-Nancy*'s last run.

"Oh, it's you, sir," Markley said from the doorway.

"Thought we had ghosts about." He saw the photographs on the light table. "A man's got to get some rest, don't you know, sir? A man can't do a proper job unless he has a good night's sleep. Sometimes I take a drop to help me sleep, sir, but I always make time for a good night's sleep."

"Yeah, I saw the bottle."

Markley coughed into his palm. "Hair of the dog, I assure you, sir."

"Must have been a Great Dane," Cole said. "What about these photographs? They're new."

"Yes, sir. Came in from Leuchars. That crew tossed the cameras but not before pulling out the film canisters. Most fortunate for us, sir."

"Yeah. It's our lucky day. There's a hell of a lot more detail here than the other photographs, but it still doesn't answer my question."

"What question would that be, sir?"

"What's all of the shooting about? If there's nothing there, why make a fuss? I need an eyewitness."

Cole watched Markley stroke his red mustache with his thumb and index finger in thought. "You know, sir. There's a Norwegian chap down in Charts and Maps. Got out just before the Germans took over. He's a sailor, I believe. At least he drinks and cusses like one."

"Get him."

"Begging your pardon, sir, but it's a bit late to be waking someone up, don't you think?"

"Now, Markley."

It was thirty minutes later that Cole heard the sound of cursing in the hall. It grew louder and more profane until a short, stocky, florid-faced man filled the doorway. Markley stood a respectful distance behind the Norwegian, his uniform disheveled and a red welt under his eye.

"Who the fuck do you think you are, getting me out of a warm bed?" the Norwegian said with a thick accent.

"Have a care with those words!" Markley roared. "You're speaking to an officer."

Cole ignored both of them. "I need your help."

"Fuck you and your help. You aren't English! Fuck you, whoever you are."

Cole waved Markley back as the big man moved at the Norwegian. "Lieutenant Jordan Cole, United States Navy."

"Now the goddamned Americans want to boss me about. First it was the Germans, and then the English. Now the goddamned Americans. What next? The Swedes?"

"Do you know anything about Leka Island?" Cole asked.

The Norwegian turned to Markley in pure despair and jerked a thumb over his shoulder. "Who is this imbecile?" he asked the gunner's mate.

Markley was about to answer when Cole jumped in. "Listen to me, you foulmouthed son of a bitch, I know you can cuss and you can probably drink, but I haven't got time to listen to your life story. So I'll ask you again and this time I'll speak slowly so that pea-sized brain of yours can wrap itself around every fucking syllable. Do you know anything about Leka Island?"

The Norwegian pursed his lips and nodded. "This is a fellow who can grow on you," he told Markley. He walked to the table. "I captained the ferry that ran between Goteboro and Alborg and I know Leka Island better than you know the hairs on your ass."

"Okay," Cole said, handing him the lens, "take a look at the photos and tell me if you see anything unusual."

The Norwegian looked at the lens in disgust and tossed it against the wall. "I don't need these fucking things." He hooked his hands behind his back, bending over the table, and began studying the photographs, blowing out great breaths through heavily veined cheeks.

Finally he stood. "Here's your problem here, sonny. You've got one too many islands in the group."

Cole almost asked if the Norwegian was sure, but he didn't want to start him on another tirade. Instead he said, "Which island shouldn't be there?"

"This one. She wasn't there before and I don't know what she's doing there now, but she doesn't belong to Leka. Probably got blown there in a storm or dropped by seagulls." He slapped Cole on the arm and announced merrily: "You've got yourself a mystery, sonny, and a big one she is. I never heard of islands sailing about, but there's a first time for everything. Now I'm going back to bed and if you send that big walrus to wake me I'll rip off his mustache and use it to polish my boots." He made his way to the door and brushed past Markley. "Oh," he said, stopping. "It was a fucking pleasure meeting you, too."

"By God, sir," Markley said, after he left, "that man deserves a good thrashing."

Cole looked over the photographs. "I need to get to Leuchars."

"I beg your pardon, sir."

"I need to get up to Leuchars. I've got to see for myself."

"You've lost me, sir."

"What the hell is so special about Leka Island and why has this island"—he stabbed the photograph with his finger—"suddenly appeared? Can you get me up there?"

Cole watched as Markley carefully prepared his response. "Harry Hamilton will have my head and my ratings if you go flying off without orders and me aiding and abetting. Sir."

"Markley?"

"Yes, sir. But—"

"You just get me up there and I'll take full responsibility. You don't need to know why."

"Too right, I don't need to know why, sir. If you take an old sailor's advice you'll stay put."

Cole remained silent, watching the petty officer's resolve melt. "I'll do it, sir. God bless my soul, I'll do it, but if this ends badly for you, and it's for certain it will, we never spoke of it."

Cole smiled. "I wouldn't have it any other way. Why don't you take what's left in the bottle?"

"Small comfort that'll be, sir. It's nearly all gone and by my own hand."

Chapter 9

The Tirpitz Pier, Kriegsmarine Base at Witt, 22 July 1941

Admiral Doenitz watched the last of the twelve U-boats disappear in the distance, a strange tableau of peace in the constant din of the active naval base. Captain Godt, his chief of staff, stood next to him, towering over the short admiral.

"What do you think of Raeder's scheme?" Doenitz asked Godt over the clatter of a passing fleet tug.

Godt noted his superior's use of the word *scheme* instead of *plan*. It could mean nothing or it could be a sign of the admiral's dislike and distrust of the whole project.

"I think that we have a very good chance of dealing the English a crippling blow," Godt said. He watched Doenitz nod and then followed him as the admiral clasped his hands behind his back and walked along the pier in thought.

"Yes. Yes," he said as if his answer were not a part of a conversation but of ideas swirling within him. Godt dropped back a pace, watching Doenitz.

Raeder's plan was simplicity itself. *Sea Lion* would dash from Leka Island, up the Kattegat, through the Korsfjord, and meet her supply and escort vessels at Grimstadfjord. There she would reprovision and refuel. No one during the meeting had brought up *Bismarck*. It was thought that one of her fatal decisions had been not to top off her tanks before proceeding into the North Atlantic. Of course, this view was delivered in hindsight, after her battered corpse had begun rusting on the bottom of the North Atlantic.

From Grimstadfjord to Hjeltefjord, Raeder's staff officer had explained easily, his pointer gliding smoothly over the map between Fjellsund and Norway, accompanied by three destroyers and a fleet tanker.

At this point Doenitz had turned and pinned the Luftwaffe staff officer with a questioning glance. The implication was obvious: what was the air cover?

"Four Condors and a squadron of FW 190s are at your disposal," he had replied. "We will clear the skies of enemy planes so that *Sea Lion* and her flotilla will remain undetected."

Again *Bismarck* was on everyone's mind. She had been caught on the high seas and denied air cover because she was out of range of the Luftwaffe. And unlike the other powers, Germany had no operational aircraft carriers.

Godt nearly jumped out of his skin when a steam whistle shrieked overhead. He looked up to find himself next to a huge crane. It rumbled slowly down a pair of glistening railway tracks, shrieking a warning as it did. Then he noticed that Doenitz was gone and he looked around frantically.

"Godt?" The voice came from behind him. Godt turned to see Doenitz looking at him quizzically.

"Where were you going?" the admiral asked, standing at the edge of the wharf.

Godt realized that he had walked past Doenitz, lost in his own thoughts. "Your pardon, Admiral," he said. "I was thinking."

"Indeed," Doenitz said. "So was I. We have a very good chance, Godt. Our chance with this operation is as good as any I've seen. That big brute of Raeder's might just bully its way past any opposition to *Prince of Wales*. With her speed and firepower it will be no contest. If . . . if everything goes as it should." Then Godt was surprised to see Doenitz smile as if the little admiral held a secret, something so cherished that he would not divulge it to anyone. Godt knew that Doenitz often left things unspoken, or revealed things in such a cryptic manner that it was difficult to determine what the admiral really meant. "If not," Doenitz continued with the idea, "we still may achieve a great victory. If a limited one."

"Admiral?"

"U-boats, Godt," Doenitz said. "They shall be where they are supposed to be, doing exactly what they were assigned. If everything goes as it should," he repeated, "then our submariners will taste blood. We are, after all, concerned with our U-boats, are we not, Godt?"

"Yes, sir."

"Yes," the little admiral said. "No one can doubt

our loyalty. No one can point at us and say that we failed in our mission. Regardless of what transpires."

Godt understood perfectly. Raeder might fail, the Kriegsmarine might fail—but Doenitz and his U-boats would triumph. So this was not merely war—it was politics. The enemy was never just the enemy—they could be one's companion in an undisclosed strategy. Godt was suddenly very happy that he was insulated from such game playing by Doenitz. He would never be as adept as Doenitz would, in a game where losing could just as easily mean execution as dismissal.

"I believe that this is the first time that I've ever increased by one-quarter my U-boat force without adding another U-boat," Doenitz said, chuckling. "Well, enough of this. We shall wait to hear from Goliath. Our boat's first messages should give us the first indications of the mission's success."

Cole watched the copilot make his way back along the pitching Dakota transport with a thermos and tin cup. He handed the cup to Cole and shouted over the roar of the engines, "Hold it out away from you, Yank. Wouldn't want to see you scald your balls."

Cole did as he was told, trying to push himself farther back into the tattered canvas and aluminum frame seat that he'd occupied for nearly five hours.

The copilot pinned himself into position by spreading his feet and wrapping his fingers around an overhead rib.

"Probably just lukewarm by now, but it might take the chill out," the copilot said as most of the liquid managed to spill into the cup. The plane bounced and a glob of tea landed on Cole's hand. He jerked back in anticipation of heat, but the tea was nearly ice cold.

"How far to Leuchars?" he asked.

"Damned if I know. This bloody Scottish soup. If it isn't the winds it's the clouds. If it's not the clouds it's the rain. Bill there"—he motioned toward the cabin with the thermos—"just aims the plane north and off we go. When he gets tired, he lets me take over, and when I get lost, I wake him up."

"Hell of a way to run a railroad."

"Isn't it though? Do you play golf?"

"What?"

"Golf? Sport of kings and such."

"I thought horse racing was the sport of kings," Cole said.

"Not in this bloody country it's not. Golf's the thing. St. Andrews. Not a stone's throw from Leuchars. Oldest golf course in the world, I'm told."

"I don't know," Cole said. "I never played the game."

"Nor have I. Well, enough chitchat. I'd best see if Bill needs me. Shall I leave the thermos with you?"

"No, thanks," Cole said, wiping his hands on the stained overalls given to him before he boarded the airplane.

Three hours later they landed in a driving rain at what Cole hoped was Leuchars. When the plane taxied to a hard stand and a lorry pulled alongside to unload the cargo, Cole was sure enough to unbuckle his seat belt, move to the rear of the aircraft, and unlatch the door. He grasped the handle and opened it slowly to keep the wind from ripping it out of his hand. A ground crewman took it from him with a nod and attached it to the holdback on the body of the aircraft.

Clamping his cap on his head with one hand, he shouted, "Where's the base commander?"

The crewman said something that was lost to the wind but pointed in the direction of a Quonset hut. It took only a few minutes of explaining to an affable colonel to allow Cole access to the crew of *N-for-Nancy*. Cole did not mention his plan to fly over Leka Island to the base commander. He was sure that if he had, the ready smile would have disappeared in a flash.

Cole found the crew of *N-for-Nancy* in the half of a Quonset hut that served as a base recreation club and social area. Off-duty crews were scattered around the few tables in the room, while several men clustered at the bar talking quietly. Four men were playing darts—*N-for-Nancy*'s crew.

Cole removed his topcoat and cap, set his briefcase on a chair next to an unoccupied table, and straightened his tie. "Gentlemen," he said to the four. "My name is Lieutenant Jordan Cole, United States Naval Reserve. I'm attached to the Royal Navy, Photographic Analysis Division."

One of the men stopped in midthrow and turned slowly. "Photographs? You aren't the chap who's been sending us over that despicable little island, are you?"

"As a matter of fact, I am."

Bunny Walker turned to his crew. "Gentlemen, here is a rare privilege. We can put to use all of those oaths that we've been muttering." Bunny threw the dart. It embedded itself deeply in the bull's-eye. "Old King Cole, is it?"

"It beats Yank," Cole said, instantly taking a dislike to the pilot.

"Well, I'm Pilot-Sergeant Douglas Walker, otherwise known as Bunny. I'm responsible for this randy bunch, which is proving more difficult each day. Especially with trips over Leka Island."

"I can appreciate that. I've seen the After Action Reports."

"Words on paper," Peter said, picking up a dart and taking his position. "Come up with us some time and see what it's really like."

"That's why I'm here."

The crew exchanged glances.

"Explain yourself, King," Bunny said.

"Let me show you something," Cole said, leading them over to an empty table. He removed the Leka Island photographs from his briefcase and laid them out on the table. "This is Leka Island," he began unnecessarily, used to briefing high-ranking Royal Navy officers who kept glancing at their watches, impatiently awaiting dinner.

"Too right it is," Peter said.

"We've seen it, King," Bunny said dryly. "But don't let that stop you."

"Okay," Cole said, "I get the picture. You don't like me coming up here to tell you what to do. But haven't you been a little curious about why the Krauts don't want you anywhere near Leka Island?"

"There's a war on, old boy," Peter said. "That should suffice."

But Bunny's curiosity was aroused. "What are you getting at?"

Cole pushed the other photographs to one side to expose the image that the Norwegian had seen. He told the RAF crew what he had been told. The men moved in closer.

Johnny, his tunic unbuttoned, with a drink in his hand, spoke first. "Now, isn't that bloody interesting? Does that Norwegian chap know what he's talking about?"

"I think so," Cole said. "That's why I came up here and why I want to go to Leka Island."

Prentice looked at Bunny. "What do you think, Skipper?"

Bunny took Johnny's glass out of his hand and downed a healthy portion. He handed it back to the dismayed gunner before speaking. "You know, King, we just don't go out on these little jaunts when it suits us. We generally wait until someone issues orders."

"Okay," Cole said. He was willing to listen until he could figure out Walker and his crew. What he hoped was that they were the sort of men who would take a chance on him.

Bunny reached for Johnny's glass again, but the gunner jerked it out of his reach. "With all due respect, get your own bloody drink, Bunny."

Cole knew that Walker was studying him, trying to determine what kind of man he was, and if he really knew what he was talking about. Neither man spoke for a moment.

"Prentice, be a good lad and fetch me a whiskey and soda," Bunny said.

"Righto, Skipper."

"Show me that island again," he said to Cole.

"Here," Cole said, tapping the photograph. "I

estimate it to be about a thousand feet long, maybe two hundred wide. It's difficult to say."

Prentice handed Bunny his drink. "You know, King, my erks are patching up poor old *N-for-Nancy* from the last go-round. We were treated a bit roughly. . . ."

"'A bit roughly,' he says," Peter said. "We threw out everything but Prentice to keep her aloft."

"Pay no mind to Peter," Bunny said. "He's half Welsh and inclined to gloominess. I should not be all that keen to go back up there because some bloke has some funny ideas about what he thinks he sees."

"I'm tired of taking your photographs," Johnny said, signaling a steward for a refill.

"Good," Cole said. "Because there won't be any photographs this time. They don't tell us anything. I need to go down on the deck."

"Are you daft?" Peter said. "We're in a Hudson IV, not a Mossie. Go get some RAF chaps who haven't been exiled to Coastal Command. We value our lives a bit more than you seem to."

"Peter," Bunny said.

"The man's mad, Bunny. Out we go again and this time with a crazy Yank and an open invitation for the Germans to shoot us down. I'll do my duty, but no one said, 'Peter, you're to go out and commit suicide.'" The bomb aimer/navigator set his glass heavily on the table, covering the mysterious island on the grainy photograph. "I'm going to sack out. Don't bother me until this bloody war is over."

"Well?" Bunny said to Cole after Peter left.

"It's the only way to find out," Cole said with certainty. "We've got to get in low. Make two passes and out again."

"Johnny?"

The gunner moved Peter's glass. "They won't be expecting us like that. We can hug the waves." He wiped the condensation off the photograph. "Can we go in at night and use flares? Better that way. Less likely to be spotted on our approach."

"King?" Bunny said.

"That might work. One pass for flares and one for a look-see."

"Prentice?"

"A bit dicey all the way round, isn't it, Skipper? I mean considering the last time. Still, if we have to go in, I'd like less of a chance for those bastards to see us. Night is fine with me."

Bunny nodded in thought. "Johnny? Run over and find out when the erks will have *N-for-Nancy* ready, will you?"

"Right, Bunny."

"What about Peter?" Cole asked. "I don't think he's sold yet."

"Peter's just being Peter," Bunny said. He looked Cole up and down. "How much do you weigh? Fourteen stone, I should say."

"Weigh? One hundred and eighty pounds, I think. Why?"

"You'll need a flight suit. It gets very cold over the Kattegat."

Chapter 10

Hardy had had his dream last night. His dream—the one that he knew would follow him forever, as the images of the Second Night were seared in his mind. Everyone aboard *Firedancer* knew about the Second Night. Convoy HBX 328 out of Halifax. The first night had been quiet, a cold black frigid following sea with a canopy of brilliant stars scattered thickly in an equally black sky. The first night had been a lark although they carried close to three hundred tons of ice, disfiguring *Firedancer*'s deck and superstructure. The extra burden meant being topside was nearly impossible and being on the bridge was barely endurable, and *Firedancer* handled like a drunken whore, staggering from port to starboard. Still, it was quiet, if uncomfortable.

The Second Night was when the U-boats had struck. In his dream he was on the bridge, alone, but somehow that never seemed odd. In reality it was crowded with signalmen and lookouts and Number One, and they all saw what he saw. They all heard what he heard. Ships exploding in the night, the harsh plaintive screams of steam whistles, the faint rumble of cargo breaking loose within the bowels of ships sliding into the depths.

He was alone on the bridge and he heard the frantic radio calls coming in, cries for help, captains begging him to come to their rescue. In the dream he thought how odd it was that he was the only escort. Shouldn't there have been others? Surely there were others? But he was alone on the bridge and *Firedancer* alone with the convoy. She raced about the dying ships, trying desperately to find and sink the U-boats, but they were phantoms. Meanwhile, ship after ship disappeared.

Now, in his dream, Land was there and the others and Hardy gave the order: "Port thirty." He gave the order because the asdic operator had made a U-boat contact off the port beam.

Port thirty.

The helmsman repeated the order as he was told and turned the wheel and *Firedancer*'s bow swung in response.

"Rudder amidships," Hardy had said.

"Rudder amidships, aye-aye, sir," the helmsman replied and then confirmed that he had done as ordered by saying, "Rudder amidships." Even in the heat of battle it was all very professional and calm without a single indication that this was anything but a superbly executed maneuver.

Out there, directly in line with *Firedancer*'s bow, was a pool of bright stars reflected in the gentle black swells. Red stars. Tiny red stars. Around them the sea turned to white froth. Red stars. Hardy, in his dream, looked at them curiously, and thought to himself, *how strange that the stars are red.*

Firedancer bore down on the pool of red stars and above all the other sounds of the night; Hardy heard the screams of the men that his ship was about to crush. Red lights on kapok vests; red, the color of blood. Arms thrashing at the water; men trying to get away from the speeding destroyer. From her hull. From her screws.

The Second Night. Fourteen ships out of a thirty-two-ship convoy, sunk.

Hardy sipped tea and watched the activity on the gray waters of Scapa Flow. The black flag had just been run up and a gun fired to recall *Firedancer*'s liberty party to the ship from Kirkwall and Stromness. As Land reported this to Hardy, Hardy just nodded.

"Number One," he said as Land was about to make his way to the wardroom to shake off this hateful Scottish cold. "Do you think a man's life is defined by a single incident?"

Hardy felt Land behind him, and sensed that his number one was taken aback by the question and was struggling with an answer.

"Never mind," Hardy said, feeling stupid and vulnerable for asking such an outlandish question. "Go about your business."

Torps Baird stood on deck near the number-one torpedo mount and drew easily on a Churchman's. There were two PR MK II mounts aboard *Firedancer*, each bearing four tubes, with a funnel and search-light platform between them. They could be fired from the bridge or from the mounts themselves, but they had to be swung into position by a hand crank. They carried the MK IX twenty-one-inch torpedoes with a maximum range of nearly fifteen thousand yards. In their blunt noses rested over seven hundred pounds of TNT. They were propelled from their tubes by compressed air pressurized to 3,100 pounds per square inch.

Seaman Blessing joined him.

"Got your fill then?" Baird said. "Straight Rush is a seaman's treat, but after we've been out awhile it'll be bully beef soaked in Alley Sloper's Sauce."

"I'm still hungry," Blessing said apologetically.

"Lord love a duck!" Baird said. "Where do you put it all, you little scupper? I'd be ashamed of myself, I would, if I ate like you and then complained I hadn't had enough to eat. Many's a time I've had nothing but a packet of Woodbines and kippers. Do you see across the way?"

"What ship is that?" Blessing said.

"*Prince of Wales*, Seaman. Isn't she the lady? *Bismarck* or not, she keeps a trim line."

"Who's that behind her? A cruiser?"

Baird looked at Blessing in disgust. "'Behind'! And I suppose that we're standing on the floor? That's *Prometheus* astern of *Prince of Wales*. She's a Diddo-class cruiser. Sir Whittlesey Martin commanding. He and our very own Captain Hardy have a history."

"A history?"

"Fire and ice. If they ever got along that well. It's been like that since they came out of Dartmouth together."

"Why?"

Baird flipped the spent cigarette over the side.

"It's a mystery. But I'm the man to ask about everything and anything, aren't I?"

"About the captain, you mean?" Blessing said.

"Him and his chum over there. Martin has family and position and poor Georgie had nobody to vouch for him. Opposites in every way except one." He let the comment hang in anticipation of Blessing's question.

"What was that?"

"Ambition, Boy Seaman," Baird said, satisfied that Blessing had sense enough to pick up the cue. "Blind ambition. They were at each other's throats in Dartmouth, so people say, and they didn't stop once they got out. Our captain and Sir Whittlesey have been at it tooth and claw, and Georgie always one step behind."

"I didn't know," Blessing said, amazed.

"It's the Lord's truth," Baird said. "Ambition fuels their fires, blind ambition. There's them that let themselves be consumed by ambition, Boy Seaman, worshiping the rewards that such brings them like them false idols that you read about in the Bible."

"What false idols?"

"Them that you read about," Baird said cryptically, "in the Bible."

"Oh."

"Now, blokes like you and me, we keep ambition safely tucked away. We go about life one day at a time, taking what it gives us. And happy we are with what we receive. We don't get greedy about it, you see. That's what ambition really is—greed. It just sounds better when a chap says that he has ambition."

"I suppose so."

"You suppose right, Boy Seaman. The problem

with captains and ambition is this: sometimes they see only what they want, not what they're meant to have, you see. So off they go, driving their ship and crew, ambition dangling fame or fortune in front of their nose like that donkey and his carrot. Greedier they get and faster they go until common sense and propriety are forgotten. Sir Whittlesey and Captain George Hardy, Royal Navy, are the same sort when it comes to ambition. But there's always a piper to pay, isn't there?"

"There is?" Blessing said.

"There is, and it's the poor sailors who pay it. Out goes *Prometheus* and *Firedancer* into the North Atlantic, with their captains afire with ambition. Mark my words, at some time or another, disaster will befall one of them—someone will have to pay the piper." Baird waited while Blessing digested the words and placed his own value on them before continuing. "They don't give a hang about us, do they? Let ten or twelve of us buy it, make it a hundred for conversation's sake, and they hardly notice. Impervious they are, hard-boiled and soaked in bile. I've seen it, lad. When Jack catches one, the high and mighty on the bridge don't feel a thing."

"How do you know so much?"

"Twenty-eight years in the Royal Navy, lad. Keep your mouth shut and your ears open and you'll do the same. Officers talk as if we seamen weren't about to hear them—bloody insolent beasts. Stripes on a man's sleeve don't give him the right to command a ship or to command the respect of those that serve. I know as much as some and more than others. 'It is upon the navy under the providence of God that the safety, honor, and welfare of this realm do chiefly depend.'"

"Who said that?"

"King Charles's preambles to the Articles of War, lad. Carved in letters as tall as a man over the arch that leads to Dartmouth. Truer words were never spoken, but half the bastards on any bridge of His Majesty's ships probably don't know it." Baird noticed a troubled look cross Blessing's face. "What is it, lad? Need the blue water cure?"

"When we were out with the convoy," Blessing said reluctantly, "I was so frightened I hardly knew what to do."

"Is that what's troubling you? Never give it a thought. That's what training is for, so that a man doesn't have to think."

"Were you frightened?"

"Me? Not a bit of it. But you see, lad, I've been at this awhile. Give yourself another ride or two on the trolley and it'll become second nature to you. I give you my word. Just follow Old Sandy."

"Will we ever get to use these things?" Blessing said, nodding toward the torpedoes slumbering in their tubes.

"Use them? Use them? Why, Boy Seaman, guns is good enough for some, but for me I'd rather get close enough to look the enemy in the face before I send them to hell. Here. When Andrews was all wooden ships and sails you had to draw alongside your enemy to kill him. Man to man. Understand? Along comes the big guns and now all of the humanity's gone out of the killing. Stand off twenty miles and let some bloke buried deep in the ship's guts tell you where to aim and when to fire. No humanity, like I said. Get me close enough and I can thread the eye of a needle with these Mark IXs. Whoosh! Off they go like the very devil himself is after them, and when they hit . . . Oh! When they hit, many a Jerry's tour is extended."

"But guns—"

"Guns! You mean those 4.5s scattered about *Firedancer*? Decoration, boy, just decoration. All they do is irritate the enemy. Keep them off balance until we can get close enough to slip one of these up their bunghole. Neatly done too. Listen, lad, *Firedancer*'s fast and nimble and even in the hands of those salt horses on the bridge she'll give a good account of herself." Baird was relieved to see Blessing smile. "That's it, lad. Keep the spirits up. Do your duty and one day you'll be torps just like me."

"I'd like that very much," Blessing said shyly.

"Well, lad," Baird said, "don't put a rush on it. I don't have a needle through me nose yet. Now, hop to and get the other blokes from the torpedo shop and we'll give oakum to the torps before Lord Nelson comes snooping about and finds us deficient. I'd take duty on a trawler before I let Number Two carry the day. Go on, lad."

Chapter 11

Above the Kattegat, 24 July 1941

Cole marveled at how quiet the crew of *N-for-Nancy* was, and how they went about their business as if it were an everyday occurrence to fly into danger. It *was* an everyday occurrence, he reminded himself, and he was one of the men who sent *N-for-Nancy* and her fragile crew into harm's way. He looked out of one of the seven fuselage windows that ran along each side of the aircraft and saw an endless night sky peppered with stars. No storms, the Meteorological Operations division at the base had told them, news that was greeted with a mixture of emotions by the crew. No thunderheads to hide in, no low banks of clouds to run for if things got . . . difficult—"No place to hide, King," Bunny had said as he made notes in his flight log. "Could be dicey all the way round." He slapped his flight log closed and said: "Still up for it, I suppose?"

"Yeah," Cole had said, but he noticed a strange tingling running through his body and he realized that it was anxiety. This was his first time in combat.

He heard the Boulton-Paul turret rotate behind him as Johnny swept the skies for enemy aircraft. Bunny had warned the gunner twice about humming into the intercom. "I can't tell if it's squelch or your own filthy humming, Johnny."

"It helps steady my nerves, Skipper," Johnny had said.

"For Christ's sake bring a flask next time. Anything but your tuneless humming."

Cole had had second thoughts about going to Leka Island when he saw the Hudson MK IV. She was a patchwork quilt of repairs and he knew that even brand-new she looked less like a warplane than the commercial aircraft she was. The addition of the ungainly turret that protruded like some obnoxious growth just forward of the twin-boom tail didn't help her lines any. *Well*, he said to himself ruefully, *you asked for it.*

Cole saw Prentice make his way back along the fuselage.

"Skipper wants you up front," he said. As they made their way forward, Prentice stopped him. "These are the beam guns," he said, pointing to the .303 machine guns projecting from small openings on either side of the aircraft. "If we get jumped, you're to take one and I'll take the other. Have you ever fired one of these before?"

"I used to shoot skeet," Cole said.

"Oh," Prentice said, a look of disappointment crossing his face. "Well, it's much like skeet except a bit faster and the clay pigeons shoot back. Come on. Skipper's waiting."

When Cole got to the cockpit, Bunny said, "Pull that jump seat down. It's where the second pilot sits if I buy it." Cole did as he was ordered and found himself in a slightly lower position than Bunny, nearly blocking the tunnel to the bomb-aimer/navigator's compartment in the nose. A row of dials filled the instrument panel in front of him and an array of throttles and knobs blossomed out of a central instrument console at Bunny's right.

"I don't suppose you know how to fly, do you, King?"

"No," Cole said, "and I've never fired a machine gun before."

"My God, is there anything you can do?"

"I'm a pretty good dancer."

Bunny shot him a glance and shook his head. "What have I gotten myself into?"

"I was just asking myself the same thing."

"Tell me that you at least believe in good luck," Bunny said.

"Sorry," Cole said. "You struck out there, too."

"My God. A heathen. Here." He reached inside his coveralls and pulled out the stuffed rabbit. "See this? This is what gets me back to base. When it gets rough, I give her three squeezes. Works every time." He jammed it back into his pocket.

Cole gazed out the windshield into the star-studded blackness. "How much trouble is this clear sky going to cause us?"

"A bit," Bunny said.

"What about getting down on the deck?"

"Getting down is a lark, old boy. It's the getting back up that gives me the shivers."

"Can you do it? I've got to get close to that island."

"You'll get close. As bloody close as I can manage it without getting us killed. One pass for flares, one pass on the deck. And then we run for Mother. Jerry's seen us come over several times at high altitude, in daylight. My guess is the flak guns are sighted and shells fused for between fifteen thousand and twenty thousand feet, so by the time they react, we'll be halfway home. Unless of course he's got the bloody thing ringed with low-altitude stuff and then that's a different matter."

"Of course."

"Of course. Jerry fighters will come tearing after us as soon as the alarm is raised, but I'm counting on the element of surprise to throw them off a bit. Now, King, you must answer a question for me."

"Okay."

"What do you expect to find?"

"A battleship," Cole said. "Or an aircraft carrier." He watched as Bunny nodded. "You don't seem impressed."

"I'm a man who's not easily impressed," he said, but then he turned to Cole. "A bloody battleship? You mean another *Tirpitz* or *Bismarck*? How on earth did you come up with that idea?"

"The size and shape of the mysterious island. It has the relative dimensions of a capital ship. I think that the Germans may even have built themselves an aircraft carrier and they've got it hidden out here. The more I think about it, the more my money's on a battleship."

"Just one? Doesn't seem sporting of them to build just one for our chaps to sink," Bunny said.

"I've always been impressed by bravado."

"I doubt they could build a battleship like that and slip it past us," Bunny said. "Even if they exiled it to this cheery place."

"Maybe you're right. Maybe it's nothing or the hulk of a vessel nowhere near completion. It could be a false alarm. But every time you fly near it, all hell breaks loose," Cole said. "That's got to mean something."

"Too right about that."

"Well," Cole said, "if it means that much to them, it means that much to us."

"Bunny?" Peter called on the intercom. "Sixty miles out."

"Can you see anything from there?" Bunny asked Cole.

"No."

"Go back up to the Astrodome. That'll give you a good view of everything. But when I shout, hop down to the beam guns."

Cole climbed into the fuselage and situated himself in the Astrodome position, staring at the stars through the clear Plexiglas bubble. It was almost peaceful here, despite the roar of the engines. The white stars glided by overhead, in the distance the sea was black and nearly invisible, and there was nothing to tell him where the horizon lay. It was a far cry from his old classrooms and the bored students who listened to him drone on about the Compromise of 1850 and the Dred Scott Decision. He was alone with his war, his place—with no one to intrude or interfere. "You're a dilettante, Cole," he remembered being told, and thought, under the guileless stars that looked down on him: *what is a dilettante except an artist in search of an art form?*

He felt *N-for-Nancy* slowly change direction and he saw the airplane's nose dip. Bunny's scratchy voice came to him through the intercom.

"All right, King, we're going down. One go-round on the flares at about fifteen hundred feet. Then we swing round and come down on the deck. Look closely because we won't be coming back."

"You bet," Cole said. He laughed at himself. His palms were sweating and his tongue seemed too large for his mouth, and his heart beat rapidly, tellingly, through his flight suit. Was it fear or exhilaration? he asked himself; and then he reverted to the scholar by trying to define the difference between the two under these circumstances—or was it an intellectual exercise that he was devising simply to remain calm? He finally resorted to telling himself to shut the fuck up. The mental gymnastics were over.

They were descending faster now, at a much steeper angle, and Cole could see a black shape ahead that blotted out the stars: Leka Island, lifeless and ominous in the night. He felt *N-for-Nancy* bank to the left, saw her right wingtip slowly rise as he steadied himself.

Searchlights came on. They began to sweep the sky, trying to trap *N-for-Nancy* in their long silver tentacles.

Nobody said anything about searchlights, Cole thought. *This is a surprise.*

"Fancy a little illumination?" Bunny said over the intercom.

"No," Cole said.

"Mustn't take them too seriously now, King. They're looking up for us. If they look down for us, it's a different story."

"How much farther?"

"Six or seven minutes, old boy. We're just reaching

two thousand feet now. Prentice will chuck the flares out of the bomb bay. We turn around and drop down to two hundred."

"Is that low enough?" Cole asked.

There was dead silence for a moment. "I say, King. Are you mad? *Nancy*'s wingspan is just over sixty-five feet. If we have to turn sharply we'll eat up a good one-third of that two hundred feet. This isn't an exact science, old chum. One little mistake and no one goes home."

"Two hundred feet is just fine with me," Cole said.

"Coming up," Peter said from the nose of the aircraft. "Ready, Prentice?"

"All set, Peter."

Cole felt the rumble of the bomb bay doors opening and suddenly he was swaddled in frigid air. It swirled madly within the Astrodome, causing his eyes to tear. The roar of the air rushing into the airplane was deafening, the howl of some enraged beast. *N-for-Nancy* shook as her sleek lines were destroyed by the protruding bomb bay doors.

"First one on three, Prentice," Cole heard Peter say over the intercom. "One, two, three, release."

He didn't know what to expect, but somehow Cole thought releasing the flare would be much more dramatic than simply words over the intercom. He saw a glint of light just to his left and realized that it was a reflection of the first flare in the Plexiglas dome.

"On three, Prentice," Peter said again. "One, two, three, release." The only noise that Cole heard this time was the rumble of the bomb bay doors closing. The stream of cold air lessened and finally disappeared. He watched the searchlights frantically sweep the sky. If those glowing eyes locked *N-for-Nancy* in their gaze, every gun on the island would target them.

"Here we go, chaps," Bunny said as the aircraft banked.

"Bunny?" Johnny said from the turret. "I don't believe that we're alone up here."

"Fighters?"

"I can't tell. Sorry, Bunny, but all I see are shapes. Two, I think."

"It'll be a fine thing if we get caught in the glare of those lights and our own flares," Peter said.

"I'll try to avoid that just for you, Peter."

Cole felt *N-for-Nancy* drop suddenly as he twisted around in the cramped quarters of the Astrodome. The flares spread an eerie, cold white light over the scene. It washed back and forth, as the flares swung rhythmically beneath the parachutes, so that shadows grew and shrunk at a fantastic rate. Cole shielded his eyes, trying to cut down the glare from the flares and the searchlights as they glowed along the soft curve of the dome.

They were virtually at sea level now and the strange island that Cole had studied in the quiet of the photo analysis room was just several thousand yards away. With the searchlights behind the island and the slowly falling flares overhead, Cole saw that it was not an island at all but a vast network of camouflage netting suspended on huge pylons that jutted out of the calm, dark waters. But the most startling sight was what lay underneath the netting: nothing.

"King!" Bunny shouted excitedly. "Time to go home."

Before Cole had a chance to answer, tracers filled

the air in front of *N-for-Nancy,* bright streaks of
angry light slicing across the sky. They looked like
fiery baseballs to Cole, coming right at his head. For
the first time he was frightened. But he wasn't satisfied with what he'd seen, either. He wanted another look.

"Take it around again," he said.

"You bloody fool," Peter said as shells began to
burst around them. "If you want to see it, get out and
walk back."

A shell exploded to Cole's right. The flash and
boom were deafening and he felt the aircraft shudder violently. There was another explosion, higher
than the first, but he felt the aircraft pushed down.
The whole night was lights, noise, and movement—
he felt as it he were in a cavern of the surreal.

"Sorry, King. Too hot here. Time to go," Bunny
said. "Hang on, chaps."

N-for-Nancy began to dance wildly through the
night, trying to throw off the searchlights and antiaircraft gunners.

There wasn't anything there, Cole thought. Nothing. Had there really been anything there to begin
with? Was it built to receive something? Had the
thing that it was built to hide never been created?

The aluminum skin in front of the Astrodome
erupted as pieces of it flew off into the night. Tracers ate into the fuselage, barely missing the Astrodome, and Cole saw Johnny swing the dorsal
turret around and the muzzles of the machine guns
flash angrily. The guns' tracers flew impotently into
the night and disappeared into the darkness.

"Two Jerry's above us," the gunner called over the
intercom.

"I saw them well enough," Bunny said. "They almost took my head off."

"We can't outrun them," Peter said.

"Beam guns," Bunny ordered. "We might get out of this yet."

Cole swung down and unhooked the left beam gun from its restraining straps. He worked the bolt twice, chambering a round. He'd seen that in a movie once; he'd never fired one of these things in his life. Prentice was at his back, manning the right-side gun.

"Nothing to it, sir," he said, "just remember to lead well ahead of the blighters and watch how the tracers fall. You'll get the hang of it, I'm sure. I just wish we had another storm to hide in."

The German fighters swept by again, one after another. They were gone before Cole saw them. He heard the harsh clatter of the turret guns and frantically searched for the enemy planes in the darkness. *N-for-Nancy* was pitching wildly as Bunny tried to throw off the fighters, but Cole knew it would be only a matter of time before the enemy returned. He dropped the gun in its harness and made his way back to the Astrodome. Behind him he could see the vast canopy of camouflage netting and he knew that they had a chance, a very slim chance to escape.

He squeezed past Prentice and into the foot of the tunnel that led to the bomb aimer/navigator's position.

"Get back to your gun," Bunny said as he kicked the rudder and added 30 percent flaps. There was nothing else that he could do—just fly like hell and hope that his gunners could keep the fighters away.

"I've got an idea," Cole said.

"I haven't the time, King. You can see I'm busy."

"Turn the ship around and fly underneath the netting. Halfway in, cut the power and let the fighters overfly us."

"Don't be foolish. I don't want to go back and there may be a hundred cables hanging from that netting. Hold on." He jerked the yoke to the left and eased it back.

"Maybe," Cole said calmly. He knew what Bunny knew: it was a chance—maybe a better chance than they had now. They wouldn't last long with the fighters—the buzzing aircraft would chew them to pieces in minutes. The netting complex held out escape for them: safety, life.

"Right," Bunny said, banking *N-for-Nancy* sharply to the left. "We're going back, chaps. Into the fire, out of the frying pan, to lose these bastards."

"Are you daft, Bunny?" Peter said. "They'll get us for sure."

"King doesn't think so, do you, King?" He turned to Cole. "Get back to your gun. If you're wrong about this I shall be very disappointed."

"You and me both, brother," Cole said. He moved behind Prentice, steadied himself, took the machine gun in his hands, and waited. He could see past the cockpit and through the windshield of the Hudson. The searchlights were out and there were no angry arcs of tracers feeling through the sky for *N-for-Nancy*. But there was a strange glow coming from the netting.

What is that? Cole thought.

"What now?" Bunny said. "More tricks?"

Prentice's gun erupted, followed immediately by the turret mounts. Cole suddenly found himself foolishly firing at nothing and jerked his finger away from the trigger.

"It's on fire," he heard Bunny say as if the pilot found the point mildly interesting. Cole looked through the Plexiglas windshield and saw the camouflage netting burning fiercely.

"For Christ's sake, Bunny, hurry," Peter said. "Those bloody bastards are on our ass."

"Here we go," Bunny said as he dropped the aircraft to wave height. The burning web awaited them like a fiery cavern. Flaming debris dripped off of the mesh foundation while strands of glowing canvas hung like demonic fingers, ready to grasp *N-for-Nancy*.

They were inside hell and could feel the heat and see the reflection of the burning structure in the water. The light was so bright that every color was burned away and their eyes hurt because of it. Cole could not get his breath, the fire had consumed all of the air, and all that was left to him was heat and smoke. He felt light-headed and he found himself falling against the bulkhead. He saw a blurry figure move in front of him and felt something that tasted of rubber clamped over his mouth. Cool, blissful air flooded his nose and mouth and he gulped it greedily. It was Prentice and he had given Cole an emergency oxygen bottle.

"Peter," Bunny said, "where are they?"

"Just over our nose, Bunny. Trying to beat us to the finish line."

"Let them run." Bunny kicked the rudder and banked the aircraft to the left, barely missing two pylon supports. *N-for-Nancy* sped out of the camouflage netting, halfway through the structure as the two German fighters waited at the far end for the Hudson to emerge.

Bunny kept the aircraft close to the water.

"Peter?" Bunny said.

"Circling like vultures," Johnny said, studying the fighters from his position in his turret, "but they haven't seen us."

"Too much excitement for you, King?" Bunny asked.

"He just needed a spot of oxygen," Prentice said as Cole struggled to his feet.

"You'll have a very nice headache in the morning, thank you," Bunny said. After they flew on for a few miles, and the crew felt more relaxed, Bunny asked Cole, "Did you find what you wanted to find, King?"

"No," Cole said.

"More's the pity," Bunny said. "But you have to understand that we won't be going back."

"Yeah," Cole said. There was more to be said but not here; not to Bunny. Cole would have to say it to his superiors. He would have to convince them that something had been under the camouflage and now it was gone. Of course they would be skeptical and rightly so. *Tell me, Lieutenant Cole, what gave you the right to go flying off to Norway? And tell me, Lieutenant Cole, what do you think the Germans were hiding there? How do you know, Lieutenant Cole—are you an expert at such things? You've done a fine job at analyzing photographs, Lieutenant Cole, and His Lordships do appreciate your hard work and they suggest that you remain in the capacity of a photo analyzer with your feet firmly planted on the ground.*

N-for-Nancy flew on, occasionally encountering a patch of bad air that batted her playfully.

Cole sat, silent, wedged against the bulkhead, thinking. There was no reason to consider that it was a capital ship; certainly no way to prove it. There had been no directives to look for additional capital ships; everyone had been accounted for—sunk, moored, or damaged. And these things didn't just spring up, and to think that one had been built and hidden from the British was impossible. Impossible.

How many times in history, the former history professor asked himself, had the impossible proved possible to the downfall of a foe? What could she be? How large was she? Forty—fifty thousand tons, nine hundred feet long? He'd remembered a conversation with Dickie.

He'd sat down with Dickie Moore over tea and some sort of pastry that tasted like cardboard on a gray, rainy London afternoon and talked about things in general. Dickie, waving his ridiculously long cigarettes like a baton, and hurriedly slurping his tea as another bit of gossip came to mind, was anything but military. But Sublieutenant Richard Moore, behind his outlandish mannerisms and air of indifference, was the most intelligent person that Cole had ever met.

"You know, Jordan," Dickie had said, crushing out a cigarette and immediately lighting another, "we ought to speak in hypotheticals."

"What's wrong with English?"

"Droll," Dickie had said, giving Cole a disappointed look. "Too, too droll. For a scholar you're very much a man of the common people, aren't you?"

"Yeah," Cole had said. "It comes with being born in a log cabin."

"Of course," Dickie had said. "So. Here is my theory. Dear Adolf causes to be built several capital ships, classes F, G, D, and E. *Bismarck, Tirpitz, Scharnhorst,* and *Gneisenau*—respectively. But wait. Dear Adolf, in a flash of Aryan pride, calls forth a behemoth— a capital ship that dwarfs all others."

"It was broken up, Dickie," Cole had said. "It never got off the ways."

"Kindly refrain from interrupting me when I'm pontificating. It's bad for my spleen. Remarkable things can be accomplished during wartime. Witness the miracle of Dunkirk." Dickie paused. "Well, I'm sure that there were other remarkable triumphs for our side, but you see what I'm getting at, don't you? The H-class lives some place in or around the Fatherland, waiting to make its presence known. It's unleashed when needed and not before."

"Why?"

"The ultimate gambit, dear boy. Don't you Americans have any imagination?"

"We don't need imagination," Cole had said, "we've got the movies." He had studied his friend's face and decided that there was enough there to warrant belief. "Okay, I'll bite. From now on I'll look for your giant battleship, but I'm not really sure what I'm looking for."

"You're a smart lad," Dickie had said with a wink. "You'll sort it out."

* * *

"How are you, sir?"

Cole looked up to see Prentice hovering over him with concern.

"Okay," Cole said and returned to his thoughts. Too big to hide? Hide it in plain sight. Whatever it was, hide it where no one would think to look, until it was time. Time for what? Why now?

Chapter 12

"Good God, Cole!" Commander Harry Hamilton shouted. "Are you mad?"

Sublieutenant Moore, standing uncertainly on his crutches next to Cole in the commander's office, said, "Easy does it, Uncle Harry, you know what Aunt Mary said about your temper."

"Don't call me Uncle Harry, Dickie."

"But what shall I call you, Uncle Harry? You haven't disowned me, have you?"

Hamilton glared at Moore, who offered nothing in return except a weak smile. "I'll deal with you later, Dickie," Hamilton said. "I'm sure your father would like to hear about this."

"Oh, don't trouble His Lordship, Uncle. I've been such a disappointment to him all of my life."

Hamilton returned to Cole. "Well? You've got something to say, I imagine? Something that would explain you disappearing into the night with one of His Majesty's aircraft?"

"I felt it was necessary to observe the situation

firsthand, Commander," Cole said. "The photographs told me only so much. I had to see for myself."

"The photographs were supposed to tell you only so much, Lieutenant Cole. That's what photographs do. The rest of it would have been decided through channels." His voice rose in volume. "Through channels, I might add, in the appropriate manner. You jeopardized your life and the lives of the air crew."

"I felt that we had a reasonable chance for success, sir."

"That was not your decision to make, Cole," Hamilton's voice boomed in the tiny office.

"Uncle Harry—" Moore began to caution.

"Oh, shut up, you little twit!"

Moore gave his uncle a hurt look. "Well, that was certainly uncalled for. Not even His Lordship calls me that and he has had ample reason to."

"Cole." Hamilton rose from his desk, barely controlling his temper. "This is a serious infraction. Serious indeed. I've had Coastal Command on the line all day wanting to know why one of theirs was commandeered by one of mine."

"May I explain, sir?" Cole said.

"Explain? Yes, explain. That's what I've been waiting for."

"With your permission, sir," Cole said, laying photographs of Leka Island on the commander's desk. He relayed the significance of the small island and told Hamilton of his conversation with the Norwegian captain. He went over the flight and the existence of the massive camouflage netting system and the incongruity of the Germans expending resources to keep British reconnaissance flights away from an uninhabited island.

"Surely it was inhabited if the bastards were shooting at you?" Hamilton said.

"Unc—" Moore's words were cut short by a curt glance from Hamilton. "Commander Hamilton, I believe Lieutenant Cole is on to something of immense proportion that deserves at least a proper hearing."

"Go on," Hamilton commanded Cole.

"The size of the camouflage complex, length, width, and height, suggests a capital ship of some sort, sir," Cole said. "A large one. Larger than a pocket battleship."

"Both *Tirpitz* and *Bismarck* are accounted for, thank God," Hamilton said, his manner softening. "So we can certainly rule them out."

"Yes, sir," Cole said. "But what if it's a ship that we've never seen before?"

"What?"

Moore laid a thick manila envelope stamped *Most Secret* on Hamilton's desk and turned it facing the commander. He opened it and said, "You had better sit down, Uncle."

"An H-class battleship, sir," Cole said. "I think that is what the Germans had hidden near Leka Island."

"H-class?"

Moore turned the folder around and began to read: "'Displacement over sixty thousand tons, length over nine hundred feet, beam 130 feet, main armament, twelve 406-millimeter cannons in four-by-three placement. She has twelve 150-mm C28 guns in a six-by-two arrangement.'" He looked up. "At least we think she does. Most of this intelligence is subject to change, you understand." He flipped through the pages. "She has a complement of 2,600 officers and ratings and an estimated speed in excess of thirty-five knots." Moore closed the folder. "Almost makes one think that she could fly, doesn't it?" he mused brightly. His smile froze when he saw the scowl on Hamilton's face.

Hamilton studied the two officers before speaking. "Let me understand you," he said, his voice low and cold. "You two think that the Germans have built and successfully hidden a ship the size of Scotland and that the Royal Navy and the Coastal Command, with all of the resources at their disposal, have failed to note its existence?"

"Yes, sir," Cole said.

Moore gave Cole a warning glance. "I think that was meant to be a rhetorical question, old man."

"Yes, sir," Cole said. "I do."

"Very well," Hamilton said calmly, sitting down. "Where is it now?"

"I don't know, sir."

Hamilton glanced at Moore for his answer.

"That is the question, isn't it, Uncle Harry?"

"There are regular reconnaissance flights over those waters by Coastal Command. If this ship exists"—his eyes dropped to the folder—"if she exists, she will not remain unobserved for long."

"Sir, may I suggest—" Cole began.

"No, Lieutenant Cole," Hamilton said. "You may not. You will return to your duties in Photo Ops. You will make no unauthorized journeys, nor will you exceed in any way those orders that bind you to this command. You may be young, Cole, but I expect mature decisions from the officers under my command. Sublieutenant Moore, you will do the same. I don't want to hear any more ridiculous nonsense of phantom ships and mysterious islands. Dismissed."

Both Moore and Cole saluted, but before Cole left, Hamilton said, "Cole. I had high hopes for you. I still do. But if you persist in unmilitary-like behavior I shall have no choice but to contact your superiors in America. They will, I'm sure, view this behavior rather unfavorably."

"Yes, sir," Cole said. He closed the office door behind him and met Moore in the hallway. They let a Wren pass before they spoke. Dickie took time to admire the slender figure of the young lady.

"Well," Moore said.

"I hate being dismissed like I'm some sort of fucking idiot," Cole said.

"Yes, it is all rather frustrating, isn't it, old boy? I've gotten used to it over the years so that I hardly ever let it concern me. Still, you haven't been cashiered or made to walk the plank or any of that nonsense."

Cole said nothing.

"Cheer up," Moore said. "Uncle Harry is generally right about things like this. I'm sure that our chaps in Coastal Command will find this blighter, and when they do, they'll dispatch her posthaste."

"Yeah," Cole said.

"Righto," Moore said cheerfully. He looked at his watch. "Party at Beth and Marie's. Mustn't be late for this one. Bound to be an available young lady or two about. Perhaps I should tag along after that Wren and invite her."

Moore was nearly at the double doors, swaying uncertainly on his crutches, when Cole called after him.

"Dickie?" he said. "What if they don't find her? What if she gets out in the Convoy Routes?"

Sublieutenant Richard Moore grew very serious and his voice took on a plaintive tone. "I suppose it will be a slaughter and thousands of men will die."

Kapitan zur See Mahlberg rubbed the sleep from his eyes. The 2,365 officers and men aboard *Sea Lion* were divided into sixteen divisions—everything from personnel for the main and secondary batteries to engineers, technicians, and stokers. Administratively, the workload was at times overwhelming, often boring, but always necessary. Even with his three office stewards, Mahlberg felt that he spent more time reading reports than commanding the ship. His *Erster Offizier*, I.O., Freganttenkapitan Werner Kadow, was a godsend. The man's memory and organizational abilities saved Mahlberg from having to do anything but the most critical administrative duties. Yet to Mahlberg, these were too much. He longed to be, he belonged on the bridge with the long graceful bow of *Sea Lion* spread out before him, gently falling and rising as she bit into the gray sea. He lost himself in the sight of plumes of white spray exploding over the North Atlantic bow, reaching well past Anton, the first of the four turrets bearing the mighty main armament of *Sea Lion*.

Cadence. That was the word. A relentless, inevitable cadence that drove *Sea Lion* through the narrow waters between Fjellsund and Norway; blasting through thick, heavy waves that came at her as if they were sent by the Norse gods themselves. But they did not stop her, they didn't even slow her

as her three mighty screws dug into the depths
and propelled the huge vessel forward. Rise and
fall—as gently as if *Sea Lion* were a wooden steed on
a carousel at a seaside resort; bit in her mouth, teeth
bared, and colorful, carved mane frozen in imag-
inary motion.

And Mahlberg on the bridge.

There was a knock on the door.

Mahlberg, stood, shook himself out of his revelry,
and made certain that his tunic buttons were properly fastened. "Come," he said, his voice crisp and
commanding.

It was Ingrid May. She closed the door behind her
and looked about casually.

"So this is where the *Kapitan zur See* finds sanctuary?"

"You shouldn't be here," he said, hardly surprised
to see her. He had avoided any contact with Ingrid
except when they were in the company of others. In
some aspects it was a very large ship—but as rumors
went it might as well have been a tiny village in some
remote province. People had a way of finding out
things. But Ingrid would not be denied anything
that she sought.

"No?" she said. "I was told by the Fuehrer that
there were to be no restrictions applied to my visit."

"With all respect to the Fuehrer," Mahlberg said,
"he has never before seen the disruptive power of
a woman aboard ship. Especially a woman such as
yourself."

"What a kind thing to say, *Kapitan zur See,*" Ingrid
said as she studied the cabin. "Couldn't the Kriegsmarine have provided one of their most illustrious

Kapitans with accommodations more befitting his stature?"

"This suits me," Mahlberg said. "What is the purpose of your visit?"

"'What is the purpose of your visit?'" Ingrid echoed. She studied the cabin. "I was certain that your tastes ran to something a little more luxurious. Exciting, perhaps."

"That was some time ago. In another place."

"Not so long ago, I should say." She was wearing a heavy wool coat, which she unbuttoned and dropped on the chair, revealing a thin white blouse underneath. She wore no bra and her ample breasts filled the material. Black, tailored wool slacks contrasted starkly with the blouse.

"Have you anything to drink?" she said as she sat on the corner of his desk. "Or have you given that comfort up as well?"

He moved to a cabinet and filled a tumbler with schnapps. He handed it to her and watched as she examined it critically.

"Not even crystal," she said. She waved the tumbler under her nose and looked at Mahlberg with mild disdain. "Diesel fuel?"

"Siphoned from the tanks just for this occasion," he said, watching her carefully, calculating how he might take advantage of her presence in his cabin. He would lock the door of course, and leave orders that he was not to be disturbed, but that would do nothing to quell the talk about her visit. It had been some time since he had been in a woman's arms; his wife's in fact. She had performed her service enthusiastically but with little talent. Her duty to the Fatherland, he liked to think—keep her

husband happy, provide him with the carnal plea-
sures that a *Kapitan zur See* required. Afterward she
had made him a splendid meal.

Ingrid sipped the schnapps delicately and placed
the tumbler on the desk. Mahlberg had always
admired that about Ingrid May—every movement
was graceful, unhurried, as if some abnormal machinery in her brain calculated each motion before
it was made. His wife lacked grace, but she was, after
all, dependable.

"You recall our previous conversation," she said,
wiping a drop of liquid from the corner of her
mouth, "about your future."

Mahlberg offered her a cigarette from a teak box
on the desk. He was curious but made every effort
to appear disinterested. She selected a cigarette as
if one were placed especially for her, her eyes never
leaving his as he lit it with a silver lighter. He chose
a cigarette for himself. She would take this as a
signal to continue, which it was. He decided to let
her speak.

"It seems that your Admiral Raeder," she said, "is
closer to . . . 'retirement' than I anticipated." She
shook her head and repeated tsk, tsk, tsk, as if she
were truly sorry to be the bearer of such news.
"How difficult it must be to command at times such
as these. There are so many casualties in war. And
not all on the battlefield."

Raeder's probable fate was apparent to Mahlberg
and was well known in the service. The surface
fleet had yet to demonstrate that they could meet
and defeat the British. *Hood* had been their one
great triumph but that at the cost of the supposedly
invincible *Bismarck*.

"Doenitz," she continued, "he is a rather short man, isn't he? I find short men distasteful. They appear always to be staring at my breasts and yet trying to appear as if they aren't. Goebbel's excepted of course. He is only interested in his wife's breasts." She changed subjects. "Doenitz and the efforts of his U-boats are well received."

"Vice Admiral Doenitz is a very capable man," Mahlberg said. "I would not be surprised if he were to succeed Grand Admiral Raeder at the appropriate time."

"But he is short," Ingrid said. She downed the contents of the tumbler and winced. "Disgusting. Your name continues to be mentioned as a potential replacement for Admiral Raeder." She examined the remnants of the glass and made a face. "Should circumstances require his retirement."

"I am sure that the Fuehrer will choose the ideal candidate."

She offered Mahlberg a look of mild disbelief. "Spoken like a loyal officer. Unfortunately loyalty is not the only ingredient needed to advance. Well, you have loyalty. That is in our favor."

"Our favor?"

Ingrid ignored his comment. "That does not change the situation, however. Positions must be cultivated, nourished. You, Kapitan zur See Mahlberg, are marked for high command," she said. She stood and moved closer to him. "I told you that I can help you. You need my help, in fact."

He could smell her expensive perfume and he noticed that the top buttons of her blouse were unbuttoned, exposing the deep valley of her breasts. She wanted to advance at his side, silently, steadily, until she joined the sacred inner circle of Nazi officialdom. She would do it too, if she demanded it as her due. She would not stop until she was truly satisfied. He knew that—he had seen it first-hand. If she wasn't satisfied after making love with Mahlberg she would ring up one of her girlfriends to join in their unrestrained lovemaking. A bitch in heat, his wife had said of her, looking at him as if she knew every detail about his affair with Ingrid May. She probably did—Kriegsmarine wives were horrible gossips.

She was that, Mahlberg had thought as his wife eyed him accusingly, and dangerous as well.

Need. The word stuck in his mind. *Do I "need" you?* "You think that I cannot achieve what is rightfully mine on my own?"

She smiled. "Eventually, perhaps. But why post-pone triumph? Especially since it need not be so. I have much to offer."

"What do you expect in return, Ingrid?" Mahlberg said.

"Everything," she said.

Anger swept over him but he did his best to con-trol it. *She forgets herself,* he thought. *She forgets who is in command aboard this vessel and the power that I pos-sess. She forgets that woman is subservient to man.* He forced his anger to dissipate.

The telephone on Mahlberg's desk rang urgently, its red light blinking. He picked up the receiver and pressed it to his ear as Ingrid placed his hand near her lips and began to kiss his fingers seductively.

"Kapitan." It was Kadow. He had the bridge watch. "We're approximately eighteen kilometers from

Kalvenes." Kalvenes was where they were to meet the refueling vessel and pick up the destroyers.

Ingrid looked up at Mahlberg expectantly, rubbing her body against his.

"I'll be right up," Mahlberg said, and replaced the receiver in its cradle. He gently pushed Ingrid back. "Duty calls," he said evenly.

"You can't delay it, *Kapitan zur See?*"

He picked up her coat and draped it over her shoulders, guiding her to the door. "Unfortunately not," he said.

"When can I see you again?" she said, expectation written on her face. "We have much to talk about." She suddenly grew petulant. "And I'm lonely. It'll be such a long voyage."

"Socially?" he said. "When we are again in port."

"But—"

"I have but one mistress at sea and she demands all of my attention."

"Don't be absurd," she said. He could see that she didn't believe him.

"I am being quite honest, Ingrid," Mahlberg said. "I have no time for frivolity and I will not undermine the morale of this ship by engaging in unprofessional activities." *Need you? Do you really think that I need a whore to vouch for my capabilities? This voyage will decide who succeeds Raeder—not your disgusting talents.*

"Who do you think you are?" she snapped. "You can't toss me aside. You had more than enough time before—"

"Before, I was not aboard ship."

"You think that makes a difference? I can have any man I want. Now the great *Kapitan zur See* suddenly has developed morals. What was it? Did you remember that you had a wife? Is it the children?"

"In the future," he said calmly, "you will be prohibited from entering all living quarters aboard ship. On any tour of the vessel you will be accompanied at all times by Korvettenkapitan Eich, our chief medical officer. He is short, fat, and has bad breath."

"You arrogant—"

"Yes," Mahlberg said. "I am. Now, if you will excuse me, I have duties to attend to." He pushed her through the door and closed it behind her.

He donned his cap and overcoat, stopping in front of the full-length mirror to consider his appearance. He was pleased with the reflection. Of course he was arrogant—he had every right to be. He was also confident, professional, and the finest officer in the Kriegsmarine. His arrogance was well founded and entirely appropriate—he commanded *Sea Lion*. Ingrid May simply did not understand. Ashore he had time for their assignations, but aboard his vessel his time, his energy, his interests were reserved for his vessel. He removed an errant piece of dust from the shoulder of his deep blue coat. He was God on *Sea Lion*: unapproachable, unassailable, unmistakably a deity. He was, he knew deep in his heart as he stared into the blue eyes in the mirror, infallible.

Chapter 13

Aboard H.M.S. Firedancer, *Scapa Flow*

Hardy, in as foul a mood as Number One had ever seen him, gave the order: "Close all watertight doors and scuttles. Hands to station for leaving harbor." Number One passed on the order to a chief bo'swain's mate, a three-badger with thirteen years of good service, who sounded the bugle over the intercom and announced: "Do you hear there? Do you hear there? The ship is under sailing orders. Special sea-duty men to their stations."

Number One followed Hardy's cold gaze as *Prometheus* swung into the Flow, preparing to take her place along with her three destroyers: *Eskimo, Windsor,* and *Firedancer*. The majestic *Prince of Wales* was astern of them.

"Depth Charge at Cruising Stations, at the stern to set the depth charges with the special key and do any electrical work necessary," the voice crackled over the speaker.

"Stand by, Engine Room, stand by, Wheelhouse,"

Hardy said without emotion. "Ready, Number One? Half ahead port."

"Half ahead port, yes, sir," Number One repeated and then called the order into the engine room voice tube. "Half ahead port," he confirmed to Hardy.

"Starboard twenty," Hardy ordered.

"Starboard twenty, sir," Number One said and passed on the course to the wheelhouse. They were pulling away from the buoy next to the filthy oiling jetty that they had sucked life from earlier that morning.

"Wheel amidships. Half ahead starboard," Hardy ordered and walked from one side of the bridge to the other, noting *Firedancer*'s station as they took position prior to entering Hoxa Sound.

Number One watched Hardy skillfully guide his ship to the entrance of the sound and wondered if he would ever have the ability to do the same. However querulous Hardy could be, and lately it seemed as if nothing were right enough for him, he was a superb sailor. But there were demons eating away at him, Number One decided, gnawing at his guts so that the only way he could find release was to unleash his anger on others.

Torps Baird waited with his party at the two TSDS Davits and three-ton winches that rose above *Firedancer*'s stern on either side of the depth charge rack.

"All right, Engleman. What's it to be? Hoxa, Hoy, or Switha? Here's a chance to make a quid. Simple as that. Here. Here's three witnesses. Let the boy seaman hold the money until we're through."

"Sod off."

"Here now! You're as cold as charity, you are. Begrudge a mate the chance to make a bit. You'd stand a better chance with me than you would playing crown and anchor."

"Hoy!" Blessing said excitedly. "I bet we're going through Hoy."

"That's it, lad," Baird said. "He's got the spirit of it."

Engleman turned to Blessing in disgust. "It's Hoxa Sound, you daft child. Can't you see the channel markers?"

"Why, bless my soul," Baird said. "So it is. Let that be a lesson to you, Boy Seaman," he said to Blessing. "You'll thank me for showing you the evils of gambling when you hand over that quid."

"Depth Charge Party, close up," Sublieutenant Morrison ordered. "Man the TSDS Davits."

Baird and his party took their stations, hooking the steel leads and cables into the eyes of the squat streaming paravanes—torpedolike devices that trailed the destroyer, snagging and cutting the suspension wires of anchored mines. Once cut, the mines would float to the surface and be detonated with gunfire.

The telephone rang shrilly, two rapid bursts, and Morrison pulled the receiver from its protective box.

Baird heard him say, "Yes, sir. Yes, sir." He turned to Baird and ordered, "Draw up the paravanes."

Baird nodded and a man on each winch cranked the handles quickly in a clockwise motion. The reduction gears spun rapidly and the paravanes, guided by other members of the crew, slowly rose and hung above the deck. Two men, one to each paravane, used cables to keep the paravanes from swinging with the motion of *Firedancer*. If they got away and fell over the side they could foul the ship's screws.

"Swing out the davits," Morrison called, and the long arms swung gracefully over the port and starboard sides. When they were fully extended they were locked into place with a pinion rod. "Play out the paravanes." They went slowly down into the water, fat fish with teeth and wings.

Firedancer was not the only vessel sweeping the channel. The other two destroyers had been ordered to do so as well, and behind them, at a safe distance, steamed *Prometheus* and *Prince of Wales*. Once they proceeded down the swept channel, escorted by a dozen Royal Air Force fighters, they would sail into the North Atlantic and begin their voyage.

"Winston's on *Prince of Wales*," Hardy said to Number One.

"Churchill?"

"He's with some American chap."

"How do you—"

"My orders said nothing beyond the fact that Their Lordships direct *Firedancer* to accompany *Prince of Wales* and render any assistance necessary. We're a small service, Number One, even with the Hostilities Only forced upon us by current condition. No secret remains a secret for very long. We don't go blabbing it to the Germans, but that doesn't mean that we can't talk among ourselves. *Prometheus* knew beforehand, I'm sure of it, but his manner was always to ingratiate himself into Their Lordships' confidence." It was a Royal Navy custom to call a captain by his ship's name, but Number One noted that Hardy said *Prometheus* as if it were distasteful to even form the word in his mouth.

"You'll know more when I relay the orders to the other officers. Until that time keep the information to yourself."

"Yes, sir."

"Damned waste of time," Hardy said, watching the other destroyers in their synchronized movements to sweep the channel.

"Sir?"

"Bloody waste of ships," Hardy said. "*Prince of Wales* can outrun anything on the sea, under the sea, or in the sky for that matter. We're just giving the enemy more targets, that's all. A flimsy Diddo and three destroyers alongside the most powerful ship afloat. What are we to do, I ask you?"

Number One knew better than to answer. Hardy was preaching his sermon. Nothing was right, everyone's decisions but his were flawed. Their Lordships were once again demonstrating their incompetence and if it wasn't obvious to anyone else, it was certainly obvious to Hardy.

Number One did not dare comment on how he felt: exhilarated, excited—marveling at this impressive flotilla as it made its way with professional grace toward the open sea. He enjoyed the majesty of it all—warships steaming in a precisely choreographed dance, Addis lights blinking rapidly, colorful signal flags streaming in the fierce Scottish wind, and above all of it, in a clear blue sky, racing clouds as gray and foreboding as the warships that filled the Flow. Even the green waters, subservient to the deadly vessels, parted in a white froth, cut in two by the bows of the ships as they sailed into the North Sea.

There could never be drama like this in the court-room, Number One decided, no matter the results of great legal minds splitting points of law into razor-thin arguments. All paled before the ceremony of war, Number One decided—even the mundane duty of escorting vast herds of convoyed ships, countless dark shapes riding easily under the orange gaze of a newborn sun—even that was drama. Of course his mood would change when the fresh food was gone and what was served in the wardroom was a questionable mix of leftovers, or when he had been at action stations for so long that sleep was only a distant memory. Or when the sea battered *Firedancer* for days at a time or the unyielding cold stole every ounce of strength left to him. But now he enjoyed the view afforded him by the advent of danger, even if Hardy did not.

It might be a waste of time and ships, Number One thought. It might be as Hardy said: there was nothing out there to challenge *Prince of Wales*.

Chapter 14

Captain Morris Prader, DSO, took the cup of steaming tea in an enameled iron cup from Yeoman Uhl and wrapped both hands around it, grateful that, despite the open windows, they were at least within the closed compass platform of the cruiser. Had he captained a destroyer, he would have no protection.

Still, it was crowded on the platform with the officers and ratings of the Watch, including dour Lieutenant Trunburrow, his number one. They were sandwiched in among the steering mechanism, dozens of dials, gauges, the voice tube station, and the engine enunciator that jutted out over the red-and-gray-checkerboard linoleum block floor. The only compromise to the starkness of the platform were the two, high-backed chairs that sat to either side, away from the polished brass compass stand. The stand itself blossomed from the deck and bloomed gracefully into a white enameled dish that held the compass. The officer of the Watch could control the entire operation of the ship from the compass platform. And even when Prader made his appearance on the platform, and to the consternation of junior officers he was there at the most inopportune times, he let the officer of the Watch control the ship. All the officer need do was to recite the ever-changing manrta: "Wind, force two, southwest to northwest," or whatever direction the wind happened to be blowing, "Barometer 30.10 to 30.20, unchanging. Visibility nine." And the course and speed. Prader might dictate change in course or speed, fine-tuning the movement of his ship, or simply reminding his officers that he was in firm control of all that transpired on the vessel. He'd read an essay from that Polish chap who gave up the sea to write—nothing to Prader's liking because it was all that philosophical and moral nonsense—but the one piece that he'd managed to wade through was "The Captain": "To each man who commands comes a severity of life that denies him everything except duty. For his crew, the passengers, for the ship on whose deck he strides, he bears responsibility. He can no more relinquish this duty, than a mortal man can live without the heart that beats within his breast." He could never remember that chap's name. Never mind, it wasn't important.

Instead, Prader would stroll, cup of tea in hand. He'd stroll out to the bridge wings and look over the 40-mm Twin Bofors MK V mountings and if the gunners were there tending to their guns, he would chat them up. There they would stand, stiff and nervous as hell: ordnance artificers and ordinary seamen alike wondering: *Christ! When is this bloody old fool going to move on?*

He would, when it suited him.

Prader might show up in sick bay, looking over the eight beds all neatly made up, and speak briefly with the acting surgeon lieutenant, a very dedicated and serious chap. He might wander through the radar and fire-direction rooms and make his way aft, deep within the ship to the stoker's mess, and from there through a 450-pound steel hatch activated by counterbalances to the transmitting station and number-two low-power room. In low-power room number two, surrounded by scores of switches, breakers, rheostats, and banks of hundreds of fuses that all hummed in expectation of action, he talked quietly with an electrical artificer and his assistant. They spoke the same language, a complicated, technical tongue that might as well have been heathen Chinese to the other ratings and seamen on board *Nottingham.* But this was Prader's world—he was proficient in all things technical. He could read the sea well enough and he could certainly captain a ship because he enjoyed learning and he had learned these things in the classroom or on the ocean. But what excited him was the electronic and mechanical things that made the ship come to life—not alive, but fulfilling its expectation to operate. *Nottingham,* to Prader, was a vast complex machine, a wondrous example of man's talents and ingenuity. He marveled at it, and took pride in its unexcelled ability to perform, and when *Nottingham* and her sister ship, *Harrogate,* were ordered up to the Denmark Strait, he was absolutely confident that she would do everything that she was designed to do.

Everything that she was designed to do.

In the end—and this was the point on which the

lives of the officers and men of *Nottingham* depended—
she was designed to fight. That was a fact about
which there was no dispute. Her four Admiralty
three-drum boilers and four steam-powered Parsons
single-reduction-geared turbines driving four shafts
at eighty thousand shaft horsepower, so that she
could close with the enemy at thirty knots and bring
her twelve 8-inch guns to bear—that was a certainty.
The uncertainty lay not with the crew, or their vessel,
or its capabilities—it lay with her captain. Would he
be willing to sacrifice the machine that he cared so
much for; would he take it where it would be horribly mutilated or destroyed; or would he, for whatever
reason, Exhibit Reluctance?

Captain Prader, DSO, was chatting with an officer
and eight ratings manning the two huge electronic
computing tables occupying half the deck space in
the transmitting room, twenty feet below the waterline. The room was aft of B Magazine and forward
of A Boiler, uncomfortably pinned between fuel
tanks—when he heard the announcement over the
Tannoy System.

"Do you hear there? Do you hear there? Captain
Prader to the compass platform, please."

It was strange because the yeoman's human voice
was converted to electronic signals and transmitted
over miles of wires to come out of a speaker box
mounted on the wall. The journey was mostly by machine and yet the message sent a chill down Prader's
spine because he could read, machine or not, wires
and speaker boxes aside, that something extraordinary was happening.

* * *

Cole had called Rebecca and offered to come over and help her clean up after the raid. She would be at work, she had said, but the front door would be unlocked. He surveyed the disheveled condition of the house after he arrived and couldn't decide where to start. It was apparent she'd managed to pick up a few things after the raid, but for the most part the place was a wreck.

Rebecca came in several hours later. She looked worn out and Cole fixed her a drink.

"The tram was out most of the way and the buses were packed," she explained as they sat on the couch.

"You should have told me. I would have picked you up."

"I didn't know when I left," she replied, cradling the glass in her hands. "It was especially bad today. Jerry's bombed the docks again. Fixing the poor souls up in the infirmary or an operating room is bad enough, but at least you can control things there. Believe it or not, it's a sort of haven. But the corridors, they must lead straight to hell. That's where we put the patients when there is no room in the wards. Blood everywhere, torn bodies, people screaming. One man stopped me, holding a little boy in his arms. He said, 'Miss? Miss? Can you see to Tommy? He's been hurt in the bombing. What shall I do?'" She took a drink and Cole could see her hands tremble. "The child's leg was gone, Jordan. There wasn't a drop of blood left in that pale little body. I can't help them, can I? Not after all the life's drained from them or there's whole pieces missing. After a while I simply get numb. But I have to, don't I?"

"It's a way to survive."

"It's not such a bad way to handle things, is it? Simply turn your emotions off. If not, I'd go mad, more so than I am now. I don't want to remember what I've seen—I don't want those chalky white faces or shattered bodies in my dreams. I'm damaged enough, Jordan. Even before I got into this bloody business, I was damaged. I thought, 'Here is something I can do. Here is a way to be me.' Just my cursed luck a war breaks out. Now life is a constant, endless carousel of death." She smiled weakly and he could see the unfathomable pain behind the mask. "So you see," she added, "if I can keep at least one part of my life from falling to pieces . . ." She was talking about her marriage, of course, and Cole had a sinking feeling that she was going to tell him that they couldn't see each other anymore.

He watched her make a drink, the silence between them saying so much more than any words could. She sat down and after taking a healthy swig fixed Cole with red-rimmed eyes.

"Doesn't ever seem to end, does it?"

He knew that she was grieving for herself as well as for those that she fought to save. He listened.

"I've something to tell you."

He watched her struggle with the words, his insides churning. He wanted to stop her from saying whatever she was going to say because he was afraid. His world was crumbling and he felt like a child again, lost, betrayed, abandoned.

"Greg'll be coming home soon. Perhaps a month."

Jordan sat back in the couch, trying to fight the panic that welled up in him.

"That's what the army tells me. Thirty days. They

sent me a cable at work." She took a drink. "He's been burned. That happens to a lot of chaps in the tank corps. He wrote me a letter when he first got there. He was afraid of being 'lit up.' That's what he called it. 'I shan't like to be in *Rebecca* if she's lit up,' he said."

She took another drink, finished it off, and made herself another. "Well, I suppose he was in *Rebecca*, when it happened. He named it after me. Ironic, don't you think?" She pulled a letter from her purse and slowly opened it. Cole watched without saying a word.

She looked at Cole and said offhandedly: "It's from Greg. It came just after the cable." She opened it tenderly, took a drink, and read. "'It won't do any good to be cheery because there is nothing to be cheery about. Colin and Angie are dead.'" She looked up. "Those were his chums," she said and continued reading. "'I wish I were. The butchers took my leg and they won't give me a mirror, so I suppose I'm burned as black as a nigger. It's all too funny, isn't it—I was such a handsome fellow on the arm of the most beautiful woman in London. Now I'll be on your arm so that you can help me walk. I cry a lot, as much for myself as the other chaps. You get close enough with your fellows in a tank so that when you hear their screams, as they are burned alive, it does something to you. I was lucky, I suppose. I got blown right out of the top hatch when the shell hit. I must have looked like a Guy Fawkes rocket. All fire and smoke. I don't know what happened. Honestly.'"

She took a drink and turned the letter over. "'We've got to come to terms with some things,

Becky. I'm not the man that left—I almost said that I'm not the man you loved, but I'm not sure that was ever the case. Maybe . . .'" She stopped reading, stuffed the letter in the pocket of her jacket, and finished off her drink.

Cole got up, fixed himself another drink, and stood nursing it.

"You're not going, are you?" Rebecca said.

"I don't know what to do," Cole said. "I know what I *want* to do, but for once in my life, maybe, I'm trying to figure out what the right thing to do is."

"You don't give yourself much credit, do you?"

Cole shrugged.

Rebecca stood and moved close to him. "I may never see you again," she said.

"You could leave your husband," Cole said, bitterly.

"Don't let's argue."

"Sure. Okay. I'm pissed off at this whole god-damned deal. I don't want to lose you but it looks like I'm going to. That makes me angry. Not at you. I couldn't be angry with you if you smacked me in the head with a whiskey bottle."

Rebecca laughed and then Cole did, too.

"I shan't do that," she said, pressing the palm of her hand against his cheek. "I don't know what to do either," she said.

"Yes, you do," Cole said, setting the glass on the mantel. He gathered her to him and kissed her tenderly. She threw her arms around him and returned the kisses, each of them lost in the pleasure.

Chapter 15

"We've picked up something on radar approximately twenty miles, three points off the port quarter, running roughly southeast," Trunburrow said without a trace of emotion. "Size is indeterminate but they appear to be moving at a considerable rate of speed."

"'They?'" Prader said.

"Radar says two, possibly three targets, but it's difficult to tell. Speed twenty-five to thirty knots. We were lucky enough to pick them up that far away."

The RDF 281 radar was temperamental and prone to detect ghosts, but to Prader it was a marvel of engineering. Eyes that see where no eyes before them could see—find an object in fog or rain; find a thing before it can be seen. Marvelous. Absolutely marvelous.

"Masthead report?"

"Nothing, sir." The lookout in the fore masthead high above the *Nottingham*'s deck might have been able to spot a wisp of smoke with his powerful

binoculars if it were not for occasional snow squalls
or patches of fog—the vagaries of weather in the
Strait.

"Well, do we know anything for certain, Number
One?" Prader said peevishly.

"'Fraid not, sir. Except they aren't ours."

"We can't be certain of that, Number One. This
won't be the first time that the right hand hasn't
told the left what it's doing. Let the Flow know
what we have. Where is *Harrogate*?"

"Eighty-five miles to the southeast, sir." *Nottingham*'s companion had experienced engine difficulties and had been instructed to return to Scapa
Flow. Her replacement had not yet been dispatched.

"Very well. Yeoman? Have W.T. send to *Harrogate*:
'Two, possibly three unidentified targets, twenty
miles southwest of my position. Stand by.' That's
all." Prader turned to Trunburrow. "Action stations,
Number One. Better to be safe than sorry." He
leaned over the voice tube to the wheel room, located
below the waterline deep in the bowels of the ship.
"Helmsman? Stand by to make a forty-five-degree
course alteration, south-southwest."

"Standing by, sir," the helmsman said.

Prader positioned himself over the compass and
nodded for Trunburrow to relay the orders to the
helmsman. Number One suppressed his irritation
at Prader. He was the captain, yes, but he had a way
of issuing commands that made a fellow feel as if
he were found wanting in every respect.

"Port twenty," Prader ordered.

"Port twenty, aye-aye, sir." Trunburrow relayed the
command into the voice tube.

The helmsman repeated it and announced: "Wheel twenty of port."

The harsh sound of a bugle over the Tannoy System called the ship's crew to action stations.

Prader studied the compass needle edge slowly to complete the course alteration, ignoring the turmoil around him. "Rudder amidships. Steady."

"Rudder amidships, aye-aye, sir."

"Number One, send to *Harrogate* that we're going over to investigate. Tell them to remain at their station should this be some sort of Jerry trick to draw us off. Have Sparks contact Scapa Flow. Give them the coordinates and the details. Ask them if *Tirpitz* has come out and see if they can scare up a few aircraft to keep track of these blighters."

"Yes, sir," Trunburrow said.

"Well, Number One," Prader said, pleased with himself. "We'll tag along with this ghost ship, keeping track of her and keeping well out her range until this whole matter is resolved. Where she moves, we move, so it's simply a matter of keeping our eyes open and our wits about us. Eh, Number One?"

"Of course, sir," Trunburrow said. The arrogance of the man was appalling and Trunburrow thought, but barely acknowledged, that once, just once, he'd like to see Prader truly shocked.

D.K.M. Sea Lion

"FuMO's picked up a target to the northeast," Erster Offizier, I.O., Freganttenkapitan Kadow said to Mahlberg. "Hydrophone confirms it. 'Steam turbine, high speed. Most likely a heavy cruiser.'"

The *Kapitan* turned easily in his leather-covered elevated chair on the bridge of *Sea Lion*, throwing his arm over its back.

"So?" he said with a smile. "How far out?"

"Twenty-five kilometers."

"Our British friends, no doubt."

The bridge telephone rang and Wachoffizer Melms answered it. He listened briefly, acknowledged the message, and reported to Mahlberg.

"B-dienst reports Morse code message to Scapa from targets."

Mahlberg nodded. "They're sounding the alarm. They don't know who we are or what we are, but they know that we shouldn't be here. Let us sound our own alarm. Kriegsmarschzustand one, Kadow."

Kadow saluted. Battle stations, Code 1. Now they might have a chance to find out what *Sea Lion* could really do. Of course it would not be a fair fight because overflights of Scapa Flow reported the presence of one aircraft carrier, three battleships, six light cruisers, four destroyers, two submarines, and a number of other vessels. Group North had been quite clear on this; the capital ships of the British Home Fleet were still in Scapa Flow. What *Sea Lion* found in the Denmark Straits was one vessel—a cruiser probably, meant to patrol the narrow passage between the ice pack and the vast minefields and sound the alarm. She had done her duty. Now the question was, would Kapitan Mahlberg take *Sea Lion* past the insolent ship and on to her assigned target or would he alter course long enough to destroy them?

To Kadow, the choice was simple: obey orders. Their objective was clearly defined and their instructions unambiguous. Everything else was a distraction. But he was not the *Kapitan*.

Kapitan zur See Mahlberg was considering the same options: test his mighty ship in battle against a lesser opponent—but nevertheless a test under combat conditions—or continue on to his ultimate target. He could do both, he reasoned, because his ship was fast and his crew well trained. He could do both because the *Prince of Wales* would be denied the opportunity to dash across the North Atlantic, the *Nord See*: he laughed to himself; the *Mord See*—Murder Sea. *Prince of Wales* would encounter a cordon of Admiral Doenitz's U-boats, strung from the ice pack at the base of Greenland down into the Atlantic. Beaters to drive *Prince of Wales* south, prolonging her voyage so that *Sea Lion* could come up astern of the British vessel and prolong her voyage indefinitely.

"Message from FuMO, Kapitan," Kadow said. "The enemy continues to shadow us. No change in course."

"I suppose he thinks that we will oblige him by allowing him to tag along. Very well," Mahlberg said. He turned to First Artillery Officer Frey, who stood expectantly at his shoulder. "Frey, I'll give you thirty minutes to destroy that British ship. She'd better be a smoking heap when we break off action or I'll send you back to Wit in a cutter. Understood?"

"Yes, sir, but I won't need thirty minutes."

"Don't be arrogant, Frey," Mahlberg cautioned. "Just sink the bastard." He turned to Kadow. "Execute zigzag pattern, Piper."

For an instant Kadow looked at Mahlberg in confusion. A zigzag pattern? In this narrow strait?

There probably wasn't an English submarine for five hundred miles. But Kadow quickly recovered himself and passed on the orders to Matrosenhauptgefreiter Rechberg. Thank God that the best quartermaster aboard *Sea Lion* was at his station— Kadow would not want anyone else at the helm. He noticed Mahlberg watching him, smiling.

"Perplexing, yes?" the *Kapitan zur See* said.

"A bit, Kapitan, but I know that you have good reason for every order that you give."

"Yes, Kadow," Mahlberg said. "That is why I wear the piston rings," he added, using the slang for the gold braid encircling his cuffs.

H.M.S. Nottingham

Trunburrow relayed the reports to Captain Prader as the parts of the ship prepared themselves for action. It was more than duty to confirm that A Turret or X Turret was ready. Or that the medical officer had taken over the wardroom and turned it into a makeshift hospital because the sick bay was much too small and exposed—it was a primal chant, each report elevating the blood's heat as the men readied themselves emotionally, and physically, for combat.

Trunburrow would not have thought of that or accepted the idea if it were proposed by anyone aboard or off the ship. He was without humor, artistic creativity, or any quality except the ability to focus on the task at hand with an intensity that, had it been examined by the medical officer driving his assistants—poultice mixers, the crew called them, to ready the wardroom—the M.O. might have shown real concern.

But the intensity was not examined by the M.O. or considered by the captain, who thought it merely a sign of dedication, and rightly so—that's what made a good number one. The captain, whose own dedication extended only as far as the machinery and workings of his vessel were concerned, misread that quality of his number one.

Trunburrow was a coward and the intensity was his own desperate attempt to muzzle the fear that churned within him.

The W.T. telephone on the bridge rang. Trunburrow answered it.

"Bridge, Trunburrow." He listened carefully, his eyebrows creeping together in concern. "Right." He hung up the receiver. "Radar reports, sir," he said as Prader glanced over his shoulder. "Targets have undertaken a zigzag pattern." He was pleased to see that Prader was as surprised as he was when he got the news.

"Out here? Do they know something that we don't know?" Prader walked to the port side of the bridge in thought. "Have W.T. contact the Flow. Find out if we have any submarines out here. I shall be very unhappy if I'm sunk by one of our own blokes. Alert the mastheads. We'll match the pattern as well. Navs? How close are we off the ice pack now?"

Nottingham's navigator, a chubby man with thinning hair, said, "Ten miles or a bit less, sir. Perhaps we should move off a mile or two."

"And put ourselves closer to that secret ship? I'd rather not, Navs. We'll speed up and cross his bow when he comes into the starboard tack of his pattern."

Trunburrow looked at Prader. Now it was Number One's turn to be surprised. "Cross his bow, sir?"

"Oh, don't be such an old woman about it, Number One. We'll get ahead and swing around to his port side. We've got him on radar, haven't we? Better than the best set of eyes in the masthead. At least fog doesn't stop radar."

D.K.M. Sea Lion

"B" Turret, Bruno, was Herbert Statz's domain. Kuhn's death was never far from Gun Commander Statz's thoughts, but when the alarm bugle sounded and he and his gun crews donned flash hoods and gauntlets and the garish white antiflash paint that protected their faces from the intense heat of the powder flash, every thought ceased.

He positioned himself at the after turret hatch under the turret mantle and counted noses as the crew for Number One Gun disappeared into Bruno. Then he followed them and behind him he could hear the men who filled the control compartment: the telephone operator, ranger officer, sight-setter, rate officer, gun layer, gun trainer, local director sighter, and the officer of the quarters, who coordinated all of their efforts.

Statz was at home in the compartment of Number One Gun, the thick outside bulkhead protecting him from shell fire, the longitudinal flashtight bulkhead on the other side of the gun offering at least a little protection if Number Two Gun exploded. Beneath the deck on which he stood were the upper and lower shell rooms, the upper and lower powder rooms, and all of the hoppers, machinery, hoists, roller conveyors, cylinders, shields, and tanks, as well as two hundred men responsible for turning the twelve-hundred-ton turret or training the one-hundred-ton guns.

They were out of sight and Statz did not care about them unless they failed to give him shells or powder.

Statz glanced up at the gun director seated in his narrow perch, a vast array of dials and switches in front of him. It was strangely silent in the cramped quarters of Number One Gun. There was almost no room for the men who served the gun, who fed her and cleaned her, and kept her in action. That was as it should be—she was the most important occupant of the room.

Suddenly a load bell sounded, shattering the silence.

"Prepare to load!" Statz shouted as the gun elevated to five degrees off the horizontal for loading. He activated the gas ejector, clearing the gun tube of any debris, and opened the breech. He inspected the bore and depressed the bore-clear switch. In the shell powder rooms, and high above him in the fire director's station, other sailors would know that Number One Gun of Bruno was ready to receive her first meal. As the signal went out he checked the mushroom stem hole and inserted the primer that would actually activate the powder. He signaled the spanning tray operator by quickly throwing a finger in his direction.

The spanning tray operator, a new man named Steiner who still seemed to remain unsure of himself despite his training and thus made Statz unsure of him, extended the spanning tray efficiently.

Statz studied the man's performance—he might yet prove to be a good gunner.

Statz heard the low rumble of the 2,700-pound projectile coming up the shell hoist. The hoist door opened and the shell slid onto the spanning tray. Statz noted the color of the shell: yellow, High Explosive. He expected Armor Piercing but let the gods up in the heaven of Fire Direction determine which lightning bolt to throw.

The shell was rammed into the breech until the locking ring fit snugly in the barrel and the ram was returned. The powder hoist door was opened in the longitudinal bulkhead and three bags of black powder rolled onto the spanning tray. They looked like big marshmallows, silk-wrapped bundles of destruction that propelled the shell on its way. The rammer pushed them into the gun and Statz signaled the hoist operator for the next three. They followed the first three bags into the breech of Number One Gun and the ram was retracted. The hoist door was closed and the spanning tray retracted.

"Close and seal the breech!" Statz ordered, although he was the one that was responsible for the action. He made the order out loud so that his gun crew understood where they were in the sequence of preparing the gun to fire. He pushed the lever home, sealing the breech, stepped back on his narrow platform, and raised both arms.

The gun director saw the signal he had been waiting for, checked the gauges to make sure that there was enough air pressure on the recoil cylinders, and turned the Bakelite knob that activated the Ready switch from Safe to Ready.

Statz looked at the gun director for confirmation.

The gun director mouthed, *three-oh.* Statz shot him a disgusted look. Thirty seconds. What a miserable performance. If they came up against *Nelson* or *KG V* they had better improve on that.

He glanced around the crowded interior to make sure that his crew was at their proper stations. Now he waited to hear the three quick rings of the fire bell. When he heard that signal, they'd be on the devil's shovel.

Kadow took the receiver and listened. He turned to Mahlberg. "Hydrophone reports the enemy vessel has turned to port and is attempting to cross our bow."

Mahlberg smiled broadly. "How accommodating of them. Confirm that with radar. Send out the range and bearing to Frey. Tell him to ready his monsters."

H.M.S. Nottingham

Tea was brought to the bridge and passed around. Kye was too heavy and made a man constipated if he drank too much of it, but the rich thick chocolate did have a way of driving out the cold. The officers and men spoke in hushed tones; orders were passed and acknowledged calmly, but under the calmness was the sharp edge of expectation. The enemy was out there.

The watch had been changed in the mastheads, the heavily clad seamen carefully climbing down the icy ladders, their replacements ringing in to the bridge to acknowledge the change and that the line still worked. Far below the mastheads the torpedo men of the exposed mounts huddled round the black-box heaters in the Oerlikon tubs. There was no reason for the Oerlikon crews, or any antiaircraft gunners, to be at their action stations so they remained below, ready to serve with the supply parties.

The gun crews of the main batteries—A, B, X, and Y Turrets—waited patiently in their damp, cold caverns. Moisture oozed from the bulkheads, decks, hatches, and pipes—from every piece of machinery aboard *Nottingham*; it was driven out of her rust-streaked gray skin by the unremitting cold and deep into the bones of her crew. If a seaman were lucky, or fast, or had rank enough, he could sling his hammock under a hot-air louver and dare a man to touch it.

Trunburrow could have used the presence of a hot-air louver and the glowing comfort of a Horse's Neck as the burning liquid slid down his throat and radiated into his numb limbs. But the hot-air louvers were deep in the bowels of the ship and he preferred to be where he could see the sky—even if it were a never-changing lifeless gray. And he did not drink. So he kept watch on the bridge with the captain and the others as *Nottingham* patiently shadowed whoever was out there.

"Number One, have we not heard from the Flow?" Prader said irritably.

Trunburrow fought back the urge to be just as disagreeable by saying, *Did anyone present you with a message? Do you think that we might have received one and kept it from you?* But he did not. "No, sir," he simply said.

"Well, we can't take on that monster on our own.

Even *Nottingham* must have a bit of help now and again."

"Yes, sir."

"She is a wonder of English engineering, wouldn't you say, Number One?"

"Indeed, sir."

"We are most fortunate, all of us, I mean, to be aboard *Nottingham.* We've our machinery and training so that we can well handle anything that comes our way. Am I right, Number One?"

"Yes, sir." *Oh, shut up, you silly old fool!*

"That is what modern naval warfare is all about. Machinery, I mean. Technology. It is unerring. When I walk about her, *Nottingham* of course, I am continually amazed at the care and forethought given to her design. Remarkable."

"Indeed, sir. I've noted it as well."

"Radar and whatnot? Technology is the ultimate weapon. Have you given attention to the new arms of the warrior?"

The masthead telephone rang as Trunburrow said: "Yes, sir." He wished vehemently that the old windbag would wander off and become engaged with examining the whatnot that he so adored. He picked up the telephone and said: "Bridge." He knew before the lookout spoke, he sensed what was coming through the telephone lines, as sure if it were a jolt of electricity, that it was a catastrophe.

"Foremast! Enemy vessel red thirty, range ten miles. Enemy vessel red thirty, range ten miles!"

Trunburrow dropped the receiver, grabbed his binoculars, and looked to port. He heard a commotion behind him, shouting, questions, and he felt others join him. The masthead was twenty feet above the bridge and the lookout had been very professional in his report—stating the information twice over as he had been trained to do. He had told Trunburrow, in an almost conversational tone, that death was in view just ten miles away.

It came into the narrow field of his binoculars, an indistinct gray mountain trailing a thin smudge of smoke behind it. Trunburrow watched it approach and was struck by the thought that the world that existed between that monster and him was, unaccountably, calm. Then he realized in terror that everything he felt, saw, and thought had happened in a matter of seconds.

Then huge clouds of black smoke erupted from the distant ship.

Chapter 16

The Admiralty, London, England

Admiral Sir Joshua Bimble entered the conference room with his secretary, an extraordinary brilliant man named Hawthorne, just in time to hear Captain Harland say: "All hell's broken loose in the Denmark Strait." At the sight of Bimble, Harland's face reddened and he and the other officers on the admiral's staff quickly took their seats around the table.

Bimble turned his attention to Captain Macready, who immediately took this signal correctly, because Bimble seldom wasted words when a glance would suffice, to bring the admiral up to date.

"At 0900 Greenwich mean time H.M.S. *Nottingham*, operating with H.M.S. *Harrogate* in the Denmark Strait, made contact with an unidentified target traveling south-southwest. Said target"—Macready littered his briefings with legal terms as if they strengthened the value of his reports—"was identified as a capital ship with two destroyers acting as escorts."

Harland was surprised to see Bimble's right eyebrow rise slightly; the old bastard seldom exhibited any reaction to any news that he received during the morning conference. The ancient badger was impressed.

"*Nottingham* closed to within twenty-five miles of the target and confirmed that it was a German battleship with a destroyer escort."

"Not *Tirpitz?*" Bimble said in a monotone.

"No, sir," Commander Elwes, his chief of intelligence, commented. "*Bismarck*'s twin sister hasn't moved."

"Who is she?" Harland wondered out loud, wanting his voice to be heard as worthy of note.

"Quiet," Bimble said, damning Harland for his obvious attempt to gain attention. "Continue," he said to Macready.

"At 0934 *Nottingham* reported that the enemy ship was engaging her. *Nottingham* reported that they were speedily, his expression exactly, trying to disengage but that the enemy appeared to be intent on a fight."

"We shall have to get some Very Long Range aircraft up there immediately," Bimble said.

"Yes, sir," Elwes said. "Unfortunately the area is socked in. Low cloud cover. Coastal Command had to call their chaps back several hours before all of this happened."

"Well," Bimble said, stroking the gray beard that earned him the nickname Father Neptune. He was no Jellicoe of Jutland and there were some reports that he and Winston, when Churchill was the first sea lord, had disagreed on nearly everything including the color of the sky, but he was imperturbable. "Give him his pipe and a cup of tea," one member of his young staff had said, "and he is quite willing to face Armageddon."

"I'll have them up and that's that. You must tell the fellows at Coastal Command," he said to Elwes, "that we have a mystery on our hands. As you gentlemen know, I don't fancy mysteries."

Harland kept quiet. He felt that he'd given the old man too much of an opportunity to make a fool of him as it was.

"Captain Harland." Bimble's voice caught him off guard. "You shall be my eyes and ears at Scapa Flow. *Nottingham* is telling them and then they are telling us, but I don't like getting my information secondhand. I trust that you'll get me everything that I need."

Harland felt his stock rise a hundredfold. "Yes, sir. Of course, sir."

"Macready," Bimble said, "we need to know who this is. She can't have materialized without someone being aware of her. Track her down, find out what you can of her. Find out what she is about and how we can destroy her."

"Yes, sir," Macready said.

"Thank you, gentlemen."

The officers quickly left the conference room, knowing that Bimble used those three words to close every meeting. When they were gone, Bimble leaned over the back of his chair and looked at his secretary. Hawthorne finished his notes and returned the admiral's glance.

"Mr. Churchill," Hawthorne said.

"Yes," Bimble said. "That bloody old fool is out there. I shall have to let Their Lordships know about this latest development. The prime minister, despite his belief in his considerable capabilities, does not control the German navy."

"Sir Joshua," Hawthorne said, "there is something else. Perhaps totally unrelated to either the German ship or Mr. Churchill's voyage."

"Yes?"

"Morning dispatches highlighted increased U-boat activity. U-boat radio transmissions indicate that something out of the ordinary is happening."

"That's all that we have, Hawthorne?"

"Yes, indeed, Sir Joshua. At the moment there aren't any more details to pass on. U-boats are on the move and they're being most vocal. That is all."

"Have you an opinion?" Bimble said, prompting his secretary.

"None worth sharing. Nothing can be done until we gather more information. I suspect, however, that we must be quick about it."

"Of course," Sir Joshua said sourly. "In other words, we wait until we know more." He turned back around and gathered the briefing notes left by his place at the conference table by his staff. "I'll meet with Their Lordships immediately. It irritates me that I have very little to tell them, but what little there is, is troubling."

H.M.S. Nottingham

Prader watched as the first shells from the distant ship landed far off the starboard quarter of H.M.S. *Nottingham.* Giant columns of white water, tinged with yellow dye from the High Explosive shells, erupted out of the sea, hung above the base of their own creation, and slowly fell away.

The huge shells sounded like locomotives when they came over—an unnerving, heavy, chugging roar that seemed to draw the air out of a man's breath. Certainly fifteen-inch guns. Perhaps sixteen-inch guns. Whatever they were and whoever mounted them, H.M.S. *Nottingham* could not match them with her puny eight-inch guns.

"Masthead reports," Trunburrow said. "Unable to determine class. Large ship, four turrets times three."

Prader slipped his binoculars to his eyes and grunted in response. "She may be powerful but we are fast. Revolutions to thirty knots, Number One. Take evasive action, stand by to make smoke. Inform *Harrogate* that we are under attack. Contact the Flow—"

Another rumble filled the air and the gray-green sea to port and starboard of *Nottingham* exploded in towering geysers seventy feet high.

Splinters from the high-explosive shells peppered *Nottingham,* beating an angry tattoo, nearly ripping off the main fire-director tower and anti-aircraft tower. They sliced through her thin skin into the for'ard galley and sick bay, and wiped out the for'ard searchlight station.

They stripped *Nottingham* of her wireless antenna. She was deaf and dumb.

"My God, they've got us straddled!" Prader shouted. "Starboard thirty. Where is my smoke? I must have my smoke." As if his voice commanded the ship itself, huge volumes of black smoke erupted from the cruiser's twin stacks, rolling down over her superstructure and then up again, masthead height.

She had to get the smoke between her and the enemy vessel; she had to make a place for herself to hide in the rolling swells of the gray waters.

The W.T. telephone rang and a yeoman of signals answered it. "Captain, sir," the yeoman said. "W.T. reports they have no signal, sir. They can't raise anyone."

"What?"

"The antennas must be down, sir."

"All of them? That's impossible. Have them checked. That can't be."

Trunburrow watched the flashes of light in the dark bulk of the distant enemy ship. Those were shells coming his way—the battleship would kill them with impunity.

D.K.M. Sea Lion

Turm Oberbootsmannmaat Statz knew himself lucky to be in Bruno. Anton was lower and closer to the bow and she leaked every time a wave rolled over the Atlantic bow and exploded against the breakwater. She had no independent sighting system because water came into the range-finder housing on either side of the turret. Statz thought little of Anton.

But Bruno was a different matter and now she was proving it.

"Enemy cruiser in sight at twenty degrees," the loudspeaker in the turret blared. "Range . . ." The rest of the message was distorted—probably a short in the speaker wiring. No matter; the range was not important to Statz. He knew that the enemy was many kilometers away and probably running as if the devil himself were after her. "Course two-four-oh degrees," the loudspeaker said.

Statz and his crew could see nothing. They depended on the loudspeaker to tell them what was happening. He could tell from practice how the turret trainer was moving the turret and about where she was pointed to port or starboard. He knew from the gun's breech when she fell or rose how many degrees the gun layer had plotted in. But for everything else he had to depend on the loudspeaker encased in a heavy steel cage behind a protective steel grid to tell him what was happening outside.

"Enemy making smoke," the speaker said.

"They're afraid of us," Hoist Operator Matrosengefreiter Manthey said. "They're running away."

"Wouldn't you be?" Steiner said.

"Request permission to fire," the speaker said. That was the gunnery officer in the forward fire-control tower. Statz could hear the excitement in his voice. There was no reply from the *Kapitan*. What was he waiting on? *Let's get this thing over with.*

"Request permission to fire," the gunnery officer said, but his voice was calmer. He'd gotten control of his emotion and perhaps that was what Mahlberg was waiting for.

"Permission to fire." It was the *Kapitan's* voice, as calm as if he were ordering a beer. Statz prepared himself. In the fire-control station were three sets of lights: lock, ready, and shoot. One set for each of the three guns in Bruno. Lock enabled the guns to be loaded, ready signaled the gunnery officer that the guns were loaded, and shoot . . . A yeoman standing to the right of the gunnery officer placed two fingers from his right hand and one from his left on the three lit buttons marked *shoot*, and pushed.

There was the brief ring of the firing bell and then it was like being in the center of a thunderstorm. The cannons roared as the two-and-a-half-ton projectiles exploded from the barrels, and the guns slid back in recoil. They immediately returned to full extension and the gun layer dropped the guns to five degrees for loading.

Statz swung the breech open and the spanning tray was dropped into position. As his crew loaded the next shell, they listened. The shell's flight was being timed, and the gunnery officer had the target locked in the stereoscopic range-finder, tracking its course and the results of the *Sea Lion*'s shooting.

"Attention," the speaker said. "Fall." The shells should impact at that moment.

"Three questionably right." It was the gunnery officer speaking. Statz knew that the officer's forehead was pressed firmly into the black foam support of the range-finder, as his eyes sought out the target. "Three wide right, questionably over." The information was being fed into the gunnery computers in the two fire-control centers deep within the ship: range, bearing, deflection—they could do everything except load the guns.

The powder hoist operator, Matrosengefreiter Scholtz, pulled open the hoist door and rolled two powder bags onto the spanning tray. Statz signaled for the ram operator, another *Matrosengefreiter* named Wurst, to push the bags into the gun's breech, but he was listening to the speaker announce firing corrections as well.

"Ten more left."

Statz knew the gunnery officer was recalibrating the range-finder. That sort of work was too fine for the gunner; it was the sort of thing that educated men did, men who kept their hands clean.

"Down four," the speaker said.

This was it.

"Full salvos good rapid."

His men let out a cheer as the last of the bags went into the breech. Fire away. Load and shoot as fast as you can. Bracket the enemy vessel and then walk the shells up until there is nothing left but an oil stain and debris coating the water.

The breechblock slammed shut and the breech screw spun, locking it into position. Statz turned to his men and shook his fist at them.

"That is the way it's done in the Kriegsmarine! We grab them by the snout and kick them in the ass."

He heard the training gear engage and felt the turret move as the gun began to elevate. He heard the fire bell ring and he grinned broadly, white teeth and shining eyes in a black-powder-covered face.

Kapitan zur See Mahlberg lowered his binoculars and turned to Kadow, expecting an answer.

"She's the *Nottingham*," Kadow said. "*Harrogate* is far to the southeast. She can't come to *Nottingham*'s assistance in less than two hours."

"We'll have to break off action very soon, sir," Korvettenkapitan Balzer said. He was *Sea Lion*'s chief navigator, a man to whom time and distance were the only true language of sailors.

Mahlberg looked at Kadow. "You see that Balzer wants to hinder our practice. I gave our first artillery officer thirty minutes, Balzer." Mahlberg studied his Tissot wristwatch. "He has five minutes left to him."

"The *Prince of Wales*, sir," Balzer reminded Mahlberg.

"We'll have time," Mahlberg said as another salvo shook the ship. The acrid, black cordite cloud rolled over the bridge. "Time us, Balzer. Five minutes. No more. Kadow? Nothing from Wilhelmshaven?"

"No, sir," Kadow said. They had sent three encoded messages to Naval Group Command North but had received no reply. This far north and nearly out into the North Atlantic, ships and radio waves were often at the mercy of the weather. Mahlberg was anxious to report his progress and his first contact with the enemy. He fully expected to be reprimanded for engaging the cruiser because it delayed his rendezvous with *Prince of Wales*, but not by much. His little excursion in no way endangered the plan laid out by Grand Admiral Raeder and the *Seekriegsleitung*—the Supreme Naval Staff. Crafting the plan was all very calm and systematic; old men studying the position of little carved wooden ships on the plotting table. But the old men shuddered mightily when you deviated from the plan, rubbing their hands together as they contemplated the disaster that might befall their beloved wooden ships.

Another salvo erupted again and Mahlberg focused his binoculars on the distant target. It was almost impossible to see anything. The sky and sea were gray and patches of fog hung close to the water.

"Balzer?" Mahlberg said.

"Three minutes."

"Kapitan?" Kadow said. "Forward fire-control

station reports, enemy vessel appears to have been hit."

H.M.S. Nottingham

They were running away. They could not fight a battleship, not without help, and the German's range-finding apparatus had them trapped no matter which way they turned.

Nottingham had been struck several hundred times by shell splinters that punctured her superstructure, and hull and supply parties were making their way to every deck to fight fires or stop leaks.

Then *the* shell struck.

The others had been near misses, throwing tons of water on the decks or razor-sharp splinters through the steel plate. This one was different.

There was a thunderous bang and the ship shook violently as if she had struck a rock at full speed. Smoke, heavy with the foul stench of smoldering metal, filled the air.

Trunburrow watched, as Prader seemed to collapse with indecision. His orders were confusing and frantic. He was truly frightened.

"For God's sake, Number One, get some chaps on that fire in the marines' mess deck. It's too close to the magazines. Something must be done. Somebody must do something."

"The aft supply party is on it, sir."

"Do they need more men? Should we detail more men?"

"They'll call if they need more, sir."

Trunburrow was no longer afraid. A new calm had

come over him, a sense of purpose and place, which he could not ascribe to any action of his own. He gave orders to steer the ship to port or starboard, to present as small a target to the enemy as possible. *Nottingham* responded beautifully, seemingly unaware of the danger just a few miles away. Trunburrow wanted her to weave through the ocean like a drunkard. No consistency in movement, no repetition in course, anything so that the Jerries couldn't anticipate your next move.

"We are making smoke, aren't we, Number One?" Prader said, moving to the port window. "I distinctly remember ordering someone to make smoke." His head and upper part of his torso were exposed when the shell struck.

There was a tremendous blast and all the air was sucked from the world of the compass platform. Trunburrow felt himself thrown against the bridge bulkhead. He knew that he was burned all over because he felt the heat and saw the clouds of flames envelop him—he marveled at the fact that he did not die. He was lying on his side on the deck, a cast-off form on the geometrically precise gray and red linoleum blocks, and across the bridge he could see some sort of bundle that couldn't have been human because there was no head or shoulders. That dark shape, and several others, littered the deck of the compass platform. They rested on and amid pieces of equipment, insulation, charts, binoculars, and life vests, helmets . . . things that had all neatly been stowed in designated locations until the shell made a mockery of order.

Trunburrow tasted cordite and black, acrid smoke

burned his eyes, but for some reason there was no sound. Not a bit of it.

He pulled himself to his feet; he was trembling uncontrollably, and looked around for the captain. Then he realized that he had been staring stupidly at the mass of flesh and cloth on the deck and that obscene bundle could only be Prader.

He tried to move and bumped into a sublieutenant named Wells. The sublieutenant's mouth was working frantically and his eyes were wide with horror and his face was an odd combination of blood, grime, and deathly pale skin. He was obviously asking Trunburrow some sort of question, but Number One had no idea what he wanted. *Ask the captain, you silly little boy*, Trunburrow thought, but then he looked down and saw the captain at his feet.

". . . house blown away," finally came through, as clearly as if the sublieutenant and he were sitting in the wardroom chatting.

"What?" Trunburrow said, suddenly aware that his head hurt horribly.

"The asdic cabinet and chart house have been carried away."

"Yes," Trunburrow acknowledged. "What else?"

"The searchlight control position, the captain's shelter and cabin."

"The important stuff, man!"

"Heavy fires in the telephone exchange and the stokers' mess deck."

"Right," Trunburrow said. "Get a supply party down to the telephone exchange immediately." He whistled into the voice tube leading to the wheelhouse. It was just aft and one deck below the telephone exchange. It was bad enough to have the exchange go out—if *Nottingham* lost the wheelhouse as well, it reduced her chance of escaping the enemy vessel. She could be steered from the engine room, but it was a cumbersome and time-consuming process.

"Wheelhouse."

"Compass Platform here. We've taken a brick just aft of the bridge on the port side. There's fire in the telephone exchange. How are you?"

"A bit of smoke, sir. She's still responding well."

"Right. Now, Helmsman, I'm going to be busy up here and the captain's dead. I want you to take her all over the bloody ocean but keep a general course of two-three-zero, until I order you to stop. Understand?"

"Yes, sir," the helmsman said. "Steer at will along a general line of two-three-zero, until further orders."

"Good man," Trunburrow said. He stepped over debris out to the starboard bridge wing. There was a fog bank five miles ahead; refuge, safety, life, five miles ahead. He got the other members of the bridge party back to their stations, except those whose wounds prevented further service.

"Sir?"

It was Wells with a young midshipman cadet . . . *what's his name? Westfield, Westmore . . . what was his name?*

"Warrant Officer Arthur has a supply party on the telephone exchange. He says that he will have it out in five minutes if . . ."

"Yes? Go on."

Wells appeared uncertain about delivering the rest of the message. "If he has to 'use teapots and soup bowls.'"

"Yes," Trunburrow said. He glanced at the midshipman cadet. "And you?"

"Westlake, sir."

"Westlake. Of course."

"Lieutenant Ames sent him forward from engineering, sir," Wells said. "He thought that you might need someone to assist you."

"Yes," Trunburrow said. "The first thing that you can do is contact engineering and have them stop all smoke. It stands out like a sore thumb against this mist. Is there any damage aft or to the ventilation system?"

"No, sir," Westlake said.

"Very well. Contact the aft fire-control tower. See if they can locate that beast. I must know where they are and what their course is. Wells, get some of the medicos up here and remove the bodies."

"Sir," Wells said apologetically, "they're all dead."

The news had no impact on Trunburrow even though they were men that he knew. "The forward supply party then. We should tidy up a bit."

Damage reports began to come in from the supply parties. The radar scanners and wireless/telegraph were inoperable—so they were blind. The fire direction room and the plot room were destroyed as were the torpedo office, sick bay, and for'ard galley.

Trunburrow took them into consideration, standing amidst the carnage in what was left of the compass platform. *Nottingham* was badly damaged, that much was obvious, but had the shell that struck just aft of the chart house been armor-piercing and come down in a plunging manner instead of a relatively flat trajectory, it would have buried itself deep in *Nottingham*'s gut before exploding. It would have been *Hood* all over again except no one would have survived.

From the aft fire-control tower came the unexpected message that the enemy ship appeared to be changing course. It was very difficult to tell; the distance was great and a thick fog hung close on the calm sea.

Trunburrow found a fog bank and turned *Nottingham* into it. W.T. reported that they could have the radio cobbled together given another hour and a bit of luck. Trunburrow needed to contact the Flow about this behemoth let loose in the North Atlantic, so he told Wireless/Telegraph to fix it and be quick about it and never mind the luck.

And then he hung up the receiver and took the binoculars handed him by Westmore, or Westport, or whatever that child's name was, and scanned the limited horizon provided him by the fog. So this was what it was like, he thought, as he trained the binocular lenses through the shattered windows of the compass platform. This was how soldiers and sailors felt when they performed those deeds that others sought to honor them for; action by which they received medals and ribbons, and toasts all around. None of that meant anything to Trunburrow.

The single thought that he settled on as the most important of those myriad considerations was: *so this is what it is like to be without fear.*

Then he heard the rumble again and looked out the shattered window of the compass platform. Another salvo was coming, maybe three shells or six; both of the enemy's forward turrets firing. But their foe couldn't see in the fog, so these were shells tossed almost as an afterthought. Perhaps they were quickly sighted, or ranged based on a guess, or the gunnery officer simply wanted to clear his guns.

It didn't make any difference because two shells landed on *Nottingham.*

The first shell struck her stern just aft of what had been the aft searchlight platform. It plunged into the wireless room and exploded, blowing out the hull of the ship on the starboard and port sides from the waterline up in a massive fountain of flame.

The second shell is the one that destroyed *Nottingham* and killed everyone aboard her not already dead. It struck amidships, forcing its way into the torpedo stores. It should have exploded on contact as any High Explosive shell was designed to do, and if it had done so, *Nottingham* and a few of her crew might have had a chance. But the fuse was defective and the shell penetrated three decks before exploding and cutting the ship in half.

Her stern, burning fiercely from the first shell, quickly drifted away from the bow, which began to fill with water and in minutes, was jutting thirty degrees out of the frigid ocean like a tombstone. This section quickly filled with water and rolled over slowly, tossing screaming sailors into the dark sea. If they lasted minutes in the water that sucked the heat from their bodies they were lucky. If they were killed instantly they were luckier still.

The bow slid into the darkness easily, without giving any indication that it marked the resting place of several hundred men. All that remained of *Nottingham* were bits of nameless debris that covered the iron-gray water, corpses of dead sailors, and a thick coating of black fuel oil that, when any light managed to break through the clouds and fog, shimmered demurely.

Chapter 17

As a young officer, Doenitz had always considered Grand Admiral Raeder the perfect Kriegsmarine officer: tall, sophisticated, resolute, kindly to his subordinates, and unwavering in his loyalty to his superiors—even Hitler. Perhaps a bit old-fashioned and certainly far too enthralled with the presence of big ships and big guns, but he was a product of the old Imperial Navy and that was to be expected. For that matter, Doenitz was pragmatic enough to recognize that his position on U-boats was that of a quiet zealot. He knew that they, not the great, lumbering targets, were Germany's true salvation.

So, knowing Grand Admiral Raeder as Doenitz knew him, and respecting him as he did, he was very surprised to enter the plotting room to find Raeder in the middle of what one would definitely describe as a tantrum.

"What has he done? What was in his mind that he has done this?" Raeder said, his tone a mixture of

Steven Wilson

frustration and barely suppressed anger. He caught sight of Doenitz, who had just handed his gray kid gloves and cap to an orderly. "The arrogance of the man!"

"What is it?" Doenitz said, approaching the large plotting table in the center of the room. He felt suddenly superior to Grand Admiral Raeder; the cool subordinate, ready to take charge and put everything back in order. A twinge of guilt accompanied his thoughts about the older man, but it was momentary—his own ambition prevented him from feeling more.

"Mahlberg has taken *Sea Lion* in pursuit of an English cruiser," Raeder said.

Doenitz studied the table. Each wooden ship was marked with a little paper flag. Male and female Kriegsmarine personnel—*Bootsmanns, Bootsmannsmaat*, and other ranks and ratings scattered about, and to make sure that all functioned as it should, a *Stabsoberbootsmann* with a *Leutnant* overseeing the activity. It was a flurry of movement and sound; sailors speaking quietly into mouthpieces, pressing W.T. headsets against their ears, hovering steadily around the table to sail the tiny vessels with wooden rods that ended in graceful hooks.

"Everything jeopardized for a cruiser," Raeder said as Doenitz reviewed the latest messages from *Sea Lion*. Mahlberg reported that he was being followed by a British cruiser and planned to sink it before it reported him. More likely had already reported *Sea Lion*'s presence. Mahlberg simply wanted to try out those big guns on an enemy vessel.

"Where is *Prince of Wales*?" Doenitz asked.

"Here, Admiral," one of the *Stabsbootsmann* said, indicating the British vessels with a rod.

"Distance from *Sea Lion?*"

"Approximately six hundred kilometers."

"Course and speed?"

"Estimates only, Admiral. Three-one-zero at twenty knots."

Doenitz locked his arms across his chest in thought. "The damage is not irreparable," he said, trying not to sound condescending. "Although it does create difficulties." He held up the message from *Sea Lion.* "Why did Mahlberg wait so long to report?"

"He didn't," Raeder said. "The one thing that he did correctly was report immediately. You know weather conditions in the Strait—it took us this long to pick up and decode the message."

But Doenitz wasn't listening to the grand admiral—he was considering the options he had left to him in the position of the U-boats spread out across *Prince of Wales*'s path. What Mahlberg did was not as catastrophic as Raeder thought. He would certainly have been detected by the British patrol vessel anyway—the Straits were far too narrow for *Sea Lion* to pass unnoticed. And the fact that he took on the cruiser meant little unless he took an inordinate amount of time to destroy the enemy. That was not yet known.

What was surprising and a stroke of good fortune for *Sea Lion* and the operation was that *Prince of Wales* was not farther along.

"Are we certain of *Prince of Wales*'s position?"

An *Oberbootsmann* clicked his heels. "Yes, Admiral. We are tracking her radio transmissions."

Her escort is slowing her down, Doenitz thought. Without them she could easily add another five knots to her speed. "Grand Admiral, I propose that we send to *Sea Lion* immediately to break off action at once and proceed on the mission. I also recommend that her escorts return to base."

"Return to base? That's a full day ahead of time, Admiral," Raeder said. "I am not comfortable with that suggestion. We are not yet certain that your U-boats are on station."

"Yes, Grand Admiral, I understand, but the British vessel cannot hope to match *Sea Lion*'s maximum speed. We yet may be in a better position than we realize. If we had difficulties receiving radio transmissions, who is to say that the British did not as well?"

Raeder saw that the idea had merit. "They may be as blind as we."

"A perfect time to add another level of confusion," Doenitz said.

Raeder shot Doenitz a troubled look. "You want to begin Operation Funker?"

"Yes."

"I must give this matter much thought before I consent to this suggestion."

"With your permission, Grand Admiral," Doenitz began calmly. "Funker will confuse and distract the British even more so. They are aware of *Sea Lion* and perhaps they are aware of what she is capable of doing to her ships. They will be distracted. The increased W.T. transmissions will create more confusion. We can immediately follow Operation Funker with Operation Umkreis. The British will never consider their Home Fleet the object of an attack. Not virtually within sight of Scapa Flow."

"We must be cautious," Raeder said hesitantly. He

nodded, confirming his own uncertainty. "Careful consideration."

He is afraid, Doenitz thought. *Bismarck* had taken away his courage and replaced it with doubts, and yet that was understandable. If *Sea Lion* failed, which was to say if *Sea Lion* were sunk, it would be more than a missed opportunity to kill Churchill.

Britain's Home Fleet might escape, and Germany's war effort would suffer another psychological blow. The vast resources that went into building *Sea Lion* and launching this operation would have been a waste. But the U-boat's reputation would remain unscathed.

Hitler tolerated the U-boat service because those vessels cost very little to build and yielded great results in comparison to their size. If a U-boat failed to return from patrols, it was seventy men lost—less than an infantry company.

"On the sea I am a coward," Doenitz heard Hitler say. The Fuehrer did not understand ships or sailors and he thought, and told Raeder often, that the huge warships that cost Germany so much, and gave back so little, were obsolete weapons.

Doenitz watched as Raeder wrestled with the suggestion. The grand admiral's face reflected his turmoil, his indecision, and Doenitz chose that moment to launch his attack.

"Grand Admiral," Doenitz said, "my U-boats are in position." He wasn't certain that they were, but neither was Raeder that they weren't. "*Prince of Wales* will be forced to turn south. *Sea Lion*'s current position places her in the ideal location to move rapidly against the English flotilla. All that is left to the English is to send heavy elements of the Home Fleet out of Scapa Flow against *Sea Lion*."

"How do you know this, Admiral?" Raeder said. "Are you quite certain that your U-boats are on station? My concern is that any move by us, at this point, might be premature and result in confusion."

He's losing his nerve, Doenitz realized, *losing his nerve at exactly the worst time. He is a sailor of the last war, overwhelmed by the complexities of a modern war. He is as obsolete as the grand ships that he loves.* "Your pardon, Grand Admiral. That is precisely the goal of *Operationsbefehl Umkreis*: to benefit from the enemy's confusion. The Home Fleet will sortie out in response to the danger. *Prince of Wales* cannot outrun *Sea Lion*, and she is now forced to turn south because of what the British perceive as a gauntlet of U-boats facing her. No matter how many cruisers and destroyers that accompany *Prince of Wales*, she cannot outgun *Sea Lion*. Soon she will be out of range of air protection. Now is the time, Grand Admiral. Let us move forward with vigor."

"I will not tolerate another *Bismarck*," Raeder said in an anguished tone. "Do you hear me, Doenitz? I will not tolerate another such defeat for the Kriegsmarine."

More turmoil, more indecision, Doenitz was rapidly growing weary of the old man's fears. Finally, Raeder came around. "Very well. I'll notify the Luftwaffe to stand by. We'll need to keep a very careful eye on Scapa Flow."

"Yes," Doenitz said. "Grand Admiral," he added in a reassuring tone, "the pieces are moving across the board precisely as we had envisioned. Soon there will be no doubt as to who is the hunted and who are the hunters."

Admiral Bimble, as passive as a Buddha, watched his staff scurry around the conference room erecting maps and huge corkboards burdened with blowups photographs that as of yet held absolutely no interest or meaning for him. Hawthorne, always at his side, leaned over and whispered something of a procedural nature to him. Bimble waved it off, certain that Hawthorne would make it right.

Commander Elwes began the briefing with: "If it pleases you, Sir Joshua," and from there launched into a minute-by-minute—as much information as they could piece together from garbled radio communications—account of the battle. "Captain Prader forwarded this information, as little as it was, prior to closing with the enemy. . . ."

Bimble leaned an ear toward Hawthorne, who discreetly reminded him: "Not much of a sailor, all machines and mechanisms."

"What would possess this captain to take a cruiser against a battleship, if it were indeed a battleship that he saw?" Bimble mused to himself. He looked up to see Elwes waiting to continue with his report. "Well. Go on."

"From Prader, 'Encounter this time, this date, with German battleship. Estimate sixty thousand tons, twelve sixteen-inch guns. Accompanied by destroyers. Severe damage to *Nottingham* . . .'" Elwes dropped the flimsy on the table. "He goes on to give details. *Nottingham*'s not been heard from since. It

stands to reason that her communications have
been lost. Or . . ." Elwes paused. "She has."

"Sixty thousand tons?" a rotund commander
said. "Surely that is a mistake."

"Quite," Bimble said sharply, silencing the out-
break. "What else?" he said to Elwes.

Captain Macready spoke instead. "There are two
inbound convoys, HX456 and HX117, and one
outbound convoy, LZ621, which, at their present
course and speed, would pass very near the enemy
vessel's last known position."

"Does this beast have a name? Do we know anything about it other than what *Nottingham* learned
by bumping into her?" Bimble said.

"No, Sir Joshua," Macready said. He returned to
the immediate subject. "We can turn these three convoys hard south and take them out of danger. Their
escorts consist of one cruiser each and five to seven
destroyers. Of course, there is a complication."

"Of course," Bimble said dryly. "There is always
a complication sucking at the teat of any simple
dilemma, isn't there?"

"U-boats," Elwes said. "In fact a level of U-boat activity that we have never seen before." He swept the
pointer that he was holding in a gentle arc across
a map of the North Atlantic. "U-boats, perhaps as
many as ten or fifteen, have been in constant contact with Goliath, apparently reporting their positions, generally corresponding with these positions."

"You've employed two words that I don't care
much for," Bimble said. "'Apparently' and 'generally.'"

"My apologies, Sir Joshua, but it can't be helped.
The messages are short, rather blunt, and we can't
hope to triangulate the U-boats' locations. They're

rattling pots and pans and we can't make anything from it. Their W.T. traffic is very aggressive but in content hardly substantial."

"Indeed," Bimble said. He shot Hawthorne a glance.

The secretary rose, opened the conference room door, and peered up and down the hallway. He shut the door and nodded at Bimble.

"Gentlemen, for your ears only," Admiral Sir Joshua Bimble said. "Our prime minister is at this very moment aboard *Prince of Wales* and on his way to the United States. He will be meeting President Roosevelt for very high-level discussions that will determine the fate of this empire. We have a responsibility to those convoys, as well as every other ship under the flag of the United Kingdom, but our primary responsibility is to prevent that enemy vessel from engaging *Prince of Wales*. The prime minister was informed about the danger of this unnamed threat steaming down from the Denmark Strait and his response, in typical Churchillian fashion, was, 'You sank *Bismarck*, sink this one as well.' I was moved beyond measure by these stirring words," he said dryly, "but the truth of the matter is we know little about what she is and where she is."

"Sir Joshua?" a voice came from the far end of the table.

Bimble noted Commander Harry Hamilton.

"Harry? You've something to add?" Hamilton wasn't the type of chap to speak up unless he felt it worthwhile.

"A couple of my lads chanced upon a large camouflage complex in the Kattegat. We did several photo reconnaissance flights over the past little while but were unable to uncover the purpose for this site. One of the lads, an impetuous American, even went so far as to commandeer a Hudson and make the trip himself. They got close enough, he tells me, to raise a hornets' nest of antiaircraft fire and German fighters, but to no avail. Whatever was under that thing, if ever there was, was gone."

"A camouflage complex, you say? How large a complex? Big enough for a battleship, Harry?"

"Perhaps that, indeed, Sir Joshua. Understand that we have nothing but circumstantial information to work with. None of our flights returned anything of substance."

"A hunch then," Sir Joshua said. "These chaps have a hunch, is that what you're telling me? I'm to mobilize the Home Fleet and God knows what else on a hunch?"

"Call it a theory, Sir Joshua," Hamilton said, refusing to be intimidated by Bimble's tone. "These two chaps come back to me with a theory. I didn't think much of it myself and told them so in no uncertain terms. Even now the idea is too fantastic to contemplate. But *Nottingham*'s encounter and distressing lack of further communication concerns me. My two chaps think that Jerry's been hiding an H-class battleship up there."

The room erupted at the news and questions began flying across the table. How was it possible? How did you hide a sixty-thousand-ton ship? Surely the intelligence services would have gotten wind of this monster?

"Quiet!" Sir Joshua roared. "I can't think with this cacophony. You shall each have a turn to speak." His bristly white eyebrows settled low over his black eyes as he scanned the table. "Now. I want your opinions one at a time with no interruptions. Each will speak his mind, no matter how outlandish. Elwes, you first."

"Sir Joshua," Elwes said, "with respect to Commander Hamilton, it's impossible for a ship this size to be commissioned and hidden. I can't even begin to think of the resources that the Germans would have to employ to accomplish this remarkable feat. Truly we don't know what happened to *Nottingham* and I'm sure that we shall shortly hear from Captain Harland on this matter, but we cannot jump to conclusions based upon an incomplete W.T. transmission and the theory posed by two low-level officers. And one of those an American who, I might add, we might rightly assume has no battle experiences and very little to do with Germans to date."

"Macready?" Bimble said.

"I think it highly unlikely, Sir Joshua. For the most part for the reasons stated by Elwes but additionally because Hitler became speedily disenchanted with large surface vessels after *Bismarck* was sunk. He has virtually ordered *Tirpitz* to remain within sight of shore. We are told that he fears the impact of another dramatic loss on the morale of the German people."

Sir Joshua nodded to the rotund commander. "Blakely?"

"With respect to all said before me I can add nothing of consequence. However," he added before Sir Joshua had a chance to move on, "what we have not considered is the presence of those U-boats. *Prince of Wales* can outrun anything afloat,

Sir Joshua, should she choose. But what about that line of U-boats?"

"Relative to speed she has nothing to fear from U-boats," Sir Joshua noted, interrupting Blakely.

"Of course, Sir Joshua," Blakely said. "But even a bear is in danger of being brought down by a pack of hounds. Let us suppose that this behemoth does not exist, for the purposes of this argument only. We are confident that there are more than a dozen U-boats poised to intercept *Prince of Wales.* Let us recommend that she chart a course to avoid that concentration of U-boats and proceed with all dispatch."

"Recall her escorts?" Hamilton said.

"Only those who can't keep up with her," Blakely said. "Destroyers and such."

"The very vessels that she needs to protect her from U-boats," Sir Joshua said.

"The very vessels which because of their inability to keep up with her," Macready jumped in, "place her in additional jeopardy from the U-boats."

Elwes joined the conversation. "No longer the bear, she now becomes the fleet stag."

Bimble gave him a cross look. The admiral found such imagery distasteful when his ships were in danger. It was unseemly—most unseemly. He said, "All right, let's continue." The others around the table gave their opinion, but it appeared if Blakely, not the brightest star in the galaxy, one admiral had commented of him, carried the day.

"I see," Bimble said. "Allow me to take a slightly different tack. Each of you having your say as to the impossibility of her being an H-class battleship, you must now answer this question. What is she? *Tirpitz* is accounted for. If she's a pocket battleship she's the first one in history mounting sixteen-inch guns."

"*Nottingham*'s report could have been in error," Elwes said.

"Yes," Bimble said. "But do we take that chance? In front of *Prince of Wales* is a large force of U-boats. Behind her, possibly, is a very fast, very powerful capital ship. Throw in three convoys that are in the wrong place at the wrong time and we have the makings of a very creditable disaster here. We can't take chances with this one, gentlemen."

"With all due respect, Sir Joshua," Macready said, "war is a matter of taking chances. Calculated risks."

"Thank you for the education about making war," Sir Joshua said. "Calculate all you like. Plan as much as you think necessary. Detail every conceivable outcome and in the end all can be thrown into a cocked hat by an unforeseen event or action. Wouldn't you agree, gentlemen?"

The men around the table were silent.

"Yes," Bimble said. "My thoughts exactly. Elwes, you will contact Coastal Command and inform them that we suspect the presence of an enemy vessel in our area of operation. Harry?"

"Sir Joshua?"

"See if that impetuous American and the other fellow have anything to add to this development."

"Indeed I will, Sir Joshua."

"Now. Hear me on this, gentlemen. If you sift through what we have accomplished today you will find very little. If you place what we know on one scale and what we don't know on the other, you can bloody well see how it will be tipped. I don't like that, not one bit. No, gentlemen, I don't. But I haven't anything else to go by, so I'll take what we have discussed to Their Lordships and they can make whatever decisions they see fit. Hold yourselves at the ready because I am fully convinced that we shall be meeting here quite often. Harry, if you please, a moment."

After the others left the room at a respectful pace, Hamilton joined Sir Joshua at the head of the table.

"How sure are these chaps," Sir Joshua asked, "and how sure of them are you?"

"I tossed them out of my office straightaway when they first came to me. Now . . ." Hamilton said, "I'm simply not sure."

"Who are they? Do I know them?"

"The American's name is Cole, a lieutenant in the Office of Naval Intelligence. Bright, excellent analysis, bit of a rogue. His companion in this affair is Sublieutenant Richard Moore."

"His Lordship's son? Good Lord, man, is that all you've got?"

"Yes. Both rather brilliant, Sir Joshua. Both unaccustomed to accepting things at face value."

"Perhaps that is what we need, because on the face of it we have a bloody awful mystery here with the potential for unmitigated disaster. Maybe they have found something of significance? Perhaps there is just a passing chance that Cole and Moore have the key to this mystery?"

Hamilton did not bother to reply.

"Yes," Sir Joshua said about his own musings. "And if my uncle had had different plumbing he would have been my aunt. What concerns me, Harry, is that I can think up a thousand questions at the drop of a hat, but it's the answers that elude me."

Chapter 18

D.K.M. Sea Lion, *the Denmark Strait*

Mahlberg took his action report on the bridge, listening as each division made its account, interested particularly in engineering and ordnance. Divisions 1–4, the main and secondary armaments, handled themselves quite ably although the second gun shell hoist in Anton and one of the elevating cylinders in Bruno malfunctioned. Repairs were being made. Division 8, Ordnance, kept the big guns fed despite mechanical difficulties. Buried deep within *Sea Lion,* Division 8's work was seldom recognized for its danger. These seamen were surrounded by hundreds of tons of explosives and one misstep on their part could destroy the ship.

Divisions 10–12, Engineering, reported a flawless performance. Kapitanleutnant Jahreis fairly beamed as he detailed the accomplishments of his departments. Mahlberg let him speak without interrupting him. Many of his men worked in sealed engineering compartments where the pressure was fifty-six times that of the outside atmosphere. They

were a very cool and confident lot who lovingly
tended the machinery that drove *Sea Lion* and gave
her power. Without them this beautiful vessel would
be nothing more than a dead world at the mercy of
her enemies and the sea. Mahlberg thanked Jahreis
for his report and asked that his thanks be passed
on to the men of Divisions 10–12. Next he wanted
to hear from his gunnery officer. They had seen a
flash and a large dirty cloud of what appeared to be
smoke just as the enemy vessel entered the fog
bank. It was then that Hydrophone had reported
sounds of a vessel breaking up. They had got her.

"We expended twenty-three rounds of High Explosive shells," Frey said. "Two, perhaps three hits
on the vessel. Six shots bracketed."

"Twenty-three? I would have thought you could
do better, Frey," Mahlberg chastised him mildly. The
reprimand was necessary not because twenty-three
rounds was an exorbitant number for the results
achieved—throw in fog, choppy seas, any of the variables in aiming and firing big guns, and you have
an inexact science—but because Mahlberg wanted
better from his men. The enemy cruiser was fast and
difficult to spot dashing in and out of its own
smoke—it was like throwing stones at a terrier. But
she need not fight back because speed was a
cruiser's defense. Had the enemy vessel been a
battleship, had her armor and armament come
close to what *Sea Lion* possessed, the two would
have entered into combat like two heavyweights, ex-
changing blow for blow. It would be fire and
maneuver—plunging fire and flat trajectory, each
ship trying to find the other's range with its shells.
The contest of speed under those circumstances was

this—whoever found the range of their enemy first had a better chance of winning. "You took over nearly thirty minutes to destroy the enemy vessel. *Bismarck* sank *Hood* in only six."

"*Bismarck* had a much larger target to shoot at."

"Nevertheless, I shall expect improvements in the future. Continue with the report."

"Our radar failed with the first salvo," Frey added. "It was completely useless by the second. We have not been able to recover it."

"I was told that it was ready for action," Mahlberg said, accepting a cup of tea from a steward. "What happened?"

"We don't know," Kadow said. "We installed extra padding and foam suspension on the radar mount. We tested it during gunnery practice and the radar functioned perfectly. The gun charges have never varied, nor the firing sequence, and the water-proofing was regularly checked. Every guideline recommended by the designers and engineers to maintain the instruments was stringently followed. Apparently it was not enough."

"Apparently," Mahlberg agreed. A salvo from the three guns of one turret was enough to send tremors throughout *Sea Lion*. Two turrets firing a salvo was more than enough to shake the senses out of any instrument. "Well, Frey, it looks as if you must resort to old-fashioned range finders. Can you make do with that?"

Frey smiled. "Of course, Kapitan. Give me a target and I will demonstrate our abilities."

"Is there no end to the man's arrogance?" Mahlberg said to Kadow.

"Message, Kapitan." A petty officer handed

Mahlberg a flimsy and stood back respectfully while Mahlberg opened and quickly read it.

"From the Seekriegsleitung. They are getting nervous," he said. "They instruct us 'with all haste to return to the predetermined course and engage the target as ordered.'" He handed the message to Kadow. "They order us to release the destroyers at once."

"That's just as well," Kadow said. "They'll just slow us down."

"Will we miss their eels, Frey," Mahlberg asked, "if we become entangled in a nest of British hornets?"

"I should be more afraid of German torpedoes racing about than British shells."

"Spoken like a true gunner. Send the destroyers on their way with my compliments, Kadow. Now, my friends, let us set a course of *Prince of Wales* and make history."

A young *Oberleutnant zur See* approached Mahlberg nervously. "Pardon me, Kapitan, but the correspondents would like to meet with you about today's action."

"I am indisposed," Mahlberg said sharply and then, mindful of the young man's impossible position as liaison to the civilians, softened his tone. "Advise them that duty requires my presence on the bridge."

The young officer saluted.

"Just a moment," Mahlberg said. "What is your name?"

The *Oberleutnant zur See* stiffened. "Jensen, sir."

"Oberleutnant Jensen, what did you think of today's victory?"

The young man tried to suppress a smile. "It was thrilling, sir."

"Do you know, Jensen, that when I was a *Leutnant zur See* in the Republic's Reichsmarine, there were only fifteen thousand of us?"

"No, sir."

"A pitiful band, was it not? We've come a long way since 1929. A very long way."

"Yes, sir."

Mahlberg smiled to himself. "Yes. Well, I doubt that you are interested in a history lesson from your *Kapitan.*"

A shocked look crossed Jensen's face. "Oh no, sir. I mean yes, sir. I am honored. Most honored, sir."

"Be at ease, Jensen. Return to the correspondents and tell them to assemble in the wardroom in one hour. I shall meet them there." Mahlberg turned to see Kadow glance at him. "You wish to say something, Kadow?"

"Only that you've never taken the time to give me a history lesson," the first officer said with a smile.

"It would be lost on you," Mahlberg said. "Have your detailing officer prepare information packets for the correspondents' briefing. Have one of the destroyers stand by to receive my launch."

"Your launch, sir?" Kadow said.

"Yes. When the correspondents have the packets, gather them and their belongings, escort them to the launch, and deposit them on the deck on whatever destroyer that you wish."

Kadow was stunned. "Kapitan, those civilians are on board at the express wish of the Ministry of Information. . . ."

"Good," Mahlberg said. "You may so inform them

that they are leaving *Sea Lion.* All of them," he said with emphasis, remembering his difficulties with Ingrid. "This is a warship. I cannot attend to the needs of noncombatants. Regardless of whom they know or what their influence is with the party. You handle it, Kadow. The less I have to say to that pack of wolves, the better off I am."

"Yes, sir," Kadow said.

Mahlberg motioned Kadow to one side and whispered. "When you give my compliments to Fraulein May, be so kind as to give her a message. Discreetly of course."

"Yes, sir?"

"Inform her that I have chosen my mistress."

"Yes, sir," Kadow said, diplomatic enough to conceal his surprise.

The Royal Navy Base, Home Fleet, Scapa Flow

Captain Harland had always been most uncomfortable in the presence of Sir Joshua Bimble, but now he stood before Admiral Townes, the man who destroyed the mighty *Bismarck.* Even the cold Scottish wind that blew across Scapa Flow was not as intimidating as this sailor.

"Bimble sent you up here?" Townes roared. "And may I ask, sir, what are you to do? Hold my hand? Wipe my nose? This is Scapa Flow, young man, we are the Home Fleet. We are certainly aware that *Nottingham* has run into difficulty and that something is about in the Denmark Strait."

Harland stood at rigid attention while Townes's staff pretended to work diligently. They had probably been at the receiving end of one of Townes's barrages and knew enough to keep low.

"Sir, if I may?" Harland said.

"What is it, young man? Speak up. Harland, correct? Captain?"

"Yes, sir."

"Well, come to, Harland. What's this all about? What's Bimble up to?"

"Sir, it is not Sir Joshua. It is information that we have come across concerning the actions in the Denmark Strait."

"Prader's 'battleship'? Nonsense. No such animal exists. Case of nerves, that's all. First time that he smells powder and he's beside himself. What we've got from him is scattered at best. Nothing of use. Nothing complete. Bits and pieces of radio messages. Suppose this German chap is a pocket battleship, maybe a battle cruiser, or perhaps a cruiser. Where is it now, Harland? What hole has he popped into? There are convoys out there that need protection, and protection I can give them if, if I know where that German chap has gone. It would bloody well please me to know what I'm fighting."

"Admiral Townes, Sir Joshua has requested reconnaissance flights from Coastal Command and the RAF. The weather."

"In the Denmark Strait," Townes said sarcastically, "a poor sailor can hardly see from port to starboard on his own ship. They must fly nevertheless. These ships of mine need service, Harland. *Bismarck* handled them roughly enough, but even before the encounter they were past due for attention. Send them out I will but with damned more in my hand than what you've given me." Suddenly Townes cooled a bit. He motioned Harland to a chair next to his nearly bare desk. "Like a squall," Townes's temper had been described to him, violent one moment, virtually nonexistent the next. Harland was relieved to see Townes becalmed.

"Now see here, Captain Harland," Townes said in a surprisingly soft tone. "I've got poor old *Repulse* out with *Kensington* and three destroyers covering a territory that rightly belongs to three battleships and a dozen cruisers. *K.G.V., Nelson,* and *Rodney* are laid up for repairs and if I send them out now they'll be cluttered with workmen. *Renown* and *Victorious* are with Force J and just coming into Gibraltar, so even if I were to recall them it would take some time before they arrive. My other carrier, *Ark Royal,* is escorting a convoy and I won't be able to get my hands on her for seventy-two hours at least. I haven't heard from *Nottingham,* which frightens me no end; and *Harrogate,* as crippled as any ship can be with out-of-date engines, is steaming back to her sister's last-known position to find out what the dickens has happened. You see my situation?"

"Yes, sir," Harland said. "Quite."

"You can stay here and report to Sir Joshua Bimble all you like," Townes said. Harland prepared himself for another outburst, but the moment passed. "I shall have some of my chaps make accommodations for you. But this is a case of I scratch your back, you scratch mine."

"Sir?"

"I need eyes, Harland. Very Long Range eyes. I've got to have Coastal Command aircraft, Royal Navy aircraft, anything that you can find that flies out there looking for what *Nottingham* tied into. If I can't find it, I can't defeat it."

"Yes, sir," Harland said. But it troubled him that Townes left out the obvious need to fight the intruder, whoever she was. They had gotten *Bismarck* right enough, but they had given up *Hood* with only three of her crew surviving the battle. At first Harland was going to chastise himself for disloyalty or at least being a pessimist, but he decided that his concerns had value. In between finding the German vessel and defeating her, lay the very uncertain matter of fighting her. And all indications were that she was a fighter.

Chapter 19

The Blair Residence, London

Cole watched Rebecca sit on the floor next to the fireplace. She had built a small fire—she was always cold, she said—and tended it carefully, lost in the effort. She searched through the coal bucket with the tongs, pushing aside piece after piece until she found one that suited her. Then she trapped it in the tongs and set it into the fire with deliberation. When she felt the need, she found a piece of wood and wedged it between lumps of glowing coal, careful not to raise a cloud of black smoke.

She sipped her drink delicately and when the mood struck her, talked. As the evening wore on and the alcohol began to take its toll, her movements were awkward. She was drinking more and late into the night she would make her way to the couch in a drunken stupor and collapse. Cole, covering her with a cotton blanket, knew that it was the only way that she could silence the screams of the wound, and hide the truth about her infidelity from herself.

"We had a bad lot today," Rebecca said, her eyes

never leaving the tiny flames that curled up around the lumps of coal. "Firemen. Six of them. Poor chaps were fighting a blaze near the museum. The UXB boys told them to fall back, that there was an unexploded bomb buried in the rubble." She took a drink. "The fire chaps said no, we can hear people in there. What did they expect to find? Everyone had been burned to a crisp. Better to let them die than try to save them." Another drink—stir the fire. "It went off. The bomb. Most were killed. The chaps we got were burned beyond recognition. They were alive, if you can call it that. But . . ." Another drink, emptying the glass. "Be a dear and make me another, will you?" she said, shaking the glass at him. "No lectures now. I'm learning how to hold my liquor, you know."

He took the glass and made her another drink, as strong as the one she would make for herself. He took it back, handed it to her, and sat down in a wing chair. She had become sullen lately and Cole knew that it was because of him, because he did not have courage enough to walk away. Because he wasn't decent enough, or strong enough, to say, "It's over, Rebecca."

"They were all burned black and torn open, you see. The strangest combination of colors—bright red on coal black. Have you ever seen such a thing?"

"No."

"No? One would have thought that you had. Do you suppose that's how Greg looks now?"

"It won't do any good to think about it. What's done is done."

"'What's done is done'? What a bloody cold thing to say," she said calmly, taking a long drink. "I worry about it though. How he will be, how I will be when he comes back." She smiled at him thinly. "How it will be with you. Do you have an answer for that question, Jordan?"

"No," he said.

"I am so very confused," she said to the fire. "Fix me another, there's a dear."

He sat motionless in the chair.

"Jordan? Well then, I shall do it myself," she said, struggling to her feet. She made her way unsteadily to the liquor cabinet and made herself another drink. "No empathy, wasn't it? Your fiancée . . ." She sat down heavily in front of the fireplace and stabbed at the fire.

"Yeah. That's me all over." He hated to see her this way. She was destroying herself and all he could do was be angry. At her. At himself.

"I could use your help, you know, sorting out this business."

"Sure. Get rid of the booze. We'll talk."

"Don't talk rubbish. One has nothing to do with the other."

"Suit yourself."

She threw the fireplace poker in the fire. "Why are you always so damned sure of yourself? Arrogant bastard. Sitting up there like some high and mighty king. On my wing chair, mind you. In my house. Some high and mighty king you are—is that it?"

"Why are you so mad at me?" Cole asked softly.

"Mad? Do you mean crazy or angry? Be precise. Speak the King's English, not that bastardized American tongue."

"You know what I mean."

"I might be both," she said bitterly. She looked

at the fire and said again, but this time in a lost voice, "I might be both." She climbed to her feet and the glass slipped out of her hand, shattering on the fireplace tiles. "Look at that. I'm almost as destructive as the Germans." Cole watched her make another drink, brush the shattered glass out of the way with the edge of her foot, and then sit down.

"You know," she said, "I lost my world twice. Once when Daddy betrayed me, and when this war came. When you came along."

"Is that right?"

"You're the war, aren't you? You see, I believed in people, in my father and mother. In Greg. And when I could no longer believe in them, I resolved to believe in myself. In my ability to help people."

"You're helping people."

"I'm not helping anyone anymore," she said. "I'm not helping myself."

"If you want answers from me, I don't have any except that you won't find answers in a bottle."

"Trite," she said. "Besides . . ." She held up the glass. "This simply helps me to sleep."

"Rebecca, sometimes there aren't any answers. We met and fell in love, your husband is wounded. That's no one's fault. You've tried to control every aspect of your life but it can't be done."

"How logical of you. One, two, three, is it? Do you always see things so clearly, Jordan? Everything except how people feel? There is no logic to how a person feels, whom a person loves, and that's why things get so messy. So bloody messy. So you eschew emotions in favor of the logic behind human beings. Except"—she said the last word as if the revelation had suddenly become overwhelmingly clear—"except humans are not neatly stacked blocks of logic. Are they? Have you an answer for that?"

"There's no use attacking me," Cole said, fighting back his anger.

"But I'm not, darling," she said, pleading that he understand her drunken rambling—trying to convince him that within the slurred words there was the truth that he had ignored for so long. "Have you replaced your feelings with logic? Is that how you live your life? No . . ." She looked down, unsure of her thoughts, until she said. "No, you're living your life by how things *should* be, how one *should* behave. What is right and what is wrong by some obscure code. That is such a cold, false world, darling."

He saw tears form in her eyes.

"No wonder you have been so terribly alone all of these years."

"I'm fine," he said.

"No, you're not," she said. "You're someone who never ventured far from the sanctuary of the world according to Jordan Cole." Her eyes were drifting shut. "But you're the chivalrous type, aren't you, Jordan? A kind man?"

Cole shrugged.

She tried to lock her gaze onto him, but her eyes were unfocused. "Yes, you are. Yes, you are, my lovely American. You're the chivalrous type because you'll do what I ask of you."

"What?"

She grew very solemn. "I want you to leave me, Jordan Cole. I have decided to give credence to my marriage vows. I know it sounds silly when I say it out loud, but it has got to mean something, I have to build my life on something. Greg isn't dead anymore. My husband is alive. He needs me. You and I were part of the war. You must go away. I could not stand the pain if you stayed. You must go away."

Cole wanted to hear the sound of his own voice saying something that would make everything all right, but all he heard was the crackle of the fire. He watched as Rebecca slowly struggled to her feet, made her way to the couch, and lay down, dragging a blanket off the back to cover herself. He felt empty inside, dead, and he wondered what good his logic and intellect did now.

He sat in the wing chair and watched the last of the fire die out, thinking about what she had said. He hadn't thought about it quite the way that she had described, but he had thought about it—about leaving her and not coming back. In his mind it was all neat and tidy; the boyfriend departs just before the husband returns. Circumstances of war and all that—the husband thought dead and the wife, the poor tormented wife, a beautiful creature awaiting his return. But he had never had the courage to leave, and that's what it took—courage.

Cole moved to the floor next to the couch and began stroking Rebecca's hair. He was ashamed because he had hurt her. He wondered if there was another way, if there was anything that he could do to stay in her life. Something held him close to her, caused him to find comfort in her presence, and he wasn't really sure what it was. It could be love, but Cole wasn't entirely sure that the thing existed, at least not for him. Then why not just leave?

he asked himself, and the answer was as puzzling as the question: *I don't know.*

The telephone shattered the silence, and Cole stumbled to his feet trying to get to it before the ringing woke Rebecca. He scooped it off the tiny hall table, pressing the earpiece against his ear and cupping the mouthpiece to trap his voice.

"Hello?" he whispered loudly.

"Lieutenant James Cole?" a very precise and professional female voice said.

He was about to answer when he heard a voice say: "Jordan, love. Jordan Cole."

"Lieutenant Jordan Cole?"

"Yes," Cole said and then he realized the other voice was Bunny.

"Please hold for a trunk call," the operator said. "Before I connect you, sir, remember that this is not a secure line."

"You mustn't worry about me, love," Bunny said. "I'm properly trained."

"Very well. I'm connecting the call now."

"King?" Bunny said. "Fancy going on a little trip?"

"Trip?"

"Remember that bauble that you misplaced? Well, seems everyone has taken an interest in it. We've been put on standby."

The operator broke in. "Gentlemen, remember that this is not a secure line. I may be forced to terminate this call under the Official Secrets Act unless you take greater care with your conversation."

"Sorry, love," Bunny said. "Didn't realize that I was giving away anyone's secrets. Here it is, King. I've got a chap who can give you a ride up here. Get out to the airport straightaway. I don't know any more than that, but I'm sure I will when you get here. King? Are you still there?"

Cole was looking at Rebecca, asleep on the couch. She said that he would fly away one day and never return. He felt it somehow, that he was never coming back. Not the premonition of death; nothing quite as dramatic as that, although he could not discount it. It was just that when he left he was not coming back and things would be changed forever.

"Yeah, I'm here. What's this guy's name?"

"Ducey. Strange bloke. Hell of a pilot. Have you here in record time."

"Okay, Bunny. I'm on my way. Thanks a lot for the call." Cole heard Bunny laughing.

"Don't thank me as of yet. By the time we get done with this business, Ole King Cole might not be quite a merry ole soul after all."

"Is this call ended?" the operator interrupted.

"Yes," Cole said.

"All done here, love."

The line went dead, apparently ended without preamble by the efficient operator. Cole placed the earpiece on the cradle and walked back into the parlor. Rebecca still slept on the couch, fitfully, and the house was silent. A car or lorry, headlights blacked out, moved slowly along the street outside. They were on official business or had ration cards, or black market gasoline, but even their gentle rumble added no life to the scene. Cole was left to his own thoughts and they were no comfort.

He was abandoning Rebecca, probably forever. He wondered if she could survive—not so much without him but without someone to be near her so that her loneliness and guilt did not overwhelm her. Her demons, those demons of her own making and the ones forced on her by life, were always her constant companions. *We all have demons,* he thought, and he realized that his were never far away, they traveled with him everywhere he went. But Rebecca paid heed to hers, allowed them to control her, and permitted them, by the monumental guilt that she carried within her, to devour her bit by bit. She tried alcohol to find peace, to find any means to numb herself to the guilt, but that was only a temporary solution, if that.

Cole pulled his ready kit out of the closet, got his cap and the car keys for the MG out of a small pewter bowl on a shelf over the umbrella stand in the hall, and quietly opened the door.

When he stepped outside he could smell smoke; not heavy, simply the trace by-product of a fire that had been subdued, the common scent of London under siege. He closed the door, carefully, and locked it from the outside. He checked the blackout tape covering the headlights on his MG, making sure that it was still in place, climbed in, slipped the gearshift into neutral, and started it. It chugged once and turned over. He released the emergency brake, depressed the clutch, and pushed the gearshift into first. Then he slowly pulled away from the house at Warren Square.

Ducey was a small man with ears packed full of hair, and the first words out of his mouth were: "Yank, aren't you?"

Cole was getting a little tired of the question.

"Yeah," he said. "For a long time now." He followed Ducey to the aircraft, a Blenheim.

"When are you chaps going to get into the war?"

"I'm here, aren't I?" Cole said.

"Not the same," Ducey said as he motioned to the hatch. "Shed some blood first and you'll be welcome into the fraternity."

"I had a paper cut the other day," Cole said, sick of being treated as a second-class citizen because his country hadn't declared war yet. "Does that count?"

"Are all Americans as cheeky as you?"

"I never bothered to ask them."

"Well, climb in and we'll make short work of getting to Scotland," Ducey said, holding the hatch open for Cole.

The takeoff was smooth and uneventful once they got clearance from the tower. There was no copilot on this flight and Cole sat next to Ducey. The aircraft was filled with spare parts and supplies, all neatly arranged and tied down securely. Ducey seemed eminently at ease in the pilot's seat, his hands wrapped loosely around the yoke, eyes scanning the instrument panel or the horizon. It was only when Cole happened to glance at the altimeter to see that they were flying just over two thousand feet that he became concerned.

"Aren't we a bit low?"

"Are you the pilot now?" Ducey said without bothering to take his eyes away from the panel.

"No," Cole said, "but if this plane smacks into a mountain I'll be just as dead."

"Listen. I've flown this route since Christ was a corporal. I know every tree, hill, stream, and town. I could climb to a proper altitude but I see it as a terrible waste of petrol and time. Waste offends me."

"Okay."

"Besides," Ducey said, "you've nothing to fear. Not only am I a superb pilot, but I am accompanied by angels."

They came into Leuchars accompanied by a light mist. Cole knew that it was near dawn, but the sun was well hidden by the clouds. There were several men scattered around a string of lorries waiting to unload the aircraft, and Cole approached one who appeared to be a noncommissioned officer. The man immediately threw his cigarette to the tarmac, ground it out with the toe of his boot, and snapped to attention.

"Sir!" He was a sergeant and responded immediately to rank.

"I'm Lieutenant Cole. I'm to meet *N-for-Nancy* here."

"Just a moment, sir," he said, his manner softening when he recognized that he was speaking to an American with no power over him. "Pinky?" he shouted to another man at the lorry behind them. "*N-for-Nancy*? Is she on the hardstand?"

"She is," Pinky said.

"Be a good sort and run this officer over to her, will you?"

"Righto," Pinky said, anxious to get out of work. He jumped in his lorry and pulled up next to Cole. "Jump in, sir. Have you there in two shakes."

Cole thanked the sergeant and climbed in beside Pinky, who gunned the engine and took off.

"American, sir?"

"Yes," Cole said, wondering how Pinky could see

in the deep gloom even with the help of the black-out lights.

"Wouldn't know any movie stars, would you, sir?"

"You don't meet many movie stars in Columbus, Ohio," Cole said.

"How far is that from Hollywood, sir?"

"About fifteen hundred miles and two centuries."

The lorry's brakes squealed in protest as they stopped in front of *N-for-Nancy*. Cole recognized the crew suiting up, nearly undistinguishable forms in the darkness. He thanked Pinky and stepped out of the lorry. It shot off before he had a chance to close the door.

"King?" It felt good to Cole to hear Bunny's voice.

"Made it," Cole said, joining the group.

"None too soon," Bunny said, shaking his hand. "We're all set to go. You remember the other chaps, don't you? Let me bring you up to speed. It seems the navy has a mystery on its hands. One of their ships had a set-to with the Germans. The Germans are supposed to have a battleship just out of the Denmark Strait. Going where, no one knows. Coastal Command has been ordered to get everything aloft and find this battleship. Yours, I believe."

"The H-class ship."

"Nobody's given it a name yet and they haven't given it a course, which makes our job doubly hard. They're afraid it's a commerce raider that'll get among the convoys and annoy them."

"We've got to be going," Prentice said.

"Right," Bunny said. "Get into your flight suit, King. It'll be a long flight and a cold one."

"Were are we headed?" Cole said, taking a bulky flying suit from Johnny.

"We fly on a course north-northwest, turn south, and then come home."

"Simple enough," Cole said, zipping up his suit. He sat on the hardstand, pulled off his shoes, and slipped his feet into the fur-lined flying boots.

"Bloody simple," Bunny said. "We're flying over the North Atlantic, King. Not a little puddle like the Kattegat."

Cole smiled and held up his hand for Bunny to help him to his feet. "But I've got all the confidence in the world in you, Bunny."

"A comedian," Peter said as he climbed in through the door.

Johnny and Prentice followed him, and Bunny motioned Cole next. Cole had one foot on the short ladder and was just about to pull himself up when he looked over his shoulder at Bunny. "You did bring that good luck rabbit of yours, didn't you?"

Bunny patted his chest. "Safe and sound close to my heart, King. Let's hope that we won't need any of her luck."

"Yeah," Cole said, pulling himself into the aircraft. "Let's hope."

Chapter 20

H.M.S. Firedancer, *the North Sea*

Chief Yeoman of Signals Dove, at his station on the starboard rail of *Firedancer*'s crowded bridge, called out: "Flagship signals to *Prometheus*, sir."

Hardy and Land turned around at the announcement. Land could see Dove's mouth moving, translating the message that he saw through his binoculars. Dove had damned good eyesight and it was said aboard *Firedancer* that he did just as well without binoculars as he did with them.

Hardy moved alongside Land. "Gentlemen shouldn't read other gentlemen's mail," he said. "But I'll not let *Prometheus* steal a march on me. Well, Dove?"

"*Prometheus*'s pennant. 'You are instructed to break off and return with all speed to Scapa. Accompanied . . .'" Dove was straining to read the message. A wisp of smoke from *Prince of Wales*'s funnels might have momentarily covered the flags. "'Accompanied by . . .'" Dove looked at Hardy. "Other ship's pennants, sir."

"Go on, man, read them," Hardy barked. He whispered in a ragged tone to Land, "Watch it be *Firedancer*. Send off with that officious bag of wind. I'll wager it's *Firedancer*. We get every rotten duty in the Royal Navy."

"'*Windsor* . . .'"

"Watch them, Number One, the bloody hypocrites. Get us out this far and have a turnaround, shepherding *Prometheus* as if we don't do enough of that with convoys."

"'*Eskimo* . . .'"

"I've had to follow Whittlesey on every turn. It wasn't enough that he was one jump ahead of me in commands. His family, you know. Filthy rich. Well bred and well bedded. It'll be *Firedancer* all right and he'll have us riding his wake."

Dove dropped the binoculars. "It's *Firedancer*, sir."

Hardy gave Land a knowing, bitter glance, hooked his hands behind his back, and made his way to the edge of the bridge.

"Keep a close eye on *Prometheus*, Dove. She'll be sending something our way." He joined Hardy. It was a moment before the captain spoke and he kept his voice low.

"Number One, you might as well know it. I can't stand the man. He goes about his business without a care and I . . ."

Land knew what Hardy was thinking. It was the night that he had run through those sailors. The Second Night.

"And I am forced to live with decisions that will haunt me for the rest of my life. I taste bile in my mouth every time that I think of the wretch and now he sails in *Prometheus*."

"Yes, sir."

Hardy turned on him. "Don't be condescending to me, Number One. I won't have it. If you must say anything, say nothing."

"I wasn't being condescending, sir."

"Your tone, Number One. That said it all."

Land glanced over his shoulder and saw the bridge party making every effort not to hear them.

"Sir, the men are listening."

"We'll let them listen," Hardy whispered hotly. "They'll learn something about how the Royal Navy works. How favorites rise in rank and how we that do our duty are merely tolerated. You can't see that because of your arrogance, Number One. Barrister or no barrister or whatever you were before coming into service, you'll go home and have a lovely life after the war while we Active Service types continue to make do."

Land thought briefly before answering. He was a barrister in civilian life, in his life before the war so long ago, and he understood how men under stress could do and say strange things. He knew, despite what Hardy said and how viciously that he attacked Whittlesey, that the stress for Hardy did not come from unrealized ambition; it came because one night he had made a perfectly logical decision—like a hundred that he had made before—and had run his ship through a patch of screaming men. It should not have happened, but *Firedancer* was trapped between two freighters and she had been called to move with all speed to the head of the convoy. Hardy gave the order, an unremarkable order like a hundred that he had given before . . . like a hundred that he had given before. Except fate had placed an obstacle in his way; fate in its own twisted, perverted game now called on Hardy and *Firedancer* to do the unspeakable—kill their own countrymen. This was Hardy's burden, Land knew, and not Whittlesey and *Prometheus* or the slights, imagined or real, he had suffered as a poor man among aristocrats.

"Captain Hardy," Land said, keeping his voice calm but making sure that his eyes were locked on Hardy's and that Hardy could read the emotion in them. "I was on the bridge that night as well. I saw the men and I heard their screams. You don't have a monopoly on that, sir." Land moved closer so that no one could overhear him. "Look here, sir. You asked me if I thought a man's life was defined by a single moment. I was taken aback when you asked me that, because if there was ever a man who did not let events define his life it is you."

"Don't try to curry favor, Number One. It doesn't become you."

"I say that, Captain Hardy, only because you seem to have forgotten it," Land said, ignoring Hardy's sarcasm. "A man's life is defined by a single event only if he allows it."

"Pleading a case, barrister? You're some distance from the Old Bailey, so I doubt your arguments have much merit out here."

"You can live your life in the shadow of the awful night," Land said. "If you choose. Or you can acknowledge it for what it was, one of the horrors of war that we are forced to encounter all too often. It will not be a single event, sir. It will be a series of events, perhaps each one worse than the last. Your choice is a simple one, sir. Choose to survive the horrors, or let them destroy you."

Land watched as the fire went out of Hardy and he leaned against the windshield. He was a proud man and a good man, if decidedly eccentric at times, but he held shame close to his heart for what he had done.

"True enough, Number One," Hardy said softly. "But you weren't the one who gave the order, were you? That shall remain with me until the day I die. And perhaps beyond. We are all judged, aren't we, Land? Each of us goes before his Maker to state his case."

"The Almighty isn't blind, sir. When you appear before him you will be judged for all actions collectively, for what you could control. Not what was beyond your power."

"You're a philosopher as well, Number One?" Hardy said with a faint smile.

"*Firedancer*'s pennant from *Prometheus*," Dove called out.

"Read the message," Hardy said, walking back to the clump of brass voice tubes. He leaned over them, spent by his conversation with Land.

"'*Prometheus* to *Firedancer*. You will kindly take position two points off my port quarter at a reasonable distance. I am turning to port now.' End of message."

"Acknowledge," Hardy said. "Number One, bring us about after *Prometheus* passes and place us fifteen hundred yards two points off her port quarter. . . ."

"Another message, sir. Aldis lamp," Dove said. "'*Prometheus* to squadron. Flagship reports communication from Scapa.'"

Hardy realized that it was straight-out Morse code; the message was in the clear with no attempt to encode it. Something strange was going on.

"'German commerce raider in the Denmark Strait. Believe to have sunk *Nottingham.* Course and location undetermined. Stand by for additional orders.' That's all, sir."

"A commerce raider?" Hardy said to Land. "Surely they aren't talking about a Q ship, are they? Nothing like that could have sunk *Nottingham.* This is nonsense. Was there anything else to that message, Dove?"

"No, sir. Nothing."

"Nonsense. Make to *Prometheus,* 'Do you suspect capital ship?' Send it off. Aldis lamp. And don't bother encoding it. If *Prometheus* can do it, so can we."

"Yes, sir."

Hardy stroked his upper lip with the side of his index finger as Land had noticed him doing when he was thinking. Hardy had every reason to be perplexed. A commerce raider could be anything from a battleship to a heavily armed merchantman— one could do *Nottingham* in, but the other would be chewed to pieces by the cruiser's guns before she got close enough to launch an attack.

"Message from *Prometheus,* sir," Dove said. "'You are to stand by for additional orders.' End of message."

A sour look crossed Hardy's face. "Well, that's plain enough if absolutely worthless. That means they don't know either, Number One. Do you have any suggestions?"

"I recommend that we double the watches. I'd like the pleasure of *Firedancer* spotting this elusive raider before anyone else does."

"But we don't know where it is, Number One."

"Yes, sir. But that works both ways. No one else does as well."

"I applaud your ambition, Number One," Hardy said. "But we'll be traveling in that big cow's wake off her port quarter."

"'At a reasonable distance.' 'At a reasonable distance,' is what our orders were. Suppose we were out far enough to have a good view of the horizon. Doesn't that improve our chances of seeing the commerce raider first?"

Hardy rubbed his lip again. "How dare you suggest that I patently ignore the spirit of my orders simply to be the first one to catch sight of the enemy? Do you think me capable of such a thing?"

Land let silence speak for him.

"You know me too well, Number One. I shall have to trade you in on someone whose ignorance plays in my favor. We'll do it your way."

"Yes, sir," Land said, trying to suppress a smile. Here was the Hardy that he had grown to admire. He did not like the other man at all. The finger on the lip again, his mind was working rapidly.

"Number One? What has gone on in the Denmark Strait?"

"Sir?"

"It's bad enough that *Nottingham* is sunk, but now we are pulled away from escorting *Prince of Wales* and sent packing."

"Returning to Scapa Flow."

"So we are told. But we have to come close to the southern end of the Strait, don't we? What goes in must come out and it might come out when we cross close to the Strait. What is it then? Big ship or little ship? My money's on a big ship, perhaps a cruiser or pocket battleship sent after convoys."

"Our being pulled away leaves little protection for *Prince of Wales*," Land said. "What has she left besides her own guns, which, I admit, are a considerable deterrent?"

"Her speed. She is a greyhound and if her speed serves her, well and good. There isn't a ship afloat that can run her down. You look perplexed."

"I'm preparing my case for His Lordship and the jury as I always did before entering the court-room. In my previous life, that is."

"Enlighten me."

"One of reasonable doubt, Your Lordship. We know of convoys to the north and south of us. Incoming and outgoing."

"One moment, Number One," Hardy said. "Helmsman? Port ten. Take us out an additional five hundred yards off that big cow's port quarter and hold us there."

"Port ten," the helmsman replied. "Wheel ten of port, sir."

"All right, Number One. Continue."

"We are told off to Scapa and as you rightly pointed out we pass to the southwest of the Denmark Strait. Precisely where this unknown vessel is expected to enter the North Atlantic."

"Or has done so," Hardy said, eyes on the binnacle.

"Exactly," Land said. "But for what purpose? Suppose she has speed to match *Prince of Wales*? This does her no good because *Prince of Wales* has a head start. Suppose her intentions are to pitch into convoys? The moment she does she gives away her cloak of invisibility. We know where our convoys are, and if she attacks them we know where she is."

Hardy crossed his arms over his broad chest and studied Land for a moment. "It's not a pleasure cruise, Number One. She's out here for a reason."

"Of course, sir. But you see I've laid out the information, as we know it. If I were defending the enemy vessel I suggest that the jury would find her not guilty because of insufficient evidence."

"Wheel amidships." Hardy shook his head. "This is surely the first time in the Royal Navy that an enemy vessel has appeared before members of a King's Bench and been declared innocent of harmful intentions. I don't fancy signaling the results of this inquiry to *Prometheus.*"

"It is not something that I recommend you do, Captain," Land said, but then he added: "I wonder what the devil she is up to. And where the devil she is. And what the devil she is."

"That's the first thing you've said to me in the last thirty minutes that makes sense," Hardy said. "The devils in this business make no mistake about that. But Coastal Command will be up if they're not already and they'll find that elusive creature soon enough. I'd bet your commission on it."

Chapter 21

The North Atlantic

The U-boat surfaced silently, accompanied only by the soft rush of water rolling from its deck. The teak decking glistened in the moonlight as the boat settled low in the water, gentle swells caressing its bow and traveling along the rust-stained hull until they slapped playfully against the conning tower.

The tower hatch creaked open and fell back on its stops with a clang. Two dark forms quickly emerged in the moonlight and took their positions atop the periscope mast. They began scanning the pale gray sky with high-power binoculars. A U-boat on the surface under a bright moon was a tempting target for British Coastal Command. Even at night the bees came and carried with them death.

Hans Webber, *Kapitan* of U-376, a Type-VII U-boat, followed the two men through the hatch. He swept the horizon as well.

"Lookouts up!" he called down into the hatch. "Ventilate the boat. Disengage E-motors, engage diesels." Webber knew that everything would be done quickly. The crew realized the danger of remaining on the surface a minute longer than they had to. Under normal circumstances the night would have given them sufficient cover—but God had seen fit to bless them with a pale moon that could draw every British bee in the area straight to them. Still, things were in balance—with a little luck they could see the approaching planes in the moonlight.

"Grubb," Webber called to his executive officer, "tell me the minute that Funker picks up anything."

Grubb's pale face appeared out of the darkness of the hatch leading to the control room. "Yes, sir."

"Have two more lookouts come up. I don't like sitting under a spotlight."

"Yes, sir."

Webber heard the additional lookouts clambering up the aluminum ladder and he pushed himself to one side of the narrow conning tower platform to allow them to pass.

"Go to the Winter Garden. One port, the other starboard. Keep your eyes open and no smoking," he reminded them. "There is enough light out here as is."

They had just started back when Grubb appeared. "Signal coming from Goliath, sir. We're getting padding now."

Webber nodded, forgetting that Grubb could not see his response. They had surfaced every night for the past week, listening for Goliath's signal— their signal. Instead the giant U-boat radio network had ignored them and they submerged into the darkness once again. It had been difficult to keep his disappointment from showing and he could

feel the frustration in the crew as they waited for a
signal that never came. Webber could not tell them
why they waited and what their mission was once
they received that elusive signal—there was always
the danger that they would be attacked and some
of them captured and then, inadvertently, someone
would say something to the British. There was too
much at stake to take chances. Too much to gain if
the mission succeeded. Maybe complete victory
over England. At least striking a blow so severe that
the island nation would never recover.

"Grubb!" Webber shouted down the hatch. "What
in hell is taking so long?" He was surprised at his
own display of nerves. "Is Funker asleep again?"

One of the lookouts snickered.

"Coming in now, sir. Funker just got our recognition signal." A moment of silence. "Funker's de-
coding the message now."

That was something—Goliath had sent a message
to them. Maybe to the other eleven boats as well.
Webber snorted at his own stupidity. If it came to
U-376 it had to go to the others; they were a wolf
pack. Good or bad, the message went to everyone.

"Grubb, goddamn it. Has he finished it or not?"

Grubb's torso, his pale face wreathed in a sparse
blond beard, appeared out of the hatch. He tore a
sheet off the message pad and handed it to Webber
with a smile.

Webber snatched it out of his hand. "Are you
trying to drive me mad? You and Funker? You come
and stand here waiting . . ." His eyes caught the
single word hastily scrawled on the sheet: *Umkreis.*

He looked at Grubb, who continued to smile.
"Was it worth waiting for, Kapitan?"

Webber nodded, making sure that the word was actually there.

"What do we do now, Kapitan?" Grubb asked.

Webber gently folded the sheet and slid it into the pocket of his gray leather coat. "We wait for a bit more, Grubb," he said calmly. "Then we destroy the British Home Fleet."

"We're not going—"

"No," Webber said. "Only Prien could have gone into Scapa Flow, God rest his soul. No. They will come to us."

"How accommodating of them."

"Yes," Webber said. "It will be the last accommodation that they make."

D.K.M. Sea Lion

Mahlberg spent most of the morning consulting with his navigation officer and the engineering staff. *Sea Lion* was running at nearly thirty-five knots, which meant that she could easily cover over eight hundred miles in a day's steaming. But thirty-five knots of continuous steaming took its toll on the engines and consumed a tremendous amount of fuel—hundreds of tons a day.

He took a cup of tea from the steward and walked around the report-strewn wardroom table, listening as his officers gave their reports. Mahlberg had reduced the ship's readiness to War Cruising Condition Two; he didn't want his men worn out by keeping them at *Kriegsmarschzustand*—battle stations—indefinitely. They had performed well against the British cruiser and he had told them as much. But the next test would be against *Prince of Wales*, and the *Prince* would not be so thin-skinned, nor would her guns lack range. She would be a challenge.

Mahlberg leaned against the sideboard as the charts were laid out on the table. He preferred the atmosphere of the wardroom to the closeted chart room. It was congenial and relaxed and reminded him of the collegial atmosphere of the classroom at Flensburg. It was a place to learn—to share information; the difference was this was not the theoretical theater of intellectual exercises—here was reality in its harshest form.

"I beg your pardon, Kapitan," Leutnant Chyla said. He was B. Dienst-wireless intelligence officer and always immersed in his electronics and codes.

"Yes?"

"Before we transferred the civilians they asked me to convey a message to you. They were quite distraught."

Mahlberg almost laughed out loud. They couldn't have picked a worse spokesperson. Chyla was a champion in his dark world of glowing tubes and humming radios, but he was strangely out of place speaking directly with another human being.

"Were they?" Mahlberg said. "What is the message?"

"They informed me that when they reached Berlin, they intended to make formal protest, Kapitan. Fruelein May was very upset. Her language was—"

"I am familiar with her vocabulary," Mahlberg said.

He saw a seaman hand a message to Kadow, who read it and then glanced quickly at Mahlberg.

"It will take them some time to reach Berlin,

and by the time they arrive we shall have accumulated enough victories to satisfy everyone. Don't concern yourself with them, Chyla. They are faraway and quite impotent. Dismissed."

Kadow approached and handed him the message, saying only: "Group North."

Mahlberg read the message. "'*Umkreis.*'" He looked at Kadow with a smile. "It is difficult not to feel at least a little pleasure over this, isn't it?"

"Of course, Kapitan."

"We are still some distance from complete victory, but this"—he held the message up—"places us a bit closer."

"We've been monitoring Operation Funker since the beginning, Kapitan. It appears to be going as planned. *Prince of Wales* had turned south. The British are not certain of our location. . . ."

"No," Mahlberg said. "But it is only a matter of time before they locate us. Don't discount the British or their abilities. We've been able to utilize this appalling weather for sanctuary, but soon we'll be out of it. We are bound to be spotted by one of their patrol aircraft." He lapsed into deep thought. "The chart," he ordered. "Let me see the chart."

He pulled a chair back from the table and moved in close, tracing the route of *Sea Lion* with his finger. He stopped and tapped the chart. "*Prince of Wales* has changed course," he said as his officers surrounded him. "B. Dienst places her here. She has no notion of our true speed and location, so she reckons if she maintains her current course and speed, she has more than an adequate margin of safety. But our calculation places us making contact with *Prince of Wales*"—he studied the chart—"here."

"What if she increases her speed," Kadow said, "or releases her escort?"

Mahlberg looked at Chyla for the answer to an unspoken question.

"If she transmits any such information," the *Leutnant* said, "we can decode it almost instantaneously. With the Funker boats we can triangulate her position, again if she transmits, and determine her speed and course."

"It's like fighting in the dark, gentlemen," Mahlberg said to his officers. "The first one who makes a noise, loses." He studied the chart in silence. "Ten hours?" he said to Kadow.

"Ten hours," his executive officer said. "There is nothing between us and *Prince of Wales*. The only threat lies behind us and they will have their hands full soon enough."

"Imagine our reception when we return home, sir," an excited *Fahnrich zur See* said. "There will be a parade in your honor."

Mahlberg smiled at the innocent. "'Policy is not made with speeches, shooting festivals, or song, it is made only by blood and iron.' You'd do well to read your Otto von Bismarck and concentrate on the duties at hand. Let the future take care of itself."

The *Fahnrich zur See*'s face reddened in embarrassment. "Of course, sir."

"Don't take it so hard," Mahlberg said with a smile. "It is my job to keep excitement sufficiently restrained. Never plan for the fortunate unless you plan for the unfortunate as well. Would you agree, Kadow?"

"Yes, sir," the executive officer said. "This is an uncertain business," he advised the *Fahnrich zur See* in a fatherly tone. "We can limit some. Some are beyond our control. Some are beyond our ability to comprehend."

"Now," Mahlberg said to the young officer, "you will return to your duty as I will return to mine. Make certain that everything is in order, as I, through my officers, will see done. Tonight, when you lie in your bunk after having checked off every duty in your mind, twice over, you can dream of parades and willing young girls. Understand?"

The *Fahnrich zur See* snapped to attention and saluted Mahlberg. "Yes, sir."

Mahlberg returned the salute and sent him on his way. He turned to Kadow, a troubled look on his face.

"Kapitan?" Kadow said.

"If we catch her here," Mahlberg said, "we can have no more than three hours with her. Our fuel reserves dictate three hours and no more."

"*Bismarck* sank *Hood*—"

"Yes, I know," Mahlberg said. "In less than six minutes. But she is a battleship and not a battle cruiser. Weren't you listening, Kadow? Plan for the unfortunate as well. We have speed, firepower, and the accuracy of our fire control. Their crew is more experienced, but we are both equally well trained. We must close quickly and overwhelm her with our guns."

"We have the advantage of range, Kapitan," Erster Artillerie Offizier I.A.O. Frey said. "We can commence firing well before we come within the range of her guns."

"Of course."

Frey continued: "If visibility permits I can gauge

range, course, and bearing in a matter of minutes. I will use the guns in bracketing groups, three salvos separated by four hundred meters. Our high-resolution optical range finders can locate the fall of the shot and adjust until we straddle the vessel. With luck, I can do that in a matter of thirty to forty-five minutes."

"That is very finely played, Frey," Kadow said. "You're certain that 'good rapid' will come immediately?"

"Yes," Frey said without emotion.

"Good. Because I will give you no more than three hours," Mahlberg said. "She will be slippery, Frey, and it will take everything that we have to keep her in range."

"Three hours, Kapitan. I need no more than that."

"So be it," Mahlberg said. "Now. The journey home. The Denmark Strait." It was a question posed as a statement. He waited for his officers to reply.

Kadow posed his own question. "Will the British have closed it off to us?"

"Possibly," Mahlberg said, "but with nothing more than cruisers and destroyers. North of the Faeroes?" He could tell by the look on his officers' faces that they considered this unlikely. He smiled. "Yes, gentlemen. I feel the same way about mines. I won't consider the Faeroe-to-Shetland passage, so you needn't offer an opinion about that. There is France."

"The Bay of Biscay?" Kadow said. "St. Nazaire or Brest?"

"A greater distance to travel but we'll have air cover. I'll give it some thought. Trenkmann?" Leutnant Trenkmann was the *Rollenoffizier*, the detailing officer who assisted Kadow with administrative duties.

"Yes, sir?" Trenkmann said.

"Contact Oberkommando der Kriegsmarine. Find out if they will detail a U-boat escort for us in the Bay of Biscay."

"Sir, if the enemy has broken our code . . ." Trenkmann said.

"Then they will be faced with a dilemma. Is the message a ruse? Would I dare radio my intentions knowing that they will most certainly intercept and decode my message? Would I be foolish enough to put this fine ship right under the guns of the English navy or within sight of their air force? Or, if *Sea Lion* is at England's doorstep can she dash out at any time and destroy her convoys? So many questions, gentlemen, and he who answers the most, wins. Send the message, Trenkmann, and let the British sort out its veracity."

Derby House, Headquarters, Western Approaches, Wireless/Telegrapher Center

Chief Petty Officer Wireless Telegrapher Watkins was a strange sort, a little man with a shock of gray hair and large, helpless eyes hidden behind thick glasses. When he spoke, which was not often, his Cockney accent distorted anything he said, so he chose to say very little. He had come into the Royal Navy during the last war when even men with eyesight such as his were welcome. He was not educated; no one in his family was educated, but the Royal Navy by sheer chance or the intuition of some enlistment officer decided that Watkins was just the sort of chap that they needed in W.T. It was in this small and little-understood division of the Royal Navy that Watkins came to know, in his very undemonstrative way, that he was quite brilliant. He heard, through the bulky earphones clamped over his ear, and he felt, through his fingertips from the clumsy black knobs on the monstrous wireless cabinets, the unseen world of radio signals. From the first year of the last war on, Watkins was content to sit in the shadow of the W.T. cabinet with its glowing dials, warm face, and gentle hum from the large glass tubes that throbbed like a hundred hearts within its body, and listen. Over the years he came to know, to understand, to appreciate, the complexity of the electronic language, and the only time that anyone saw Watkins excited was when he spoke with other supplicates of the wondrous machines and their ability.

Now it was his second war and as was the case with all wars, all things became much more complicated and required even more devotion of the warriors; those who fought with guns, and those who listened. And Watkins had been listening. For U-boats. And the U-boats had been talking; a great many U-boats chattering away as if their only purpose at sea was to gossip. This was a mystery to Watkins, who prided himself on understanding things. He had been told by his superiors, and had confirmed by listening, that Mr. Doenitz's boats were expected to communicate regularly through Goliath—the giant U-boat radio network. Watkins expected, as one in his line of work would expect, that the U-boats would do exactly that:

send regular W.T. transmissions to inform Mr. Doenitz where they were and what they were doing.

But one night Watkins, his uniform disheveled, his half-empty stained mug of tea perched dangerously close to his elbow, a company of dead cigarette butts lying in and around a cheap tin ashtray, leaned slowly into his W.T. cabinet and pressed the Bakelite earphones tightly against his ears. He had found something—something strange, something that at first did not make any sense and was so unusual that he thought, perhaps, he was mistaken. So he listened. For seven hours, his hunched shoulders burning, his tobacco-stained fingers curled around the earphones, he listened. After seven hours he reached without looking and found the pad and pencil that he always kept on the narrow shelf next to his desk, and he began to write.

The U-boat W.T. transmissions were certainly in code, but Watkins was not concerned with that because he simply copied down the message as it was transmitted and he sent the whole thing up to the chaps in Crypto. He knew what was padding, that segment of the message before and after the true transmission that was supposed to throw off anyone listening. He knew that. And he knew the call signs of the various U-boats; he judged fifteen in all, because he had heard thousands of call signs over the years and that was the first thing that he had picked up.

That wasn't what troubled him and for an instant caused him to doubt his ears, and his experience. So on his pad he wrote down fifteen names; good, strong English names like William, John, Paul, and Robert. And then for the next ten hours, as Mr.

Doenitz's U-boats cluttered the airwaves with W.T. transmissions, he placed a checkmark beside the name of each enemy W.T. he identified. Not beside each call sign, but beside the English name of every U-boat W.T. *operator*, the flesh-and-blood human being that tapped out the message. After Watkins had heard enough, after he was satisfied that he had solved a mystery, and a very curious one at that, he lit a cigarette and, looking over his shoulder, called to the young duty officer: "Sir? If you don't mind, sir, I've run across something that I think you should have a listen to."

Chapter 22

Scapa Flow

Captain Harland had tried for the better part of an hour to ring through to Sir Joshua, but for one reason or another, he was unsuccessful. Radio was out of the question; there was a violent storm raging just outside the squat brick administrative building of the Home Fleet and every signal transmitted or received was garbled beyond comprehension. Drops of cold rain peppered the windows accompanied by the low, mournful howl of the wind as Harland agonized over his inability to speak with his superiors. The message that he had for Sir Joshua was critical: the Home Fleet was going out.

Admiral Townes and his staff had gone over the reports from *Harrogate* when she got to the last reported position of *Nottingham*. There was nothing, *Harrogate* had reported, some bodies, Carley rafts, and the few pitiful things that had once made up the life of one of His Majesty's ships.

"Send *Birmingham* to join *Harrogate*," Townes had said. "In case the bastard turns round and comes

back out the Strait." Then he turned to Harland
and said: "You may inform Sir Joshua that the
Home Fleet is lighting off boilers in preparation to
sail. *Rodney, King George V,* the cruisers *Hermione,
Kenya,* and *Neptune* will accompany them."

"*Neptune* has had to stand down, Admiral," one
of the officers had reminded him.

"*Norfolk* can go in her stead," Townes said.

"When can you sail, sir?" Harland had asked.

Townes glanced at an aide for the answer.

"Four to six hours, sir," the aide said crisply.

"I can see from the look of disappointment on
your face, Captain Harland, that you are not satisfied with the answer. Nor am I, but we simply can't
turn the key on these ships and drive them into the
North Atlantic. There is preparation after all. You
can help and make no mistake about that. Find the
German ship for us. If I know where it is I will go
and destroy it. Put everything that flies into the air
and find that bastard for me. I shall feel much
better once I avenge *Nottingham.*"

Harland had been trying to reach Sir Joshua to
inform him of Admiral Townes's intentions. He
slammed the telephone down in disgust. Millions
of pounds invested in the finest naval base in the
realm and he could not even make a trunk call to
London.

He lit a cigarette to calm himself and walked to
the window overlooking the bay. Even in the gloom
he could see them, huge black machines, their
mute forms punctuated by signal lights, turrets,
funnels, superstructures, and guns. The might of
the Royal Navy, the great ships that had destroyed
Bismarck and would now venture out to destroy

another German vessel. He felt pride at what he saw—he was staff and not line and there was an unspoken agreement that one seldom acknowledged the contribution of the other. Still, there was the real Royal Navy and in just a few hours they would go in harm's way.

Harland dropped the cigarette on the rough-board floor, ground it out, and reached for the telephone. How he hated Scotland.

Cole stood uncertainly in the tight confines of *N-for-Nancy*, trying to force the stiffness out of his legs. The constant vibration of the twin engines and the cramped quarters had combined to numb his legs so that they felt as if they were blocks of wood. When he rose, hunched over because he was too tall to stand upright in the Hudson, he walked on two rubbery limbs with the ponderous weight of the flying suit bearing down on him. The others in the aircraft, Bunny, Peter, Johnny, and Prentice, might have felt as numb as he did but they didn't show it. He made his way awkwardly to Prentice and held on to the W.T.'s shoulders for support.

"Where the hell are we?" Cole asked and then realized that the question was as ridiculous as the answer was useless to him. They were in the middle of the ocean and the only location of any importance would be where they found the Germans' ship. He noticed Prentice glancing at him quizzically. He was holding Cole's intercom plug.

Cole nodded his understanding, too tired to curse himself for being stupid, and slipped the plug into the intercom system. "Sorry," he said, his own voice coming to him with a distant metallic ring. "My butt's numb and that goes right to my brain. Where are we anyway?"

Prentice pulled out a small chart. "Just here, sir, about five hundred miles out. Of course Peter is our navigator, so by rights his is the chart we follow. I just keep mine as a bit of a hobby, you understand. If I'm right we fly on for a bit more and then turn south-southwest on a course of two-two-oh. I think I'm close enough to Peter's reckoning."

"Okay," Cole said, mildly disgusted that he still had no idea where they were. "Let me get back to my window."

"Bit of a strain on the eyes, isn't it, sir?" They had all been staring through the marred Plexiglas windows for any sign of the enemy. The only thing in sight was the unending ocean.

"A bit."

Prentice handed Cole a canteen. "Dash some of this on your face. It'll bring you around."

Cole nodded, unscrewed the lid on the canteen, poured a handful of water into his palm, and rubbed it into his face. It was ice cold and it almost took his breath away. He handed the canteen back to Prentice with a smile and struggled aft to his position. He lowered himself carefully into place, grimacing as the muscles of his thighs and lower legs burned when he tried to fold them into position. He heard the Boulton-Paul dorsal turret swing rhythmically back and forth as Johnny swept the sky, looking for enemy aircraft. There wouldn't be any German fighters out this far, but there was always the possibility of a graceful German Condor or squat flying boats making an appearance. Either one would be an unwelcome, and most dangerous, intruder.

Something hit him on the leg; it was a coin. He looked up to see Prentice pointing to his intercom plug.

"Shit," Cole said to himself. He slipped it into the receptacle and heard Bunny's voice crackle in his ears.

". . . just received word that *Prince of Wales* has released some of her escorts. We're to be on the lookout for them. We ought to pass close by, although I have no exact location. We're to turn south in approximately ten minutes. King, old chum. If you don't remember to keep your intercom plugged in, I shall be forced to shove it up your bum. Now come up here like a good chap so we can talk."

Cole rose again, struggled forward, and sat down in the entrance to the tunnel that led to the bomb-aimer/navigator's compartment in the nose. He showed Bunny the plug-in and slid it into the receptacle.

"You don't have to tell me something more than twelve to fifteen times before I get it."

"That's heartening, King," Bunny said. "I thought you'd like a bit of a break. Constant searching can deaden a man's eyes and brain."

"Thanks. It was hell on my ass as well."

"Is your ship as big as all that? Larger than *Bismarck*?"

"Yeah. From what we know of her. Big and fast. I'd hate to think what would happen if she ran into a convoy." He noticed Bunny had lost interest in what he was saying. "What's the matter?"

Bunny was tapping one of the dials on the

instrument panel. "This bloody thing is dancing up and down. I thought my erks fixed it."

"What is it?"

Bunny twisted to look out the window. "My oil pressure. Left engine. She's not leaking oil unless it's coming out underneath." He turned back to the instrument panel. "Now the bastard's running just fine." He tapped the dial again. "Prentice? Radio back to base, will you? Tell them that we're having a spot of trouble out here and we're turning around. Give them our location. King? You'd better go back to your station."

As he started to rise, Cole heard a bang. Not loud enough to create concerns; more like the sound someone makes when they slam their fist on a desk. It was the explosion that followed that was loud.

The blast threw him back against the wireless operator's table. Cole felt bits of aluminum, rubber, plastic, and flaming debris, all wrapped in an intense smoke, engulf him. He heard shouting and saw Bunny clawing at the yoke. But there was something wrong—it was like the pilot couldn't see.

Cole pulled himself forward until he was even with Bunny.

The pilot had no face. It was nothing more than a mass of bloody meat.

"Get out of the way, you fool!"

It was Peter, covered with blood, pushing his way through the bomb-aimer/navigator's tunnel.

Cole moved back as Peter saw Bunny.

"Jesus wept!" he said. "What happened?"

"The left engine exploded," Cole said.

The plane started to descend and twist to the right.

"Get him out of there," Peter ordered Cole. "I'll try to fly her from the second pilot's station."

Cole nodded. He felt a hand on his shoulder. It was Prentice. His mask was gone and blood streamed from his nose.

"I'll help," he shouted. "Let me get the quick release." Prentice moved between Cole and Peter and reaching under Bunny's waving arms punched the quick-release switch for the pilot's harness.

"Will you two hurry, please!" Peter said. "I can't keep this rock in the air much longer."

Prentice glanced at Cole in alarm. "His legs have gone all stiff. They're wrapped up in the rudder assembly."

"Get him out!" Peter screamed. "He's going to kill us all."

Cole looked around. "Give me that map case."

Prentice handed it to him and Cole ripped off Bunny's flight cap.

The wireless operator grabbed his arm. "What are you going to do?"

"It's the only way."

"You'll kill him!"

"For bloody sake, Prentice," Peter said. "He's dead already. Do you want him to kill the rest of us?"

Prentice, tears rolling down his cheeks, released Cole's arm.

Cole brought the metal case down hard on Bunny's head and the pilot went limp. He tossed the map case to one side.

"All right," he said to the stunned Prentice. "We pull him out on three. One, two, three." They lifted the unconscious pilot over the back of the seat and let him drop on the floor next to the transmitter.

"Get Johnny," Cole said to Prentice. The boy's haunted eyes were locked on the faceless form on the deck. "Prentice? Get Johnny out of the turret. Now."

"King!" Peter shouted over his shoulder. "Under the pilot's seat are smoke floats. We'll need them when we go down. I think we're losing hydraulic fluid as well. She's becoming difficult to handle. Did Prentice send out a distress signal?"

"I'll find out."

"Do it bloody quickly, Yank. We won't survive long in that water."

"Right," he said, reaching under the seat. He felt two canisters and their release mechanisms. He also felt hunks of flesh and warm sticky liquid. He focused on the mechanisms, found the latch, pictured its operation in his mind, and flipped it open.

Cole staggered back to the bulkhead just forward of the Boulton-Paul turret, carrying the canisters. It was becoming almost impossible to move in the gyrating aircraft and he was thrown from side to side. Prentice was helping Johnny slide out from under the dorsal cutout former and onto the step by the entry door.

Johnny was shaken but not hurt. "Bastard jammed on me. Thought I was going to have to squeeze out the aft flare tube."

"Prentice told you?"

The gunner nodded.

"Did you get out an SOS?" Cole asked Prentice.

"Yes, sir. But no one answered, or if they did, it won't help. Wireless is out, sir."

"See if you can get it going again," Cole said. "You

take these." He handed the canisters to Johnny. "Where's the life raft?"

"You're standing on it, chum," Johnny said. "The hand lever for the dinghy release cylinder is right behind you. We land, pop the door, and step in Won't even get our feet wet."

"Yeah," Cole said, certain it was going to be a lot more difficult than that. "You say."

N-for-Nancy seemed to have settled into a more or less level flight when Cole passed Prentice on his way up front. He patted the wireless operator on the shoulder. "How's it going, Prentice?"

"Let you know in a bit, sir. I'm afraid everything's scrambled."

"Okay," Cole said, kneeling on the deck behind Peter.

"How's Bunny?" Peter said, his eyes on the glowing dials of the instrument panel.

Cole glanced back at the pilot. The man was barely breathing.

"I don't know. Not well."

"King?" Peter said. "Bunny's got his good luck token in the inside pocket of his flight suit. He may not be able to see the ridiculous thing, but it might help him to feel it."

"Sure," Cole said. "Sure thing." He turned and, careful not to look at the destroyed face, unzipped the blood-soaked flight suit and felt inside for the stuffed bunny. He found it, covered in blood, pulled it out, and tried to wipe some of the blood on the leg of his flight suit. When he was satisfied that he had done all that he could, he placed it carefully in Bunny's right hand and closed his fingers around it. "Okay," he said to Peter.

N-for-Nancy shuddered violently.

"I've got them!" Prentice shouted. "And they've got me, I believe. Some Royal Navy chaps. Everything's garbled. There's a lot of static but I think they've got me."

There was a high-pitched whine from *N-for-Nancy*'s right engine, as if the aircraft were calling for help. The engine was straining to keep *N-for-Nancy* aloft.

"I think this is it, chaps," Peter shouted over the shrill noise. "She's behaving badly now. Everyone to the rear and latch on to anything not moving."

"What are you going to do?" Cole said.

"Someone's got to drive the bus, haven't they? I'll be right along when it's my time. Just get back there and hold on to something. Hold tight, King. When we hit, it'll be like slamming into a brick wall. Then we'll skip free and things won't be bad at all. Then we'll hit again and that'll be the worst part."

"Sounds like you've done this before," Cole said.

"Once or twice, King. Bunny was at the controls then. I wish to hell he was now. Get aft and take Prentice with you."

"Okay," Cole said. "Good luck."

"Fuck off, Yank."

Cole slapped Prentice on the back. "We're closing up shop. Let's get aft."

"But the wireless—"

"Forget it." Cole followed Prentice's gaze to Bunny. "It's no good, Prentice," he said. He didn't want to abandon the pilot on the floor either, but it was apparent that Bunny wouldn't last long. "Come on. Let's get cracking."

They found Johnny stuffing parachutes against the bulkhead. He had jettisoned the door and the frigid wind roaring through the opening made it almost impossible to hear. Debris whipped wildly around the interior of the aircraft until it was near enough to the door for the slipstream to suck it out.

"Stay clear of that bastard," Johnny shouted, pointing at the turret. "She might come loose when we land and crush you. Get on either side of the fuselage and cushion yourself with these parachutes." *N-for-Nancy* gave a lurch. It was a warning, she was dying and she could give her crew no more time. "Where's Bunny?" Johnny asked Cole. Cole shook his head.

"Right," Johnny said sharply. "Right. Get settled in. It won't be long now. Peter will try to keep her nose up as long as possible. If she hits a wave head-on she'll explode. If he can drag her tail we'll have some time to inflate the dinghy and get out."

Cole felt his stomach drop. They were going in now. They were going to ditch. He wedged himself against a parachute and pushed his feet against the step that led up to the turret. Johnny and Prentice were on the other side of the cabin, each waiting for the impact.

Cole wondered what would happen and for the first time in his life he was frightened, really frightened. He had no control over what was going to happen or if he would survive it. He felt his heart pumping wildly and he thought he could feel every movement of every rivet in *N-for-Nancy*. For a moment he thought the aircraft was alive and he wondered if fear was causing him to hallucinate.

He thought of Rebecca and the last time that he had seen her, asleep on the couch, and he wished that he had left a note or awakened her to say good-bye, or something. But he didn't and he wondered how much of a bastard he had been to her and if perhaps he could have done more to help her.

He thought about praying but he didn't believe in God, not in any real sense, just some nebulous unformed entity that people spoke of with reverence but to his logical, educated mind simply could not exist. No atheists in foxholes, he had heard before, and maybe that was right but he did not seek God as *N-for-Nancy* dropped slowly to oblivion; he inventoried his failures and regrets. There they were, listed on a tally sheet for him to check off, and it seemed that he had more than his share on the negative side of the ledger.

What have I given my life for? he wondered, and the answer came immediately: *to satisfy my own ambition*— an ambition that had nearly consumed him and did destroy any relationship that he was fortunate to have. But inside, as *N-for-Nancy* lost altitude and he saw Prentice's lips moving rapidly in prayer, he knew his arrogance would never permit him regrets. Regrets meant that he had been fallible and he just couldn't accept that notion when he was this close to death.

But that didn't silence the fear.

Oh God, he could see through the open door and the waves were becoming larger, becoming more distinct, taking on shape and character—blue-green hillocks with white, frothy crests. The plane was getting lower and soon it would be even with the waves and an instant after that, impact.

N-for-Nancy fell slowly and Cole watched the waves rise to meet them, and as the waves neared, his nerves grew taut, twisted so tight that he knew they would snap.

They were lower now, skimming over the tops of the waves. They must be biting into hillocks, destroying the crests, but there was no sound except the roar of the open door and the high-pitched whine of *N-for-Nancy*'s one, pitiful engine. He could smell the sea. The scent was sharp, clean, and for some reason it comforted him.

Atlantic City. His parents took him to Atlantic City when he was a boy and he let the waves roll him onto the shore, feeling his body scrape along the sand, giving himself up to the power of the ocean.

There was a bump behind them and *N-for-Nancy* shuddered harshly as the fixed tail wheel dug into the waves.

A second later *N-for-Nancy* collided with the sea.

Chapter 23

The Admiralty, London, England

A low light from the hallway flooded Bimble's office, followed by a soft knock on the door. Bimble, who had been working at his desk by the light of a small lamp, looked up wearily. The moon might crash into the sun, German ships might gobble up British cruisers, and the end of the world might be on hand, but nothing, nothing must interfere with the reports required by Their Lords of the Admiralty, completed in the proscribed manner, and within the specified time. Bloody nuisance, Bimble labeled it, sailing a wooden desk with paper sails.

"Sir Joshua?" It was Hawthorne. The light gathered around the outline of his body like a halo.

"Yes," Bimble said, rubbing his sore eyes. "What's the time?"

"Just after four."

"A.M. or P.M.?"

"In the morning, Sir Joshua. We've received some news. Harland has called to say the Home Fleet's going out."

"High time. Never known Townes to be so slow about things."

"Not all of them," Hawthorne said. "*KG V* and *Rodney*. Three cruisers and assorted destroyers."

Something in Hawthorne's tone told Bimble that he had more information.

"Well?" Bimble said curtly.

"Our intelligence chaps picked up a transmission from the German vessel and a return message from Group North. Our chaps have finally been able to determine her name. She's the D.K.M. *Sea Lion.*"

"*Sea Lion?*" Bimble said. "She's not on the registry."

"She's not any place, sir. No one has heard of her so we're left to suppose that she is the vessel that Commander Hamilton's men happened upon. The H-class."

"The class that was never built?" Bimble said, his irritation rising. "We know nothing more than her name, do we, Hawthorne? We don't know where she is or what she intends to do?"

"We do know from the transmissions that it appears that she wants to return home by way of the Bay of Biscay."

"Brest or St. Nazaire?"

"We don't know," Hawthorne said. "But our chaps are on it. They feel that they can determine that and her location from her radio transmissions."

"For them to do so," Bimble said, searching through the clutter for a cigarette box, "she must do something that she has not shown a penchant for doing as yet."

"Sir Joshua?"

"She must fill the airwaves with continued transmissions. She has been maddeningly closemouthed.

We can't count on her becoming talkative now, can we?"

"No."

"No. Indeed. All right, Hawthorne. Let me get back to this foolishness."

"There is something else, Sir Joshua."

Bimble lit a cigarette, took a deep draw, and blew the smoke into the darkness. "Go on."

Hawthorne stepped aside and motioned into the hallway. A thin figure stood in the doorway. Even in the gloom Bimble could see that it was a Royal Navy officer.

"With your permission, Sir Joshua, this is Lieutenant Anthony. He's with the Wireless Telegrapher section. Shall I turn on the light?"

"No."

Hawthorne nodded at Anthony to begin.

"My division survails U-boat transmissions, Sir Joshua. We keep pretty close tabs on who is out there and what they have to say. Of course these are all coded messages so we detect and copy the messages, in code, and send the information up to Crypto. They are the fellows who actually determine what's being said. My best man at that sort of thing is Watkins. Twenty years in W.T., sir." Anthony hesitated. "He's come up with some information, Sir Joshua. I'm not quite sure what it means."

"Continue," Hawthorne prodded the officer.

"Yes, sir. Everything that goes out for U-boat W.T. transmissions goes through Goliath, that's their network, and everything that comes in from them takes the same route."

"I understand what you're saying, Anthony," Bimble said. "What is the point?"

"Yes, sir," Anthony said. "Watkins was told to monitor those fifteen boats lined up west of Greenland. These U-boats kept the air burning with W.T. transmissions. Watkins got their call signs easily enough. It's very odd, you see, because U-boats are naturally chatty, but these blokes are working overtime at it. So he began to track them."

"That's what he's paid to do, isn't it?" Bimble said.

"Yes, sir. Of course, sir. Fifteen U-boats, fifteen call signs, all matched up. He was quite certain about that."

"We know there are U-boats out there," Bimble said, pinning Hawthorne with a fierce glare for wasting his time with this nonsense. "We know the number and the general location and for reasons that you aren't to know they are causing us some concern." Bimble's tone became harsh. "That is why you are doing your job, but for the life of me I don't know why you are here at this ungodly hour wasting my time."

"Well, sir, this is where it gets a bit queer," Anthony said, unfazed by Bimble's outburst. "You see, every W.T. has his own way of keying, fisting, we call it. That is to say, how he taps out a message. Watkins can close his eyes and tell who's on the other end by just listening to the transmission."

"And?"

"He noticed something very odd and started keeping track, giving the operators' names, you know. Fifteen U-boats, fifteen call signs, fifteen operators, fifteen names." Anthony handed a slip of paper to Hawthorne, who handed it to Bimble.

"What does this mean?" Bimble said, holding the list under the feeble light of the desk lamp.

"It's the enemy W.T. operators that Watkins named. Those that he identified. The W.T.'s sending out all of those transmissions."

"William," Bimble read, "Robert, and Thomas." Anthony nodded.

"Are you telling me," Bimble said, "that you've only been able to account for three U-boats?"

"In a manner of speaking, sir," Anthony said. "But more to the point—Watkins has been able to account for three W.T.s. There's three chaps out there pretending to be fifteen. They switch call signs but it's three W.T.s and only three. I'd stake a month's pay on it."

"Three U-boats masquerading as fifteen," Bimble said thoughtfully. He looked up. "How sure are you about your chap? Watkins?"

"Sir Joshua, I've worked with Watkins for eight years and he's got the keenest mind when it comes to wireless telegraphy that I've ever seen. The man's ability to understand the nuances of radio transmissions is absolutely frightening. When he told me what he'd found I spent nearly ten hours listening to the transmissions with him to see if he might be mistaken. He identified the elements of each that I was to listen to, at almost the moment that the transmission began. There are three, Sir Joshua. I'm convinced of it. Three W.T.'s sending those messages."

Bimble studied the list of names again and nodded. "Thank you, Anthony," he said. He leaned back in the chair and tossed the paper on his desk as the young officer left. "What a bloody mess."

Hawthorne waited for a signal to speak. It came with a simple "Well?" from Bimble.

He moved to the desk, took a sheet of stationery

from a pad, and sketched out the situation. "Here is where we thought the fifteen U-boats were."

"And may still be," Bimble said.

"Perhaps, Sir Joshua. Here is *Prince of Wales.*" He drew an X. "Here is where we think *Sea Lion* is." He drew a large circle. "If those chaps are right, *Prince of Wales* can turn west now and make a high-speed run to Newfoundland, chancing the U-boats."

"If there are only three U-boats. But see here, suppose Jerry has his three out front as skirmishers, with twelve behind covering a much smaller area with a much better chance of getting *Prince of Wales?*"

"Perhaps the U-boats are within range of air reconnaissance from St. Johns. Surely the Americans will help us with air reconnaissance? They did with *Bismarck.*"

"Perhaps," Bimble said. "But the fact is we don't know where the missing twelve U-boats are or what they plan to do."

"They could have been arrayed south of *Prince of Wales* as a means of trapping her if she continues on that course. The three to the west acting as beaters, if you will, driving *Prince of Wales* south. So if *Prince* turns west now, she is safe."

"Yes," Bimble said. "From the U-boats. But with *Sea Lion* behind her, and we have no idea where, she can then turn southwest and cut *Prince of Wales* off."

"But she has no idea where *Prince of Wales* is."

"If we can pick up W.T. transmissions between Group North and *Sea Lion,*" Bimble said, "the Germans can pick up W.T. transmissions between us and *Prince of Wales.* Besides," he said, picking up the stationery, crumbling it into a ball, and throwing it into the dustbin next to his desk, "we don't know

where *Sea Lion* is. She could be within sight of
Prince of Wales at this very moment. Have you at least
some good news to share with me about Coastal
Command's search?"

"I'm afraid not, Sir Joshua. They've got everything
capable of flying aloft. The only news that they
passed on is that one of their Hudsons went down."

Bimble crushed out the spent cigarette in the
blackened glass ashtray at his elbow. "I suppose it
would be too much to hope that she crashed into
that damned German battleship, wouldn't it?"

Cole felt himself being swept along. He had no
idea where he was, no recollection of anything; just
a sense of movement. He couldn't see anything, but
that wasn't important, not that he shouldn't be
troubled by it—just that for some reason sight was
out of his control as was a sense of danger, or fear,
or even concern. It was all very strange. He bumped
against something solid and woke up.

He was outside *N-for-Nancy*, or at least the back
half of her. Her tail was hanging in the air and he
saw the trailing edge of her wings just below the surface of the water. *She must be intact*, Cole thought,
but he couldn't see her nose.

He pushed away from the fuselage and looked for
the door. Most of it was underwater and he suddenly realized that he was alone.

"Johnny! Prentice!" he shouted. A wave slapped
him in the face for disturbing the tranquility of the
wreck site with his shouting and he swallowed a
stomachful of water. It tasted of gasoline and oil. He
retched heavily and vomited. The stench of it almost

281 BETWEEN THE HUNTERS AND THE HUNTED

made him vomit again. He paddled away from the scene, thankful for the buoyancy provided by his Mae West. "Peter?" He spun around, searching the water. "Hey!" He looked back at *N-for-Nancy* and saw that she was settling lower into the water. He thought for a moment about swimming back and trying to get inside the aircraft. Maybe one of the men was trapped inside, or maybe he could find the life raft. But he shrank from the thought of entering *N-for-Nancy* for any reason. She could suddenly sink and he would be trapped in her forever.

"King!"

Cole looked around frantically, trying to locate the source of the voice.

"King. Over here."

It was Johnny. He was in the bright yellow life raft about thirty yards behind Cole. The gunner was alone.

Cole heard a gurgling noise and saw *N-for-Nancy* slowly slide beneath the waves. He was still staring at the site when Johnny called to him.

"For Christ's sake get into the dinghy, King. You'll freeze to death in no time if you don't get out of the water."

Cole thought it strange that Johnny was worried about him freezing to death as he swam to the raft. He wasn't cold at all. He thought it would be worse if he got out of the water and into the life raft, but he didn't have time to consider it—he felt Johnny's hands grasp the fabric of his flying suit and drag him into the life raft.

"Help me along, will you?" Johnny pleaded.

Cole slapped heavily at the life raft until he managed a handhold, and pulled himself in—falling awkwardly into the tiny craft. He lay still for a moment, drained from the exertion, sucking in great gulps of air. "Where's . . . ?" he managed to gasp.

"Dead," Johnny said. "We're it. Poor young Prentice smashed his brains against the gun support frame. The other two never had a chance. We must have bounced off our tail and driven the nose right into the sea. Bloody bad end for good men. How about you? Anything broken or cut?"

Cole shook his head, surprised at how exhausted he was. Worse, he was beginning to chill. He was trembling and the cold seemed to pour into him, invading every part of his body.

"The adrenaline's wearing off," Johnny said. "Felt just fine in the water, didn't you? It was the shock of all that happened. Now that that's passed, you'll feel the cold."

"I can't talk you into building a fire, can I?" Cole said, his teeth chattering.

Johnny smiled. "Swallow much water?"

"Just enough to throw up. Now I guess we sit and wait, huh?"

"Nothing to do but that. Prentice got our emergency call out. If there was anyone close enough to hear it and come to our rescue, we'll have a warm bed and hot rum in no time."

Cole wrapped himself in his own arms, trying to control the shivering. "It's a big ocean. May take a while. How are we fixed?"

Johnny unzipped a waterproof pouch and pulled back the flaps. "Tins of food. Small jug of water, enough of that, I hope." He pushed the contents to one side, searching. "Flares. Line and hooks for fishing. You any good at that, King? Fishing?"

"I couldn't catch a cold in a snowstorm, let alone catch a fish."

"Pity. I'm no good either," he said, continuing. "Bits of material to catch rainwater. Enough odds and ends to keep us going." He grew somber. "They counted on four chaps."

The death of Peter, Bunny, and Prentice suddenly hit Cole hard. It was Peter that Cole focused on. He didn't like Peter much and it was apparent to Cole that the feeling was mutual. But Peter had taken over the controls of *N-for-Nancy* when Bunny had been wounded and he had fought to keep the aircraft aloft to give the others a chance to prepare for ditching. Peter was a hero. Peter was dead.

"It's no good, King."

Cole looked at Johnny.

"Thinking about the others," Johnny said. "It'll give you nothing but hurt and it won't change things. They're gone, the poor blighters, and we're alive. All we can do is try to stay alive until someone comes and pick us up."

"I've never been through this before. Knowing guys that were killed."

"It's a bloody tough thing to deal with. You never really forget," Johnny said. "Blokes I know who bought it, I see their faces right out of the blue. I don't know why, they just pop up in my mind. I hate it. Maybe that's my penance. That's what I pay for living when they died. So don't you go dwelling on it. They'll come back to you often enough without you making a habit of thinking of the poor bastards. All we need to do is stay alive until someone comes and finds us."

Cole nodded, scanning the endless ocean,

knowing that he was unlikely to see anything. He heard a strange noise coming from Johnny's end of the raft.

"Are you humming?" Cole said.

"I am," Johnny said. "Takes my mind off things. Never learned to whistle, so I hum. I hum everything."

"I don't hum and I don't whistle," Cole said.

"Deprived, are you?" Johnny said. "Fancy a sing, then?"

"What?"

"To keep our spirits up," Johnny said. "Normally, I'd have a pint in me hand with me mates down at the pub, but this will have to do. I'll sing one and then you sing one."

Cole laughed. It seemed somehow disrespectful to laugh so soon after men had died. *Perhaps*, Cole thought, *I'm laughing out of relief that I didn't die like the others.* Regardless of the reason, he decided, it felt good.

"King," Johnny said with a look of contrived pity, "do you think it makes a bloody difference out here whether a chap can sing or not? There's nothing but fish and mermaids. Now, here I go—

> "My uncle's a hell of a hunter,
> He hunts up big bottles of gin.
> For ten bob he'll save you a good one.
> My God, how the money rolls in,
> Rolls in, rolls in.
> My God, how the money rolls in, rolls in,
> Rolls in, rolls in.
> My God, how the money rolls in."

Johnny beamed at Cole. "Well?"

"Sounds like someone squeezing a cat," Cole said.

"Can you do any better?"

"I can recite poetry."

"Go on."

> "There was a tall lady from Ender,
> Whose big bosom nearly upend 'er.
> Hiring Willy and Ted,
> With a breast on each head,
> She then had a human suspender."

"That was bloody pathetic," Johnny deadpanned. "God help us if that's all you Yanks bring to this war."

"I told you I couldn't sing," Cole said, smiling.

"You've proved it, haven't you? How does that bloody limerick go?"

"What?" Cole laughed.

"Teach me yours and I'll teach you mine," Johnny said.

Despite everything that had happened, Cole smiled again. "Okay, listen up." He repeated the limerick several times before Johnny said that he knew it.

"You got it?" Cole said.

"It isn't Ode to a bloody Grecian Urn, is it now, King?" Johnny cleared his throat dramatically. "You lead off and I'll jump in."

"Okay," Cole said. "Ready?"

> "There was a tall woman from Ender,
> Whose big bosom . . ."

Johnny joined in, their voices drifting over the

waves, accompanied by the green waves slapping against the sides of the yellow life raft.

> "Nearly upend 'er.
> Hiring Willy and Ted,
> With a breast on each head . . ."

The little raft slid down a gentle swell, into a shallow trough, and up another wave, pausing briefly at the crest.

> "She then had a human suspender."

The raft spun slightly, a tiny craft on the vast open plain of the inhospitable sea; settling into another trough, carefully tended, for the moment, by the endless waves.

"I've got one," Johnny said. "There was a young virgin from Glasgow. . . ."

The voices of the men grew fainter as they laughed at the ridiculous words, the wind gently pushing the raft over the waves, farther away from the unmarked grave of *N-for-Nancy* and the men that lay entombed within her.

Chapter 24

H.M.S. Firedancer, *the North Atlantic*

Land rubbed the stiffness out of the back of his neck and paced the narrow confines of the tiny bridge. He glanced at the stoic form of *Prometheus,* beating her way through the sea, two points off the port bow of *Firedancer.*

Hardy had tried to edge *Firedancer* well off the cruiser's starboard bow after *Firedancer* had switched stations with *Windsor* and *Eskimo.* He was going to place her far ahead of the position prescribed by Whittlesey, but *Prometheus* caught on and sent *Firedancer*'s pennants up the yardarm. Resume your station, *Firedancer* had been told, and not once, but three times.

Each time Hardy had cursed the signalman's message and replied, simply: "Tell the bastard, 'Acknowledged.'" He had reluctantly ordered Land to make the necessary course alterations, rather than to perform the distasteful duty himself.

"Number One," Hardy said, squeezing between

the chief yeoman of signals and the voice tubes, "are we properly stationed for His Majesty over there?"

"We appear to be, sir," Land said. "At least our pennant hasn't made an appearance in the last hour."

"We must be thankful for small miracles, mustn't we?" Hardy said. "I am blind to port because of *Prometheus*, so let us hope that the enemy has the good sense to come from starboard."

"Signal from flagship, sir," the chief yeoman of signals reported.

"Oh, what the bloody hell is it now?" Hardy exploded. "We're where we should be, aren't we? Number One, have you taken her one point out of station without my permission?"

"No, sir."

"'Flagship to *Firedancer*.'" The yeoman read the Morse lamp signal. "'Aircraft down. Sixty miles, bearing 183 degrees. Proceed to rescue. Rejoin squadron when rescue effected. End of message.'"

Hardy said: "Number One, prepare a boat party. Yeoman, reply to *Prometheus*, 'Message received, acknowledged. Proceeding as instructed.'" Hardy flipped open the brass cover of the engine room voice tube. "Engine Room? Bridge here. Light off number three. Let me know when she's ready. Stand by for increase in revolutions. Quartermaster?" he called. "Bridge here. Starboard thirty. We shall become an ambulance."

"Bridge, Quartermaster. Starboard thirty," the helmsman confirmed. "Wheel starboard thirty."

Hardy made his way to the binnacle and watched the compass needle swing. Smartly done, he thought. At least he was free of *Prometheus* and could act on his own. He didn't like to take orders and could barely stomach suggestions, and his irritation at being nudged in one direction or another had increased significantly since the Second Night. But he remembered his heated conversation with Land, especially when Number One had said: "I was there, too." It was a relief that Land said it aloud. For some reason, and Hardy had thought this through and could find no logical reason for it, it was as if the burden of his actions had been shared by Land's acknowledgment, and it did not lie all on his shoulders alone. Stupid, bloody emotions. No sense to any of it.

Now I can do something positive. I can go and pull some poor bastards out of the cold sea and give them a warm place to lay their head. He suddenly remembered his comment about *Firedancer* being an ambulance and he felt a twinge of shame. *What's wrong with the old girl being an ambulance?* he told himself. *Change of pace for her—do her a bit of good.*

Do yourself some good, you mean, old bastard, he told himself. *Good God,* he thought. *Now I'm a philosopher as well!*

D.K.M. Sea Lion

Turm Oberbootsmannmaat Herbert Statz had been proud of Bruno's performance against the English vessel although he couldn't see anything more than the crowded confines of the turret during the battle. He had heard of course; the loudspeaker within the turret kept Statz and the others informed of the action.

Statz had taken time to visit the crews of the

other two guns and speak to them about the victory. He spoke to them as if Bruno alone had destroyed the English cruiser while the crews of the other turrets did little. Those who listened understood the pride that Statz felt because they felt it as well. They could feel nothing else. *Sea Lion* was almost too big, too fast, and too powerful to conceive of. She was a complex city that functioned perfectly, that performed beyond anyone's expectations, and there was nothing like her on the seas. That is the reason that Statz took the time to speak to the other sailors: he wanted to share his pride, and exalt in theirs, of *Sea Lion*.

Statz found Bootsmannsmaat Otto Liebs calmly sitting on a shell-transfer capstan near the upper revolving shell ring, eating potted meat from a tin. He alternated between the meat and a stack of crackers poised precariously on his knee.

"How can you eat that shit, Liebs?" Statz said.

Liebs dipped a piece of cracker in the tin, scooped out some potted meat, and popped it into his mouth. "I can eat anything. I'm not so fancy as you gunners."

Statz glanced at the racks of high-explosive shells surrounding the room. They were two decks down and encased in an armored barbette, but one lucky shot piercing this room would send the turret above them straight up into the air.

"Keep your hands off my children," Liebs said, digging in the tin.

"Children?" Statz said.

"I'd give them all names but there are too many of them. You fellows above don't have the sensibilities that we shell handlers do. We do the real work. My children are the real heroes."

"What about my guns?"

"They are of no consequence," Liebs said.

"What do the fellows in the powder rooms say, then?"

Liebs shrugged. "Who listens to them? That reminds me." He set the tin on the deck, rose, and made his way to the shell hoist shutter casing. He turned a butterfly knob and opened an access panel. Taking a flashlight from his overall back pocket, he peered into the shell hoist trunking. Apparently satisfied with its condition, he closed and locked the panel. "Have you seen Kuhn lately?"

The question shocked Statz. "What?"

Liebs turned off the light and slid the flashlight into his back pocket. "They say Kuhn is wandering the ship at night."

"That's not funny," Statz said. "He was my friend."

"Mine as well," Liebs said. "You forget that we had liberty together quite often. That doesn't change things. Eich saw him near the hydraulic accumulator. Hillen said that he saw Kuhn in one of the cordite storage bays."

"Hillen is a fool."

"Of course he is. But he's not the only one who says that he saw Kuhn."

"What of it?"

Liebs shrugged again. "Nothing. Some sailors are concerned about such things. It means nothing to me."

"All we need to be concerned with," Statz said, "is our duty. We serve the guns and think of nothing else."

"You needn't lecture me," Liebs said abruptly.
"Have you ever wanted for shells? I do my job and
keep my machines clean. But this could be bad luck,
you know."

Statz turned away from Liebs. "It's nonsense," he
said. But he found the talk disturbing.

"For you and me, yes. For others, I'm not so sure."

"You'd better not let the officers hear about this."

Liebs snorted. "What would I tell them? The ghost
of a sailor is wandering the ship? Better I keep my
mouth shut and come face-to-face with Kuhn. But the
others call it bad luck, Statz. You know that."

"Bad luck?" Statz said. "On this ship? Nothing can
harm her, Liebs. Nothing can sink her."

"Fine," Liebs said, ending the conversation. "For
my part, I don't believe in ghosts. I believe in high-
explosive and armor-piercing and big guns that
sink enemy ships. I believe in cordite and steel,
Statz, and the Kreigsmarine."

"That is all you should believe in, Liebs," Statz said.
"Trust to those things and German optics and we
need not fear ghosts, the devil, or the Royal Navy."

The twin-engine Heinkle 111H settled nicely in
a cloud while the observer crawled forward into the
bombardier's position. He could see nothing of
course through the Plexiglas panels except the
wispy shroud of gray cloud that protected the
German aircraft from the British far below.

The Heinkle was a medium bomber, a very fast aircraft that swooped in quickly and dropped its small
but respectable load of bombs on the enemy, and
then fled. This Heinkle 111H, with red propeller

hub covers and a large yellow A painted aft was not over Scapa Flow to bomb or even to be seen. Its crew had been given specific instructions and as the pilot ordered his crew to get ready, the Heinkle fell like a stone out of the thick clouds and into the open skies of the Flow, twelve thousand feet below them.

Flak started almost immediately, dirty clouds that exploded all around the Heinkle 111H. The pilot, a veteran of Spain, Poland, and France, cursed softly as he maneuvered the aircraft across the sky, trying to throw off the antiaircraft gunners' aim. They were persistent though and anxious to kill him.

"Do you see anything?" the pilot asked through his intercom, the tension he felt obvious in his voice.

"Nothing," the observer said calmly, "there's too much cloud cover. We must go lower."

"Lower," the pilot muttered fiercely. "Lower. Lower. We must always go lower." He had lost his nerves long before, but he was a veteran and proud so that he would not admit to himself or anyone else that his hands trembled too much and he felt as if he were going to fill his oxygen mask with puke every time he heard the Junkers JUmo 211F-2 engines turn over.

Speed was their only salvation. They had seven 7.92mm machine guns that protruded from the fuselage like stingers, but it was the 1,350 horsepower generated by each engine that was what the pilot counted on.

He eased the Heinkle down two thousand feet, feeling slight satisfaction that the antiaircraft gunners would have to adjust their aim, trying to locate the intruder again. Their instructions had been simple. They were to radio back one of two words depending on the situation that they observed in Scapa Flow. That was it; the entire mission centered on what the enemy was doing far below and the word that was selected for transmission.

The pilot had flown missions before when he did not drop bombs or strafe the enemy. After years in Spain, Poland, and France, one becomes used to carrying out orders that do not make sense, with unquestioning loyalty. Regardless of the fear.

"Lower," the observer said.

"I gave you lower," the pilot snapped. "Do you want me to land?"

"I can't see," the observer said. "The clouds aren't as heavy but I still can't be sure. I want to be sure. You want to be sure, don't you?"

"Lower," the pilot said angrily, and pushed the wheel down, keeping his eye on the altimeter. He kicked the left rudder and banked slightly, thinking that he'd fly a figure-eight as he descended and leveled out, giving that idiot of an observer time to see everything that he wanted to see.

"I've got it," the observer said excitedly. "I can see them now. One. Three battleships. Looks like three cruisers. Many destroyers. Many." The man paused and the pilot waited. He had stopped breathing and it seemed that his heart had stopped and he knew that the radio operator and gunner were waiting for that one word as well.

"Dresden," the observer said.

There it was.

"Are you sure?" the pilot asked.

"Yes. Dresden. Dresden. Send the message."

"You heard him," the pilot said to the radio operator. "Send it."

As the operator tapped out the word *Dresden* in code on his Fu-10 radio, the pilot pulled heavily on the wheel, pushed the throttles forward, and as the aircraft gained speed, settled into his seat, a little more relaxed than he was before.

Below him was the Royal Navy, but it couldn't reach him anymore, and somewhere out there was the Royal Air Force, but his Heinkle 111H was fast enough, with some skill and luck, to outrun them. There was always the danger of mechanical failure, but his ground crew was superb so the pilot never gave that possibility much thought.

Dresden. They were to transmit that word, they were told by the squadron commander, if they observed the British Home Fleet on the move. They were to be absolutely sure that the enemy fleet was moving. Beyond a doubt. But if the fleet was static; if the vessels were moored and there were no smoke plumes hanging lazily above them, then they were to transmit the word *Belgrade*.

The pilot had no idea of the importance of either word and as far as he was concerned his radio operator had just informed high command of some disastrous news. Or it was the best possible news and those martinets who traveled by long gray, Mercedes-Benzes and stuffed their oversized bodies in ribbon-covered uniforms might be dancing with joy.

He didn't know and he didn't care. All he cared about was that he had survived Spain, Poland, and France, and perhaps he would survive England as well.

The pilot adjusted the fuel mix as the observer made his way up from the nose and sat on the narrow step next to him.

"I wonder what it means," the observer said.

The pilot said: "I don't know," but he said it in such a way that he didn't care very much one way or the other what word was sent—that he was above such things—that his attention was on nothing except flying the aircraft. He was a professional after all.

"It must mean something to someone," the observer said. "Why else would they send us out here?"

This time the pilot reinforced his superiority by saying nothing. He sat calmly, eyes scanning the instrument panel, then the sky ahead and above him, then the small mirrors that let him see aft. He listened to the engines with a professional air, careful to keep at least a portion of his arrogance concealed so he did not overplay his hand, and glanced at the magnetic compass.

He did all of these things because he wanted to bury the fear that so recently before had nearly consumed him. He could not permit the observer to see it, because then the squadron would know and the pilot could not accept that. So, now that his hands did not shake, and his mouth was no longer dry, and he did not have to fear that his voice would tremble uncontrollably, he wondered along with the observer.

Why did high command risk the lives of a Heinkle 111H crew for the sake of one word?

Doenitz stood on one side of the plotting table sipping a cup of tea and watching the young lieutenant approach Raeder. He held a message in his hand and he stopped a respectful distance from the grand admiral, waiting for Raeder to acknowledge his presence. The grand admiral was heavily engaged in a conversation over something or other with someone from Jodl's staff. Whoever it was and whatever was being discussed would be reported directly to General Jodl, who would then rush immediately to whisper the results of the conversation in Hitler's ear. That was why Jodl existed, why Hitler kept him close by, and why most professional soldiers and sailors found it distasteful to speak with the man.

Doenitz took a sip of tea and savored the taste, watching the conversation between the two become more animated. Raeder would have done better to take the discussion to one of the offices where it would not look so unseemly. It was not that the Kreigsmarine staff around the plotting table was unused to confrontations—it was a regular occurrence as the tension of tracking unseen naval battles became too much for some. The little wooden ships on the large glass ocean were sometimes silently removed by plotting officers to acknowledge that the real ships filled with real sailors would not be coming back to port. The strain to keep the little wooden ships sailing smoothly on the large glass ocean could be considerable.

But to have one of Jodl's lackeys accost the grand admiral of the Kreigsmarine was an affront to the service and to Raeder as well. It did not bode well for Raeder. It could mean that Hitler was losing his patience with the navy—that he was losing his patience with the grand admiral.

Doenitz looked into the empty cup and smiled to himself. *If only I could read tea leaves,* he thought. *Perhaps I would know what is to transpire from this adventure. Perhaps I could see my own future as well.*

"Doenitz?"

It was Raeder. Jodl's messenger was gone and now the Kriegsmarine lieutenant stood rigidly at Raeder's elbow. In the grand admiral's hand was the flimsy.

"Come, come," Raeder said excitedly, waving Doenitz to his side of the table.

Admiral Doenitz patted his lips with a napkin, draped it across the teacup, and handed the cup and saucer to a steward. He walked around the plotting table to the beaming grand admiral.

"Jodl?" Doenitz said, hoping Raeder would share the subject of the discussion with him. The grand admiral's face darkened.

"Jodl," he spat, shaking his head in disgust. "The Fuehrer's poodle. He sends one of his subordinates here seeking answers. He won't come himself and he wouldn't dare ask me to report to Hitler. No. He wants me to speak here and then my words are twisted beyond recognition by the time that the Fuehrer hears them. The Fuehrer knows me well enough to know that I am a loyal German. Those around him attempt to distort everything that he sees or hears. He must take care that they do not harm him. Who knows how things are misrepresented to him?"

The old man has no idea, Doenitz thought. *The grand admiral of the Kreigsmarine does not realize how close he has come to being dismissed by Hitler. He is a kindly old soul from another century, another war—he is the innocent pensioner who spins tales of noble sailors to impatient grandchildren.* Doenitz suspected that Hitler cared no more for Raeder's loyalty than he did Raeder's fleet, but the grand admiral was blissfully unaware of the Fuehrer's feelings.

"Admiral Doenitz," the grand admiral said, shaking off Jodl's scent. He held up the paper. "It is Dresden."

Doenitz's fists tightened and a smile crossed his face. "Truly," he said, his eyes growing hard with victory. "Dresden."

"Two hours ago," Raeder said. "Look." He tapped the glass at Scapa Flow with a wooden rod. "The reconnaissance aircraft reports perhaps two, perhaps three battleships, three cruisers, and numerous destroyers moving out. They might be holding a capital ship in reserve. Then, they will turn slightly south-southwest in pursuit of *Sea Lion*." He looked at Doenitz. His question was obvious; where are your U-boats?

Doenitz took the rod from him. "Webber and the others are here. The Home Fleet must pass through them."

"How far are they from Scapa Flow?"

"A hundred kilometers. Any closer would be suicide. The British will have aircraft up to protect the fleet and scout ahead of them. They may suspect a U-boat of being in the area, but they could not possibly conceive of a wolf pack of twelve. If the attack is properly coordinated and Webber knows what I want of him, then the British Home Fleet will run a gauntlet of German torpedoes for nearly eighty kilometers."

Raeder nodded soberly and studied the plotting table. "*Sea Lion*, there," he said. "*Prince of Wales*?"

"There," Doenitz said, pointing with the rod. "Well beyond air coverage from Canada. *Sea Lion* will quickly overtake her, from this angle." Doenitz laid the rod on the table.

"I'm almost afraid to believe it," Raeder said,

trying to suppress his exuberance. "Look at this. Here we snatch the *Prince of Wales* and the prime minister from the British and here"—he swept his hand over the table—"we destroy the British Home Fleet." He grew silent, his eyes darting over the table. He turned to a tall *Oberbootsmann.* "Is there any surface force reported between *Sea Lion* and *Prince of Wales?*"

"No, Grand Admiral," the man said.

"She released her escort, did she not?" Raeder said, a note of concern in his voice. "The *Prince of Wales?*"

"Yes, Grand Admiral," the *Oberbootsmann* said. "A cruiser and several destroyers, according to messages intercepted by B-dienst."

"They are a small force at best and some distance from *Sea Lion,*" Raeder said as if to settle the issue and his nerves. "They pose no danger."

Doenitz watched Raeder relax.

"Good, good," the grand admiral said. "Very good, indeed. We wait now. Eh, Admiral?"

"Yes," Doenitz said, scanning the plotting table. "It is out of our hands. We wait."

Wait. For Doenitz it meant one of two outcomes. Complete success—*Sea Lion* would sink *Prince of Wales* and his U-boats slaughter the Home Fleet. Or, *Sea Lion* would fail in her mission and his U-boats succeed. Wait. Wait for Raeder to fail; wait for the opportunities that would come to Doenitz when he did.

Chapter 25

The North Atlantic

Cole vomited over the side of the life raft. When he was finished he wiped his mouth and chin with the back of his hand and then washed his hand in the cold water.

Johnny sat at the other end of the raft, watching him. "You can't have anything left, King."

"I felt my toenails come up that time," Cole said. He was ashamed to admit it but he was seasick. He thought at first that it was because of the mouthful of water that he'd swallowed, but decided that wasn't it. He was seasick. Hell of a condition for a sailor.

The little raft had been bobbing up and down in the rolling swells of the North Atlantic for over twenty hours. The weather had been fair, a slight breeze under a pale blue sky dotted with wispy clouds. Johnny and Cole had congratulated themselves on their good fortune. What Cole thought but did not say, and what he knew the gunner must be thinking as well, was that the

North Atlantic was fickle; she would just as soon suffer a storm as not. If the weather changed for the worst, even if that worst were nothing more than heavier seas and a respectable wind, chances of survival for Cole and the gunner dropped significantly.

Cole laughed at himself—chances of survival dropped significantly. *You sound like you're lecturing a bunch of freshmen.* Analyze, synthesize, and interpret the facts. That's what he used to tell his students: read and consider. He looked at the endless sky. He read a pleasant day in a tiny rubber craft on a huge ocean. He read the chances of being found as slight, perhaps nonexistent. *You should be scared,* he told himself. He glanced at his companion. Johnny was asleep.

You should at least be scared, you dumb son of a bitch. But that was the irony of the situation. He was cold, miserable, and if he had anything left in his stomach he'd throw that up as well, and that was all he felt. He remembered everything that happened just before *N-for-Nancy* crashed and he knew how frightened he was then—he knew it but the feeling was long gone. What he did remember was telescoped into some sort of fractured image that, if he were asked to describe it, would come out disjointed and incoherent. Not a telescope—a kaleidoscope.

Analyze and synthesize. He decided that the classroom was hardly the place to learn.

"If they could only see me now," Cole said, chuckling.

"King?"

Johnny was awake and looking at him questioningly.

"I was thinking about my students. I just wondered what my students would think if they could see me now."

"They'd have to be in another dinghy, wouldn't they? They'd have enough to keep them busy. How are you feeling?"

Cole cupped some water in his hand and splashed it on his face. "Like hell."

"I had a refreshing nap."

"I saw that."

"I can sleep anywhere, anytime," Johnny said. "I used to sleep on the Underground. You'd think a bloke would find that bloody well impossible, wouldn't you? Not me. Slept like a baby, I did. Got on at Hobb's End, rode to Victoria Station. Slept from one end to the other."

"What'd you do before the war?" Cole said.

"Mechanic. Kept the trains running. The war comes and I thinks, 'Well, that's it for you, Johnny. You've got a nice cushy job keeping the trains running. They'll not touch you.' So I'm called up right off. And then I told myself, 'They've got to keep you some place safe working on engines, now, don't they?'"

Cole laughed. "So they made you a gunner."

"Bloody bastards. Never been near a gun in my life. You?"

"Teacher. College."

"Took you for an educated man right off. What'd you teach?"

"American history. Government."

"Make a right good living, then?"

"You don't know anything about teachers, do you?"

"I knew to keep on their good side. Had my ears cuffed more than once. Got out of school first chance I got. Still, sounds cushy. Never got your hands dirty, I suspect."

Cole noticed something over Johnny's shoulder.

"What is it?" the gunner said, turning around.

"I thought I saw something."

"What?"

"I don't know."

"Here," Johnny said, tossing Cole one of the small plastic paddles. "Let's get on top of a wave. We can see from there."

Cole felt the paddle bite reassuringly into the water as he and Johnny worked to guide the raft to the crest of a swell. He tried to envision what he'd seen. It was very far away, sitting on the horizon; narrow, very narrow. It could have been a ship, a small ship. Maybe it was nothing. The sun was getting higher in the sky and its rays created a glare off the water. At least they were doing something to help themselves.

Johnny pulled the flare gun and a flare out of their waterproof pouch. He snapped open the breech and dropped the thick cartridge into the barrel.

They cleared a swell and sat briefly on the crest. Cole searched for the ship; it had to be a ship of some kind. There it was.

"There!" Cole shouted. "Over there." Suddenly he heard a pop and then a loud whoosh as the flare shot high into the sky, followed by a thin trail of brown smoke. Cole and Johnny watched it make its wobbly ascent and then begin its slow fall.

The raft slid down into a wave trough, blinding them, and they came up again, the ocean taunting them first with a glimpse of the faraway ship, and then by denying it to them.

"Over there," Johnny shouted, pointing across the waves. "It is a ship. They'd bloody well better come here and take us in."

"Is she turning?" Cole asked. "I can't tell if she sees us."

Johnny shot another flare into the sky. "Come on, you bloody, blind bastards. We're over here."

A wave cut off their view.

It was a ship all right. Not a big one, Cole decided. A destroyer or maybe a corvette. It had to be a destroyer; they were too far out for a corvette.

"They're searching for us," Cole said. "Prentice got his message off. That's a destroyer. I'm sure of it. Probably from a convoy."

They rode to a crest again. There was no doubt of it now; the destroyer was closing on them.

Johnny slumped back against the soft rubber wall of the raft. He looked at his watch, tapped the crystal, held it to his ear, and then shrugged. "Gone," he said. "A perfectly good two-quid watch rendered absolutely useless."

"It's a small price to pay," Cole said.

"I wish the other chaps had made it. I'm going to miss them terribly. It just won't be the same without them. I'm feeling a bit guilty. I mean them having bought it and me alive."

"What did you tell me?" Cole said. "Something about not looking back. There's nothing that you can do, Johnny. I guess just be glad you're alive."

* * *

H.M.S. Firedancer

Hardy lowered the binoculars and turned to Land. "Number One, assemble a party to help those men aboard. Too choppy for a ship's boat to retrieve them. I'm sure they'll need treatment of some kind or another, so see to that as well."

"Yes, sir."

"And, Land?" Hardy added. "I don't fancy stopping long in U-boat country, so have the men snap to." Hardy resumed his watch, picking out the bobbing life raft in the rolling swells.

Number One rejoined Hardy on the bridge. "All set, sir. I've detailed a party on either side of the ship. That will leave us free to approach from port or starboard."

Hardy looked at his number one in appreciation. "Well done, Number One. That's thinking, all right. You might find yourself on *Prometheus* one of these days with initiative like that."

"No, thank you, sir," Land said. "I prefer *Firedancer.*"

"That answer has considerably reduced my confidence in you, Number One. Let us go and fetch those poor bastards out of the water."

Her hull was scarred and rusted and her numbers were nearly invisible, bleached by the harsh sun and scouring salt spray of the North Atlantic, but to Cole the British destroyer looked as large and imposing as a battleship. When the ship was close enough he saw a party of sailors lining her deck, ropes in hand, waving at the raft. He had never seen sailors of the Royal Navy at sea before and he was amazed at their dress—they were wearing castoffs of every description, except for the two officers standing by the men of course. They were properly dressed. If any American sailor had reported for duty looking like this crew, he would have been tossed into the brig.

But he didn't really care. They had come to rescue him and as far as he was concerned, they could have been dressed like the Rockettes and the ship could have been the Staten Island Ferry.

"I hope they don't run us down," Johnny said. "Wouldn't that be just the proper end to this disaster?"

"She's doing fine," Cole said appreciatively. Her captain, whoever he was and whoever she was, worked her steering and engines masterfully.

When the ship was close enough, Cole saw ropes shoot lazily into the air, uncoiling against the pale sky. He caught a line as Johnny pulled one out of the water next to the raft.

"Pull yourselves in, can you?" a faint voice asked from the ship. "Or shall we come and get you?"

Cole waved off the second question as Johnny and he began to pull. When they were close enough to the vessel Cole realized that it was going to be tricky getting aboard. The sea was moderate and the swells unimposing when the life raft was on her own. But when she got close to the destroyer, there was a fair chance that she would be thrown against the hull and ripped to pieces by the barnacles that ran along the ship's side. There was a good chance as well that Johnny and he could be seriously injured.

"You chaps need to leave the dinghy," an officer

shouted through a voice trumpet. "Hang on to the ropes and we'll pull you in."

"Well, that's that, then," Johnny said, stripping off his flying suit. "In we go."

Cole did the same. He felt confident enough pulling his own weight up the ropes, but the thought of a bulky flying suit saturated with water concerned him. Still, it would offer quite a bit of padding if he ended up slamming into the hull.

"Hang on tight," the officer called. "We are going to pull you up now. Mind the hull, will you? We don't want you injured."

"Who's he kidding?" Cole said as he and Johnny slipped into the icy water. He wrapped the rope firmly around his hands and immediately felt the line tighten. There were two brawny sailors on each rope, pulling away in unison. The rolling destroyer began to fill his vision as he glided through the water. He tried to keep his head up; one mouthful of the North Atlantic was plenty. They were several feet from the rust-stained hull when the sea tried one last time to kill them.

A burst of wind caught the destroyer's bow and drove it to port while a stiff wave caught them from behind and threw them against the hull. Cole felt it happen; felt the waves grab him and throw him at the ship, so he pulled his legs up, bending his knees, and landed against the hull with the balls of his feet. His legs took the force of the wave and other than the impact on his feet, he was uninjured. He heard Johnny cry out.

Cole twisted on his rope to see Johnny's deathly white face.

"I've broken my bloody hip," the gunner gasped. "All of this just to end up a cripple."

"He's been hurt," Cole shouted to the men above him. All he could see were their heads peering anxiously over the side.

"Can you tie him off?" the officer called through the voice trumpet.

"Yeah," Cole said, making his way to Johnny. "Give me a minute."

"Do you need a hand?"

Cole didn't answer. He had the rope looped under Johnny's arms and tightly knotted in a matter of seconds. He knew that he had to work quickly; he was losing the feeling in his hands from the icy water. Finally, he gave a thumbs-up and shouted: "Okay."

Cole watched Johnny magically rise out of the water as the sailors pulled him up. He felt his rope grow taut and he walked up the side of the vessel as he was hoisted aboard. A dozen hands grasped him and lifted him over the cables and stays. When they set him down Cole was amazed to find how unsteady he was.

He looked over to find Johnny on a stretcher, unconscious, being examined by a sailor that Cole could only hope was a corpsman. "Is he okay?" he asked.

"Banged up a bit, I'm afraid," the sailor said, examining Johnny. He pushed the gunner's damp hair off his forehead. "Nasty bump here. Broke his leg, I suspect. Don't you worry, sir. He's in good hands now. Wouldn't hurt a bit for you to get out of those wet clothes and get a spot of rum."

"What is this ship?" Cole asked.

"H.M.S. *Firedancer*," the pitifully young officer with the voice trumpet announced with dignity. "Captain George Hardy, commanding."

"My compliments to Captain Hardy," Cole said as a sailor threw a musty-smelling blanket over his shoulders. "My thanks as well."

Cole was startled at the flat crack of a rifle. A seaman, his cap pushed back off his forehead, carefully aimed an Enfield over the side. Cole followed the line of the weapon and realized what the sailor was shooting at. The life raft. It could not be left floating about the ocean—it was decreed a hazard to navigation once it was abandoned. There was another report and a small column of water jumped into the air near the edge of the raft. It looked as if the man had completely missed his target, but it was only an illusion. Cole watched as the raft slowly lost form and seawater rushed into the interior over the deflating walls.

He felt a twinge of regret as the sea consumed the little craft that had given him life. It had been part of *N-for-Nancy* and now it too was going to disappear into the depths. He was alive, he remembered, and in war that was the ultimate triumph.

"Come along, sir," the sailor said. "We'll have you fit in no time."

Chapter 26

Mahlberg leaned over the chart, resting his hands on the chart table. He studied the calculations generated by his navigation officer—neatly written letters and numbers that nearly filled one page of the navigation log. He compared those to the course settings on the chart for *Sea Lion* and *Prince of Wales* while his officers waited.

The log was a history of the movements of the two ships, a record of a closely followed chess game in which each action was dutifully recorded. Time, speed, course; knight to bishop one, check . . . checkmate. Mahlberg straightened and accepted the numbers with a sharp nod.

"Just over three hours," he confirmed, glancing at the navigation officer for a response. He wanted the officer to answer the statement. He wanted the calculations to be sure and without error and he wanted the navigation officer's answer to be strong and unhesitant.

"Yes, sir. Three hours."

Mahlberg turned to Kadow, who had been watching the drama from the other end of the table. "Three hours and *Prince of Wales* is ours."

"And the Home Fleet belongs to the submariners," Kadow said.

"Cheer up, old friend," Mahlberg said. "If we've done quickly with *Prince of Wales* we can turn and take on the Home Fleet as well." He saw that the idea troubled Kadow. It was apparent that his first officer was uncertain if Mahlberg was jesting.

"Of course," Kadow said, keeping his opinion to himself.

"You don't think it beyond us, do you? Pick up a load of fuel on the way to the party and show those U-boats what high-seas action really is."

"We had not planned for that. We have no instructions regarding the Home Fleet."

"Nor had we planned to encounter that British cruiser so early in the voyage. We did and we are still on schedule. We simply radio Group North with our intentions and location and have a tanker meet us." He turned to his navigation officer. "There are two tankers, about here," he said, tapping the chart. "Am I correct?"

The navigation officer nodded. "Yes, sir. At last reports, undetected. I can contact them and arrange a rendezvous if you so order, sir."

"Don't be premature," Kadow reprimanded the navigation officer.

Mahlberg smiled. "Don't tell me that you've grown cautious, Kadow. Between Frey's guns and *Sea Lion*'s speed we can accomplish our mission and still give the Home Fleet a bloody nose."

"I was not being cautious," Kadow said, obviously stung by Mahlberg's comment.

"'But'?" Mahlberg said, foreseeing Kadow's concern.

"I do not wish to see us overextended. If we sink *Prince of Wales* and kill the prime minister of England with his staff, we have accomplished a great victory for the Fatherland."

"'*Patriae inserviendo consumor,*'" Mahlberg said.

"'I am consumed in the service of the Fatherland,'" a young *Leutnant zur See* said proudly. "Von Bismarck."

"And so it shall be," Mahlberg said. "It does no harm to consider the other options that may be open to us. Especially if those options include dealing the British an even greater blow."

"Yes, sir," Kadow said.

Mahlberg smiled graciously and clapped his hands together with satisfaction. "Now, gentlemen, let us double the lookouts and put our best men on radar and hydrophones."

"Kriegsmarschustand One, sir?" Kadow asked. The others in the chart room did not miss his formal tone.

"No," Mahlberg said. "I think that we can remain at Battle Station Two for a while. Let's not excite the men just yet. There will be excitement enough to go around in a short time."

All of the officers, except Kadow, chuckled at Mahlberg's joke.

"You may return to your stations, gentlemen," Mahlberg said. "Kadow. Join me on deck, won't you?"

Kadow and Mahlberg walked along the narrow

deck below the conning tower, a cool wind washing
over them. They stopped near a quadruple 20mm
mount. The ship was silent except for the soft blast
of a wave disintegrating under her bow, and the
rush of water against her gray hull.

"All my life I've dreamed of commanding such a
ship," Mahlberg said, looking out to sea. He turned
to his executive officer, absentmindedly rubbing his
left elbow with his right hand. It was a habit that he
had had since he was a child. "To command a
vessel such as this and to take her against the
enemy. I despaired under the republic. We were allowed only ships of no consequence. I could not
think of our great fleet scuttled under the nose of
the British at Scapa Flow. Resting deep in the darkness of enemy waters. But now"—he looked around
proudly—"here is the Fatherland's future. The
power of the Kriegsmarine." He waited for Kadow
to speak but his executive officer merely listened.
"You have reservations?" Mahlberg said. "About
my intentions?"

"Yes, sir."

"Kadow," Mahlberg said kindly, "I have never
denied you the opportunity to speak freely."

"Yes, sir," Kadow said. "I appreciate your confidence in me."

"There is another one of your infernal 'buts'
hanging there. I could order you to speak, you
know. If you were not so obstinate."

"Kapitan," Kadow began, "I sometimes have difficulty following your rationale. We have been fortunate. We have remained undetected since our
encounter with the British cruiser. We are set to
overtake and destroy *Prince of Wales*. I have every

confidence that when she falls within range of our guns we will sink her. But . . ." Mahlberg saw Kadow troubled by his own use of the word. "But are you really planning to then turn and attack the Home Fleet?"

"Why not? Why settle for half a victory when we have complete victory within our grasp?"

"Because it may be beyond our reach."

"Now we have stumbled into the realm of the philosophical, Kadow," Mahlberg said. "We have the greatest warship ever built. The most powerful weapon on earth. I vowed to myself that I would undertake a voyage so amazing that nothing whatsoever could match it. From the moment I heard 'Muss I denn' played at our departure, I knew that Sea Lion was indestructible." He placed a fatherly hand on Kadow's shoulder. "We are warriors, old friend. Sailors in service to the Fatherland. Our nation has given us a wondrous vessel by which we can give her victories. Don't be reluctant. We must be bold. Cunning. When the British expect us there, we will be here. When Doenitz reports to Grand Admiral Raeder that his tiny boats have encountered the Home Fleet, Raeder can reply, yes, but it is Sea Lion who destroyed them."

Kadow hesitated and finally answered, "Yes, sir."

"We will triumph," Mahlberg reassured his executive officer. "The British will encounter the unexpected on both sides of the North Atlantic. They will face Sea Lion."

"Yes, sir."

"Good," Mahlberg said, clapping Kadow on the shoulder. "Good. Now have our famous Kapitanleutnant of engineering come to the bridge. I wish to speak to him. Our ship is fast but she is also thirsty. I will charge him to give us more speed with less fuel consumption."

"Yes, sir," Kadow said. He watched Mahlberg walk away. A single idea was gnawing at him, an elusive voice that whispered foreboding in his ear; doubt sitting on his shoulder. Mahlberg had placed it there with a phrase—encounter the unexpected.

Bismarck had done so. A single torpedo striking her bow allowing tons of seawater to rush into her hull, fouling fuel and driving her down at the head. From that injury she is denied the fuel in her bow tanks, and that which leaks leaves an oily path— blood in the water for the hungry sharks to find her. Now her speed is reduced as the vengeful waves of the North Atlantic batter her, sensing that the great ship is wounded. But that is not the worst blow. Another aerial torpedo strikes her during an attack by flimsy enemy aircraft and her rudder is jammed. A one in a thousand chance that this could have happened. One in ten thousand. A hundred thousand. Now *Bismarck* is condemned to death because she cannot maneuver; with her rudders jammed she steams around in lazy circles, waiting for death. Waiting for the Home Fleet. They come, distant vessels across a gray plain. *Rodney, King George V,* others. Ninety minutes. In ninety minutes *Bismarck* is gone.

Kadow had been there when the band played "*Muss I denn*"; the song played as all capital ships of the Kriegsmarine prepared to set sail on extended voyages. He was moved as well by the music and the pageantry. One could not help but be moved by it. *See Lowe, Sea Lion*—a magnificent vessel of unimaginable abilities. He felt the pride in her, in the

Kriegsmarine, in the valor of the crew that every man felt. But they had played "*Muss I denn*" for *Bismarck* as well and she was never coming home.

Encounter the unexpected, Kadow thought. *How does one prepare for the unexpected?*

H.M.S. Firedancer

Cole was shown to the tiny bridge by a yeoman. It was no bigger and perhaps a bit smaller than the open bridge on the old flush-decker on which Cole had trained. He noted the location of the binnacle and the clump of brass voice tubes amidships and forward. Directly behind him was the wheelhouse, the pale face of the helmsman visible through one of the large portholes. In one corner of the bridge were thin stanchions to hold life vests and helmets and in the other corner was a mount for a pair of Lewis guns. The windscreen was down and the man that Cole supposed to be the captain, a short stocky man with a bull neck, stood to port, eyes pressed to binoculars. There was another officer, younger, thinner, taller, reading a message just handed to him by a seaman.

The younger man looked up and smiled. "Cole, is it?"

"Yes, sir," Cole said.

"Captain," the younger man said to the stocky figure, "here is our visitor."

"Well," the man said. "None the worse for wear, I trust. Came as quick as we could. Bit of luck finding you right off. George Hardy, captain, Royal

Navy. This is my number one, executive officer to you chaps. Land."

Cole saluted. "Jordan Cole, lieutenant J.G., United States Naval Reserve."

Hardy waved off the compliment. "Let's do away with all of that saluting nonsense. Doubt if I'd recognize one aboard old *Firedancer* if I saw it. Not likely to get one, eh, Number One?"

"On the contrary, sir. The officers and men respect you deeply."

"Bullocks, Number One. The officers are insolent and the crew can barely tolerate me. But let's not air our dirty laundry in front of Cole. Do you know what you've dropped into, young man? What we're about?"

"No, sir," Cole said. "We assumed that you were part of a convoy."

"Never assume, Cole," Hardy said. "Makes an ass of you and me. Understand? Ass-u-me? Ever heard that one before, Cole?"

"No, sir," Cole said, but no one on the bridge missed the trace of sarcasm in his reply. Except Hardy.

"Well, we're bound for home. We're rejoining two other destroyers and a cruiser and have set our course for Scapa Flow. You were out here looking for that commerce raider then? Not that I believe it's a commerce raider. This one's a capital ship, eh, Land?"

"Yes, sir."

"It's a battleship," Cole said. "I'd bet my bottom dollar that you're going to be in the hunt as well, sir."

"So you know all about her? I suppose, as soon

as someone takes the bloody time to let us know what's going on, we'll be after her. We were escorting another vessel, so I'll give you half a point for your guess about the convoy, but we got pulled off that. For your information the enemy ship's name is *Sea Lion*. We got that over the W.T."

"Have they told you anything about her, sir?" Cole asked.

"She sank poor *Nottingham* so she's a bloody threat, isn't she?"

"What do you know, Cole?" Land asked.

"She's over sixty thousand tons with a speed in excess of thirty knots, sir. Her main armament is twelve sixteen-inch guns and maybe twenty five- or six-inch guns."

"How the bloody hell do you know—" Hardy began.

"I'm with Photo Ops. We picked up intelligence about the vessel and her class. She's an H-class, Captain Hardy."

"Good Lord!" Hardy said. "No wonder she cut us loose."

"Sir?" Cole said.

"You might as well know it. We were escorting *Prince of Wales* to America. The prime minister is on board and he is to meet your President Roosevelt." Hardy looked at Land knowingly. "She cut us loose to outrun the bastard. That's her only hope. She has to get out of the Mid-Atlantic Air Gap and under Canadian air cover faster than you can say Jack Sprat." Air coverage from England, Canada, or Iceland, when it wasn't socked in, could only reach a small portion of the vast reaches of the North Atlantic. It was the area in between, the Mid-Atlantic

Air Gap, that was the most dangerous. "We'll have
to return to the Flow for fuel," Hardy said. "Unless
we can pick up a spot along the way."

"*Prometheus* can stay out a bit longer," Land noted.

"Oh, *Prometheus* can fly around the world without
bumping her arse," Hardy said.

Cole lowered his head to hide his grin. He was beginning to like this guy—he was the sort of man that
said the first thing that came to mind and said it the
way that he felt and to hell with everything else. He
watched as the captain regained his composure.

"Yes, of course *Prometheus* can stay out longer
and we're the better for it. If Cole here is correct,
and no offense to you, sir," Hardy said.

"Not at all, Captain," Cole replied.

"The Royal Navy has its hands full, doesn't it?"
Hardy continued. A telephone in a box on the
wheelhouse bulkhead behind Cole jangled heavily. A yeoman of signals quickly answered it, listened
for a moment, and reported to Hardy: "Foremast
starboard lookout reports ships sighted green oh-
eight, sir."

Land and Hardy immediately swung their binoculars to that location.

"Can you see anything, Number One?" Hardy
said.

"Not yet, sir."

"Yeoman," Hardy said, "confirm to the lookout.
Number of ships."

"Right, sir."

"Mr. Cole," Hardy said, adjusting the focus on the
binoculars. "What was an American naval officer
doing aboard an English bomber?"

"I'm an observer with Coastal Command, sir."

"I see," Hardy said, dropping his binoculars and fixing Cole with a sly grin. "And now you're an observer with H.M.S. *Firedancer*, aren't you?"

"Yes, sir."

Hardy searched the horizon again and said merrily: "I wonder what we will all observe together."

It was a magnificent sight. Gray ships big and small, their dazzle-pattern camouflage, wild slashes of black, white, and gray paint that destroyed the order of the vessels, as it was meant to do. It was meant to challenge the enemy gunners so that at a distance the symmetry of the vessels' shapes would be destroyed. Their size, speed, power, and direction would be safely hidden like an actor's face behind greasepaint.

First came six destroyers, two each coming out of Scapa Flow from the Sounds of Hoxa, Hoy, and Switha; small ships whose names were far from intimidating and, despite their 4.5-inch rapid-firing guns and torpedo tubes running fore and aft, might not be taken seriously. They were paired, sweeping the channels leading out of the Flow and into the three channels of the huge main field that protected the ships within the Flow from U-boats. In the North Channel were *Icarus* and *Nestor*, *Icarus* slightly in the lead so that her paravanes weren't fouled by *Nestor*. If the German Condors or U-boats had seeded the channel with mines, either vessel's paravanes might cut the anchoring cable, and the mine would float to the surface. It was then that the antiaircraft gun crews had their fun, shooting the bobbing sphere, only a small part of its glistening, algae-covered black hide, studded with prongs, visible above the surface. But there was not fun for the gunners today; the destroyers plowed the depths to no avail.

Astern of the destroyers came H.M.S. *Hermione*, a cruiser and veteran of the *Bismarck* chase, although to her crew's disgust she had only been posted to block *Bismarck*'s path and had never had the chance to engage her.

Astern of her, regal, calm, her thirty-seven thousand tons driven easily through the black, icy waters by the 4x Parsons single-reduction-geared turbines spinning four three-bladed manganese-bronze 14.5-foot-diameter screws, was H.M.S. *Rodney*. She was two decades old but she carried herself as well as she did when she came out of the Cornwell-Laird-Birkenhead Shipyard. She was stately, as she sailed out the North Channel, and when the sea parted before her bows in respect it did so knowing that it was *Rodney* who sank *Bismarck*. Perhaps it was H.M.S. *Dorsetshire* who dashed in to let go a few torpedoes at the smoldering wreck, but the cruiser could not have done it; by God, she couldn't have gotten close to the mighty ship had not *Rodney* with her nine 406mm guns pounded *Bismarck* into submission. It was H.M.S. *Rodney* who had sunk the mighty Kriegsmarine vessel, not H.M.S. *Dormouse*, *Rodney*'s crew proclaimed, and they were more than willing to fight for her honor.

But there was a problem with H.M.S. *Rodney*, a very apparent flaw in her beautiful lines, brought about by a gaggle of haggling politicians who did not know a ship from a sheep. To meet the requirements of various naval treaties her main armament, all of it, was placed forward. There was nothing of consequence aft except a truncated stern that gave her a very ungainly appearance. But appearances aside, because appearances can be deceiving, the problem, the flaw, was that the three-by-three-turret arrangement meant that A Turret, well forward, was nearly flush with the deck. And B Turret, right behind the first turret, was high up over A, sitting on an armored barbette so that she could shoot over her sister turret. Well enough designed because that brought six guns to bear straight ahead. But C Turret was placed directly behind B Turret, flush on the deck as if the Admiralty was ashamed to acknowledge its presence. So C Turret could shoot to port or starboard but not forward. And none of the three turrets could protect the exposed stern.

In the Middle Channel steamed the destroyers *Tarter* and *Active*, mimicking the actions of their sisters in the North Channel. Behind them at a respectful distance were the cruisers H.M.S. *Kenya* and H.M.S. *Norfolk*. They, like *Hermione*, were fast and in surface actions they would be the spoilers, waiting to slip in and unleash torpedoes at capital ships, laying down smoke with the destroyers; hounds after a boar.

In the South Channel came *Lance* and *Anthony* and behind them, towering over the destroyers, was H.M.S. *King George V. KGV*. Vickers-Armstrong, Walker Navy Yard, Newcastle-upon-Tyne, and only a child. Laid down on 1 January 1937, she was completed in 1940 and after her working up trails, she was accepted by a grateful Royal Navy. She had ten fourteen-inch .45-caliber MK VII guns and she'd fought *Bismarck*, but she was young and arrogant and wanted more. She wanted *Sea Lion*. She wanted to be the first in and the first to draw blood, and the one to send *Sea Lion* to the bottom of the North Sea.

Out of the three channels, North, Middle, and South, steamed the Home Fleet and when they were well clear of the channels they would increase speed and seek out the enemy. At a time that would be most opportune for the mission, the six destroyers would fall out and return to Scapa Flow because this was an emergency, and the three cruisers and two battleships would make a high-speed run, traveling much farther, to save *Prince of Wales* and sink the enemy, and the destroyers could not keep pace.

The six destroyers would turn once the others were safe out to sea and, bidding a farewell to the larger ships, sail home. Destroyers—born many years before to destroy torpedo boats that could quickly run up and launch torpedoes into the side of slower vessels, adapted to fight U-boats during the First World War, now designed to find and sink the descendents of those U-boats. The natural enemy of U-boats: fast, loaded with depth charges, vicious little predators that bit happily into the green seas with a bone between their teeth so that they could run up on the U-boats and kill them—destroyers.

Irony.

Twelve U-boats, in the hands of twelve skilled *Kapitan*s waiting precisely in the path of the Home Fleet; targets aplenty for the six veteran destroyers of the Royal Navy that escorted the battleships to sea. Battleships not nearly as maneuverable as destroyers and cruisers not as adept at fighting

U-boats as destroyers. Big targets for U-boat torpedoes.

Soon the vessels that could best fight and certainly defeat the U-boats that lurked in the depths of the ocean would be turning their backs to their traditional enemies and steaming back to Scapa Flow.

Chapter 27

"It's called kye," Land said to Cole as a rating handed the American a cup of thick hot chocolate.

"It'll foul your plumbing if you take too much of it," Hardy added in disgust. "Best to stick to tea. You've got to piss a pot full every ten minutes, but you can do that over the side if times demand it."

"I don't suppose you have any coffee," Cole said, deciding against the kye. He found the only use for the sludge with a thin sheen of grease floating on the top was to wrap his hands around the chipped porcelain cup for warmth.

"You suppose right, Mr. Cole," Hardy said. "The Royal Navy does not have the luxuries that you're used to in the American Navy. We're smaller and not as wealthy, but we're as keen as mustard when it comes to a go at Jerry."

"Yes, sir," Cole said, handing the kye back to the seaman.

"For God's sake we're civilized enough to have alcohol on board. Well managed of course. Takes the edge off the excitement a bit. Smoothes a man's nerves when the time's right. You chaps don't go in for that sort of thing, do you? Prohibition and all that. Uncivilized practice. Goes against nature."

"I believe Prohibition was repealed some time ago," Land offered.

"What?" Hardy said. He turned to Cole for confirmation. "Is he right about this? You Americans finally came to your senses?"

"Yes, sir," Cole said.

"Well," Hardy said with satisfaction, as if his comments had had something to do with the turnaround in attitude. "High time, I say. Puritans, wasn't it? Mormons? Who brought about that silly practice in the first place? Methodists, by God, it must have been the Methodists. Never find a member of the Church of England even contemplating such a thing."

"You're Methodist, aren't you, sir?" Land said.

"Shut up, Number One."

Cole watched as Land moved diplomatically back to the wheelhouse. He was on his own with this strange man.

"I can't say, sir," Cole replied.

Hardy gave his suggestion some thought before announcing his decision. "Puritans," he said emphatically.

"Fleet in sight, sir," the starboard bridge lookout called out. "Green oh-two."

"There they are," Hardy confirmed through his binoculars. "Mr. Cole, soon you will be introduced to *Prometheus*, *Windsor*, and *Eskimo*. The latter two are of no matter—only Sir Whittlesey Bloody Martin and his big cow." Hardy lowered his glasses and fixed Cole with a hard glance. "Kindly note the ranker, will you?"

"Of course, sir," Cole said, trying to hide his amusement. *This guy is a first-rate character*, he thought. Probably a little insane.

Number One handed Cole a pair of binoculars. "See for yourself." Cole let his eyes adjust and swept the horizon with the binoculars. He picked up the vessels, thin black smudges on the gray-green tabletop.

"You must not accept everything that our captain says at face value," Land said with a smile. "He can be eccentric at times, but his skills as a seaman can't be denied."

"The best sailors are a little odd," Cole said, returning the binoculars.

"He's a fighter as well," Land said thoughtfully, wrapping the straps around the binocular frame. "He's had a bad time of it lately, but he's a fighter."

"Dove?" Hardy called to the chief yeoman of signals. "When we're within Aldis lamp range make to the flagship, 'Mission accomplished. Two on board.'" He joined Land and Cole. "Your fellow survivor is resting comfortably, I'm told. No danger of a needle through the nose."

"That's how we tell if a chap is dead," Land said. "Destroyers don't carry medicos, so we stitch a fellow's nose closed and if he protests, he's alive. A bit barbaric, but it does the job."

"Beats the alternative," Cole said.

"Beats the . . ." Hardy said and then laughed loudly. "By God, he's right. It would be a crying shame to send a man to his doom when he wasn't ready. Eh, Number One?"

Before Land had a chance to answer, there was a loud whistle through the voice tube. "Bridge? W.T."

Land answered it. "Bridge here. What is it?"

"Straight-out message from *Prometheus*, sir. Plain language. 'Single vessel bearing 243 degrees. Unidentified. Rejoin with all dispatch.'"

Hardy joined Land. "What's that, W.T.? Repeat that." Cole watched Hardy closely while the message was repeated. The captain turned to Land. "God's holy trousers, it can't be. We couldn't have just run into her? W.T.? Send to *Prometheus*, 'Will join you immediately.'" Hardy walked to the windscreen in thought before turning quickly. "Well, Number One. You heard him. Action stations and look lively."

"Yes, sir," Land said and called for the chief bo'swain's mate.

"You had better retire below, Mr. Cole," Hardy said.

"I'd like to stay, sir," Cole said.

"This is a small bridge, Mr. Cole. There's barely enough room for those who should be here when things get hot. And if you don't mind me saying so, you're a big man and you'd make a lovely target."

"I understand, sir, but with all due respect I'd like to stay," Cole said. "After all, you said I was an observer on board *Firedancer*."

Hardy's eyes narrowed. "You aren't a barrister, are you? Turning my own words against me? I get enough of that from my own number one."

"No, sir," Cole said. "Just a sailor."

* * *

D.K.M. Sea Lion

Kommandant K, D.K.M. *Sea Lion*, Kapitan zur See
Mahlberg, had just dismissed his engineering officer and was about to send for his nautical officer
to recheck the computations when the bridge telephone clattered three times in rapid succession. An
Obersignalmaat answered it quickly. It was the *Obersignalmaat*'s tone that caught Mahlberg's attention.

"Hydrophones, sir," the *Obersignalmaat* said, cupping
the receiver. "They say they are picking up high-
speed turbines. Very faint, fine off the port bow."

Mahlberg smiled broadly. "Ahead of schedule. I
must speak to the nautical officer about his calculations. How far is *Prince of Wales?*"

"It's not *Prince of Wales*, sir. It's a smaller ship.
Ships, sir."

"What?" Mahlberg snapped. "Where?"

"He can't be certain yet, sir. Perhaps eighty kilometers. There is a great deal of distortion. He estimates two to four vessels."

Mahlberg glanced at Kadow.

The executive officer took the telephone from
the seaman and identified himself. "Kadow," he
snapped. "Repeat."

Mahlberg watched his executive officer concentrate on the information.

"What size?" Kadow said. "Are you sure? Could it
be an echo of some sort?" Kadow listened. "I need
the distance, man, make a guess if nothing else."

Another telephone clattered insistently and an
Oberleutnant zur See picked it up.

"Bridge. Yes? Please repeat that." The *Oberleutnant*
cupped the mouthpiece and caught Mahlberg's

attention. "It's radar, sir. They report three vessels at sixty to eighty kilometers to the southwest. There appears to be another vessel just beyond them."

"Size and speed?" Mahlberg said calmly.

Kadow hung up the telephone. "A cruiser, possibly Diddo class. Two destroyers, perhaps three."

"Possibly a cruiser," the *Oberleutnant* reported. "Radar can't determine the class. Likely three destroyers, one of those trailing the others."

"*Prince of Wales* escorts," Kadow said. "Shall I set a course around them, sir?"

"Around them?" Mahlberg said. "We're going through them."

"Kapitan—"

"My God, Kadow. A light cruiser and a handful of destroyers. The best they can offer are six-inch guns. They might as well spit on us as shoot at us."

"Torpedoes, sir," Kadow said, but he saw immediately that his arguing only made matters worse.

"They won't get close enough to use them," Mahlberg said tersely. "Twelve thousand meters? Is that their range? Every man aboard those vessels will be dead before they get close enough to launch torpedoes. This ship does not turn aside for any vessel. This ship will never run away or retreat. Is that understood?" Mahlberg looked around the bridge. "*Sea Lion* is the greatest vessel that has ever put to sea and I will never"—he turned to Kadow—"never order her to avoid battle. Is that clear?"

"Yes, sir," the executive officer said.

"Kriegsmarschzustand One," Mahlberg ordered Kadow, "notify Oberkommando der Kriegsmarine that we've run into an irritant."

The executive officer stepped to the bulkhead

and pushed the large red button that set off the alarm bells throughout *Sea Lion*. The crew burst into activity, dropping whatever they were doing and rushing along corridors and through hatchways with a cry of "Warsaw! Warsaw"—*make way*. This was no *Rollenschwoof*—no drill. This was real.

Statz was just coming on deck when the alarm sounded and he sprinted toward Bruno, dodging other sailors running to their stations. It was pandemonium to the uninitiated, but the men were trained to get to their stations any way possible, in the fastest way possible. They knew which corridors to take, which to avoid, and how to dash through the passageways before the heavy watertight doors were closed behind them with the warning shouts of "tuy-tuy-tuy-tuy." Once those doors were closed, that way was denied to the sailors so that they had to find an alternative route, and God help them if they arrived at their battle stations to find their *Oberbootsmannmaat* waiting for them.

Statz dropped to all fours and scampered under the turret counterweight, climbing into Bruno through the after hatch. He dodged pipes, ducked under the thick steel trunk of the range-finding mechanism, swung around the squat analog computer station that was used if fire control were denied them, turned sharply right, and slipped through the narrow hatch that led to the gun room.

He was off the control platform in an instant, down the ladder, around the breech of the big gun, and at his station. As Statz smeared his face with antiflash cream and donned his flash gloves and hood he heard the others rush in.

"You're late," he called to them good-naturedly.

"Do you expect me to run this thing all by myself?" The gunners took their stations, preparing themselves for battle. Statz watched them appreciatively—they were good men and they had trained well.

Matrosenobergefreiter Scholtz, positioned at the powder doors, pushed the button that let the powder rooms know that he was ready. Then he stood, arms folded, waiting patiently for whatever was to happen.

Matrosenhauptgefreiter Steiner, who did his best to show disdain for Statz whenever he had an opportunity, checked over the spanning tray, the trough that dropped down to accept the shells and powder bags.

Next to him was Matrosengefreiter Manthey, a naturally funny sailor who loved doing discreet impersonations of officers, and did them quite well. He was the hoist operator and it was his job to bring the one-ton shells from the shell rooms deep within the vessel and guide them onto the spanning tray.

And Matrosengefreiter Wurst, the smallest and youngest man in the crew who suffered under Steiner's attacks when Statz was not around, triggered the ramming mechanism, pushing first the shell and then the bags of powder into the gun's breech.

When the rammer cleared and the spanning tray was pulled back, Statz signaled to the gun controller, a distant man named Gran who never really seemed to fit in, and Gran turned the thick, black knob through the sequences on the gun-indicator of lock-ready-shoot. When Gran signaled that the gun was ready for action, it was up to the gunnery officer in his cathedral high above Bruno to find the target, and compute the half dozen variables that decided the gun's elevation and position. After the speed and course of the enemy vessel, and after *Sea Lion*'s speed and course, deflection, the wind, the weight of the shell and the powder charge, even the relative humidity, had been calculated, there remained only permission to fire.

"Is it *Prince of Wales*?" Wurst asked.

"They'll let us know in good time," Steiner said, stifling a belch. "Just tend to your business."

"We'll hear soon enough," Statz said gently, hating to agree with anything that Steiner had to say, but it was true. Someone, probably the *Kapitan*, would come over the loudspeaker and tell them who they faced.

Wurst merely nodded and joined the others in waiting.

In the cluttered room behind the three gun rooms the gun layers, each man responsible for the elevation of a gun, and the turret trainer, who rotated the huge gun housing on the thick rollers secreted in the rings embedded in the barbette, waited. The gun sighters, who peered through the eyepieces, and the gun plotter, who stood by the turrine that bore the crude computer, waited. They were a redundancy because all of those actions were firmly and expertly in the hands of the gunnery officers in the forward, amidships, and aft fire-control centers. These three stations together, or any one if only one remained undamaged, could provide the information, sent through the transmitting rooms to the four turrets, that would give a coordinated fire at enemy vessels. Situated far above *Sea Lion*'s deck, the gunnery officers peering through their sensitive range finders could see great distances. No enemy ship could hide below the horizon. But if the fire-control centers were knocked out or their links to the transmitting rooms were severed, it was up to the men behind the gun rooms in Bruno to find the targets, calculate the speed and distance, make the necessary adjustments, and shoot the guns.

"I wonder who it is," Statz whispered.

H.M.S. Prince of Wales

John Leach, captain of the *Prince of Wales,* handed the message to Prime Minister Winston Churchill but didn't wait for him to read it.

"It's from *Prometheus,*" Leach said. "She's run right into *Sea Lion.*"

Louis Hoffman watched Churchill roll the stout cigar to one side of his mouth, considering the news.

"How far is *Prometheus* behind us?" Churchill said.

"Just about two hours' hard running," Leach said, dismissing the yeoman who brought the message.

"Then I suggest that you waste no time in turning this vessel about."

"No, sir," Captain Leach said. "My mission is to carry you and the others safely to meet with President Roosevelt. I will not deter from that course until you are safely in Placentia Bay."

"Captain Leach, you seem to forget that I was once First Sea Lord and as such quite capable of making a sound tactical decision, and inasmuch as I am the prime minister and your superior, I order you to turn this vessel about and engage the enemy."

"With all due respect, Prime Minister," Leach said, "I will not endanger your life and I will not

forfeit my mission. There are seventeen hundred
seamen aboard this vessel who would gladly join me
in taking on *Sea Lion*, but I am not at liberty to do
so. Those poor bastards out there won't have a
chance against that behemoth. It will be a slaughter. You will get to Placentia Bay, sir, to meet with
Mr. Roosevelt and I will be haunted for the rest of
my life by the souls of those seaman."

Churchill jerked the half-consumed cigar from his
mouth and threw it to the deck. "Sir Dudley?"

Admiral Sir Dudley Pound shook his head. "Not
this time, Prime Minister. This time discretion is the
better part of valor. Those ships might delay *Sea Lion*
long enough for us to get away. They might, if one
is to believe in miracles, so damage *Sea Lion* that she
is forced to turn back. Regardless of the outcome
of that contest, John is right. You will meet with President Roosevelt and *Sea Lion* will be dealt with another time."

Churchill patted his coat, searching for a cigar.
"How I hate to turn my backside on the enemy," he
said, giving up the quest. He walked to the port
wing, letting the stiff North Atlantic wind wrap
around him. Hoffman joined him.

"Do you believe in the Almighty, Louis?" Churchill
asked him. "Pray to him in desperate times?"

"Once every four years," Hoffman said. "In
November."

"I am thinking of your President Lincoln. During
the Civil War."

"The one good thing that ever came out of the
Republican Party."

"After the Battle of Fredericksburg, December
1862. After the terrible losses suffered by the Union

Army of the Potomac at the hands of the more skill-fully led Confederate Army of Northern Virginia, Lincoln, in deep despair over another Union defeat in a seemingly endless series of Union defeats, ut-tered, 'What will the people say? What will the people say?'"

Hoffman listened.

"Sometimes, Louis, despite the public image of my iron resolve in the face of great odds, I despair, at times, as well."

"Prime Minister, I'm a cockeyed optimist. I don't believe in that bullshit about going down fighting. I believe in winning. Like you. Like Franklin. You can't win if you're not in the game, that's what your captain's telling you. Let those boys behind us throw a few blocks and keep you in the game. Then we'll lick those Nazi sons of bitches. That's what I think."

"Well, Louis," Churchill whispered, "I do pray that our chaps behind us live to see the game completed."

Home of Admiral Wilhelm Canaris,
Kaiserstrasse, Berlin

Captain Eberhardt Godt stood uncomfortably in the library of the home of the *Abwehr* chief. He could hear the sound of a piano and the mingled voices of the guests invited to the Canaris dinner party. He was not a guest. He had come to deliver some rather bad news to his superior.

The library doors were pulled open by a butler and Admiral Doenitz entered, obviously surprised to see his chief of staff. He waited until the doors were closed.

"What is it?" Doenitz said.

"*Sea Lion* is about to engage the *Prince of Wales* escort. We received Mahlberg's message not an hour ago."

Doenitz looked away in thought. "This message cannot mean that our valiant Mahlberg is about to engage *Prince of Wales*? She has released her escort, has she not? *Prince of Wales*?"

"Yes, some time ago. It appears as if they simply stumbled into one another."

"Mahlberg plans to engage those vessels before he reaches *Prince of Wales*?"

Godt knew that it was a rhetorical question. He had been with Doenitz long enough to know that the slight admiral simply tossed questions into the air and then studied them as they floated to the ground.

"Does Raeder know?" Doenitz asked.

Godt nodded. "He is livid. He threatened to court-martial Mahlberg when he returns."

Doenitz shook his head in wonderment. "The gold ring within his grasp and Mahlberg's vision is filled with the gleam of brass. Raeder has every reason to be concerned. The grand admiral knows that sometimes a warrior sees only as far as the point of his sword."

"Grand Admiral Raeder will surely instruct . . ." Godt offered.

"Oh yes. Yes, he will. But will our headstrong *Kapitan* respond? Mahlberg would not be the first man whose ambitions led him astray. Still," Doenitz said, "we want to be selective about the concerns that we address. Our world lies beneath the sea, does it not?"

Godt suddenly realized that Doenitz had introduced his own interests into the conversation. "We are," the vice admiral said carefully, "to concern ourselves only with the U-boats."

"Are we?" Doenitz said. "We are Kriegsmarine officers, Godt. Our loyalties cannot be divided between branches of the service. Of course we hope that *Sea Lion* accomplishes her mission, Godt. Our role, the U-boats' role, is clearly defined. My hope is that the entire mission be a success."

It was a lovely speech given with no conviction, and there was the question of hope; it was such a fragile commodity, such an elusive entity—surely one did not rely on hope alone.

"Yes, sir," Godt said, content to let the discussion die away.

"Besides," Doenitz said, airily, "how can those tiny vessels stop *Sea Lion*? Destroyers and cruisers. She will crush them and proceed on to *Prince of Wales*. Isn't that what we are told?"

"Your pardon, Admiral, but I detect reservation in your tone."

"Yes, well," Doenitz said wryly, "I always approach foregone conclusions with a healthy degree of reservation. What about Webber?"

"Nothing, sir. It should only be a matter of hours before he engages the Home Fleet."

"One day," Doenitz said with a look of disgust, "I shall invent a radio that can send messages from deep underwater so that I won't have to wait for U-boat *Kapitans* to surface when they deem fit and contact me. Raeder has one prima donna. I have dozens. Send for my coat. I've had enough of parties for tonight."

Bimble was gardening when Hawthorne brought the news. The admiral asked his wife, a plump, matronly woman who had been helping him tend to the roses, to excuse them.

"*Prince of Wales* is going on?" Bimble said.

"What else can she do, Sir Joshua?" Hawthorne said, sighting a pitted stone bench. The days had been endless for both of them and he had been the one to encourage Bimble to come home for a bit and rest. He knew that the only way that Bimble found relaxation was in the quiet surroundings of his tiny garden. Hawthorne sat down and waited for Bimble's reply.

"If those poor sods can slow that bloody bastard, they might give the Home Fleet time to get to her," Bimble said, joining Hawthorne on the bench. "Unlikely though. Damned unlikely." The admiral laid his arms across his round stomach. "God! What will happen to this country if we lost *Prince of Wales* and the prime minister as well?"

"The escorts. A cruiser and three destroyers," Hawthorne said. "They might offer some resistance."

"They won't last five minutes under that fire," Bimble said. "What did Hamilton tell us? Twelve sixteen-inch guns? A score of lesser guns and a hide as thick as an elephant's."

Hawthorne stood and stretched, letting his mind mull over the situation. Bimble kept a good garden. It was neat and colorful and although he couldn't tell a buttercup from a blade of grass Hawthorne appreciated the care that went into the creation and nurturing of this tiny plot of land behind a modest house surrounded by an ancient brick wall. He noticed a movement in the corner and he saw a pair of ears.

"You have a rabbit," he noted.

Bimble jumped up. "Is that bloody creature back in here? By God, I'll shoot him next time. He eats everything in sight. Does me no good to toil over this bloody garden if that little furry bastard eats everything. I'll get a gun, I tell you, and lie in wait and when he shows up, bang! I'll spring on him . . ." The words stopped.

"Sir Joshua?" Hawthorne said. The admiral looked at the stone pathway leading to a potting shed, and then to the plants on either side, and then at Hawthorne.

"Sir Joshua?"

"Those bloody bastards! Those deceitful underhanded, bloody bastards."

"Sir Joshua?"

"It's a trap, Hawthorne. The Home Fleet, by God."

"A trap?"

"The other twelve U-boats. They're nowhere near *Prince of Wales* or anybody else," Bimble said. "They're lying in wait for the Home Fleet to go rushing to the rescue."

"Are you certain?" Hawthorne said.

Bimble gave him an irritated look. "Of course I'm not certain, you silly ass, but I'd be willing to bet my bloody garden on it. Those others, the ones that that W.T. identified, were beaters. Don't you see that? They kept *Prince of Wales* running southerly to give *Sea Lion* a chance to catch up with her. But they convinced us that they were fifteen instead of three. So we calculated the truth but not the location of the other twelve boats. They are hiding, man, lying in ambush for the Home Fleet to steam like great, fat rabbits into their sights. When the Fleet's close enough, they spring the bloody trap."

"Yes," Hawthorne said, digesting the information. "Yes. That's it."

"Get back to the admiralty," Bimble said, taking him by the elbow and guiding him toward the back door. "Contact Scapa Flow and have them alert the Home Fleet. I'll be in as soon as I rinse off this grime and change." He shoved Hawthorne through the door. "Hurry, man. I'll be right behind you." Bimble shook his head at the possibilities. A complex plan: back *Prince of Wales* and the prime minister, and throw in the Home Fleet as well. Why not? Use *Prince of Wales* as the stalking goat and when the snare is sprung, destroy her as well. The damned, efficient Germans. He saw the rabbit venture tentatively across the stone pathway. "All right," Bimble said. "You can stay, you bloody hare. I suppose I owe you that much."

H.M.S. Firedancer

The bo'sun's whistle and alarm bell had sent *Firedancer*'s crew dashing for their action stations as the destroyer sliced through the North Atlantic, spray exploding over the bows and whipping around A Turret. They pounded down ladders and along passageways, emerging from the confines of the vessel to slap Kelly helmets on their heads and take up position. Excitement charged through the ship, men racing about, shouting directions and orders; warrant officers, chief petty officers, and petty officers cursing the men: faster, faster. The crews of the 4.5-inch guns pulled the tampions that protected the barrels from saltwater spray out of the muzzles, opened the doors for the ready-access magazines located in the front of the turret, and removed the canvas coverings from the breach mechanisms. The rear of the turrets were open, the men unprotected. In reality it made no difference because the turret shields did nothing more than partially protect the men from the cold wind. It was too thin to stop splinters, and if they were unlucky enough to be hit by a shell of any size the whole thing would disintegrate. She was not *Sea Lion*, and her turrets did not weigh one thousand tons each.

Firedancer bit into the waves playfully as if she had been too long under restraint and now given her head and was pleased at the ability to run. Her bow came up and with it a taste of North Sea as she flung high into the air in a moment of pure joy. Down her bow went again for another gulp and all the time men raced about her preparing for battle. This was not *Firedancer*'s concern—she was at full speed and that seldom happened in her voyages. She was either tied to plodding merchant ships in cumbersome convoys or forced to sail under two boilers instead of all three because fuel was low or she had too far to travel or one of her boilers needed replacement and it could not be counted on to perform. Now, now was a different matter entirely. *Firedancer*'s captain had finally come to his senses and unleashed her, given her her head so that she could stretch out; screws driving hard, bow slicing cleanly, engines humming contentedly.

Cole saw the other British vessels clearly now. No need for binoculars—they were close enough now for him to make out details. The cruiser was in plain sight, larger than the others—the destroyers that hovered just beyond *Prometheus*—but still a pitifully small ship. She was a light cruiser all right, strikingly similar to the light cruisers that he had seen tied up at Norfolk. They were fast, lightly armored, lightly gunned—a compromise between a heavy cruiser that stood at least a fighting chance with a capital ship and a destroyer that stood no chance at all. She was a compromise vessel—giving up armor and armament so that her speed would take her well clear of danger. But this was to be a fight and she would have no choice but to engage the enemy, however uneven the odds might be.

He glanced around the bridge, careful to keep to his corner of the tiny area. Hardy was almost taciturn, giving orders minimally, doling out the words as if they were rationed to him. His temper exploded once or twice; once when he called for more revolutions from the engines and once when he was asked if *Prometheus* had signaled them yet.

"Just now, sir," the yeoman of signals had replied.

"Well, goddamn it," Hardy had flared. "What is it? Do I have to call for messages before they are given to me?"

"Message from *Prometheus*, sir," Dove had returned calmly, used to his captain's outbursts. "'Glad to

see you could join the party, signed, *Prometheus.*'
Any reply, sir?"

"Reply," Hardy exploded, directing his frustration
toward Land. "Reply, Number One! Party. He's
talking as if I'm late again. Well, by God, I'll let
him know that we're not late. You tell that . . ." He
reconsidered and pinned Dove with a glare. "Make
to *Prometheus*," he said, gritting his teeth, "'I have
brought the champagne. Trust you have not ne-
glected to invite the guest of honor. Signed,
Firedancer.' Ha!" he said and then turned to Land.
"Ha, Number One. Guest of honor. I'll warrant
that will send that pompous ass around the bend."

"Right you are, sir," Land said, peering through
a pair of binoculars. "I think I have the guest in
sight, just now."

Cole, holding tightly to the binoculars that Land
had given him earlier just in case someone claimed
them, searched the horizon.

"Four points off the starboard bow," Land said
calmly.

"Jesus!" a lookout above him said. "She's a whole
country unto herself."

"Belay that talk, Taffy," a petty officer said. "You
sound like a bloody Hostilities Only. Now give it to
the officers quick and give it to them right."

"Green twenty. Green twenty," Taffy said. "Enemy
vessel in sight. Unable to determine range or speed,
sir."

Cole found her in his lens. "Holy shit," he said.
"That is a big son of a bitch."

The petty officer eased next to him. "Begging
your pardon, sir, but that sort of talk sends the
wrong message to the boys."

"My apologies, Petty Officer," Cole said.

The seaman had just turned away when he added: "But she is the biggest fucking ship that I've ever seen, if you pardon the observation, sir."

"Message from *Prometheus*, sir," Dove said. "'Take station two miles off my starboard quarter. We shall move in, in unison, and engage. End message.'"

"Well, that's the first sensible thing that I've known Sir Whittlesey to say in years. Make to *Prometheus*, 'Message received and acknowledged.' Well, Mr. Cole," he said over his shoulder, "what do you think of our chances?"

"I think it would be wise to shoot and scoot, Captain Hardy."

"Shoot and scoot?"

"Run in quickly, launch your torpedoes. Then get the hell away from her before she can target you."

"Oh, that won't do, Mr. Cole," Hardy said. "*Prince of Wales* is just over the horizon. *Sea Lion* can go through us like shit through a goose. We shall have to do more than that, I'm afraid. What, exactly, I'm not certain." He took a deep breath and resumed his watch. "Perhaps we can slip in and irritate the great ship, eh, Number One?"

"I wouldn't have it any other way, sir," Land said.

Chapter 28

D.K.M. Sea Lion, *Quadrant XC 38*

Kadow, standing next to the communication's bank in the conning tower, hung up the telephone.

"Foremast lookout reports that the enemy ships appear to be deploying for action. Hydrophone and radar report no other ships in the vicinity."

"But *Prince of Wales* is just beyond them," Mahlberg said, peering through the slits cut into the sixteen-inch steel walls of the conning tower. It was a small circular room, heavily armored, cramped; from which the *Kapitan* and a few men could direct the actions of *Sea Lion* during battle. It was a relatively safe place to be, as only a direct or very close hit could destroy it, but Mahlberg had to observe the action through those strategically placed tiny openings. He could control the engines, the steering, and communicate to any part of the ship from the round, steel citadel. But Mahlberg preferred to be on the bridge.

The telephone rang again and Kadow answered it. After a moment he reported to Mahlberg:

"Foremast reports cruiser bearing two-six-two, one destroyer to her starboard, two to port. Distance, approximately seventy kilometers and closing."

"Come to two-seven-oh," Mahlberg said. "That's the only variation these gnats will wring from me. Inform Frey that he may engage his main battery when the enemy is within range."

The blast of the alarm bell filled Bruno and called the crew of number-one gun to action.

Statz heard the rumble of shells coming up the hoist and watched as Steiner extended and locked the spanning tray into position. Manthey opened the hoist door and the blunt nose of the one-ton shell slid onto the spanning tray, anxious to be employed. As the door closed, Statz signaled Wurst, who activated the rammer, pushing the shell gently but resolutely into the gun breech until the locking ring settled snugly into the barrel.

At the same time Scholtz pulled hard on the gray lever that rolled open the barrel-shaped doors that led to the powder hoist. The two silk bags that fell onto the spanning tray were immediately guided into the breech by the rammer. Three more silk bags followed before Statz closed the breach and signaled to Gran. The gun was ready.

The loudspeaker above them crackled to life.

"Sailors of *Sea Lion*. This is your *Kapitan*. We are about to engage an enemy light cruiser and three destroyers, the only defense that the British have managed to throw up between us and *Prince of Wales*."

The men smiled at one another. What they would do to those tiny ships!

"We will rush through this pitiful force," Mahlberg continued, "and sink *Prince of Wales*. We will achieve a great victory for the Fatherland and avenge our brothers who perished on *Bismarck*."

Statz bowed his head and said a short prayer. He had known and trained with some of the gunners on *Bismarck*. Only luck, and the Kriegsmarine's unfathomable system of ship assignments, had kept him off the doomed vessel.

"We sail aboard the greatest warship ever built," the *Kapitan* continued. "Our guns shoot farther, our vessel is faster, and our men are better trained than any that have sailed before us. Even our name denotes our power. We are the Lion of the Seas."

Just as Mahlberg finished and the loudspeaker crackled off, there was a sharp clang and distant rumble as the turret gear was engaged and the turret began to move. At the same time Statz heard the pump motors engage and the wild hiss of hydraulic fluid being released so that the gun's heavy breech slowly dropped, and her muzzle began to elevate.

Statz felt pride overwhelm him as the turret trained and the guns laid in a beautiful choreography of destruction. He dared not look at the others because he was the gun captain and must remain professional at all times; but think of it! Feel the movement of the turret and the majesty of the gun as it sought out its enemy, and how could a man not know that he was a part of something so powerful and awe-inspiring that God himself must have had a hand in making it?

* * *

"Starboard thirty," Hardy ordered the helmsman in response to orders from *Prometheus*.

Cole felt the tension rising as Hardy concentrated on the scene unfolding before him. The captain dropped the binoculars from his eyes only long enough to bark an order.

"*Prometheus* wants us to go end around," Hardy said. "She'll have *Eskimo* and *Windsor* make smoke for her and then God only knows what Sir Whittlesey has up his sleeve. If he thinks that *Sea Lion* is going to be unnerved by *Firedancer*'s presence, he is being highly optimistic."

Cole spotted *Eskimo* and *Windsor* turning hard to starboard. Suddenly black smoke began belching from their stacks. The engine room had been ordered to dump extra fuel oil into the burners—they were making smoke to shield *Prometheus*'s move.

"There's the smoke," Cole said.

"Yes. Lovely pattern at that," Hardy noted professionally. "Let's hope the wind helps out. Keeping a sharp eye on Sir Whittlesey, Number One?"

"Yes, sir," Land said. "Nothing yet." Hardy wanted both Land and Dove to watch the flagship for signals—less danger of missing any of Sir Whittlesey's pearls of wisdom.

"Message from *Prometheus*," Dove called. "'You will demonstrate with vigor at the enemy's stern.' End message."

"Acknowledged and received, Dove," Hardy said in what Cole thought was a surprisingly calm manner. No explosions, no denunciations—very cool and professional. "Number One, I shall want the port engine up twenty revolutions and starboard fifteen on the wheel."

"Yes, sir," Land said, giving the commands to the helmsman and engine room.

"Any sea duty with the navy, Mr. Cole?" Hardy asked.

"A flush-deck destroyer," Cole said, trying to watch everything.

"The old four stackers. First war vintage. What was your station?"

"Gunnery officer," Cole said as he saw *Prometheus* turn hard to port. She was going to come in under the smoke that the destroyers were laying but from a different course than *Sea Lion* had observed her. Not much of a surprise to the enemy vessel but the only one that *Prometheus* had.

"Guns, were you?" Hardy said. "I'll have the wheel amidships, Number One, and starboard engines up twenty."

"Twenty millimeters aft of the well deck," Cole said, focusing on the German ship. He dropped the binoculars and rubbed his eyes roughly. They were starting to feel the strain. "Seconded as the torpedo officer."

"*Windsor* and *Eskimo* are just now pulling to starboard, sir," Land noted.

Hardy acknowledged the observation with a grunt. "*Prometheus* will cross *Sea Lion*'s bow, drawing fire, no doubt. He'll send *Eskimo* and *Windsor* in with torpedoes. Nicely done, Sir Whittlesey. All of this is textbook, Cole," Hardy said. "Until the shooting starts."

Cole swung his binoculars back to *Sea Lion*. There was an incredible flash that nearly covered her forward area and then a great mass of oily black smoke. Before he could say anything, Land shouted: "*Sea Lion*'s firing. A and B Turrets." Cole turned his head to one side, the only way to see shells in flight, an old gunner had told him. Look out of the corner of your eye, don't look directly for them, and you'll be able to catch them as they head for their target. Now, of course, the gunner told him wryly, if you're the target, you'll get a real close look at them anyway.

"Thank you, Number One," Hardy said with some irritation. "I am perfectly aware of this latest development."

Cole began calculating, his mind frantically working the puzzle—*fifteen-inch shells can travel 25,000 yards in fifty seconds. But these are sixteen-inch shells and I have no idea how far away they are. How many thousands of yards separate* Sea Lion *from* Prometheus? *Speed.* Sea Lion's *eating up the distance at twenty yards a second and* Prometheus *is closing as well but with an angle of deflection. What happens when one of those shells strikes* Prometheus? *What about two shells? Not this quickly, they can't find the range this quickly.*

"The ball has started, Mr. Cole," Hardy said grimly, "and we are hardly dressed yet."

"Hits," Land said. "Beyond the destroyers. My God, those columns must be a hundred feet tall. It's high explosives all right. Their fall is over by a thousand yards."

The telephone next to Cole's shoulder jangled urgently as the thunderous sound of *Sea Lion's* guns reached *Firedancer*. Cole jumped at the sound of the telephone and then cursed softly at his own nervousness.

"Masthead reports, Captain," Land said with the receiver in his hand. "X Turret is training on us." It would have been Dora—the British were unimaginative in designating their turrets. Instead of Anton and Bruno forward, and Caesar and Dora aft, it was A, B and X, Y. The name was of little consequence; the fact that *Sea Lion* had singled *Firedancer* out as a recipient for upwards of six tons of high explosives was a matter of some concern.

Hardy flipped open the voice tube cover to the wheelhouse. "Quartermaster, Bridge. Port thirty and make it lively."

"Masthead reports," Land said. "Y Turret is training on us."

"Has she reduced her speed?" Hardy said.

"No, sir," Cole threw in. "She hasn't backed down an ounce."

"Thank you for that report, Mr. Cole," Hardy said. "You may now consider yourself a member of the crew."

"She'll have a hard time judging our speed and course," Land said, joining them.

"All she need do is get close with those big monsters and our speed and course will be the least of our worries," Hardy said.

"There's another salvo, sir," Cole said as *Sea Lion* flashed brilliantly. She was trying to knock out the destroyers. *Windsor* and *Eskimo* were just separating to launch a torpedo attack and they made just as enticing a target as *Prometheus.* And if one or both of the destroyers were disabled, *Prometheus* could not call on them for smoke and she could not return to the smoke that they had just lain down, because the oily plumes that had obscured her position were dissipating. *Prometheus* would have nowhere to hide from *Sea Lion.*

* * *

D.K.M. Sea Lion

Statz heard the loudspeaker call out the first salvo over, but he wasn't concerned because he was sure that the fire-control station would find the range, deflection, and speed of the enemy vessels and he would hear: Good Rapid—fire for effect.

He could taste the cordite and his ears rang from the explosion of number-one gun and he felt, as he always felt when they first fired the gun, a little dizzy. The breech swung open and the spanning tray clanked into place and Statz heard the distant rumble of the heavy shell as it sped up the hoist. The hoist door flew open and the shell, dull gray except for its brilliant yellow nose, dropped easily on the spanning tray, waiting impatiently for the rammer to slide it gently into the breech.

"Come on, boys," Statz urged happily. "Don't lag. Just like training. One foot in front of the other. One, two, one, two."

"Now he's got us in the army," Wurst chimed in, pulling the rammer back.

"Not me," Scholtz said, allowing three powder bags to roll onto the spanning tray. "I'm a sailor."

"You're a shit!" Manthey offered loudly, and the gun crew burst into laughter.

They worked like a machine, Statz noted proudly. They were happy because they were no longer training. This was not simply the routine of load, fire, load, fire with the 8.8cc subcaliber gun that was inserted in the sixteen-inch barrel for practice firing; this was battle.

When Bruno fired, it was the Fellow Upstairs speaking to them in a voice that shook not only the turret but also the entire ship. God in heaven shouting encouragement to them in words that traveled down to the shell flats where *Bootsmanns-maats* directed teams at each shell hoist to send the shells to the gun rooms. And each hoist team was supported by three *Matrosenhauptgefreiters* in the forward part of the shell room who replenished the shell supply on the inner ring near the hoists from the fixed storage area. They were big men, strong men who used lashing chains and bucklers, applying a snubbing rope below the shell's rotating band so that they could slide the shell across the steel deck plates and into position.

Each step in the turret, each movement, each action related to another until the gun controller sitting on his tiny platform switched the indicator to lock, ready, shoot.

The firing bell shattered the interior of gun number one. Statz turned away from the gun, clamped his hands over his ears, and opened his mouth to lessen the chance of having his eardrums burst. Despite all of this, he still managed a contorted grin of satisfaction.

H.M.S. Firedancer

Things started getting very interesting for *Firedancer* when *Sea Lion*'s port secondary battery of 150mm L55 SK-C/28 and 105mm L65 SK-C/33 guns began to fire. The sea around *Firedancer* erupted in fountains of angry foam.

"Bloody hell," Hardy shouted as cold sea spray

rained across the bridge. "Are we the only bloody bastards out here? Shoot at someone else, won't you?"

Land was guiding the ship through the voice tube to the quartermaster on a wildly erratic course to throw off the German gunners. So far they had been remarkably successful at dodging the shells. But the noose was tightening. *Firedancer* had to get close enough to *Sea Lion* to launch her torpedoes. *Firedancer* had to engage the enemy—*Firedancer* had to offer up herself as a tempting target.

Cole knew that it was a matter of percentages— X number of German shells fired in Y amount of time from Z number of German guns against an overage British destroyer darting about the ocean for its life, and each minute trying to get close enough to fire its torpedoes, equals. Equals . . .

"Well, Mr. Cole," Hardy shouted to him above the crash of shells and the fiendish hiss of the towers of spray falling back into the sea, "fancy a transfer back to Coastal Command?"

"I'll fill out the papers tomorrow," Cole said.

"It'll get worse, Mr. Cole," Hardy said. "We're not within range of their quadruple-mount anti-aircraft guns yet." He staggered back to the bulkhead, trying to keep his footing on the slippery deck, and cranked the handset. "Torpedo Station? Bridge. Captain here. Deploy your tubes to port. Repeat, deploy your tubes to port. I shall fire them from the bridge. Acknowledge. Right."

"They haven't fired their aft main batteries yet," Land noted.

"Indeed," Hardy agreed. "Some trick, I assume."

"You've got to steer a relatively straight course in for the torpedo run," Cole said, shaking his head with admiration at the patience and skill of the German gunners. "They'll let go when we start our run because they know that we can't vary our course."

"Why, the bloody bastards!" Hardy said. "It's not enough that they try and kill me with everything they've got. Now they want to trick me in the bargain. Well done, Mr. Cole. Well done, indeed."

"Not at all, Captain," Cole said, wiping the salt spray from his face. "I was once told never to assume anything. It makes an ass—"

"Go to Hades!" Hardy snapped.

It was then a 150mm shell landed close to *Firedancer*, peppering her with shrapnel. The explosion startled the little ship and she hove to, throwing the bridge party against the bulkhead.

Cole heard the splinters hit, a rapid barrage of thuds—some sounds thick where the splinters hit the hull, some quick, innocent rips where the splinters sheered through the thin steel of gun tubs, funnels, or deck housings. He felt his heart beating against the walls of his chest. It was the feeling that he had felt aboard *N-for-Nancy*. He was scared again.

Hardy pulled himself to the voice tubes. "Wheelhouse, Bridge. Port ten. Port ten, do you hear?" Cole could tell from Hardy's voice that he wasn't the only one who had been frightened by that close call.

"Can anyone see *Prometheus*, for God's sake?" Hardy shouted.

"Here, sir," Land said, blood streaming down a gash near his temple. Cole watched as Number One ignored his wound and trained his binoculars back to the smudge of smoke aft. "I've got her masthead, sir. She's just coming around." He scanned to the left. "*Windsor* and *Eskimo* are both turning to starboard. They've stopped making smoke."

"Salvo from *Sea Lion*," Cole called out at the telling flash, followed instantly by the rolling cloud of gun smoke that seemed to consume *Sea Lion.*

Three sets of binoculars trained on *Prometheus.*

"They'll have her straddled this time," Hardy said bitterly. "Or close to it."

The six German shells hit within a split second of one another, far off *Prometheus*'s starboard quarter but close to *Eskimo* and *Windsor*. There were five fountains of yellow water thrown high into the air. They hung for a moment as if observing the battle and then fell lazily, harmlessly back into the sea. It was the sixth shell, maybe one of the first fired, or the last, maybe from Anton or Bruno; but it was the one that killed a destroyer. There was a huge explosion followed by a blast of smoke and debris that filled the sky.

"Who is it?" Hardy shouted. "Who got it?"

Land's glasses dropped and he said: "*Windsor.* Direct hit."

Cole found the stricken ship through the lenses of his binoculars. Black-brown smoke boiled from within her, fed by fierce yellow flames that raged from the bridge to the second funnel. She appeared distorted somehow and he was about to adjust the focus when he realized her back was broken. Her bow jutted out of the sea a good fifteen degrees and her stern only five degrees, but it was twisted to port, wrenched from the body of the ship by the explosion. She would not die slowly. The sea would claim her through shattered bulkheads and sprung watertight doors, or the fires would reach magazines and set off shells and torpedoes. There would be no survivors. If the explosions did not kill them, then the sailors of H.M.S. *Windsor* would die in the frigid waters of the North Atlantic, falling into a deep, comforting sleep that led to death.

"God help those men," Hardy said and then called down the voice tube. "Starboard thirty." He moved to the other tube. "Engine Room, Bridge. Smoke, and lots of it. Now, unless you want to end up like poor *Windsor*."

Cole threw Land a questioning glance. *We're turning away from* Sea Lion, he thought. *What the hell's going on?* Turning away, he asked himself, *Or running away?*

"Captain?" Land said.

"We're showing *Sea Lion* our stern, Number One. We've gone and joined the Reciprocal Club. She can't tell our bow from our stern at this angle, so she can't tell if we're coming or going, and by God, I want them to see us going."

"Captain—"

"Did you see the size of those bricks, Cole? Big as houses, they were. Poor *Windsor*. Cunningham was a fine man. No drinker he, but a fine man. Wheel amidships if you please, Number One."

What the hell is going on? Cole wondered. *Has this guy gone crazy? First he pumps smoke into the air and then begins a big circle as if he's hightailing it out of here and now* . . . Cole couldn't help the smile.

"Ah, you've got it, Cole," Hardy said. "Kudos to you, young man. Number One, we shall go out a bit with the smoke covering our movements and then turn sharply to starboard and run with all speed at

the enemy. At the appropriate time we shall turn
hard to port and being just off her bow, launch a full
spread of torpedoes. That should give her pause."

"Yes, sir."

"Surely you did not think I had intentions of
running from the enemy?" Hardy said.

"I had my doubts, sir," Land said.

"Yes," Hardy said slowly, gazing at the smoke
plume that marked *Windsor*'s grave. "After seeing
what happened to that poor devil, I had my doubts
as well."

"Swing them to starboard, swing them to port,
and now the bloody simpleton on the bridge wants
them amidships again," Chief Torpedo Gunner's
Mate Baird said as he sat in the cramped cockpit on
top of the four torpedo tubes and cranked number
one back into position. He leaned over the back of
the cockpit, a low tub that housed the compressed
air indicators, training gear, and backup firing
mechanism, and called to Engleman.

"Did you see her go up?" he shouted.

"Too right, I did," Engleman said, standing by at
the torpedo shack. He led the sailors who winched
the additional torpedoes deep within the stores,
up through the open doors of the shack, and into
the tubes. Once they were loaded and the compressed air was charged, number-one station would
be ready to fire a spread again. "Was it Cunningham
on the *Windsor*? That tall skinny chap with an Adam's
apple as big as a coconut?"

"As if you've seen a coconut," Baird said. "He—"

"Number One Station," Sublieutenant Morrison

called crossly as he quickly passed the station. "You will direct the tubes to starboard."

Baird watched him disappear beyond the funnel, making for the second torpedo station. "Lord Nelson always favored those bastards on Number Two Station," he said, pressing the brake lever and gripping the handles of the turning wheel in each hand firmly. It was geared to the machinery that spun the tubes in the proper direction and moved smoothly enough considering that all the power called upon to move it was located in the muscles of one man. "Tommy Blessing? Are you standing by, Boy Seaman?"

"Yes, Torps," Blessing said, stationed at the thick compressed air hoses that fed the tanks of the torpedo tubes. It was a blast of compressed air that shot the torpedoes out of the tubes and engaged their onboard engines so that once the torpedoes hit the water their screws were spinning in a blur. The torpedoes should right themselves and come to a proper depth and cut a straight line to their target and with any luck one of four would hit, or with better luck make it two, or with phenomenal luck and the help of the sea gods there would be three deep explosions. And if someone on board *Firedancer* had sold his soul to the devil or the Royal Navy, then all four might hit.

"Don't worry about bricks," Baird said. "*Firedancer*'s too small and too fast for that nonsense. You just keep your mind on my air and all will be right in the end." The condition of the compressed air tanks was critical. If the pounds-per-square-inch were inadequate due to the tanks or hoses being pierced, the

torpedoes would rest impotently in their tubes—
useless.

The number-one torpedo station swung into
position and locked with a clang. Baird released the
brake, licked his lips, and waited. Glancing around
for Lord Nelson, he pulled a cigarette and a pack of
matches from his coat. He pulled the smoke deep into
his lungs and exhaled appreciatively. "Boy Seaman,"
he called to Blessing, "run down to the pub and get
me a pail of Guinness and a blowsy barmaid."

Chapter 29

"She's cleared the smoke," Kadow said.

An *Oberleutnant zur See* reported: "Forward top-mast reports enemy cruiser fine off our port bow. Distance, thirty kilometers, speed, thirty knots."

"She's too close for Anton to get a good shot," Kadow said.

"Then Frey has to make do with Bruno because *Sea Lion*'s course will remain unaltered," Mahlberg said. "Let them snap at our heels, Kadow. They can do nothing more."

"They have torpedoes, sir," Kadow reminded Mahlberg.

Mahlberg gave the statement a disdainful look and said nothing.

Kadow remembered a book that he had read long ago. It was about Rome and the ancient generals and their triumphant return to the Eternal City after far-off victories. They were entitled to ride in a grand parade in their honor, and to receive the adulation of the population. Their greatness, their invincibility was acknowledged by all as they rode in their splendid chariots down the broad avenues lined with cheering crowds. But riding behind them in the chariots, so close that the generals must have felt their hot breath, was a servant who whispered, so that pride did not blind the triumphant to their own inadequacies, "Remember, thou art mortal."

Statz and his gun crew cheered loudly when the speaker announced the destruction of the enemy destroyer.

"We got that one," Steiner said. "Anton can't see that far. She can't even see over our bow."

"Perhaps when she grows up," Manthey said. The red shell hoist light blinked rapidly. "Shell coming!"

The shell slid onto the tray and was pushed into the breech, followed immediately by the powder bags. Statz shut the huge breechblock and listened with satisfaction as it spun closed and locked. He heard the gearing mechanism engage and felt the turret move to starboard as the gun rose. The turret slid to a stop.

"Over the bow?" Scholtz said. "We're going to give Anton a headache."

"British cruiser dead ahead. Distance thirty kilometers. We'll wait until she turns and fire," the loudspeaker said.

"We haven't slowed a bit," Steiner said. "How can we hit anything at this speed?"

"We hit that destroyer," Manthey said.

"Don't worry about Kapitan Mahlberg," Statz said to Steiner. "He wants *Prince of Wales*. He won't waste his time with these shits. Besides, they can't hurt us, Steiner."

"She's turning to port, Kapitan," Kadow said, watching the progress of the cruiser through the narrow slits of the conning tower.

"Frey will get her," Mahlberg said.

"Kapitan!" a *Kapitanleutnant* called from the other side of the conning tower. "British destroyer just clearing our bow. At ten thousand kilometers. She looks as if she's preparing for a torpedo run."

"Let the secondary batteries deal with her," Mahlberg said calmly.

"Kapitan, we must prepare for evasive action," Kadow reminded Mahlberg. It was standard procedure in the face of an impending torpedo attack.

Mahlberg put a pair of binoculars to his eyes and said nothing.

"The cruiser's making smoke," a *Leutnant zur See* said, perplexed. Cruisers didn't make smoke.

"She's going to turn back into that to hide after she unleashes her torpedoes," Mahlberg said. "Except she won't have time to fire her torpedoes or run and hide."

A thought struck Kadow. "Where's the second destroyer?"

"What?" Mahlberg said, lowering his glasses. "We sank her, Kadow. . . ."

"No. There were three." For the first time Kadow saw a hint of concern on Mahlberg's face.

"British destroyer," a lookout called. "Two points off the starboard bow. Twelve thousand kilometers."

"The cruiser's firing," a *Leutnant* reported.

"Port twenty," Mahlberg said. "Now!"

"Destroyer to starboard is launching torpedoes," the *Leutnant* said.

"We're showing them our beam," Kadow said. They were exposing their length to the torpedoes and fire of the cruiser. The cruiser's guns would have little effect, but the torpedoes would have a much larger target in which to bury themselves.

"We're bringing our secondary batteries to bear," Mahlberg said irritably. "Neither one of those vessels can survive that. And then we'll be on our way."

"Yes, sir," Kadow said. *Remember, thou art mortal.*

H.M.S. Firedancer

"*Prometheus* is going in," Land called out. "There's *Eskimo. Prometheus* is drawing fire to give *Eskimo* a chance."

"They're spoiling our shot!" Hardy railed. "By God, I can't shoot with those two on the other side. Those glory-seeking bastards. All right, all right," he said, calming. "We can at least give *Sea Lion* pause. We'll make a false run of it. Let's hope the mere sight of *Firedancer* will frighten them."

Cole watched as the secondary batteries along *Sea Lion*'s port twinkled ominously. *It's going to be the other way around,* he thought. *Those bastards have got our range.* "This is going to be close," he said to anyone listening as he tracked the blur of the shells through the air. "Close," he said again and then the sea exploded around them. It was worse than before. Splinters screamed through the air like banshees, peppering the superstructure and hull of *Firedancer*.

Cole heard screams and shouts of alarm and a huge crash as the foremast fell over the side, shot completely off the ship. There was a secondary explosion as the ready ammunition of a 20mm Oerlikon exploded just below and aft of the bridge.

"Land," Hardy said as he picked himself up off the deck, "get the supply parties topside." He looked at Cole in horror.

Cole quickly examined himself. He was covered in blood. *Am I wounded? I don't feel anything.* He tore at his clothes, trying to find the injury. His trembling hands were covered in blood and bits of flesh as he pulled away his coat.

"It's not you," Hardy said. "Behind you."

Cole turned to see Dove and the other two signalmen slumped over their stations just above him. They were sliced open, their bowels hanging in bloody coils from their stomachs. Their intestines, covered in blood and strewn over the deck, glistened obscenely in the dull light.

"Check the telephone, will you, Cole?" Hardy said, his voice shaking.

Cole wiped his bloody hands over his trousers and cranked the handle of the bridge telephone. There was nothing. No sound. He tried the Tannoy system, but it was dead as well. He caught Hardy's attention and shook his head.

"At least we have the bloody voice tubes," Hardy said. He checked the relays for the torpedo-release buttons. "Nothing here as well. Land? Detail a man to act as runner to the torpedo stations."

"I can do it, sir," Cole said. "I know how they work."

"Very well, Mr. Cole," Hardy said. He was sober now, as if the sight of the dead men hanging from their stations had finally driven home the horror of this moment. "Go down and tell them to stand by. I don't know from which direction we shall attack, so one blast of the ship's whistle will be to port, two blasts starboard. If the bloody whistle works at all. You're to report to Morrison. He's the fellow in charge down there."

"Aye-aye, sir," Cole said. He made his way down the narrow ladder that led to the main deck. Along the way to the torpedo stations he saw the damage that the splinters had done. There were holes punched through deck housings and Oerlikon tubs, jackstays hung over the side of the vessel, Carley floats were shredded, and her hull was caved in where the foremast had fallen and then been pulled off the *Firedancer* by the force of the rushing water. There were dead men too, lifeless bundles of blood and fabric, some missing arms, legs, heads. The supply parties, fire control, and damage control moved methodically over the ship, removing the dead and wounded and assessing the condition of the destroyer.

Cole saw that the forward funnel had been pierced a dozen times, smoke pouring from the gaping holes. Her antennas were down as well, the wires scattered over what remained of the rigging.

He found a seaman helping another to his feet at torpedo station number one.

"Where's Morrison?" he asked.

"Dead," the uninjured seaman said. "That makes me the bloody headmaster. Baird." He looked at Cole closely. "You're the American we fished out of the water. You're covered in blood, sir."

"Somebody else's," Cole said. "Communications

are out with the bridge. So is the fire-control system. The captain sent me down here to help."

"Fair enough, sir," Baird said. "First you can help me get Boy Seaman Blessing to his feet. He took a sharp right to the chin from the deck there. Didn't you, Boy Seaman?"

"When we go in for a torpedo run, one blast from the ship's whistle means port, two means starboard," Cole said, looking around. "Any damage?"

"Not to the gears and tubes, thank God," Baird said. "But my compressed air is a mess, sir. Two of the hoses are sliced through-and-through and the tank for tube four had a bloody elephant sit on it. Squashed flat, she is, and no hope of resurrection. Number Two Station's just as bad. Worse. There's not a man back there who isn't wounded or dead."

"I trained on torpedoes. I can help."

Baird slapped Blessing lightly on both cheeks, trying to get him to come around. "Do you hear that, Boy Seaman Blessing? The Yanks are here and ready as well. I've sent Engleman after some tools to get us up and running again, sir. A couple of spanners and a roll of tape and we should be as right as rain."

"Okay," Cole said. "If you keep things going here I'll go check on Number Two Station. We might end up serving both of them, Baird."

"Nothing to it, sir," Baird said. "Just as long as our bloody captain can keep us away from those bloody bricks long enough to get these bloody things ready."

"Amen to that," Cole said.

When Cole saw number-two torpedo station it was a glimpse into hell. A supply party was trying to remove parts of the after-searchlight platform and engine room vents to get to the dead and wounded men scattered on the deck. So much blood covered the deck that the men of the supply party had difficulty standing. They worked rapidly, cutting away the entanglement with torches, huge bolt cutters, and hacksaws, trying to get to the poor bastards who lay dying in a grotesque spider's web of destruction.

Ignore it, ignore it, Cole thought, forcing himself to look away from the carnage. He climbed aboard the tubes, carefully inspecting each one as he walked to the cockpit. The sounds of the rescue, the screams of the men, the horrific thunder of exploding shells, and the sledgehammer beat of his own heart; he ignored them all. He was looking for shrapnel holes. If the tubes were pierced, then the torpedo was pierced and it was useless. If the hole was aft on the tube, then it could have pierced the compressed-air chamber and the tube was useless.

Clear, he told himself with satisfaction. *They're all clear.* He moved to check the cockpit when he saw the sailor. Half a sailor. He had his right arm and most of his torso, but the head, shoulder, and left arm had been sliced off. Cole walked gingerly to the cockpit, careful not to let his foot slip off the curved combing of the tube, and wondered why he didn't feel sick, or horrified, at the sight. Here was a man, what was left of a man, mutilated beyond comprehension, by a hunk of metal going a thousand miles an hour. *Why don't I feel anything?* Cole thought.

Once he reached the cockpit he steadied himself on the back of the shield and tried to read the gauges. It was impossible. They were covered with blood. He spotted a sailor who had just cleared a piece of twisted metal from the deck.

"Hey, buddy?" he called. "Give me a hand, will you?"

"Right," the man said and joined Cole. "God help that poor soul," he added, looking at the remnant of the sailor. "I suppose you'll be wanting him out of there, sir."

"Yeah," Cole said. "I've got to check the gauges."

"Stand back a bit, will you, sir? Bill? Marcus? Come and lend a hand." Two other sailors joined Cole and the four of them managed to remove the body. Cole wiped the blood off the compressed air gauges and rapped them with his knuckle to make sure that the needles were free to read. Three registered; the gauge for the fourth tube remained at zero. The tank was ruptured, a line was cut, the compressed-air chamber was pierced, the gauge simply didn't work—it could be anything. He looked at the supply party frantically trying to remove the wreckage. Until they had most of that cleared away to allow him access to the tanks and hoses he couldn't be sure what it was. *Firedancer* had three weapons at her disposal: her speed, her agility, and her torpedoes. The first two were defensive, the last offensive, and she could not afford to lose any portion of the meager weapon that remained to her.

Chapter 30

D.K.M. Sea Lion, *Quadrant XC 38*

"Hits on the cruiser!" an excited *Oberleutnant zur See* called out.

Kadow hung up the telephone. "Foremast reports several hits from the secondary battery on the destroyers. Frey confirms at least one hit on the cruiser from the main battery, somewhere forward of the bridge."

"Where are your concerns now, Kadow?" Mahlberg said.

"Perhaps they were unfounded," Kadow replied, certain that the concerns were still valid.

"Kapitan?" a *Kapitanleutnant* said. "Radar room reports possible target bearing two-five-four, distance eighty kilometers."

Mahlberg turned. "*Prince of Wales?*"

"He can't be sure, Kapitan. The radar equipment is being shaken about by the gunfire. At this range, lookouts can't make out anything in the haze."

Mahlberg grinned triumphantly at Kadow. "It's

her. It has to be her. We have her now, Kadow. *Prince of Wales.* Winston Churchill and lesser dignitaries. Contact hydrophones and see what they can tell me. I want confirmation immediately. Tell radar that they are not to lose contact with the target. Order them to maintain contact. I won't be denied my victory. *Sea Lion*'s victory."

H.M.S. Firedancer

Cole pulled himself up the bridge ladder to find Land ordering another group of lookouts and signalmen into position and Hardy giving sharp orders into the voice tubes. He was taking *Firedancer* in a wild, twisting race through the sea, and frantically trying to stay out of reach of *Sea Lion*'s guns.

"Captain?" Cole said. "Number One Torpedo Station is ready with three tubes. Maybe we can get four. Number Two Torpedo Station is damaged, sir. We're repairing it now."

"Oh, are we?" Hardy said in a blustery manner that Cole had gotten used to. "Well, we are still in shit up to our necks, Mr. Cole, torpedoes or not. *Eskimo* and *Prometheus* just took a hard knocking from *Sea Lion* and I can't see a damned thing for all of this smoke. I can't hear much of anything as well. Can you fire those bloody bastards when I tell you?"

"Yes, sir," Cole said.

"Good. *Sea Lion*'s change in course gave us a chance to get ahead of her a bit, so perhaps we can reposition ourselves for another go at her. Considering that we didn't get the first go."

"Signal from *Prometheus*, sir," a lookout called.

"'Severe damage forward. Many dead, wounded. *Eskimo* reports damage. Can you make smoke? Will turn away in preparation.'"

"'In preparation'?" Hardy said. "What the hell is he talking about? Preparation of what?"

"Message continues, sir," the lookout said. He dropped his glasses with a puzzled look on his face.

"Well," Hardy said. "What is it, man?"

"I'm sorry, sir," the lookout said, peering through his glasses again. "I don't think I got it right the first time—"

"What the bloody hell was it?" Hardy exploded.

"Sir," the lookout said, "it is 'Remember the Athenians.' I'm sorry, sir. I must have read it wrong."

Cole saw shock on Hardy's face.

Land stepped forward in concern and said: "Sir?"

Hardy came to. "Signalman," he said sharply, "make to *Prometheus*, 'Message received and confirmed. Here's one for Old Amoss.' End message. Number One, you will have the engine room give me all the power and smoke they can when I call for it. They mustn't keep back an ounce of either, do you understand?"

"No, sir," Land said, "but I'll do as you order."

"Good," Hardy said. "Signalman, make to *Eskimo*. They will make a hard turn to port and commence making smoke immediately to cover *Prometheus*. Mr. Cole, you may return to your station and prepare to engage the enemy. I'll signal from the bridge whether it's to be port or starboard, but that's all that I can do."

"Aye-aye, sir," Cole said and hurried down the bridge ladder.

"Helmsman, Bridge," Hardy called into the voice

tube. "Take us hard to starboard, Quartermaster. Lay us on our beam."

Land steadied himself as the ship veered sharply to starboard and hoved over. That was as close to a ninety-degree course change as he had ever experienced.

"All right, Number One," Hardy said. "Both engines full ahead emergency. Make smoke from the engines and the smoke generators."

"Yes, sir." Land passed the information on. "Sir . . . ?"

"We're preparing a stage, Number One," Hardy said in response. "We'll have the curtain ready in no time for *Prometheus*. It will be her last performance, God rest her soul."

Cole arrived at number-one torpedo station to see the last of the debris cleared away. Baird and two other seamen, including Blessing, were struggling to get the hose connections securely tightened to the compressed-air tanks on the port side.

"Is the old man trying to stand the poor girl on her head, sir?" Baird said. "I almost fell ass over teakettle off the bleeding ship."

"He's trying to keep us alive," Cole said. "What do we have?"

"Three here and three on Number Two. We can get old Number One loaded again from the torpedo shed, but it'll take just over ten minutes to do it, sir. The bloody supply party's got me stores for Number Two blocked, so she gets one shot at it."

"We've got to get to those stores," Cole said.

"They can't throw that mess over the side, sir,"

Engleman said. "Afraid they'll foul the propellers and rudder."

"Wouldn't that be lovely?" Baird said. "Here it is then, sir. Engleman's got the stores and hoist. Blessing's got the compressed-air tanks and I'll take the cockpit. I can crank her into position in twenty-two seconds. You stand by to pitch in wherever you're needed, sir."

"Okay."

"When we fire off this lot, sir, Blessing and I go to Number Two and you and Engleman load us again."

"Got a taste of power, have you, Torps?" Engleman said sourly. "Ordering an officer about. Even if he is only a Yank."

"You just do what Torps tells you," Baird said, "or you'll be right after those MK IXs."

D.K.M. Sea Lion

Kadow noticed the maneuvers first. "The two remaining destroyers are changing course. Crossing our bow." He adjusted the focus. "They're making smoke."

"The cruiser's trying to get away from us, Kadow," Mahlberg said confidently. "Our guns surely dealt her a hard blow."

"Radar confirms it, sir," a *Kapitanleutnant* said. "The British cruiser is moving away at high speed. Hydrophone can't read anything because of the gunfire and constant movement of the other ships."

"Well," Mahlberg said, tossing a glance of satisfaction to Kadow, "send a message to Oberkommando der Kriegsmarine, 'Defeated *Prince of Wales* escort.

Sank one destroyer. Damaged a cruiser and two destroyers.' No, make that, 'heavily damaged a cruiser and two destroyers. Proceeding to engage *Prince of Wales*.' Sign it, Mahlberg."

"Those two British destroyers will pass close to one another just off our port bow," Kadow said, still tracking them through his binoculars.

"Get me Frey," Mahlberg ordered. An *Oberboots-mann* handed him the telephone. "Frey? What are you going to do about those destroyers? I am pleased that you are tracking them. However, I would be more pleased if they were destroyed. Don't worry about the cruiser, we shall sink her on the way to *Prince of Wales*."

H.M.S. Firedancer

Cole and the other members of number-one torpedo station helped Engleman hoist the ready torpedoes into position at the edge of the torpedo shack. It was dangerous having them exposed on deck, but the shack walls offered so little protection from the splinters of the High Explosive shells that it seemed ridiculous to consider any location on *Firedancer* less dangerous than another.

Firedancer bore heavily into the waves, running at top speed. Spray whipped over her foc'sle and fell like ice-cold rain as far back as her forward tunnel. Cole could feel the ship throb with excitement, her engines beating a mad rhythm that vibrated throughout the ship. Black, oily smoke poured from her stacks, creating a vast dark cloud that hung close to the surface of the ocean.

He and the others took hold of the thick lines fed through the squealing pulleys and eased the sleeping torpedoes up from the depths of the little destroyer. They did it by count and Cole felt the strain on his shoulders and in his arms as Baird cursed them on.

"Get them up," Baird shouted. "Get them in place where I can get to them, you lubbers." He looked at Cole apologetically. "Present company excluded, sir."

All Cole could do was smile in return. His arms burned and his back hurt and for once in his life he had no glib response.

"All right," Engleman called. "Tie them off and get to your stations." There might have been more for him to say, perhaps something stirring and meaningful, but more likely profane, when they heard the shells.

The men scrambled to their stations when the shells began landing around them. There was the roar of the raging sea as it sent columns high above *Firedancer*. Splinters shot through the air, slicing through cables, cutting through deck housing, and ricocheting with wild screams across the water. Finally came the malevolent hiss as the water descended with serpentlike satisfaction back into its home.

Cole found himself on the deck—he didn't remember how he got there, but as he looked around he was glad to see that none of the number-one torpedo station crew was injured. Blessing was game enough to give him a thumbs-up, even if his hand was trembling so violently he had to hold it still with the other hand.

The ship's whistle screamed twice, its high-pitched

wail piercing Cole's heart. Train the tubes to starboard. He waited for the telltale rumble as the gears rotated the PR MK II mount into position. But he heard nothing.

"Mr. Cole? Mr. Cole, sir?" It was Baird.

Cole scrambled over the edge of the mount and ran along the edge of the tube to the cockpit. Baird was out of his seat, straining to turn the training wheel.

"Of all of the bloody times for this pile of shit to let me down," Baird said. "Take the other handle, sir. Take the other handle. I'll crank clockwise, you crank counterclockwise. We've got to hurry or we won't have a shot. Put your back into it, sir."

Cole leaned against the handle that was attached to the training wheel. It wouldn't budge. The gears were jammed. He locked his feet against the restraining bands on the tube, gripped the handle, and using his body weight, pushed against the frozen wheel.

It moved, slowly, each movement a protesting jerk.

"That's it! That's it," Baird said. "Put your back into it, sir."

Another salvo of enemy shells straddled *Firedancer*, drenching the vessel with tons of water and soaking everyone topside. Cole's foot slipped and he fell unevenly, banging his chin on the cockpit spray shield. He tasted blood as he repositioned his foot and continued to crank. His eyes stung from the coarse smoke that whipped past them and a stream of tears rolled down both cheeks. The muscles of his arms burned in protest and his hands began to cramp on the handle.

Somehow the noise of the exploding shells and

the force of the torrents of water assaulting *Firedancer* and her crew drove all feeling from Cole's body. He was numb and removed from everything except turning the training wheel. They were making progress, the blunt snouts of the tubes nearly extended over the side of the vessel.

"That's it, sir," Baird shouted over the turmoil. "Give us some more. Just a bit more and she's ready. Almost there."

Suddenly *Eskimo* filled their vision, racing with a roar in the opposite direction, her hull just feet from *Firedancer*'s, trailing a cloud of smoke. Baird cried out in surprise and lost his footing. The two destroyers roared past each other with a thin river of water separating their hulls, weaving a thick curtain of smoke behind them.

"You bloody assassins," Baird screamed, regaining his hold. "I didn't come all this way to be killed by the likes of you. Bloody cheese-eating bastards." The mount locked in place and Baird hopped into the cockpit. Cole knelt behind him.

Baird quickly flipped a set of four switches up and down, three alternating between red lights and green lights. The fourth refused to change color. There were four piston levers in the confined deck area between his knees and the spray shield. He released the triggers of the three tubes that worked.

"Now it's instinct and eyesight, sir," Baird said. "When she's where I want her to be and we're where we're supposed to be, I pull up those handles—if they all work as they should, from outside to inside. Use both hands and pull one-four, two-three. Off they go, hungry little hounds." He grimaced at Cole. "If they work."

Firedancer cleared the smoke and there was *Sea Lion*, running a bit to starboard, maybe ten thousand yards away. Baird's hands were gripping the two outside handles so tightly that it looked as if there was no blood in them. The man's focus was on *Sea Lion* and the course that the huge ship was making through the water.

"God help us," he shouted and pulled the levers. "One-four"—his hands moved to the inside levers— "two-three!" The first two torpedoes shot gracefully out of the tubes with a sudden rush of compressed air. Three joined them, but two remained motionless in her tube. "All right, sir. Time to take her around for loading. We're out of position anyway, so Number Two's of no use to us now. We'll get this one turned and get to Two. Right? Take hold, sir."

D.K.M. Sea Lion

An *Oberleutnant zur See* took the call in the crowded conning tower. Despite the ventilation ducts the tiny space was hot and often filled with smoke from *Sea Lion*'s own guns.

"Foremast reports, sir," the *Oberleutnant* said excitedly. "Destroyer to starboard has fired torpedoes."

Another telephone rang and Kadow answered it. "Forward fire-control tower reports, sir. Destroyer to port has fired torpedoes."

"Where is Frey?" Mahlberg exploded. "Can't he destroy those gnats? Did starboard fire first? Well? Answer me, for Christ's sake."

"Yes, sir," Kadow said calmly, hanging up the telephone.

"Hard turn to port," Mahlberg ordered. "Emergency. Take the wheel over as far as she'll go. We'll get ahead of those torpedoes and let the others pass up. Kadow. You are to order Frey to sink those vessels immediately. I will not change course, I will not give up my pursuit."

The telephone rang again and as Kadow picked it up he heard a *Kapitanleutnant* report that the two enemy destroyers had fallen back to enter the thick bank of smoke that hung close to the surface of the water. Cat and mouse, he thought. Dart out and fire torpedoes and then run for safety. It was a risky business—for the mice. *Sea Lion*'s guns would eventually find them, and when they did they would be crushed. It was inevitable.

"Kadow," he said into the receiver.

"Radar Room, sir. The British cruiser is changing course to starboard."

"One moment," Kadow said. "Kapitan? Radar reports that the British cruiser is changing course to starboard."

"Well, what of it?" Mahlberg said. "They don't want to lead us to *Prince of Wales*, that's all. They're acting as a decoy, Kadow. I'm surprised that you haven't thought of that."

"Yes, sir," Kadow said and was about to end the call when he thought better of it. "Radar Room? Stay on this line and let me know what course she settles on."

"Yes, sir."

Anton fired a full salvo of three shells to port, the tremendous blast and concussion shaking the conning tower. A wild rush of air and smoke, stinking of cordite, blew in through the slits and the conning tower crew turned away and closed their eyes. Bruno fired a full salvo to starboard and the conning tower shook even more from the thunderous voice of the huge guns. Bits of paint and insulation flecked from the bulkheads, raining down on the shoulders of the conning tower crew. When the smoke had cleared and the men shook off the effect of the tremendous explosion, Mahlberg turned to the men.

"She speaks loudly, doesn't she?" he said cheerfully, brushing the debris from his shoulders. "Now if we can only get the British to be kind enough to sail under those shells, our job would be done."

Kadow heard his name being called and realized that it came through the telephone.

"Kadow," he said. "What is it?"

"Radar Room, sir. The British cruiser is coming about, sir. Making very high speed."

"Hold," Kadow said and covered the mouthpiece with his palm. "Kapitan? Radar reports the British cruiser is coming about." Kadow saw a mixture of bewilderment and concern in Mahlberg's eyes.

"What?" the *Kapitan zur See* said.

Chapter 31

H.M.S. Firedancer

Firedancer cut through the sea, white foam wings curling up from either side of her bow. She was a wreck topside. Both funnels had been pierced, her aft searchlight platform was a mangled mass of indefinable features, and so much debris cluttered her deck that she looked like a derelict rather than a vessel of His Majesty's Navy. A large-caliber shell had struck A Turret so that most of the spray shield was gone and the gun cocked at a ridiculously high angle. The gun's crew, or parts of them, lay near their station.

Hardy turned away from the sight. "No hits, Number One?"

"No, sir. I'm afraid not. She avoided our torpedoes quiet handily."

Firedancer had ducked back into the smoke to hide from *Sea Lion*'s guns and to pick up *Prometheus*. *Eskimo* had joined her, just emerging from the smoke screen followed by a salvo of enemy shells.

"*Prometheus* green thirty, sir," a lookout called.

"She's got a bone in her teeth all right. Thirty knots or more, sir."

"She's coming back?" Land said. "How can she—"

"She's coming back, Number One, because I truly underestimated her captain. For that, I am heartily ashamed. 'Remember the Athenians,' Number One."

"Sir?"

Hardy didn't reply. "Well," he said, "that's that, then. Yeoman of Signals? Make to *Prometheus*, 'I am honored to join your party. *Eskimo* will take the starboard, I will take the port. God bless you, sir.' Sign it *Firedancer*. Bring us around, Number One. We are going to join *Prometheus* for another run at those bastards."

"Yes, sir."

D.K.M. Sea Lion

Kadow listened and then repeated the information. "The cruiser is moving toward us at a high rate of speed three points off our starboard bow. Distance approximately twenty-five thousand kilometers. The destroyers have taken up stations on either side of her."

"Well, be that as it may, I'm not turning aside," Mahlberg said. "It's up to Frey to deal with those vessels before they get close enough to launch torpedoes. We are only an hour or so behind *Prince of Wales*, but every minute that we dally with this insignificant force is another minute wasted. Maintain current course."

"But, Kapitan?" Kadow said.

"But, but, but! Is that all that you say? A cruiser and two destroyers, all badly damaged, and you have reservations. What should I do, turn away? How would that look if the greatest ship in the world fled from a cruiser and two destroyers?"

The telephone rang and a shaken *Fahnrich zur See* answered it. The exchange between Kadow and Mahlberg was unprecedented and it shocked even the veteran seamen.

"Frey, sir," the *Fahnrich zur See* said. "He requests permission to fire."

"Permission to fire," Mahlberg said, returning to his post at the center slit.

H.M.S. Firedancer

Cole heard the shells traveling overhead, loud rumbling things, like the sound of overladen freight trains rumbling across a trestle. He looked up, expecting to see something, but all he saw were patches of smoke from the battle.

"There," Baird said, pointing astern. Six huge columns of water rose above the surface of the sea about two thousand yards off the fantail. "That's a dreadful waste of good explosives for a little scud like *Firedancer.*"

Cole saw a dozen lesser columns dot the water from the enemy's secondary battery. Suddenly he felt the vibration from the deck increase.

"Now she's a racehorse. Old Georgie's got her all out." Baird cupped his hands over his eyes. "*Eskimo,* too. She's picked up speed as well." He swung his makeshift binoculars to the stern. "*Prometheus*! Look at her run. By God, she's sailing all right."

"The Charge of the Light Brigade," Cole said.

"How's that, sir?"

"A poem. 'Into the valley of Death rode the six hundred.' Alfred Lloyd Tennyson."

"Was he a sailor, sir?"

"No."

"Well, then bugger him."

The three ships, *Firedancer*, *Prometheus*, and *Eskimo*, gained speed, racing through the gray water of the North Atlantic like thoroughbreds bound for an unseen finish line. They rose and fell over swells, clean white foam boiling against their bows, broken waves rolling along their sides, the broad bands of their wakes streaming out behind them. More shells from *Sea Lion* came at them, tearing at the sea, hunting them, trying to stop and destroy them.

Cole stood on the deck near number-one torpedo station, his legs like springs as *Firedancer* dug into the waves and came up again, throwing clouds of spray into the air. It would have been fun, it would have been like an exhilarating ride at Cedar Point back in Ohio with the cold, sharp wind coming off Lake Erie and a shiver that was part excitement and the rest just trying to keep warm. It would have been fun like that except for one thing: the shells were getting closer.

The blast knocked Cole to the deck and almost immediately he was soaked by an ice-cold shower of water. He rolled over on his back and staggered to his feet. There was no damage to the tubes of the station as far as he could see.

"Baird?"

He saw the seaman slowly get to his feet. "Here, sir," he called back groggily. "What happened?"

"I think we were hit forward."

"Any more of those and it won't matter where we're hit," Baird said. He looked around. "Have they given us the signal, sir? Are we going in port or starboard?"

"No," Cole said. "Nothing yet."

"What the hell is taking those simpletons so bleeding long? They've only got two sides to choose from. I for one would like to know what's going on, sir. Just this one time I'd like to know what those grand lords have got planned for us."

The shelling increased and became more accurate. Columns of water peppered the sea around the three vessels and *Prometheus* took a brick at B Turret, which blew the gun mount and crew overboard. *Eskimo* lost her aft funnel, and smoke boiled from her deck housing. *Firedancer*, battered and unsightly as a Fleet Street whore, remained strong and resolute, closing with the enemy as if nothing else on earth mattered. And to Hardy nothing else did because he knew what Sir Whittlesey Martin intended to do; what the captain of the *Prometheus* had planned as a last wild maneuver to keep *Sea Lion* from its target. It was a bold, valiant, desperate move, foolish in the extreme, but there was nothing else to be done. *Firedancer* and *Eskimo* displaced little more than the weight of two of *Sea Lion*'s turrets; *Prometheus*, armed with six-inch guns and torpedoes, was fast enough to dodge *Sea Lion*'s bricks—for a time, that is. But none of them, singly or as a pitiful little squadron, could affect *Sea Lion*'s voyage with any conventional tactic. Any conventional tactic.

D.K.M. Sea Lion

The rapid crescendo of secondary and main batteries firing made it almost impossible to communicate in the conning tower. Kadow manned the telephones, speaking first to Frey, urging him to sink the enemy vessels, and then with the radar room, trying to anticipate what the British cruiser and two destroyers planned.

"A torpedo run," a *Korvettenkapitan* offered as Kadow laid out the scenario to Mahlberg.

"Obviously," Mahlberg said. "They want us to turn one way or the other to expose our beam. But we won't turn at all. We'll head straight for the cruiser. She'll have to turn to keep from being run over. When she does—Frey can have her. We'll be past the other two before they have time to react. Once we've cleared them, they can't possibly catch up."

"Kapitan," Kadow said, "wouldn't it be better to turn slightly off the cruiser's course to bring at least some of our guns to bear?"

"We'll have the forward 150-millimeter mounts available as well as Bruno. That's all we need."

"Kapitan—"

"That is all that we need, Executive Officer," Mahlberg said.

"Kapitan," a *Stabsoberbootsmann* serving as a lookout said, "the enemy ships are just clearing the smoke field now."

Kadow grabbed a pair of binoculars and focused on the ships. They were steaming to their destruction. They had to break to port or starboard to begin their torpedo runs, and then the guns of

Sea Lion would chew them to pieces, all without slowing her speed.

"Kapitan," the *Stabsoberbootsmann* said, "enemy cruiser dead ahead."

"Shall I change course, sir?" Kadow said.

"No."

"But she's coming straight at us, sir."

"Leave it to the guns, Kadow. Frey knows what to do."

Kadow stepped to the rear of the conning tower, troubled by a thought that remained hidden. He heard the rapid fire of the 150mm guns and knew that they were biting huge hunks out of the cruiser. All along the enemy vessel there would be a flash and a cloud of smoke and debris would erupt as the big shells pierced her skin and exploded within her. She was too close for the main batteries—they could not depress the big guns to reach her, but the secondary batteries were enough for the thin-skinned vessel. She was racing to her doom. Why? What was the British cruiser doing? Why rush directly at *Sea Lion* without maneuvering to avoid shellfire? Her torpedoes were useless at this angle and her small guns ineffectual even if she were alongside *Sea Lion*; but the British cruiser had not reduced her speed. The answer struck him.

"Kapitan," Kadow cried out, "she's going to ram us."

Mahlberg turned in disgust. "For God's sake, Kadow, this isn't the fifteenth century! What good would it possibly do her to . . ." Kadow saw the look of realization in Mahlberg's eyes. "Hard aport! All back port engines, full head starboard engines. Get Frey. Concentrate on the cruiser. Stop her."

H.M.S. Firedancer

Hardy squinted through the binoculars, following *Prometheus*'s path, watching *Sea Lion*'s guns turn her into smoking wreckage, pieces of flaming metal shooting high into the air every time she was struck. And yet the ship did not waver. He watched and was aware that he was quietly crying. He kept his glasses in place so that no one could see his tears.

When *Prometheus* struck *Sea Lion* just aft of A Turret, it was when the big ship was just beginning her turn. *Prometheus*'s bow dug deeply into *Sea Lion*'s body, the loud crash of the collision finally reaching Hardy long after the impact. The motion of both ships, coming at one another at high speed, combined to drive *Prometheus*'s knifelike bow into *Sea Lion* like a dagger. Hardy watched as the two ships shuddered from the crash, the bigger ship dragging the cruiser backward through the water, both twisting like wounded animals. Black smoke erupted around the cruiser's bow, followed by a series of explosions.

She had crushed *Sea Lion*'s decks, Hardy knew, and ruptured fuel tanks, and mains and lines, and sprung watertight bulkheads and doors, and started cataclysmic fires deep within the ship. Hundreds of tons of ice-cold water tore into the interior, flooding decks and compartments, killing sailors, pounding at the weakened steel bulkheads. It was hell belowdecks for those poor bastards—enemy or not. They would drown or the force of the water jetting through the ruptured hull would crush them. They would die in the darkness with only the flickering red emergency lights to comfort them.

"Orders, sir?"

Hardy turned to find Land waiting. "Make to *Eskimo*, 'Come up on her starboard side and attack with torpedoes. Be careful, she is still lethal. *Firedancer*.' We will attack from the port side, Number One. Quick in, quick out. Please inform the torpedo stations of my intentions."

"At once, sir."

D.K.M. Sea Lion

It was an explosion of some kind, Statz knew, a tremendous bang that shook the entire ship and threw everyone off their feet, splitting steam lines, blowing circuits, throwing tools and unsecured minutia in every direction. Smoke instantly filled the turret from below and the one sickening feeling that Statz had as he pulled himself to his feet was, the powder rooms. If they were damaged, there was danger of explosion and the blast would send Bruno tumbling end over end through the air.

"What happened? What happened?" It was Steiner, but his voice came from the ladder near the gun-control platform. "Were we hit?"

The others came around, frightened voices calling from somewhere in the smoke-filled turret.

"Statz?" It was Scholtz. "I think I broke my fucking leg!"

"Where are you?"

"Under the spanning tray. Get me out of here."

Soon the cries for help began to fill the interior of the turret and Statz realized that he had to regain some control. "Shut up. Shut up, all of you. Answer when your name is called. Scholtz?"

"Here."

"Steiner?"

"Here, Mien Fuehrer."

"Wurst?"

No reply.

"Wurst?" he said again, urgently. There were a dozen places an unconscious man could fall within the turret and, in the darkness and smoke, remain hidden for hours.

"When we fall out I'll look for Wurst," Statz said. "Manthey?"

"I think I shit my pants, but I'm here," Manthey said.

"Gran?"

"Yes. Here"

"Gran, contact Turm Befehishaber and let him know that we'll have a damage report ready for him in five minutes."

"Find out what happened," Steiner said.

"That's none of our concern," Statz said sharply. "We man this gun, Steiner. Those who can, return to your stations and break out the extinguishers. Scholtz? Where in the hell are you?"

"In the same place, Statz."

The smoke was becoming thicker and worse, yet it was coming from below. What had hit them? Certainly not an enemy shell, there was nobody out there but cruisers and destroyers. Suddenly it came to Statz; they'd been torpedoed. But that didn't make any sense—Sea Lion carried a sixteen-inch armor belt at the waterline. He heard the hatch off the gun-control platform swing open with a clang and saw the head of one of the range-finder crew in the eerie red emergency light.

"We've been rammed!" he shouted down into the turret. "That bastard has rammed us."

Then the air exploded with a rapid crescendo of gunfire.

The collision knocked everyone in the conning tower to the deck and suddenly the air was filled with the wail of a dozen alarm bells. Kadow spun the wheel on the conning tower hatch and made his way onto the deck. He couldn't see anything through those devilish slits, but the scene that lay before him was indescribable. The enemy cruiser was buried deep into the starboard side of *Sea Lion*, listing slightly to port, and acting as a sea anchor, her length and bulk slowing *Sea Lion*'s progress to a crawl. Smoke poured from around the point of impact, obscuring the extent of the cruiser's penetration into *Sea Lion*. But Kadow knew that it had to be at least fifteen meters.

Then he saw the cruiser's guns elevating to bear on *Sea Lion*. She was still full of fight and at this range even her six-inch guns could cause considerable damage by raking the superstructure and upper decks of *Sea Lion*.

He ran back to the conning tower and was about to close and secure the hatch when he looked down. He was standing at an angle. He was a seaman so long used to this sort of thing, the constant roll and toss of a vessel at sea, that it came as second nature to him. But this was different. *Sea Lion* was listing to starboard, maybe as much as five degrees. She was taking on water.

The cruiser's guns opened fire, cutting into *Sea*

Lion's bridge, forward fire-control centers, the FuMO 23 radar tower and masts, and sweeping the area around the conning tower. Kadow should have been safe. He was on the opposite side of the conning tower with the hatch partially closed, but an errant splinter slipped through the tiny crack between the edge of the door and the casing and buried itself in Kadow's heart.

There was very little blood and as his hold on the door weakened and some odd, gray fog covered his eyes, he slid to the deck and died. His last thought was that he wanted to warn Mahlberg about the list, but that became impossible due to his death on the cold, steel deck of the conning tower.

Chapter 32

H.M.S. Firedancer

There was no noise, no thunder of guns, or the shrill screams of the wounded. For Hardy, it was as if God had lowered a shroud of silence over the scene and left only the image of two ships caught up in a death struggle; one embedded in another, a wounded hound valiantly tearing at a boar's throat, trying to bring him down. It was the most fantastic thing that Hardy had ever witnessed and he had seen so much in this war.

Sea Lion and *Prometheus* surrounded by columns of smoke that rolled into the sky, engulfed in flames that licked impartially at both vessels, trading gunfire. And then gradually he heard the roar of the storm as his senses returned to him: explosion after explosion, the blasts of shells exploding against steel, the high-pitched demonic whine of ricochets echoing across the sea. It was unadulterated savagery, with *Eskimo* and *Firedancer* reluctant observers of the struggle.

"Yeoman?" Hardy called, trying to suppress the

emotion in his voice. "*Firedancer* to *Prometheus*, 'Can you withdraw?' End message."

"Yes, sir."

"Number One," Hardy said, "she is as much a sitting duck with *Prometheus* in her as any I've seen. We'll come in off her starboard quarter and give her a brace of torpedoes. Kindly inform Mr. Cole and whoever else is left down there what I plan to do."

"Yes, sir," Land said. "She's listing badly, sir. *Sea Lion*. Nearly ten degrees, I'd say, and she's down some at the head."

"*Prometheus?*"

"Well down at the head, sir."

"Captain," the yeoman of signals said, "reply from *Prometheus*. 'We are here for the duration. Shoot straight. Will hold her as long as possible. *Prometheus*.'"

Hardy was silent for a moment before he spoke. "We shall do as he bids, Number One. Inform the torpedo stations, I will send on to *Eskimo* to lead off the attack to port."

"Yes, sir. I'll have Torps prepare."

"Number One? Tell those chaps that we're going in very quickly and we're going to get rather close. I don't want them to fire until they see more of *Sea Lion* than they do the sky."

"How bloody close is that lunatic going to get, sir?" Baird said after Land delivered the instructions and returned to the bridge.

"'Don't fire until you see the whites of their eyes,'" Cole said, following Baird along the deck to what was left of number-two torpedo station. *Firedancer* was steaming at full speed, bucking the waves so that each swell threw a cloud of spray over the deck in protest.

"Look at those lovely bastards, sir," Baird said, nodding at *Prometheus*, her guns blazing at *Sea Lion*, the ragged sound of gunfire echoing across the water to *Firedancer*. "Up to their neck in Nazis and they're still dishing it out. Coo, they've got courage, they have. All we have to do is stand off a couple of dozen yards and throw torpedoes at that big bloody mountain."

"You know for us to make this work, we've got to throw everything but the kitchen sink at them," Cole said. "We've got to do it at one time because we may not have a second chance."

"That's a lovely thought, but what the hell does it mean, sir?"

"You take Number One. I'll take Number Two."

"Well, you're daft, man. Meaning no disrespect, sir," Baird said. "You've no idea how these things work. I've spent years—"

"Look, Baird, I don't need your resume. I saw what you did and these aren't that different from the tubes I trained on. Besides, you can get any of those guys to help you lay the tubes."

"You won't know when—"

"I'll fire when you fire."

They both heard the roar of incoming shells and dropped to the deck. Caesar, followed by Dora, fired a salvo. The huge shells landed well beyond the speeding destroyer, but now the secondary battery began to fire and geysers sprung up all around *Firedancer*.

"All right, sir," Baird said. He spat in the palm of his hand and offered it to Cole. As Cole spat in his palm and took the seaman's hand in his, Baird said: "Now let's hope that both of us come out of this with our heads firmly attached to our shoulders."

"I'm more concerned about getting my nuts cracked," Cole said, jumping over the edge of the torpedo platform. "Let's go." He slid into the cockpit and tested the laying mechanism, traversing it back and forth. The wheel cranked freely. He flipped the switch on the torpedo tubes, from neutral to off and then to on, and was relieved to see that they functioned properly. He didn't know what the hell he would do if they didn't—he'd never gotten that far in his training. He heard someone call his name. It was Blessing.

"Beg your pardon, sir, but Torps sent me over in case you ran into any trouble."

"Very thoughtful of him," Cole said as Blessing knelt down next to the cockpit. "If I were you, I'd find something a little more substantial to hide behind. This doesn't look like it's much more than half an inch."

"Orders, sir," Blessing said apologetically. "'If the torpedo operator is rendered'—"

"Okay," Cole said. "I get it. Just don't set your mind on getting my job."

"Oh no, sir. Never, sir."

Cole wiped his damp hands along his trousers. He was scared but his nerves seemed to have settled—strange, he thought, to feel fear so completely that it was a part of him, like the simple action of breathing. He felt *Firedancer* turn quickly to port, rolling heavily on her side, and the only thing he felt now was exhilaration. *When I get out of this*, he promised himself, *I'm going to sign up for destroyers. If I get out of this,* the thought repeated itself. *Death. Maybe I am a coldhearted son of a bitch. I get scared, shouldn't that count for something?*

"Sir?" Blessing said.

Cole was thankful that Blessing interrupted his thoughts. "Yeah?"

"I think I just pissed myself."

Cole smiled and turned to the back of the cockpit so that Blessing could see his face. "Boy Seaman, you're a better man than I am. I did that about an hour ago."

"Did you really, sir?" Blessing said, brightening at the revelation.

"Yeah," Cole said. "But let's just keep that between us seamen. What do you say?"

"Oh yes, sir. Yes, sir. Mum's the word."

D.K.M. Sea Lion

One of the *Oberbootsmanns* dragged Kadow's body into the conning tower and pulled the heavy door shut, spinning the locking wheel.

Mahlberg quickly dismissed all thoughts of his friend's death and ordered: "Engines, full ahead emergency. Rudder hard to starboard. We've got to break her grip on us."

"Kapitan," a *Stabsbootsmann* manning the telephones called out, "forward fire-control reports British destroyer three points off the port quarter preparing a torpedo run."

"Well, sink her, for God's sake!" Mahlberg shouted. He calmed himself and lowered his voice. "Inform fire control that they are ordered to concentrate all guns that can brought to bear on that destroyer. Where is the other one?" He waited for the reply.

"Forward fire control reports the other destroyer off the starboard beam at a distance of approximately fifteen kilometers. She appears to be in distress."

Suddenly *Sea Lion* lurched forward, shaking with effort as she began to break *Prometheus*'s hold on her. The sound of tortured metal ripping metal filled the air, the scream of a wounded animal tearing itself free from the jaws of a predator. The noise of constant gunfire and the screeching of metal against metal made it nearly impossible to hear. Mahlberg had to shout his orders and the conning tower crew had to shout their responses so that it seemed the whole world had gone completely mad and demanded that the men in the conning tower join it.

Despite himself, Mahlberg did what he had avoided the minute that his executive officer's body had been dragged into the conning tower: he looked at Kadow's face. The sight shocked Mahlberg— Kadow's eyes were partially closed and the silent form appeared to be asleep. *How peaceful he looks,* Mahlberg thought, but then he looked away. *I have no time for the dead,* he told himself, and turned back to the command of his ship.

But—a word that Kadow used to Mahlberg's constant disgust—the *Kapitan zur See* would not admit the obvious. *Sea Lion,* his magnificent ship, was critically wounded and at the mercy of those pathetic little jackals darting about the sea.

"She's breaking free!"

Mahlberg turned to the *Kapitanleutnant* who had shouted the news.

"Kapitan! We're breaking free of the cruiser."

Mahlberg nodded as if he expected nothing else, and the old arrogance that had driven him relentlessly all of his life returned to fill the void of uncertainty.

"Very well," he shouted above the din. "Make ready to draw off and sink the cruiser."

H.M.S. Firedancer

Land and Hardy had watched *Sea Lion* drag the barely living carcass of poor *Prometheus* through the water. What they saw next horrified them.

"*Sea Lion*'s breaking free," Land said in alarm.

"Right. We must stop them," Hardy said. His calm manner surprised Land. "We're going in, *Eskimo* or no *Eskimo*. Go and tell Cole and whoever is left back there that no one fires until they hear the ship's whistle. We can't risk missing and hitting *Eskimo*, and to do any damage we've got to get every one of those torpedoes into *Sea Lion*'s vitals. She can't get away, Number One. If I can't sink her with torpedoes, then by God we'll pull a *Prometheus* on her."

Cole looked up from the cockpit in response to Land's statement. His eyes stung and his voice was ragged from shouting and from the smoke that he had inhaled. Every part of his body ached so much that he could hardly move, but there was something in Land's desperate words that made him forget all of that.

"Yeah," Cole said. "You get us close enough to that big son of a bitch and I'll lay these goddamned things right on her deck."

Land smiled. "Well said, Mr. Cole."

It seemed just minutes after Land left that *Firedancer* picked up speed and began to twist violently, trying to throw off the German gunners. It worked for the most part, but the gunners guessed *Firedancer*'s intentions and the firing increased. Cole watched as huge columns of water began to inch closer to the speeding destroyer. It was the secondary battery and any second the main battery would swing into action. He remembered *Windsor* and what one sixteen-inch shell had done to her.

Firedancer jerked to starboard and then whipped to port, throwing spray over Cole and Blessing. Cole pushed his legs against the walls of the cockpit to keep from getting thrown about, taking his hands off the torpedo-release levers only long enough to wipe the salt water from his face. He felt *Firedancer* tremble as a shell struck her a glancing blow aft and then the destroyer leaped to starboard again.

Sea Lion, with *Prometheus* dragging along her hull, grew larger. Details emerged in between the flashes of the guns and the tentacles of smoke that trailed over her: turrets, life rafts, masts, and portholes— the thousand features that defined her size. She was magnificent, Cole decided, and terrible; and for a moment he was torn between admiration and hate. But all of that quickly disappeared when *Firedancer* jumped quickly to starboard to avoid another salvo of *Sea Lion*'s guns. Now all Cole concentrated on was the signal to fire.

It had to come soon. Any minute now. They couldn't get any closer. And then he saw *Prometheus* begin to twist, her stern slowly swinging into *Sea Lion*'s hull as the cruiser's bow was being forced out of the wound that she had made in the German ship. He realized that if the cruiser continued to swing like that she would block any chance of getting at *Sea Lion*; her body would protect that of her killer.

They were so close now that *Sea Lion*'s antiaircraft batteries began to fire at them; huge golden balls—tracers—heading directly at Cole. When they landed they ripped through the water, making erratic stitches. Happy little spouts filled the sea between them as *Sea Lion* grew closer. The ocean was ripped to pieces as *Firedancer* frantically dodged the hundreds of shells fired at her.

Firedancer's whistle screamed above the din.

Cole heard the soft whoosh of Baird's torpedoes leave their tubes. One, three, two. He gripped the release levers and pulled up. One, three, two. The mount shuddered with a gasp of compressed air as the torpedoes leaped out of the tubes and seemed to hang suspended in the air. Then they splashed into the sea.

Firedancer veered sharply to starboard, turning her fantail to the enemy. Shoot and scoot, Cole thought, but he regretted not being able to track the torpedoes as they sped toward their target.

He heard the explosions. Far off, he thought, muffled somehow but still distinct enough to count. Four, he thought, maybe five. He leaned over the back of the cockpit to ask Blessing, but the young man's lifeless body lay awkwardly over the tube combing. Cole stared at the body surrounded by a swath of bright red blood that had pumped from the jagged hole in his neck. He watched as the tiny droplets of spray washed the tubes of the blood and he wondered why Blessing was dead and he wasn't. They were within inches of one another. One alive. One dead.

H.M.S. Firedancer

"Hits!" Land cried, tracking the torpedoes. "At least three, sir. *Sea Lion*'s listing heavily. Down by the head, sir. There's another explosion, sir. Magazines."

Hardy watched as smoke billowed from the mortally wounded ship and secondary explosions consumed her amidships. Huge pieces of wreckage were thrown into the air with each blast and deep, black smoke covered a good three-quarters of her length. He put his binoculars to his eyes and noted: "She's taking *Prometheus* with her."

"What?" Land said, and then focused on the cruiser. The force of the explosions had driven *Prometheus* out from *Sea Lion* but they had not saved her. She listed heavily to port and her superstructure was blazing, the bright yellow flames framed by columns of dirty brown smoke. "The poor bastards," Land whispered. "The poor bastards. Can we—"

"No," Hardy said without emotion. "We cannot. We'll have to stand off and wait. Otherwise," he added, lowering the binoculars and turning away, "we will lose *Firedancer* as well."

* * *

D.K.M. Sea Lion

Bruno was a madhouse. Statz heard screams and shouts for help, but he could do nothing because he was in complete darkness. The British cruiser striking *Sea Lion* had been catastrophic; the explosions aft and amidships, torpedoes, Statz knew, had doomed the ship. He had called for his crew when the emergency lights went out and dense smoke filled the turret, but in the confusion and noise he could not hear their replies. He felt *Sea Lion* listing and he knew that she would quickly continue until she turned turtle, showing her broad, glistening belly to the sun before she sank. Unless the explosions tore her apart. The magazines were erupting and several hundred tons of high-explosives were right below his feet. Time to get out.

He reached out and felt the open breechblock of the gun—they had been in the process of loading when the torpedoes struck. Now he knew where he was. He could follow the shape of the gun across the extended spanning tray and get to the gun controller's platform, out the small hatch, through the turret, and exit the deck hatch. If they weren't jammed closed.

Maybe he could go down through the shell hoist and through the shell room and come up by way of the passageways alongside the barbette. No, he could not force himself to go deep into the doomed ship.

"Statz," a familiar voice came from the smoke.

"Here!" he shouted. "Who is it? Where are you?"

"Statz," the voice said again. "Here. Come this way."

He looked in the direction of the voice and saw

daylight. The gun bloomer, the flexible hard rubber collar that covered the barrel of the gun and was attached to the turret to keep spray from entering, was shredded.

"This way," Statz called to anyone in the turret who could hear him. "The bloomer's gone. We can get out this way." He carefully crawled up the huge barrel, holding a dirty handkerchief to his nose and mouth to filter out the noxious fumes of the fires. He called out behind him once more, hoping that others would hear him and follow. He pulled himself along the barrel. The list was increasing. *Sea Lion* was dying.

Statz pushed his way through the bloomer and into daylight and sanctuary. He dropped to Anton, slid down her side to the tilting deck, made his way to port, and saw the sea below him littered with men, living and dead. Someone had lashed a rope to one of the deck stays. He climbed over the cable, took a firm grip on the rope, and slowly lowered himself into the sea. As he did so he realized whose voice had led him to safety. He knew it with all the certainty that he possessed as his strong arms pulled him away from the doomed ship. It was Kuhn.

Mahlberg staggered to his feet and cried out at the tremendous pain in his lifeless right arm. He must have broken it when he was thrown against the bulkhead. The others on the conning tower were just beginning to rise when he forced the cloud of pain away.

"Report!"

One by one the other sections of the ship were

contacted and each replied, in turn, that the situation was hopeless. Only engineering continued to function at more than half performance, supplying power to the pumps, electrical system, communications, and firefighting. There was power for the guns as well, but *Prometheus* was too close for the main battery and the secondary battery could do nothing but saw away the superstructure down to the boat deck. At least there was no one to command her, Mahlberg knew. The bridge of the British cruiser had long ago been destroyed.

Smoke seeped into the conning tower, heat and noise accompanying the sharp stench that came from steel heated almost to melting. *Sea Lion*'s fine white-oak deck was charring, and her sturdy gray paint was lifting itself off bulkheads, peeling away from intense flames until the feathered edges blackened and the paint was consumed. The flat cracks of both ships' secondary batteries sounded strangely like bells tolling in the metal cavern of the conning tower. The fire was so rapid that it was almost impossible to separate the guns, one from another. Above all, Mahlberg could hear the screams of the men, injured men, dying men, frightened men, men desperate to leave *Sea Lion* and take their chances in the ice-cold sea.

"Shall I order abandon ship, Kapitan?" It was a *Leutnant zur See* who spoke.

Mahlberg looked at him incredulously. Abandon? What was the man talking about? Surely he must be injured? A concussion. "No!" Mahlberg said. "No, of course not." He looked around, trying to get his bearing, taking a quick survey of those men who remained to him. All but three. Kadow and two others lay on the deck, unmoving. All but three. Pride swelled in him. Only three dead. "We'll move to the sea bridge," Mahlberg ordered, holding his injured arm carefully. Any movement sent excruciating pain shooting to his shoulder. "I can't see anything in this cave." He issued orders quickly, knowing that the ship's salvation lay in his skills as a ship handler. He ordered the rudders thrown over full and the engines increased to emergency power so that they could wrench themselves free of that hateful ship embedded in their side. He ordered that calls for assistance be sent out so that the might of the Kriegsmarine could be mobilized to come to *Sea Lion*'s rescue. His pride did not interfere because the challenge, his challenge, the supreme opportunity was at hand: save *Sea Lion*. He relished the role; he reveled in the chance to snatch *Sea Lion* from the cold, icy depths of the North Atlantic. His arrogance, his confidence were all-powerful, unfailing, and he was the *Kapitan* of the greatest warship in the history of the world.

And then when he was on the narrow walkway just outside the conning tower, a chance breeze parted the thick black smoke that boiled with impunity from the guts of the ship, and he saw the truth.

Anton was pointed to port, all three guns angled lifelessly toward the sea. Bruno looked straight ahead but her three guns, like gnarled fingers of an arthritic hand, jutted in three different directions. A scythe had swept whole sections of *Sea Lion*'s deck and what remained was carnage. Bodies, parts of bodies, blood soaked darkly into the oak deck timbers. Men raced to port, madly tying off lines so that they could lower themselves into the water to escape the maelstrom that was overtaking their ship and threatened to overtake them.

Sea Lion jerked to starboard as hundreds of tons of seawater continued to rush in and some unknown place within her body a bulkhead gave way, and the water gained another victory. She was dying.

Mahlberg, stunned, staggered against the list to the starboard wing and looked aft. Everything was on fire; turrets were destroyed, boats dislodged, gun mounts swept away, deck structures missing, and over all of it, a raging fire, rich with hunger, fed on the still-living carcass of his vessel. He looked at the lower deck in time to see two officers, Luftwaffe officers that he knew flew the scouting planes aboard *Sea Lion*, put pistols to their heads and blow their brains out. He did not hear the gunshots. He saw the jets of blood and tissue spurt out one side of the men's head and then their bodies drop silently to the deck. Death before dishonor.

The sight did not affect him. He was losing *Sea Lion*—what was the death of two cowardly officers that he hardly knew?

The bridge—get to the bridge.

There was a blast and he was engulfed in flames and smoke and he slid into darkness. It must have been for only a moment, because when he came to, nothing had changed. He was still on the walkway near the conning tower, except now he knew that he was lying on his side and he could feel the reassuring steel curve of a gun tub at his back. He slowly pushed himself into a sitting position with his one good arm and stared stupidly at the clutter on the deck. It was a mass of arms, torsos, and legs, all intertwined, with some movement, and some sound.

He heard whimpering, moans, really, although one of the conning tower crew managed to cry softly for help. It might have been a six-inch shell, Mahlberg thought dully, his mind trying to find something to focus on that made sense. Everyone was down. He was down.

He swallowed heavily and fought to clear himself of the stupor that would not let him think clearly, see clearly. Or rise.

Get up, Mahlberg ordered himself sharply. *Get on your feet. Get to the bridge.* He was like a drunk whose mind appears to work perfectly well but has been disconnected from his body because his body would not respond.

"Get up!" he ordered again, in a ragged voice, the sound of his words giving him determination. "Get up. Get on your feet! Get . . ." And then he saw the problem. It was very clear now and he was mildly surprised that he had somehow overlooked it. His legs were gone. He concentrated on their absence as though that action would magically return them to him. He was having difficulty holding himself erect and thought, *If I can only rest for a bit, I can get to the bridge. What about the others? You'll need help manning the ship.* Mahlberg studied the silent forms before him. *They'll be along. They're good men.*

He felt himself sliding sideways down the gun tub wall and he landed heavily on the deck. He willed his good arm to support him, to push him erect, but his one limb was insubordinate and chose to lie lifeless at his side. He was cold, and darkness, a kind and gentle entity, wrapped Mahlberg in an impervious blanket. All around him was silence and then that, too, was removed.

H.M.S. Firedancer

Hardy watched as *Prometheus* sank slowly, with little drama, as if knowing that she must surely die, she was determined to do so with dignity. She went down bow first after having floated free of *Sea Lion*, her stern guns firing at the enemy in a futile, valiant, courageous act. Hardy was proud of those men, proud of their selfless, mad attempts to inflict more damage on the steel walls of their enemy. The noise was part of it, a terrific din of explosions, roaring flames, and the deep thunder of *Sea Lion* dying.

Hardy discovered Land standing next to him, his uniform rank with sweat and the smell of oil smoke.

"We shall go in shortly," Hardy said.

"Very well, sir," Land said.

"I wonder what was so important," Hardy said, "that Martin and I never got on together."

"Personalities, perhaps," Land said. "Two strong-willed men—that usually leads to conflict."

"I shall always regret that I was not charitable to that man. Never were my own shortcomings made more apparent than at the death of Sir Whittlesey. You are always a good man for words, Number One. Nothing to say about heroes and sacrifice?"

"No, sir," Land said. "There are no words to describe what I saw today."

D.K.M. *Sea Lion*, her towering flames extinguished only when she suddenly rolled over, disappeared in a tremendous explosion that sent smoke and debris hundreds of feet into the air, protesting her death. The concussion raced across the water and slapped *Firedancer*. She trembled at the power of the big ship's end, but when the destroyer settled back, she did so with satisfaction of the knowledge that, although severely injured, she remained afloat.

Firedancer led *Eskimo* in a search for survivors when it was safe, but by that time the summer sun had tired of the day's events and retired below the horizon. In the end both destroyers could only account for a total of 123 survivors from *Prometheus* and eighty-five survivors from D.K.M. *Sea Lion*. Darkness, the threat of U-boats, and the fact that both ships were dangerously overloaded forced them to depart the area.

Chapter 33

President Franklin D. Roosevelt, his arms locked in those of two straight-backed naval officers, smiled as Prime Minister Winston Churchill was piped aboard. He held out his hand and the prime minister shook it heartily.

"My dear Mr. President, I'm glad to finally speak with you in person," Churchill said.

"Call me Franklin," Roosevelt said, "and with your permission, I shall call you Winston. Or do you prefer Former Naval Person?"

"Winston will do nicely, thank you, Franklin."

"How was your voyage, Winston?"

"Uneventful," Churchill said. "Remarkably uneventful. Now, before I introduce you to the members of my party, it is my pleasure to return Louis to you, none the worse for wear."

Louis Hoffman pulled himself unsteadily up onto the deck and eyed Roosevelt with a mixture of disgust and irritation.

"Well, Louis," Roosevelt said with a broad grin, "what have you to say for yourself?"

Hoffman jerked a ragged cigarette from his mouth and flipped it overboard. "Where can a guy get a drink on this goddamned boat?"

Supreme Naval Staff Seekriegsleitung,
Tirpitzufer, Berlin

Admiral Doenitz watched as a *Bootsmann* calmly removed the tiny wooden ship that represented D.K.M. *Sea Lion* from the plotting table. He glanced at the haggard face of Grand Admiral Raeder and wondered if the man knew that Hitler would relieve him. The grand admiral had to know it was the end, Doenitz thought. He lost *Sea Lion*, and the Home Fleet, having no reason to sortie out, turned back before the U-boats had a chance to engage them. Webber and his wolf pack had been reassigned, some to look for survivors from *Sea Lion*, others to lie quietly along convoy routes for targets to sail into range.

Doenitz thought that he should say something to Raeder. Something comforting perhaps, but no words were forthcoming. It was a disaster and that was that. The finest ship in the Kriegsmarine, destroyed on her first voyage. Again. First *Bismarck*, now *Sea Lion*. Doenitz conscientiously ran several phrases through his mind that he thought appropriate to say to the shattered Raeder. None seemed right so he concentrated instead on whom he would name to positions of command within the

Kriegsmarine when he was named to replace
Raeder.

Royal Navy Base, Home Fleet, Scapa Flow

H.M.S. *Firedancer* sat quietly in the sound, an old
hound home from the hunt, licking its wounds. She
would be called in for refitting, but now a rusting
barge, filled with the wreckage that had been removed from the destroyer by a crane, nursed at her
side while she lay tied off to a buoy in the middle
of the sound. The violence and din of battle were
replaced by the hiss of acetylene torches as the
repair crew cut through the twisted metal of the destroyer, trying to remove the abomination that had
once been functioning parts of the ship. The heavy,
constant thundering of sledgehammers echoed
across the flat waters of Scapa Flow until a man
almost became accustomed to the sound.

Number One and Hardy walked over *Firedancer*,
inspecting the vessel, sharing opinions about what
she should have done to return her to service, accompanied by a yard superintendent armed with
a clipboard, sheets of paper, and a sharp manner.

"He behaves as if our opinion doesn't matter,"
Number One had said to Hardy.

"Yes," Hardy had said. "Perhaps it doesn't. We only
sail *Firedancer*. He must heal her."

The superintendent was very efficient and
demonstrated a remarkable grasp of what should
be replaced or what could be repaired, or what
could be gotten by without. It was certain that
Firedancer would not go out for some time, and it

was equally certain that *Eskimo* would suffer the same fate. They had been too roughly handled.

Hardy and Number One stood near what had once been A Turret but was now a mass of scorched metal. The superintendent was gone, speeding back to the yard in his dilapidated launch, bearing his reports, calculations, and estimates. The crane astride the barge, surrounded by bits and pieces of *Firedancer* in the well of the ugly box, continued to swing casually back and forth, carrying the dead parts of the destroyer. The yard workers, large men in filthy dungarees, dismantled portions of *Firedancer*, and she—she remained stoic through it all, immune to the humiliation.

"Those poor chaps never had a chance," Land said, kicking a piece of metal to one side, glancing at the pitiful memorial to the gun's crew.

"No," Hardy said. "They did not. Still, we've had our chances and a few more, haven't we?"

"It seems so long ago. Does it feel that way to you as well?"

"Oh yes," Hardy said thoughtfully. "Centuries ago." He stopped to watch *Norfolk* steam toward the North Channel. "When Whittlesey and I were at Dartmouth together, centuries past, we had Amoss as a teacher. One of those brilliant idiots, more brains than anyone has a right to possess, and not a sliver of common sense to go with them. He taught ancient history, Romans, Greeks, that sort of thing. When he became excited, which, thank God, was not often, he had a habit of throwing both arms in the air and hopping up and down. He did so only when he thought it most important that we cadets pay strict attention to what he was saying.

One morning, I shall never forget it, his lesson was on the Athenians, on their seamanship, courage, and service. He spoke of the Athenian rams, the finest of their kind. Swift, deadly. Naturally, he became excited and began hopping, arms straight up in the air. Well, the exertion caused his braces to give way and down came his trousers. We cadets remembered that of course. We were young, foolish boys. But we were enchanted by the Athenians and we saw them as mystical souls. When Whittlesey sent his message, I knew exactly what he proposed, and I knew the consequences."

Land said nothing as Hardy watched *Norfolk* disappear into the distance.

After a moment, Hardy, relieved of the need to talk, said: "Come on, Number One. We shall have plenty to do to get the old girl ready to put to sea."

Cole waited patiently for the pilot of the battered Hudson to climb out of the lorry. He must have been sixty, Cole thought, with a flowing white mustache and a round belly.

Another man waited on the hardstand with Cole, a British naval officer who looked as if he had been through hell. His uniform was wrinkled and he needed a shave, and his eyes were sunken in their sockets. Cole suddenly realized that he probably looked worse.

"Well, chaps," the pilot said brightly, "just two this flight. Not to worry, not to worry. Tubby's old but experienced. We'll get you there, me and my Sal. She's old too, but she's dependable." He dug into a haversack and pulled out two tins as the ground crew opened the door and attached the steps leading into the aircraft. "Presents. Presents galore. One for you." He handed a tin to Cole. "And one for you," he said, giving a tin to the other man.

Cole looked at his. Sardines.

"Time to get aboard," the pilot said. "Tubby's never late. You chaps follow Tubby. He's got to fly the plane, you know."

The two passengers exchanged glances and followed the pilot into the plane. As the door was closed and locked the Royal Navy officer extended his hand.

"Harland," he said.

"Cole."

"Are you stationed with the Home Fleet?"

"Heavens no," Harland said. "My chief sent me up to this horrible place. I think it was some sort of object lesson. Some punishment or other."

Cole thought of his own assignment to Royal Navy Photographic Operations by his superior. You aren't navy, he had been told. Not part of the team— someone who didn't belong.

"If you don't mind me saying," Harland said, fastening his seat belt, "you look a bit used."

"Yeah," Cole said, looking at the tin. "What did you get?"

"Cheese," Harland said, stuffing the tin into the seat next to him. "Fancy meeting old Saint Nick on this trip."

The left engine turned over with a backfire and Cole jumped. He looked at Harland to see if he had noticed, but the man was almost asleep. Thankfully the right engine started smoothly and Cole felt the aircraft taxi to the runway.

He looked around the interior of the old Hudson. Some of her ribs were bent and several of her windows had been replaced by sheets of aluminum. There were patches along her roof and Cole wondered if she had seen action.

He settled into his seat and thought of *N-for-Nancy*. Up there where the W.T. station had once been he saw Prentice working diligently. He glanced over his shoulder to see that the turret had been removed and wondered how Johnny was getting along. He remembered the gunner's watch and the death of the tiny raft alongside *Firedancer*. Past the odd pilot up front was the tunnel leading to the bomb aimer/navigator's station and he saw Peter's scowling face and recalled how the man had stayed at the controls so that the others had a chance to live.

Cole remembered lifting the lifeless form of Bunny from the pilot's seat and dropping him, dying, to the floor of *N-for-Nancy*.

He regretted that he had not been gentler with the pilot. That he had not taken the time to treat the horribly wounded man with the compassion that he had deserved. Cole hoped that he would one day be able to quiet that regret and that he would remember those men as they lived.

Before he fell asleep, Cole remembered *Firedancer* and Hardy, Land, Baird, and Blessing, but most of all he recalled the excitement mixed with fear that he'd felt as the destroyer raced through the North Atlantic, trembling with anticipation at closing with the enemy. It was a strange place to find one's purpose, at sea, but he knew that's what he had found. He never really belonged anywhere, he had told Rebecca. He had always been, and he thought of this with real irony because of how he had come to be on the deck of that destroyer: an observer. He had stood aside life, content to watch without becoming involved. He had remained uncommitted because there was nothing that had interested him. *Or I had not made it my business to become interested*, he thought—knowing that it was more the latter than the former. In this way he knew that he had been a coward. But that was in his life, Before. Now, this was the life, After.

He had read about men going to war—he had taught his students about men at war, but it had been themes, trends, facts and figures that were nothing more than cold notations on a crisp, white field. *You cannot go into it*, he had often told himself, *you cannot go into war and come out the other side the same man.* He knew this.

He knew also that he would not be content with his life in any form, until he was on the deck of a warship in time of war. Despite the fear, death, and carnage— he knew.

Rebecca. He would go and see her when he got to London. He had had time to think about her and his life without her, and he knew that nothing would have meaning unless he could share it with her. Her husband wouldn't be back for some time, so he had a chance. He had planned what he was going to say, discarded that, and created a new speech. She had to understand, she had to take him back.

As the Hudson cleared the runway and banked slowly to gain altitude, Lieutenant Jordan Cole, United States Navy, was deep asleep, teetering on the edge of his dreams.

Chapter 34

London, England

Dickie drove. Cole was simply too tired to concentrate on the road. The Royal Navy officer began pumping Cole for information about *Sea Lion* and the battle before Cole had even cleared the aircraft.

Finally, Cole said in exasperation: "Jesus Christ, Dickie. Can't you wait until I get a decent cup of coffee in me?"

"I can't help it," Dickie said, "I was born an inquisitive child."

Cole had told him where he wanted to go when Dickie picked him up at the base. "You're mad," was all that Dickie had said but agreed to drive him despite his injured leg. He was going to see Rebecca of course and he had everything planned out—what to say and how to say it, and what not to say; that was perhaps the most important point—that the wrong thing not be said.

"If I'd known what you were about I should have refused to drive you," Dickie said with indignation.

"Shut up."

"I do have standards, you know. I'm not completely amoral. I was raised with principles, I'll have you know."

"You must keep them in the top drawer because I've never seen them," Cole said, and then the anticipation was too much to bear. "Have you talked to her lately?"

"I haven't seen her," Dickie said. "We've taken quite a pasting, so I'm sure that she has spent all of her time at hospital. You know we've developed quite a friendship, she and I. Brother and sister, that sort of thing. I do hope you two children find happiness with each other. Your dilemma is getting worrisome."

"Have you heard about her husband? When he's due in?"

"Not for some time, I'm told."

The car turned the corner into Warren Square and Cole was relieved to see Rebecca's house untouched by the raids. He half thought that he would be enveloped in a melodrama: one lover killed before the other had a chance to declare himself. He was nervous, excited, and anxious to see her, to hold her tightly in his arms. Dickie pulled up in front of the house and laid his hand on Cole's shoulder as he started to get out.

"Listen," Dickie said. "You are both my very dear friends and I shouldn't like to see either one of you hurt."

Cole nodded.

"You must be very gentle with her, Jordan."

"I will," Cole said and climbed out of the car. He walked up the steps and rang the doorbell. There was no answer. He rang it again. He thought he heard a noise inside and thought perhaps he should open the door and simply call for Rebecca. He rang again and almost instantly the door opened.

She stood there and Cole's heart raced. He was about to speak when he heard someone call from inside the house.

"Becky? Who is it, dear?" It was a man's voice.

She looked at Cole, desperation in her eyes.

"Becky?"

"A friend of Dickie's, dear."

Cole felt cold.

"Have the poor chap come in. We can't have any friend of Dickie's standing at the door."

"Yes, dear," Rebecca said, her voice weak. "Won't you come in, Lieutenant Cole?"

Cole found himself moving into the house in a daze. There was the staircase and next to it was the telephone table with the black instrument sitting on the white lace doily. Nothing had changed, he thought dully as he walked into the parlor. There was the large oak table that had served as their bomb shelter, and the fireplace and the sofa where Rebecca lay the last night that he had seen her.

"Can I take your hat, Lieutenant Cole?"

"Cap, Becks. Hats are for civilians, aren't they, Lieutenant?" The words came from a small form, bundled in blankets, sitting in a wheelchair near the fireplace. White bandages, stained brown along the edges, covered the man's head and one side of his face. The skin that was exposed was red and mottled. One of the man's legs was missing. A pair of crutches were propped against the wall behind him.

"This is my husband, Lieutenant Cole. This is Gregory."

Cole's mouth was dry but he tried to sound as

natural as possible. It was then that he noticed the smell. It was the faint scent of charred flesh and salve.

"How do you do?" Cole said. He forced himself to add: "Call me, Jordan."

"Royal Navy, are you?" Gregory said. "Is he Royal Navy, Becks?"

"American, Greg," Rebecca said with strained pleasantry.

"Of course he is. Sit down, Jordan. Would you like a drink? Becks can make one for you, can't you, Becks? She's developed a taste for it herself. I'd do it, you see"—he gestured to the missing leg—"but part of me is still in North Africa."

"No," Cole said. "Nothing for me."

"Nothing? Never heard that from a Royal Navy chap—"

"He's an American sailor," Rebecca said. "Don't you remember—"

"Of course I do," Gregory said curtly. "Friend of Dickie's. Well, he won't mind if I have a drink."

Cole saw Rebecca's chin tremble. "The doctor—"

"The doctor, the doctor, the doctor," Gregory mimicked in a shrill voice. "Fix me a drink and be quick about it. And have a double yourself, my dear." He turned to Cole. "Hardly took a sip when we were married, now she drinks enough for both of us." Rebecca handed him a glass. "If I let her."

"I just came by looking for Dickie," Cole said. "I don't want to intrude."

"Of course you were looking for him," Gregory said, staring into his drink. "Why else would you be here?"

Rebecca knocked over her glass. "Please don't be rude, Greg."

"Rude? Was I rude?" He looked at Cole, the burned skin on his face seeming to glow angrily as he attempted a smile. "Was I being rude, Jordan?" The words came out slowly, bitingly.

Cole stood. "I should be going. It was a pleasure meeting you, Gregory."

"Of course it was. You were charmed by my presence. Forgive me if I was terse. Time for my pills, you know. The only way to manage the pain. Pop a few pills, down a few scotches. Come back again."

Cole nodded.

"Becks?" Gregory called out. "See our visitor to the door, won't you? Then hurry back and make me another."

Rebecca followed Cole into the hall and handed him his cap.

"Why did you come here?" she said, her voice breaking.

Cole swallowed heavily, trying to fight back his anger. "I came here to tell you that I love you and I want you to marry me. You've got to get away from that bastard."

"He's just bitter. He lost his leg and his friends. It's going to be very difficult for him. I can help. I can help him."

"No," he said, shaking his head.

"Becky? I say, Becks? Can you come in and give me a hand? I've got to piss like a racehorse."

"Don't do it, Rebecca. Don't throw your life away."

"I've got to go to him."

"I love you."

"Oh, Jordan," Rebecca said. "I know that. I love you as well. When I sent you away before I thought that I should die, but when Greg came home I realized what I had to do—where my duty lies. You've got to understand that. You've got to understand that I can't continue to live with the guilt of betrayal. I know that you love me as much as I love you. Every part of me feels the love of that lost little boy." She took his hand in hers, tears streaming down her cheeks. "We can no longer see each other. We were just something that happened during the war, that's all. You must believe that. You'd better go." She began closing the door when she stopped and tenderly touched his cheek. "Goodbye, darling."

Cole felt nothing as he walked down the steps. Dickie must have been talking to him for several moments before he realized he was at the car.

"Her husband's home," Cole managed.

"Bloody hell!" Dickie said.

"He's a son of a bitch. He's going to sap every bit of life right out of her. She's going to let him."

Dickie lit a cigarette and offered one to Cole, who refused it.

"That's that, then," Dickie said.

"The hell it is," Cole said angrily. "I'm going to get her back. I don't know how, but I'm going to get her back. If I ever saw anything worth fighting for, it's that lady in there."

"Cole! For God's sake, think of her feelings."

"She doesn't know which way is up. I'll do it. I'll get her back come hell or high water. . . ." Then Cole remembered what she asked of him and the agony that he had brought to her life. He turned and looked at the closed door, her words ringing in his mind, and exhaled a ragged breath; the fight was out of him. He choked back the tears that he knew were close.

"Jordan?" Dickie said.

"'When I was a child, I spoke like a child,'" Cole whispered. "'I thought like a child, I reasoned like a child. When I became a man, I gave up childish ways.'"

Dickie remained silent.

Cole remembered the hospital where he first saw her, and the picnic in Hyde Park, and the terror that he felt when he thought that she had been killed in the bombing raid. And he knew, despite his soul screaming that he must not go back, that she was right.

"Come on," Cole said to his friend. "Let's go get a drink."

Acknowledgments

The following have helped in the preparation of this book and deserve special mention.

Kay Davis
Karen Loving
The Royal Air Force Museum, Herndon; G. Leith, Curator
Michaela Hamilton
Bob Mecoy
Michael Lynch
Thomas Ross Wilson
Denton Loving

BOOK YOUR PLACE ON OUR WEBSITE AND MAKE THE READING CONNECTION!

We've created a customized website just for our very special readers, where you can get the inside scoop on everything that's going on with Zebra, Pinnacle and Kensington books.

When you come online, you'll have the exciting opportunity to:

- View covers of upcoming books
- Read sample chapters
- Learn about our future publishing schedule (listed by publication month *and author*)
- Find out when your favorite authors will be visiting a city near you
- Search for and order backlist books from our online catalog
- Check out author bios and background information
- Send e-mail to your favorite authors
- Meet the Kensington staff online
- Join us in weekly chats with authors, readers and other guests
- Get writing guidelines
- AND MUCH MORE!

**Visit our website at
http://www.kensingtonbooks.com**